TREE OF LIFE

TREE OF LIFE

TREE TRILOGY – BOOK ONE

CHRIS LOVEWAY

YAV PUBLICATIONS
LUTHERVILLE-TIMONIUM, MARYLAND

Published in the United States by YAV Publications, Lutherville-Timonium, Maryland.

First Edition

Library of Congress Control Number: 2006938259

ISBN-13:   978-0-9790221-0-4
ISBN-10:   0-9790221-0-X

YAV books may be purchased in bulk for educational, business, fund-raising, or sales promotional use. For information, please contact Books@yav.com Visit our website: www.InterestingWriting.com

1 3 5 7 9 10 8 6 4 2

For Celie and Steph

ONE

MAY 28-JUNE 21, AD 33

THE HOLY LAND

O N THE SIXTIETH DAY, shortly before dawn, three men rushed up the hill and took the cross: James, son of Alphaeus; Thaddaeus, called Jude; and Simon the Zealot—three disciples of the Son of Man, whom his followers called The Christ.

They didn't stop running until the sun had fully risen. They ran silently, not out of fear, but out of expediency. The carefully memorized route was parallel to, yet far enough from, the road to Damascus; they traveled unseen, leaving no tracks.

Alexander, barely fourteen years old, ran close behind. His job was to make certain that no one else was following them. And, if someone were, to lead that person away from the men and their burden. Much was at stake. He spent most of the journey looking over his shoulder.

THANKFULLY, THEY ARRIVED at the meeting place without incident. Alexander joined the men under the outcropping of rock, bathing in the coolness of the shade.

They prayed.

Bartholomew and Joseph, the Joseph they called Barsabbas came next. Throughout the day, more people came, some alone, some in groups.

Alexander stared at the path and waited.

Finally, his father was there, stretching out his arms for a hug that would be soft and gentle even though his arms were thick and powerful. Alexander ran to him; he was proud of his father—Simon of Cyrene had carried the crossbar through Jerusalem for the Son of Man. Many who had stood and watched on either side had wept. Some were among the daughters and wives who now made their way to this secret gap—a steady procession, including donkeys. One of the women was pregnant.

The donkeys brayed in relief when their riders relinquished them. The children took this as a signal to let loose their own brand of cacophony they had obediently suppressed throughout the journey.

As the pandemonium grew, Alexander's father gave him a telling look and motioned toward the top of the rock with his head. Alexander scurried up the promontory where he commanded a 360-degree view from the summit. This time, there was no pretence as he watched for unexpected intruders.

Here, the noise was not as loud as in the rock basin below. Most of the people were savoring the shade under the stone shelf upon which he stood. Down below, the rock reverberated as a natural amphitheater.

The massive wooden horror lay in the center of the bowl-like arena; blood side up again. The sun, now directly overhead, glinted off each drop of blood, the reflected brilliance casting rays in all directions. Alexander was reminded of the first time he had seen a faceted gemstone hanging outside a shop in Jerusalem. Now, as it had been then, a wonderful flash occurred—all the refracted beams of light focused along his line of sight, and the brightness was too much to bear, forcing him to look away.

He averted his eyes to the path, and saw a large man breach the horizon. By the width of the man's shoulders and length of his stride, Alexander immediately identified him: "Philip," he mouthed silently.

Alexander saw his father gazing up at him; a nod acknowledged that he understood their *de facto* leader had arrived.

His father hushed the rest of the group, and when Philip entered the clearing everyone was quiet, even the animals. The babies and children, too, seemed to comprehend that this was a solemn moment.

Philip was the last of the men to arrive. Surveying the scene with calm assurance, he turned to the people and spoke at length. Perched above, Alexander did not have to strain to hear; even Philip's softest whispers prevailed over the soughing wind and rustling brush. When the Apostle finished, the boy knew that the plan had been carried out exactly as Philip and his father had devised it. Furthermore, it was all because of a dream his father had had on Passover—a dream of great armies in century-long wars, fighting and dying because of the thing lying in the natural theater. He glanced again at the blood-soaked timber on the ground in front of him.

The charged air seemed to dissipate, and the disciples gathered to wrap the beams with bolts of cloth the women had brought. Alexander wondered how they could be so cheerful—he had once seen a body being wrapped in a burial shroud; the scene before his eyes was disturbingly similar, and he could almost smell the scent of myrrh. When they finished, they prayed.

Everyone was now standing in the light, and he took this opportunity to count the group. Thirty-three: seven couples and nineteen children, some too young to walk. He saw Philip smile in a way that seemed to say "so far, so good."

Alexander climbed down to join the others.

They ate a meal and prayed again. Excitement grew as the sun moved closer to the horizon.

Philip talked quietly with the men while the women prepared the children for the journey. Now and then, someone glanced in the direction of the sun as if doing so would hasten the group's departure.

PHILIP PRODUCED THREE slings from a hiding place under the rocks. Alexander remembered helping the older men prepare them.

They had started with three ropes, each the diameter of his wrist and twice as long as he was tall. "Do you see how the strands are braided together to make the rope?" Thaddaeus had asked.

Alexander did.

Bartholomew and the two Simons—Simon of Cyrene and Simon the Zealot—had stretched a sheepskin nearby. One by one, Thaddaeus and Alexander brought each rope to them and placed it on top of the stretched sheepskin. Two of the men pulled the central cords in opposite directions while the other two held the knotted ends fast.

"Trace the open part of the rope onto the sheepskin," Thaddaeus said to Alexander. "Use a piece of limestone."

Thaddaeus cut out the shape from the leather, making it slightly larger, just enough to allow it to be folded back around the inner cords. Then they sewed the edges to the insides of the fish-shape, the seam forming a channel enclosing a cord on either side.

"We will oil the exposed parts of the cords, and seal their ends with wax, but be careful with the knots—we'll need to be able to grip those without slipping."

Now, as they laid out all the pieces on the ground, Alexander understood the purpose of the slings they had constructed.

When the last rays of light disappeared, Philip motioned to Bartholomew and Simon of Cyrene. They slid the leather part of one of the slings under the thickly wrapped base beam, each picking up a knotted stub of rope. Thaddaeus and Barsabbas did the same with another sling at one end of the crossbar; James and Simon the Zealot copied their actions at the other.

On Philip's signal, the men crouched and, grasping the bulky ropes by the knots, placed them over their shoulders. They stood, distributing the weight of their burden between them.

The others gathered around. Besides the adults, there were eleven donkeys, seven for the wives and infants, four for provisions. The younger girls and boys walked next to their mothers. The older boys led the donkeys or positioned themselves on either side of the small, mule-drawn wagons.

They traveled by night for secrecy; they slept through the days. Besides concealment, temperature was an added incentive: the night breezes made the sand cool enough to walk upon with bare feet.

None of them knew where they were going, although Philip led the way, and he was led by God.

A short distance behind Philip, Simon of Cyrene and Bartholomew carried the main sling supporting the base beam, facing forward. The two men chatted in low voices with Alexander, who walked proudly beside his father.

Periodically, Philip glanced over his shoulder. Whenever he did this, Alexander ran ahead to walk beside him. They would talk for a while, and then the boy would prance back to the group, darting from person to person, relaying Philip's message.

◆ ◆ ◆

ON THE ELEVENTH NIGHT, the caravan crossed the Euphrates River. Four days later, they camped on the banks of the Tigris. Then the band headed northwest, crossing the river as soon as they were able.

Philip stopped at sunrise on the eighteenth day. A tributary joined the racing Tigris, directly in their path, and he signaled that they would sleep at this junction.

As the women readied the tents, the children played in the shallows at the spot where the two rushing currents collided. Whirling eddies spun around their feet, and they giggled from the tickling bubbles; their giggles mixed with the low roar of the turbulent rivers.

Philip stared at the intersection in front of him, struck by the thought of faraway Jerusalem. It seemed only yesterday that they had all been together in an upstairs room at Mark's house.

Barsabbas and Simon of Cyrene joined him. They talked well into the morning. Too excited to sleep, Philip stayed awake long after the others.

When the group reassembled at sundown, Philip announced that they would be leaving the path along the Tigris and following the tributary into the wilderness. No one questioned his instructions.

Their route began to climb. Two nights later, they came to the tributary's apparent source, a sizable pool in front of a vertical wall of rock. Strewn on both of its banks where the pool abutted the wall, were piles of boulders, all bigger than a man. The rocks extended in either direction to the horizon, blurring endlessly skyward, casting sharp reflections in the stillness of the pond.

The travelers set up camp, exhausted from their climb, perplexed at the dead end, but trusting nonetheless.

The sun rose while they prepared to sleep, prompting Philip to study the wall of rock across the pond. What had appeared to be a sheer cliff in the dark looked all the more impenetrable at dawn.

Lord, where do we go from here?

He struggled to fall asleep, staring across the water, watching the play of light reflected onto the rock. Although the water of the pool did not seem to be moving, the reflections of the sun danced on the wall of rock in an ever-changing embroidery of light. The sunbeams combined with the vertical stripes of the off-white granite to produce a dazzling, radiant design.

The moment the lower rim of the sun cleared the horizon, the diagonal rays of sunlight appeared to straighten out, aligning with the grain of the rock. This happened quickly and with a unique visual effect: two-thirds of the wall to the left appeared to suddenly melt into one shade of chalk white, smooth and polished, no longer reflecting the water. At the same time, the rest of the wall appeared to drop backward as its shadows became more pronounced and the color darkened. The illusion of melting crossed the wall from left to right, making it appear as if the patterns of the light interplaying with the grain of rock were sliding—transferring all their roughness over to the stone wall behind. It was all the more breathtaking because the right-hand third of the wall was offset a dozen feet behind the front barrier. The cumulative result was that anyone present perceived a curtain being pulled open from left to right, and a section of rock dropping back as if a door were opening.

Philip jumped up and waded through the water to peer around the vertical barrier. He discovered the beginning of a chasm through which the stream continued, easily wide enough for the group to pass through, even carrying their burden. Looking skyward, he saw bushes sheared apart on either side of the gorge, as if the rift had been created recently. *Well, maybe it had.* Earthquakes were common in this region. As the thought crossed his mind, he flushed with shame; *this was no coincidence.*

He rushed back to the camp, but everyone was sleeping. He decided to tell them of his discovery when they awoke that evening. There would be plenty of time to explore. After all, it was the longest day of the year—the summer solstice.

THE FIRST WEEK

"I tell you the truth, whatever you bind on earth will be bound in heaven, and whatever you loose on earth will be loosed in heaven." (Matthew 18:18)

TWO

MONDAY, JUNE 20, PRESENT DAY

TURKEY

STUART WATCHED HIS FRIEND push a large pile of Turkish lire across the ticket counter at the Ankara bus station. "You said we were going to find Noah's Ark."

"I know I did, but check out the map," Roger said as he handed Stuart his ticket. "We can't just pass *by* the town of Batman without doing some exploring." He drew out the word "by" and traced a semicircle in the air with his finger, as if it were taking a detour around something.

"Look." Roger's finger landed on the map of Turkey, audibly crinkling the paper. "Here's Mount Ararat, and here's Batman." He jabbed his thumb down, then lifted his hand while maintaining the distance between his thumb and index finger. "We're this close! And I have a *feeling* about it."

Stuart shook his head at Roger's latest crazy plan. He drew in an exaggerated sniff. "Why do I suddenly smell bulls?"

Last summer, after their freshman year at college, Stuart and Roger had traveled throughout Spain and Portugal, the first trip to Europe for both of them. They began in Barcelona at Christopher Columbus' ship, and then explored a good deal of art nouveau architecture by Antonio Gaudi. Roger discovered the local bull-fighting stadium. After a few days watching bullfights—rooting for the bull—Roger said, "You know, Stuart, every day so far we've only been *looking* at things; as if we're tourists or something."

"We *are* tourists," Stuart had replied warily.

"I want to *do* things… You know, immersive reality."

The next day they heard about the annual bull run in Pamplona. They traveled there immediately; Roger had insisted. And he made sure that they *did it,* instead of just watching it.

After donning red scarves and nearly being trampled by stampeding bulls, Roger had taken out his withered map of the world. That's when they had decided to spend this summer searching for Noah's Ark. Stuart was all for it. An archeology student, the quest for ancient relics was in his blood; however, this expedition could quench a vital thirst for something else he'd been seeking his whole life: faith.

"But," Roger had announced with great confidence, "we're not just going to *look* for Noah's Ark. We're going to *find* it! I have a *feeling* about it."

Later, on the flight home from Europe, Stuart had met Meredith Montgomery. The chance encounter seemed so long ago; hard to believe it was a mere ten months. Ever the tease, her first words were, "Sorry, I tried to get two seats, but they wouldn't let me make a reservation for hair." He did a double take. *Had she said "hair" or "her"?* She'd deliberately mispronounced the word. Stuart laughed when he saw her expression. He was already tangled up in it: the longest, most voluminous, and most beautiful hair he had ever seen. Yes, Meredith's hair could have filled a separate seat.

As they chatted through the flight, they discovered they were the same age and attending the same university. By October, they were a "couple"—his first real girlfriend—and by the end of the academic year, the only times they weren't together were when they were in class or sleeping. Even then, he dreamt of her at night, and daydreamed of her during class. Meredith had bid them *bon voyage* at the airport less than a week ago. He already missed her.

STUART FOCUSED on the map of Turkey. Sure enough, there was a town called Batman on the way to Mount Ararat. He remembered how he and Roger had played super-heroes as children. Roger was always Batman; he was always Batman's sidekick, Robin. In grade school, their nicknames were Batman and Robin. At college, they had new nicknames: "War and Peace," from Roger Warren and Stuart Pierce. It suited their personalities much better.

"See these rivers?" Roger pointed at the map again. "The Tigris and the Euphrates—these are the rivers that watered the Garden of Eden."

"But what about Mount Ararat?" Stuart had spent the past few weeks reading everything he could find about the ancient Ark's purported landing place, their destination.

"We have plenty of time for this side trip," Roger said. "To-morrow is the longest day of the year."

"I know. It's the summer solstice. I'm the one who got an 'A' in astronomy, don't forget." Stuart studied the map, adding the kilometers and converting them to miles. "OK. Let's check out Batman, but don't call me Robin—that's ancient history."

◆ ◆ ◆

ON THE BUS RIDE to Batman, Stuart and Roger joked in Turkish accents. The ticket agent had pronounced the name of the city "Baht-mahn." Now, Roger was "Baht-mahn"; Stuart, of course, was "Raw-bean." They reminisced while they gazed out the windows, trying to incorporate the passing scenes into their fantasy.

Stuart saw dismal poverty alternating with shiny, ultra-modern developments, and then, vast expanses of uninhabited plateau reaching toward stunning mountains in the distance. After this pattern repeated several times, he realized that the poverty wasn't so dismal, nor the developments so ultra-modern; they appeared that way only because they were displayed in stark contrast to each other, as if the new and modern had been purposely placed next to the old and ancient with the intention of emphasizing their disparity. He recalled Ankara, where he had been fascinated by farmers on donkeys obliviously stopping beside shining, late-model automobiles, both waiting for the traffic signals to turn green.

Outside the window, the heat waves distorted the distant mountains and reminded Stuart that he was hot—hotter than he could remember ever having been in Southern California.

"Hey. These windows don't open."

"Because of the air conditioner… Duh!"

"But it's not on." Stuart felt a drop of sweat roll down his forehead. He smelled the perspiration glistening on the neck of the bus-driver; they were seated directly behind him.

"Did you get a whiff of this?" Roger held up the bowl of lemon toilet water the attendant had passed to them.

"It reeks."

"Not as much as the tobacco. Haven't they heard of second-hand smoke?"

The two nauseating smells competed for Stuart's air space. Then he smelled the people—women who probably couldn't remember the last time they had bathed and men wearing sweaters in the summer for some unfathomable reason, sweaters drenched in sweat. In a moment of panic, he couldn't breathe.

He snapped back to reality at the slight movement of air produced when his companion opened the map of Turkey again with a flourish. Roger took out the tiny pocket Bible he always carried. For luck, he said.

Stuart knew that under Roger's shirt hung a gold crucifix. He had asked him about it once.

"It's to be sure I'll receive the last rites if I'm in an accident and don't regain consciousness."

"No, really."

"Well, you know, the cross is still working in the world."

"What's that supposed to mean?"

"No idea. Father Romero used to say that."

THE LAST TIME STUART had accompanied Roger to Mass, Father Romero's sermon had focused on Golgotha, the Hebrew name for the hill where Jesus had been crucified between two criminals. Right before they died, one of the criminals made it clear that he believed Jesus to be the Son of God, even as the other continued to mock him. Jesus promised that the believer would be together with him in Heaven that very day. Father Romero had tied the story into choices people make in life—right versus wrong. The part that stuck in Stuart's mind was the priest pointing out the window, directing the congregation's attention to the three antennae towers atop a small hill known affectionately around campus as "Marconi Mountain." Although the satellite dish on the right was huge, the central microwave tower dwarfed both it and the aging A.M. radio mast. The bald-pated priest compared the technological tableau to the three crosses, noting that the antiquated radio tower was like the criminal who refused to change, refused to make the right choice; the satellite dish represented the one who decided to repent. Stuart suspected that the good father was unaware that the satellite dish was part of Professor Bryce Brinkman's non-optical imaging project, and that, although better known for being a "hottie," she was an outspoken agnostic. Nor would Father Romero have been aware that the elderly caretaker of the ancient A.M. radio antenna sat several pews away in the chapel, not looking very happy with the analogy.

Come to think of it, he recalled another occasion when Father Romero had projected a photograph and used a similar analogy. The photo had been of three single-crossbar telephone poles stark against the setting sun, and yes, the image had been striking.

Both times, Father Romero had led the parishioners in prayer following the homily, and both times, he'd closed the prayer with a moment of "personal reflection." The first time, Stuart hadn't realized protocol insisted he keep his head bowed and eyes closed during that part too; the second time he'd sneaked a peek out of curiosity; both times he'd glimpsed the Reverend taking a moistened towelette from behind the pulpit and furiously washing his hands while mumbling what appeared to be another prayer.

ROGER FOUND the page he had been searching for and started reading.

"A river watering the garden flowed from Eden; from there it was separated into four headwaters. The name of the first is the Pishon; it winds through the entire land of Havilah, where there is gold... The name of the second river is the Gihon... the third river is the Tigris... And the fourth river is the Euphrates. (Genesis 2:10-14)

"According to this, four warrior angels are bound in the Euphrates River. They will be released at the end of time to kill one third of the people on the planet," Roger added matter-of-factly, then grinned.

Stuart envied Roger's religious upbringing. His own parents were confirmed agnostics. Thus, church and Sunday school hadn't been part of his life. His father was firm in his beliefs. "Religion is a crutch for weak people," Brad Pierce bellowed whenever the topic arose. He intended that to end any discussion on the matter. As far as Stuart could remember, it had.

Until his parents separated, that is.

Stuart's parents had been fighting more and more each week. He would lie in bed at night, listening to the escalating "discussions" they'd postponed until after he was asleep in a vain attempt to spare him. Then, there had been that time he was caught shoplifting with some kids from shantytown; to confound things, it was during school hours and they were playing hooky. That night, he overheard his mother accuse his father of not having raised him with proper morals. The next day, his father went away on a "business trip." He was gone five months. Even as a boy of twelve, Stuart suspected all was not as he was being led to believe—his father showed up regularly for a change of clothes and more fighting. His parents no longer saved their battles for "after the children were asleep." Stuart heard the word "divorce," and realized they were separated; the so-called "business trip" was a cover story.

With the horror of his parent's impending divorce pounding in his brain, Stuart imagined the whole separation was his fault—that his brush with the law had somehow caused it. He prayed a child's prayer to God, begging that the Lord would bring his parents back together; that somehow they would reconcile. Shortly thereafter, they did, and things appeared to be growing better between them. Nevertheless, Stuart was left with questions about God: *Had God done that in answer to his prayer? Was he under an obligation to God now? Should he go to church? Why would God patch up his parents marriage when his father continued to proclaim that religion was a crutch for weak people? Was the shoplifting incident going to count against him in Heaven...if there was a Heaven? Was God going to do anything else in his life?* Of course, none of this mattered if there were no God.

Yet, when these questions arose, Stuart often heard a rustling, sometimes in the wind, sometimes in the waves at the beach. It seemed to answer *Yes,* and urge *Come to me,* or *Come and see.* He couldn't make it out. At other times: *Some to be…Someone he…From one three…From one tree…*? No way to make sense of it. Often, he thought the voice was saying many things at once; the exact words were just below the threshold of audibility.

He'd even asked Roger whether it was possible that God would have deemed to answer his prayer, "being as I'm not properly church-going and all."

Roger replied, "Father Romero says God hears all prayers. I guess he hears those from heathens like you, too. Of course, you *should* learn the Rosary, and it helps to be named after one of the Apostles, which you aren't!"

Stuart knew how Roger's mother had planned for a large family, but her plans had been blotted out permanently that year she'd been so sick.

"Matthew and John: those would have been the names of my brothers," Roger often explained, "and Mary, Esther, and Ruth would have been the names of my sisters." He would then put on a solemn countenance and intone, "Now I'm the last of the line…Or the first of the new line, depending on how you choose to look at it."

WHILE THEY WERE growing up, Stuart attended Mass with Roger more than once, but the ritual had done nothing for him. He even checked out the CYO—the Catholic Youth Organization—at Roger's church, but there he discovered that Catholic teens were just like all the other kids from school. When he got to college, everyone in the dorm professed to have been "through that church thing." They immersed themselves in contemplating Buddhism, or meditating on their inner oneness, or communing with the "Goddess," whoever that was.

Stuart believed in God—at least he thought he did—but he didn't know what he should do about it. What was the next step?

Some Sunday mornings, he sneaked into the back of the university chapel and observed. It seemed like a club, and he wasn't a member. The songs were usually about Jesus.

Stuart knew he was seeking something, and that it had to do with God. Deep down, he also knew that Roger wasn't very pious, but liked being around someone who was a paid up member of the club.

SEATTLE

Richard Roebuck funded researchers throughout the world. His projects included scientists on the *Gansu Kansu* mountains in central China, others in the heart of Africa—on the *Kotto River* in the Central African Republic, more in the ice caves of Antarctica, and an outpost on the smallest of the *Tarawa Islands* in the southern Pacific—so small it didn't have a name. His project in the South American rainforest gave him the most reason for optimism.

The group he had sent to the Amazon basin consisted of eight promising biotechnologists; among them several biochemists, a microbiologist, a cytologist, a geneticist, an immunologist, and two general botanists. There had been reports of seemingly miraculous cures by a certain shaman whose magic reportedly healed everything from the common cold to cancer. Further testing raised hopes that the people of the village in question might be immune to cancer—none of them ever "got skinny and died" like the natives of surrounding villages. This fact made that village very important to Richard.

Creativity, subterfuge, and an overwhelming desire to possess a pocket laser-pointer induced the village shaman to disclose his secret: one merely had to dig underneath a certain tree and gently coerce the presumed miracle elixir from the tips of its living roots without disturbing or severing the root system—a very delicate process. The shaman used eucalyptus oil to separate the organic compounds; hence, the strong smell of breath-mints. This, coupled with the tree's striking resemblance to a Boab, had prompted Richard to name it a *Boalyptus* tree.

His research team believed they had isolated the compound responsible for the "miraculous cures." Soaking root-drippings in aromatic oils like the Shaman did was far too unpredictable to produce consistent results. After HPLC (High Performance Liquid Chromatography) and molecular modeling, they detected a substance with a chemical structure similar to Quinolone class antibiotics. Unfortunately, the medicine had a little "something extra" that the FDA would surely balk at. There was a side-effect with the *mu*-opiate receptor—something that passed readily across the blood-brain barrier—a powerful heroin-like substance that could be used orally: no IVs, no skin-popping, smoking, or snorting required, and it was very stable.

At first, his team-leader had recommended cutting their losses and getting out of the rainforest. Richard expected no less from his scientists; they were good, ethical people. However, he also knew there were other people who needed the healing properties of this drug—people who didn't care whether the FDA had approved it or not, and who didn't care whether the side effects included euphoria. Richard had no need for the Boalyptus tree; what he needed was the chemical formula he'd paid his researchers to discover. Eventually, it might figure into his "retirement plan."

AS HE DID WITH ALL his researchers, Richard kept a constant satellite link to the young scientists in South America. Further, the Global Positioning System they used in the field accessed his personal satellite network while transmitting real-time coordinates. The GPS technology allowed Richard to pinpoint their location with a precision measured in inches.

During one of their weekly reports the team leader signed off saying, "I'm expecting that we'll have even better news next week." As the link was shutting down, Richard thought he overheard one of the women say, "Do you think he believed you?"

Richard replayed the recording a dozen times until he was sure he had heard the words correctly. He remembered interviewing all eight researchers; he'd already spent millions on this project. They were more than a year into their research—nine months stateside and now four months in the field.

He replayed the past fifteen communications…in his mind. Richard had what scientists call an eidetic memory, and others, a photographic memory. At the age of twelve, he had memorized one hundred verses of the Bible to win two tickets to a baseball game. He heard some church-going kids discussing the contest and rightly deduced that his memory abilities would make the task a piece of cake. He rushed to his grandmother's house and, opening her old Bible approximately to the center, read a hundred verses. As quickly as he read them, he committed them to memory. The day he retrieved his baseball tickets was the first day he had set foot in church.

Justin Robinson, who had placed second in the contest, happily accepted Richard's invitation to attend the game, but when Richard told him how he'd won the tickets, Justin said, "You can't do that sort of thing with a church; you're going to end up in Hell. You're a cheater!"

Richard noticed Justin move several inches down the bench, so their coats wouldn't touch, as if such contact might condemn the boy to a similar fate. However, he knew that Justin had extraordinary peripheral vision; the boy regularly copied from Richard during examinations. In an instant, he understood the definition of a word they'd learned in school the previous week: hypocrisy. He vowed revenge.

Richard was patient. He stopped clipping the nail on his left index finger. Then, on the day of their final science exam, he carefully fashioned it into a sharp point. Fully aware that Justin was copying his answers, Richard answered everything incorrectly. Three minutes before the end of the exam, he picked his nose with the sharpened fingernail to provoke a nosebleed, the drippings of which rendered his answer sheet unreadable. With two minutes left to go, he approached the proctor, and displayed his blood-soaked page. He received a blank answer form, and made certain Justin was watching while he crumbled the original and dropped it in the circular file. He pointed to the clock, whispered something to the proctor, and was allowed to sit in the chair beside the teacher's desk. In less than 90 seconds Richard entered an 'X' in all the correct squares, duplicating the ones he'd written on the eidetic page inside his head—not the ones he'd allowed Justin to copy.

Justin's grades never recovered; his personality took a turn for the worse, and the episode marked the day his life began sliding downhill: he didn't get into college. While the outcome turned out to be much greater than Richard expected—merely an annoying blot on Justin's "permanent record"—Richard had no remorse regarding the event. He had manipulated the boy's beliefs to such a degree of blind faith that Justin hadn't even bothered to apply the "test of reasonableness" on a single one of the answers.

Richard's mantra had long been, *you get what you deserve*. And usually, the sword of retribution cut with a blade that could have more than two sharp edges. Gullible people deserved the consequences of their own stupidity.

THE PROGRESS of the South American research team seemed to be escalating; he had doubled their budget three weeks ago. Even so, the whispered, "Do you think he believed you?" echoed in his mind.

The thought made him very uncomfortable. "Do you think he believed you?"

Could they be milking him?

The thought became a taunt. "Do you think he believed you?"

He sighed the sigh his underlings hated, the one guaranteed to make them feel brainless, guaranteed to make them believe that their stupidity was the sole source of Richard's frustration, and that the "great man" had every right to laud over their sniveling insignificance—the sigh that sounded as though he were planning to spit.

After a sleepless night, Richard decided to fly to Brazil and check out the situation.

THREE

TURKEY

ROGER'S PRONOUNCEMENT WAS meant to be a caption to their situation: "The town of Batman is dead—deader than the 'Joker' after he was vanquished by Batman."

"Batman and Robin, you mean."

"You told me not to mention him…"

Touché.

"And that smell— " Stuart said.

"Yeah. I saw the oil refinery."

They didn't get off the bus until Batman was miles behind them and the odor had disappeared.

"We have at least seven hours of daylight left." Roger pointed to the sun. "And it *is* cooling down." The temperatures had been above 103 since their arrival in Turkey.

They hitched a ride to Cattakkopru with a farmer whose only compensation was the last of the licorice that Roger had bought when they changed planes in Amsterdam. It had seemed like a good arrangement, yet by the time they stepped off the wagon, the old man had given them far more rose-flavored Turkish delight—he called it *locum*—than the licorice he had received for his troubles.

While they sat in the back of the horse-drawn cart, two vegetable crates separated them from a half-dozen goats; Roger took photos of the farmer. "I'm going to sell these to National Geographic," he said, "and we can use the money to finance our trip to Norway next year."

Stuart's ears perked up. Finances were customarily a taboo topic for them. Roger was, in a word, rich. His father was the chairman of the medieval something-or-other department at the university, but the job wasn't necessary. Roger's mother had inherited a fortune from her own mother, a sixties rock star who had died of vegetarianism and whose name was never mentioned. Stuart tried to pull his weight as best he could, but without Roger's limitless credit card, this vacation and last year's too, would have been considerably more rugged.

They shared another taboo topic: Stuart's younger sister, Cindy; Roger had dated her in high school. Cindy was small for her age, with wavy hair framing her face, a constant dimpled smile, and beautiful, sparkling eyes. If she weren't so cute, she might have appeared mousy. Eventually, Roger had broken Cindy's heart, at least temporarily.

Leaning against the inside of the wagon, Roger strummed their three-stringed *baglama*. They had bought it in Ankara; Roger's credit card had come in handy again.

Stuart gazed at his best friend. Their birthdays were only a week apart, yet their physical differences were striking—he had an average build and wispy brown hair, while Roger was tall and muscular, his curly hair coarse and almost blond. Roger exercised regularly—it showed—and Stuart knew that his friend considered him a wimp for not doing likewise. All the same, he believed that if the two of them ever came to blows, while Roger might inflict the most damage, Stuart would surely win by virtue of the strength of his convictions, for any conceivable disagreement would be rooted in a difference of principles.

Stuart's reverie was broken by a crescendo of honking and hooting through which he could discern the Beach Boys tune, "I Get Around"—strangely incongruous in such a foreign land.

I'm getting bugged driving up and down this same old strip.
I'm gonna find a new place where the kids are hip.

He straightened, craning to see, as their driver pulled over to let the cars pass. The extra bumping caused Roger's camera to fall by his side.

They stared as the procession approached.

"Check out those cars."

"American antiques."

"Do you think they're shiny enough?"

Stuart recognized an ancient Chevy Impala and a Chrysler Le Baron. Both were polished to look as if they had left the showroom that very day.

"Those are taxis in the back, the beat-up ones with the yellow stripe."

"Older than you are."

"Yeah, but classic."

The motorcade decelerated to navigate the small edge of pavement between the archaic wagon and the sandy shoulder on the other side of the road.

The cars were overflowing with youths their age. The hooting stopped as the young Turks noticed the Americans—a meeting of two cultures, one caught exploring the other without the benefit of a guide. While they stared at the party on wheels, Stuart wondered what they must think of Roger holding the *baglama*. The Turks stared back. They seemed to be traveling in slow motion. The only thing continuing in real-time was the music of the Beach Boys, but even that played with their sense of time; they were stuck in the sixties—the seventies might never have reached this remote locale, much less the millennium.

The young people were dressed very sharply in American-style clothes which Stuart could tell at a glance were Taiwanese knock-offs. One young woman's entire face was covered with a red veil. Although Stuart couldn't see through the veil, he sensed her eyes locked onto his.

He wondered what was behind the red lace. Was she hiding childhood scars? She turned to follow his eyes and the gracefulness of her movements convinced him she was beautiful.

No one spoke. The montage etched itself into Stuart's mind with a focus sharper than any snapshot he might have taken.

After the cars squeezed by, the old man turned to the travelers and said, "Wedding." They were accustomed to the farmer's one-word sentences by now. The cart started moving again, and neither Stuart nor Roger spoke as they watched the wedding party disappear over the horizon.

A crunch of gravel accompanied by a sudden lurch brought Stuart back to reality. He looked forward, realizing that neither of them had any idea where the farmer was taking them, and the sun was falling lower by the minute.

◆◆◆

THE GOAT FARMER dropped Stuart and Roger at the eastern bank of the Malabi Bridge. He gestured his willingness to take a picture of the two young men; Roger waved away the photo-op—his customary rebuff. From Roger's perception, the most prominent feature on his face was a scar from a childhood injury; he had no desire to capture that memory again with a photograph.

The two companions continued beside the shore of a small lake; it had undoubtedly been the beginning of the Batman River in earlier times. The water narrowed north of Ormandisi and the young men were able to wade to the other side.

They stayed by the water until arriving at the village of Kulp. There, they bought some kebab from a roadside vendor who continued to turn his ancient spit with one hand while negotiating the sale with the other. The smell of coriander was intense.

Roger stretched out the map and studied it while they ate. He suddenly threw down his kebab stick. "See how these rivers start, right here around the Cotele Mountain?" He stabbed the map with his finger.

"Look at the name of the village closest to the top of the mountain. Look at it!"

Clearly, he wasn't going to say another word until Stuart looked at the map and read the name aloud.

Stuart followed Roger's finger. *Godis*. "Goh-deeze."

"Yeah. Look at the spelling: *Godis*. GOD IS! Do you think that's a coincidence?"

"Hmm…"

"And this stream must be the original source of the Batman River."

He folded the map and started hiking. Stuart hastened to catch up.

◆ ◆ ◆

THEY FOLLOWED the small brook to its apparent source: a pool nearly forty feet in diameter abutting a wall of smooth rock. Stuart wanted to camp there. He felt comfortable for the first time in days. The moss at the edge of the sparkling water was warm in the light of the setting sun. He played with the spongy vegetation where it met the water—the temperature had dropped to acceptable levels.

"I don't think you want to spend the night here," Roger said.

"Yes I do. This moss is softer than my air mattress."

"Do you have any idea what happens at pools of water like this in the middle of the night?"

"I haven't given it much thought."

"Then let me tell you. Wild animals come to the pool for a drink of water. That's what happens. Wolves, bears, jackals, and even leopards! And do you know what they do if they find a couple of juicy humans wrapped in sleeping bags next to their water hole?"

"I can imagine."

"Anyway, we can't climb here—the rocks are too smooth. We want to be farther north, where all those boulders are."

"Climb?"

"Naturally. Don't you want to see what's up there?" Roger pointed to the top of the wall of rock.

"Of course I do."

Stuart and Roger continued hiking and set up camp five hundred feet beyond the small oasis. This was just far enough away to prevent them from noticing Achmed bin Cyrene, descendant of Simon of Cyrene, bearer of the cross, when he and his eldest son, Matthias, approached the moss-rimmed pool less than six hours later, the morning after the shortest night of the year.

FOUR

TUESDAY, JUNE 21

DAWN

MATTHIAS AND HIS FATHER, Achmed, arrived at the pool, as they had every month for as long as Matthias could remember, and his memory reached back twenty years. Their cart, pulled by a strong workhorse, was laden with an apparently arbitrary array of items: bags of grain; dried cat food and dog food; a month's worth of newspapers and a dozen books; medical supplies; reams of paper, art materials, and photographic film; an assortment of wooden toys; and six cases full of large bottles of the latest carbonated iced-tea rage. They were three-hours from their home near Diyarbakir.

Matthias realized that the bottles would be quite warm by now. *Too bad they have no ice.*

Because this was the longest day of the year, the secret crevice would be visible to anyone who happened to be near the pool at sunrise. Instead of proceeding directly through the hidden entrance of the gorge, the two men stopped at the water.

Matthias loved this spectacle as much as his father did. They rested quietly on the moss in anticipation while the sun rose. Deep indentations from Stuart and Roger's hiking boots marred the spongy ground cover, but the men were so engrossed in the wall of rock on the other side of the pool, they did not notice. Instead they stared, transfixed by the annual occultation that never failed to blur the boundary between the real and the spiritual. That this peculiar solar anomaly happened only once each year made the experience even more precious.

"Beautiful!" Matthias exclaimed. Like his father, Matthias had the dark, swarthy, middle-eastern look indicative of a bloodline stretching back to the Patriarchs. Hair blanketed the exposed areas of his flesh. Both men had a keen sense of, and appreciation for, beauty.

His father smiled as he stood. "Let's go."

They led the horse and cart to a shady natural stable beside the entrance to the gorge. Apparently, the removal of one of the massive boulders had created the shady shelter. Matthias theorized that the selfsame boulder had formed the depression in the earth that became the pool, landing hard before bouncing, but so far, he had been unable to find the missing stone.

They uncovered the back of the wagon, and Achmed calculated the weight of its contents. He had not yet divulged his system to Matthias.

"Six trips," said Achmed, referring to how many times they would have to pass through the ravine while transferring the wagon's contents to its destination.

They each grabbed an end of the sturdy stick attached to the top of the largest sack of grain. As always, the heavy items were the first to be transported.

◆ ◆ ◆

A MERE 150 YARDS to the northeast, Stuart and Roger were awakening. Or, more accurately, Roger was. Stuart heard a "Tsk, tsk," opened one eye a sliver, focused, and saw that Roger had decided to let him continue to sleep.

Peeking again, Stuart saw Roger moving silently around the camp, packing delicately. Obviously, he planned to have as much ready as possible before *accidentally* making a noise loud enough to wake his friend. Then, Roger would be able to gloat while Stuart scurried around frantically getting his gear in shape. He'd been through this before: groggy eyes, Roger standing over him, ready to go. Probably, he would go explore, looking for a climbing route while Stuart readied himself. Again, it was right in character.

Stuart knew that his friend wasn't being particularly malicious; they really were best friends. Roger treated everyone like that.

Roger craned his neck to study the giant rocks that towered over their camp. He walked toward the east, then returned with a determined look, continuing west in the direction of the pool. He still didn't suspect that Stuart was merely pretending to sleep. Fifty feet from their campsite, Stuart heard him let out a cry and he came running back, hooting the whole way.

If Stuart hadn't been awake by now, Roger's racket would have roused him.

"Hey, slacker," Roger said smugly. "Get a move on."

Stuart stared at him fuzzily. "Did you make coffee?"

"I forgot." Roger put on his most penitent face, and then changed the subject. "I did some scouting around while you were asleep." Roger paused for effect. "I found the perfect path."

"Perfect path?"

"Hurry up! *I'm* already packed and ready to go."

Stuart glared and gathered his things as quickly as possible. "Ready," he said five minutes later.

"Aren't you forgetting something?"

"Huh?"

Roger gave him a spacious grin, and the rising sun reflected off his pearly white teeth. They were perfect, without a single cavity, and he reminded Stuart of that fact whenever he had an opportunity.

"OK. OK." Stuart opened his knapsack and took out his toothbrush.

◆ ◆ ◆

ACHMED AND MATTHIAS stepped behind the rock baffle for the third time that day. Matthias heard a whooping sound. He stopped, turned back, and peered around the corner of the baffle. A large bird was flying off; he could hear the beating of its wings.

The two men hadn't spoken much during the first two trips, but Matthias knew his father expected him to break the silence when they returned to transport the lighter, but bulkier packages. Family tradition was powerful about the day of the solstice: the younger of the Cyrenes would recite the story of the crater settlement while they traversed from one end of the ravine to the other. The recitation ensured that Matthias would be able to pass on the story to his own son when it became necessary.

As the two of them waded through the pool for the fifth time and Matthias began, "On the sixtieth day, shortly before dawn, three men rushed up the hill and took the cross..."

His father's eyes lit up.

Achmed studied the sides of the gorge while his son recounted the history of the settlement. He tried to remember the times he had walked this route with his own father, his *baba*. He tried to recall which bushes had been where—or hadn't been—and how much they had grown. When they reached "the corner," a place where the gorge made a forty-five-degree turn, he focused.

Matthias was precisely at the spot in his narrative where he should be at the bend in the stream: *Philip didn't know that the hidden entrance to the gorge was visible only on one day of the year, the summer solstice, and only in the first three hours of the morning sun. But God did.*

The young man felt his father reach around and give his shoulder a hug.

◆ ◆ ◆

MATTHIAS STOPPED his recitation to marvel at the curving of the stream around the corner. His thoughts clouded as he contemplated the settlers whose actions 2,000 years ago had so irrevocably set the course of his own life. In a flash, a seed of doubt ripened into full-blown uncertainty. He hesitated as images of other places; other lives—the might-have-beens—erupted before his mind's eye. As quickly as this apprehension had swept over him, it subsided, replaced by a strong, purposeful sense of duty.

He continued intoning the ancient Aramaic words of the bin Cyrene oral tradition: *Philip bade everyone line up in the late afternoon. They would travel singly or in pairs through the gorge, wading through the rushing waters, where required.*

A full two hours did it take to traverse the ravine. Wet and tired, they quickly moved to one side of the stream and gazed upon the sight before them.

What they saw resembled a large bowl, one with a flat bottom roughly 7,000 cubits [2 miles] in diameter and over 600 cubits deep [900 feet]. The stream flowed from the north of the valley. To the east was a grove of orange trees; across the stream, a large field of wheat. Sheep grazed on the grass-covered northern half of the valley.

The thirty-three weary pilgrims did not question whether this was the destination God had planned for them. They knelt and prayed.

With two hours of daylight left, the men carried the cross to the source of the stream, a small bubbling spring close to the far northern wall of the crater.

Philip and the other six men talked at length.

Soon they had unwrapped and planted the cross in the soil beyond the spring—a monument to the greatest act of sacrifice since the beginning of the universe.

Beneath the earth and unbeknownst to all, rivulets of the blood of Jesus on the base of the cross sprouted roots and reached outward.

"Friends," said Philip. "Eighty-one days ago, our Lord was nailed to that tree. When Simon of Cyrene came to me with this idea two months ago, I confess I was perplexed. Yet, Simon carried the cross for Jesus on that final day, and God had given him a vision of what needed to be done—a vision of wars that would be fought over the cross if it stayed where it lay.

"When we embarked on this journey three weeks ago, our destination was unclear to me. I trusted the Lord to lead us, and you trusted me. Now, I believe that we have arrived where the Lord would have us stay. In His infinite grace and generosity, He provides a safe refuge for us.

"People, let us all thank the Lord from our hearts, and praise Him with our souls. For He alone is holy.

"In the blessed name of Jesus Christ."

"Amen," they said, as one.

Then they heard a loud voice exhort, "You have done a great thing. For whatever is loosed on earth is loosed in Heaven, and whatever is bound on earth is bound in Heaven. What you have done has been done in Heaven. For though this place is here, it is also in Heaven. This sanctuary is but a copy and shadow of what is in Heaven.

"Philip, James, Bartholomew, Thaddaeus, Simon, and Barsabbas, You and your families and descendants are blessed—blessed that you do not have to return to the world but can live out your days here. This is a great honor. The Lord is well pleased. You have been placed under the protection of the Lamb of God. You have nothing to fear. No evil will befall you. The King of Kings has need of this place when He returns."

For the second time this day, Matthias sensed the seeds of uncertainty stirring within. He wondered what his father would say if he suddenly announced that he wanted out. That he wanted to travel, to explore the rest of the world, to go to America, to have a *real* life—something more than this month-after-month journey from Diyarbakir to the settlement, this so-called "blessing."

Nonetheless, he persevered with the Heavenly pronouncement: *"Simon of Cyrene, you who took upon the burden of the Son of Man in His final hour, you and your family and descendants are blessed. You are blessed that you can come and go from this place to minister to the needs of those who remain. This is a great honor. The Lord is well pleased. You have been placed under the protection of the Lamb of God. You have nothing to fear. No evil will befall you. The King of Kings has need of this place when He returns.*

"Hail King Jesus. Righteous is the Son of Man. Worthy is the Lamb of God. Holy is the Lord of Hosts."

AGAIN, A FAMILIAR IDEA raced through Matthias' mind. His own ancestor, Simon of Cyrene, had started this mess.

Matthias had lost count of the number of times he had heard the family legend: When Simon of Cyrene carried the cross for Jesus on the Via Dolorosa two thousand years ago, he had been filled with a revelation. As they neared Golgotha, God showed him a vision of what would happen if the cross were left there—the blood of Jesus was on it after all. God had wanted Simon to remove it and hide it.

With Philip's help, Simon refined the plan. Then, the remaining Apostles were brought in on the secret.

Now, two thousand years later, *I'm* locked into this life. Thanks a lot Grandpa.

Matthias and Achmed stepped forth from the ravine into the crater. The young man wondered how long it would be before his father became too frail to make this journey. After that, his lot in life would be fixed for good.

FIVE

LOS ANGELES

BRYCE BRINKMAN had come a long way from Harmony, Pennsylvania. The middle girl between an older and younger sister, and an older and younger brother, Bryce had grown up with the opinion that she had to do something very special for anyone around her to take notice.

A word of advice from her grandmother, "The squeaky wheel gets the grease," once grasped, quickly became one of the central principles in her personal philosophy. Bryce tested this theory on all manner of things, in and around the house—anything that managed to attract attention by making a reasonable facsimile of a squeaking sound.

Bryce surmised that nearly everyone's perception was limited to the edges of things. People would look at the outside of something—a house—for hours without giving a moment's thought to what was inside. They were looking at the house's edges. Merely looking through the windows of a house wasn't enough. That only provided more edges to ponder. However, upon the detection of life—a shout, someone practicing piano—a person's perception changed. They no longer were seeing only the edges.

She hypothesized that the only requirement for most people to jump the mental hurdle between looking at something's edges, to perceiving it in three dimensions, was awareness of life inside.

FAMILIES WERE LIKE THAT, too. Sissy (the youngest) and Heather (the oldest) were the "edges" of her family. The boys, C.J. and Scott, were closer to those edges than to the center. She was in the middle, and that made it difficult to be noticed unless she took steps to go that extra distance.

It all tied into the way one perceived space.

She had learned much about the perception of space from her father. John Brinkman collected old fire engines. When Bryce had become old enough to appreciate this fact, having noticed that all of her friends collected manageable items like stamps, or dolls, or bottle caps, she asked her father why.

"Because I have the space," he said.

They lived on a 300-acre farm. Her parents weren't farmers, although they rented the fields out to honest-to-God farmers whose land abutted theirs. This arrangement left the Brinkmans with a couple of empty barns and nothing to put in them. Her father gradually filled the empty space with antique fire engines. Now fire engines were parked all around the barns as well.

Bryce deduced that the extent to which people's thoughts, dreams, and aspirations reached out from their deep insides to the farthest boundaries of their imagination depended upon the amount of space they had in their own environment.

Later in her life, economists would apply her theories to national frontiers and construct complex models defining the outer limits of the global marketplace. At the age of fourteen, Bryce applied her theory to the allocation of bedrooms among her siblings.

Bryce was aware that her hypothesis about "edges" and her father's notion of "space" had much in common. For her high school science project, she hoped to tie these two ideas together and confirm something for herself at the same time.

She borrowed Heather's and her mother's old dollhouses, and Sissy's, too. Ten-year-old Sissy had agreed to this with great reluctance and made her sign a paper guaranteeing the safe return of her dollhouse. Bryce could tell she was genuinely worried; she had twiddled all eight of her braids while negotiating the contract. Adding Bryce's own dollhouse, made four.

Bryce affixed the four houses to a large piece of plywood and began to work on the interiors.

Dollhouse number one didn't call for any alteration; she simply closed all of its curtains, making sure there was no way to determine its contents.

Dollhouse number two's curtains were completely open, the intricate miniature furniture inside displayed for all to see.

The third dollhouse had some curtains open, and other curtains closed. She placed a layer of wax paper behind the living room windows. Then she installed a light bulb in the tiny living room. Having laid flat a little old clock whose second hand still worked, Bryce attached cardboard cutouts resembling paper dolls to create a mechanism that gave the illusion of activity taking place in the house—silhouettes of people walking back and forth appeared periodically on the wax paper lining the living room windows.

Inside the fourth dollhouse, she placed her small cassette recorder and inserted a recording of herself practicing the piano. It started with exercises and scales and gradually advanced to works of Bach, Mozart, and Chopin, sometimes repeating a measure twenty times, as one would expect during practice.

The four houses could have been in the middle of a typical street anywhere in rural America.

Satisfied, she drafted a brief questionnaire aimed at finding out and quantifying what people perceived of the spaces inside the houses, between the edges.

When Bryce returned from the copy-center with three hundred copies of her questionnaire, she discovered that C.J. and Scott had painted a sidewalk and a road in front of her houses. C.J. had donated four of his model cars to the project, and each house now had a vehicle parked in front of it. Installed at one end of the street was a crudely-lettered sign proclaiming ENTERING BRYCE-VILLE, POPULATION: 18. She was obliged to admit that their enhancements created a positive effect.

During the next two months, she took Bryceville, firmly fastened to an old red wagon, to various school and community activities where she entreated people to take part in her survey by filling in her questionnaire. "Have you visited Bryceville yet?" she asked passing strangers, as if she were a travel agent.

After tabulating all the data she collected, she entered the project, titled, "Spacious Thinking," into her high school Science Fair.

She won easily—the judges had all visited Bryceville.

Her father had been very proud.

How she wished she had someone to be proud of her now, and hold her, calling her "Bry" as her father used to.

Bryce's "Spacious Thinking" project had netted her the scholarship to Radcliff, from which she graduated *Summa Cum Laude*.

In her junior year, she made the leap from dollhouses and fire engines, to photography and satellites. Her senior thesis, "Inside the Edges—On the Superiority of Non-Optical Imaging," had been published in the Journal of Astronomical Research. All this, from an attempt to rationalize her position as the middle child, or so she once reasoned during a moment of clarity brought on by a bottle of Pomerol wine.

Next came a full Carnegie fellowship for her doctorate at M.I.T. Then, post-doc, and her first RRR grant—Richard Roebuck Research, "Triple-R" as everyone called it.

The grant had prompted her to move to California. There, she received a second "Triple-R," then another, and another, and another, until she lost count.

Three years ago, the university knocked out the walls of five adjacent classrooms in her building to make room for the lab adjoining her office.

My lab... She said to herself proudly.

Richard—by then she was on a first name basis with the CEO of Richard Roebuck Research—had donated a large endowment to the university the year they extended the lab. Through a complex series of circumstances, many deliberate, Bryce passed the first two years in her new lab unaware of that fact.

She owned her house in Pacific Palisades, had her own parking space on campus, and a brand new Lexus to park in it. She held a platinum membership to her health club. At 34, she had it all, and the looks to go with it. Moreover, as she was fond of reminding herself, she had never had to sleep with anyone to climb this ladder of success. So why did she feel so empty?

SIX

TURKEY

STUART AND ROGER began their climb about ten minutes after sunrise. It wasn't serious rock-climbing calling for ropes and crampons; it was more of a you-hoist-me-then-I'll-pull-you-up type of affair. An occasional funnel required working their way upward, wedged between two sides of a split boulder from antiquity. They came upon some disturbing bottomless crevices, big enough to swallow a man. Certain rock formations were too large to hoist each other over, and these necessitated nerve-racking inch-by-inch circumnavigation, clinging to its outer edge of the obstacle, slowly moving from handhold to handhold.

By noon, their route had required them to switch back and forth several times, each time returning them farther west. On one side of a flat rock shelf, roughly twenty feet wide by six feet deep, scrub grass dotted the against the mountainside. They walked to the other end of it and peered down.

Below them, they could barely make out the small pond that they had seen the night before. It wasn't straight down but, looking down made Stuart dizzy.

"I think we're at the top, Sir Hilary," Roger teased. "Give me a boost."

Stuart studied the ridge above them. "It looks too high for that."

"Nah. But this one's going to require your shoulders for a second."

STUART FELT Roger's weight lift from his shoulders. He heard Roger shout, "Hey, *Raw-bean*. I can see *Baht-mahn*."

"Help me up."

"Wait a second. I want to check out the other side."

Stuart waited on the rock shelf below. *This was just like Roger. First check out the other side*, and then *help me up*. The order of the tasks was significant. Stuart exhaled long and audibly, pausing to lose himself in the stillness of his empty lungs.

Roger's head popped over the edge above. "Robin, get the Batmobile!"

Stuart glared.

"Pass me my bag. We have to take some photos of this."

Stuart detected the excitement in Roger's voice. He attached his own knapsack to the hook at the end of the strap Roger had lowered.

"No. Pass mine up first. It has the camera in it."

"And get left behind. I don't think so," Stuart said, as he slipped Roger's knapsack over his shoulder.

Finally, Roger pulled him up to the flat plateau; it was thirty feet wide.

Roger grabbed for his knapsack and took out his camera. "Check this out," he said. He rushed to the other side of the rim, readying his camera on the way, and Stuart followed him to the other side of the plateau. He couldn't believe his eyes. It was tremendous.

Probably two miles across. A thousand feet deep. Definitely a crater!

He wondered why it wasn't on the map. In the center of the crater was a church with a gold dome; in front of it were dwellings—a small village. Despite the distance, he could make out people walking. A farm extended from the church to the bottom of the rim below him, and in the other direction, far beyond the church, was a garden. At first glance, it appeared to consist of purple-green trees, arranged concentrically around a mammoth bush. The blood-red centerpiece pushed skyward through rolling puffs of mist—a pulsing haze that originated from the base of the far right crater wall. Soft pillows of steam accumulated and detached themselves with the regularity of cresting waves in an ocean made of clouds. Obviously, this flow of moisture nurtured the garden continuously, and the result was spectacular. He had never seen anything like it; he had a strong feeling that no one else had either.

ROGER COULD barely contain himself. "It's some sort of meteor crater or something. I've been to one like it in Arizona, but this one's even bigger."

The panorama was overwhelming. Stuart's eyes followed the rim down to the crater floor. On the inside, it was smooth, the complete opposite to the rocky rubble they had just scaled. There would be no way to climb down from where they stood.

Roger snapped a photo. "I want to get some shots of what we climbed." He rushed to the other side of the rim.

Precisely at that moment, the ground began to tremble. Residents of California, Stuart and Roger were accustomed to frequent earthquakes. They knew that earthquakes were also common in Turkey. Unfortunately, at the instant this one struck, Stuart was straining to look over one side of the rim, and Roger was running toward the other. Although the quake was small, the young men went flying in opposite directions.

About twenty feet down from the rim on the inside, Stuart hit the side of the crater with an *oomph*, his breath knocked out of him. He started sliding over the tightly tangled scrub covering the slope. He continued to slide all the way to the bottom.

He landed flat on his back on a soft bed of grass, and lay there for a while looking up at the sky. Full of billowing white clouds, it evoked a fleeting memory of Meredith. How often they had lain on their backs staring at the clouds, and describing to each other what fantastic creatures they saw in the shifting shapes.

Stuart patted his chest. Under his shirt, a crystal heart the size of his thumb hung from a leather cord. Meredith had given it to him on his birthday. You couldn't see through it, but you could see into it. The dangling adornment was divided into two compartments, vertically. One side appeared empty—actually, it was full of air; the other contained three apple seeds. Meredith had a similar pendant, but hers had dirt on one side, and water on the other. "Without you, I'm just mud," she said. "Or at the very least, uprooted," Stuart had replied.

Theoretically, by putting their hearts together, they could grow an orchard; nourish themselves in times of need; feed the nations; and if the necessity arose, restore food to the human race if everything else were to disappear. Earth, air, water, life—their lavalieres were a simple symbol of puppy love, and it comforted Stuart to know he hadn't lost his; he imagined an invisible connection that caused Meredith to touch hers, whenever he touched his.

Dazed, he rested in the warmth of the sun. He rolled his head and studied the tops of a grove of fruit trees close by. He tried to focus on the crater rim; Roger was up there, or so he presumed—he pictured Roger scanning the floor of the crater with his binoculars, inch by inch. He waved in the direction of the rim and gave a thumbs-up sign. *Roger will find a way down…*

He noticed he was hungry. He vaguely wondered why he wasn't in pain after such a fall. Yet, he was delightfully comfortable; he didn't want to move.

He thought he heard laughter, and the lilt of young voices speaking in a strange tongue. Three faces entered his field of view. Two girls and a boy, all under the age of seven, all well tanned. They peered and pointed, then whispered and stared with puzzled looks upon their faces. Suddenly, they giggled some more, and spoke in a language he couldn't understand.

Stuart sat up with great difficulty, noting that he could not move his legs. *Broken or paralyzed?* He couldn't tell. The children jumped back in surprise at Stuart's efforts.

"Are your parents around?" he asked. This generated a fresh onslaught of giggles and more comments in the strange language. He realized they didn't understand him. He wished Roger would hurry up and join him; Roger had such a great knack for getting his point across a language barrier. Again, Stuart studied the crater rim, looking for a sign of his friend. Finding nothing, his eyes moved back and forth over the crater wall, expecting to see his friend climbing down to find him.

The young boy turned and shouted something. A half dozen other children ran to the group. Two older boys motioned for Stuart to follow. Again, he attempted to stand without success. They understood the problem immediately.

The older boy said something and rushed away, returning minutes later with a hammock-like device: a leather sling, wide in the middle, with thick ropes at either end. He fed this under Stuart's legs and worked it up to his thighs. They placed another sling under his calves. Next, the two tallest boys crouched on either side of him and positioned their shoulders snugly under Stuart's arms. After what must have been a count of three, the six boys stood. Stuart's weight was distributed among them, and they started walking through the orange grove. The younger children skipped beside them.

Oh well, this is a crater after all; Roger will find me soon enough—it's not as though one can get lost in a crater. Stuart reassured himself. *If they try to take me outside the crater, then I'll protest.*

Stuart didn't think about his injuries. The parts of his body that weren't bruised or broken felt renewed. The chattering children carried him like a royal sultan; he could easily get used to this attention.

"Wait," he said, and pointed to an orange tree.

One of the little kids climbed the tree lickety-split and returned with an orange.

"Wait," the child said, as he handed the orange to Stuart.

Stuart burst out laughing when he realized the child had taken the word for "orange" to be "wait." The rest of the children laughed harder than ever at Stuart's amusement.

The merry band headed to the church in the center of the crater. Sunlight reflected from the golden dome, momentarily blinding him.

◆ ◆ ◆

ROGER WASN'T AS FORTUNATE. He went sailing off into space—the space above the pool. He flailed at the rock shelf as he passed it, but found nothing to grasp.

He continued past the shelf. A loud crack came from the direction of his leg as he bounced off the boulder it. This continued all the way down the side of the mountain.

Crack! Bounce...

Crack! Bounce...

Mercifully, he passed out after the third crack.

Roger landed with a thud in the moss beside the pool. His shattered camera came to rest not far from his head. Had they been open, his eyes would have been staring at the smooth wall of rock. Blood trickled from his mouth and from one of his knees.

He woke several hours later, passing in and out of consciousness from the pain. Once when he opened his eyes, he imagined he saw two people walk right out of the wall across the pond.

Then, blackness.

SEVEN

ANTARCTICA

INSIDE THE USCPS—the U.S. Center for Predictive Seismology—near the South Pole on the edge of Antarctica, the eerie light of a hundred computer screens was a welcome relief to the uninterrupted darkness of the six-month polar night. Bursts of clattering computer keyboards punctuated a continual murmuring as Tuesday's earthquake was replayed, studied, modeled, simulated, and analyzed repeatedly.

The facility was the brainchild of Chief Science Officer Chester A. Morgenstern; the "A" was for "Aristotle" and his nickname, "Cam," derived from his initials—people named Chester usually adopted a nickname.

The first officer pointed to a computer monitor. "It's still right on the line!"

Cam, at six-foot-five, had to bend over to study the screen. What he saw bothered him. "No earthquake has stayed at fifty-percent this long."

"What's your guess? Foreshock or mainshock?"

Guess! Cam hated the word. He had devoted his whole life to removing the probability factor from the science of predictive seismology. *Fifty-percent meant random. Fifty-percent meant the 'null hypothesis.'* To Cam, fifty-percent meant failure.

Cam's work had taken off at the end of the twentieth century, a time when most other seismologists were throwing up their hands in defeat; traditional methods of earthquake prediction had yielded results no better than the null hypothesis—random choice had been proven to be just as reliable as the intricacies of mathematical modeling. The scientific community acknowledged that they had reached an impenetrable wall—one that would permit no entry into the realm of earthquake prediction beyond rudimentary forecasting, the statistical determination of the rate of future seismological activity within a specified time-period. Cam had discarded those tried-and-failed approaches—computer simulations based upon time sequence analysis of seismic reflections, predictive deconvolution, elastic wave propagation, various flavors of ray-based tomography, the "seismic gap" hypothesis, and the vertical profiling of borehole logging—in favor of an approach that relied upon the fractal analysis of minute fluctuations within the earth's magnetic field.

A new recruit entered the lab and interrupted his reverie. "What's the forecast?"

Cam glared at her. "We don't use the 'F' word around here," he said. "An earthquake forecast is like a weather forecast: it states nothing more than the probability of an event in a particular area based upon the past seismological history of that area. It might say something like, 'there is a sixty percent chance of a magnitude eight earthquake somewhere on the San Andreas Fault sometime during the next thirty years,' in the same way a weatherman might say, 'there is a sixty percent chance of rain or thunderstorms somewhere in the Bay area during the next week.'"

"Sorry…"

"What we make are *predictions*," Cam stressed. "A prediction must fulfill several rigorous requirements: the predicted earthquake must be of a magnitude seven-point-five or greater, the location and focal point must be specific, and the date must be accurate to a time-period of less than one year. Most importantly, the predicted earthquake must actually happen—any reasonable prequake response implies a colossal financial expenditure."

"Why is this one so important?"

"Because lives are at stake," interjected the first officer.

Cam continued: "We need to know whether this quake was a foreshock or a mainshock. If it was a mainshock, aftershocks will come soon, and if it was a foreshock, we can expect a mainshock—a big one, judging from the size of the tremor."

"Six-point-seven," the first officer said.

"On August seventeenth, 1999, a seven-point-four rocked the same fault—the Izmit Quake; that one killed more than seventeen thousand people. It was the largest quake of 1999; less than two months later an aftershock killed another thousand.

"If Tuesday's quake was a foreshock, then we can expect a huge mainshock. A seven-point-seven would produce ten times as much surface motion, thirty-two times as much energy—"

"—I'm thinking more along the lines of an eight-point-seven," the first officer interjected again.

"That would mean one-hundred times as much surface disturbance, and a thousand times as much energy," the recruit said.

Cam led the young woman to the nearest computer. "That's why we have to determine if it was a foreshock or a mainshock."

"And…"

"And we can't do that with reasonable accuracy until the moon reaches full apogee—when it is at its greatest distance from the center of the earth—and thus exerting its minimal gravitational interference."

"You're not saying that the tidal-effect has anything to do with earthquakes, are you?"

"Not at all. Although the gravitational pull of the moon *does* affect the magnetic response of…" he hesitated, not wanting to disclose too much too soon, "…the little crystals we're monitoring to make our predictions."

The young women accessed an ephemeris on her computer; the accuracy of astronomical data displayed by its tables was updated in real time.

"The moon won't reach apogee for another seven days," she said.

"Precisely! That's when we'll know."

EIGHT

TURKEY

LATE AFTERNOON

ACHMED AND MATTHIAS stepped out from the ravine and into the cool water of the pond after a long day toiling for the people in the crater. The two men had traversed the rock fissure as quickly as possible; the morning's tremor reminded them that an earthquake could close the ravine as easily as one had created it.

They proceeded directly to the wagon, hidden in the rock-hewn stable immediately to their left. Taking a feedbag from under the wagon seat, they fed the horse.

Matthias carried a water pail to the edge of the pool. When he bent down to fill it a flash of sunlight blinded him. Covering his eyes with one hand, he looked around. Lying on the moss several yards away, he saw a camera; the sun reflected off its broken lens. *That's curious...*

His eyes traveled farther and came to rest on Roger.

He froze.

Eyes fixed on Roger, Matthias edged backward to the wagon. He put his finger to his lips to signal silence, and pulled on his father's tunic. Achmed stopped humming and eyed him questioningly. The older man's gaze followed his son's outstretched arm to the tip of his pointing finger.

Then he saw it.

His mind rushed through a dozen scenarios. In an instant, he recalled generations of oral history. This had never happened before. He straightened and took control, motioning his son to follow. They crept cautiously to the young man's broken body.

"He's still alive," Achmed said.

"I'll get the wagon." Matthias started to run back to the horse.

"Wait! What if he saw the entrance? The valley?"

"Well, what do you propose to do? Leave him here? He's hurt. He's unconscious!"

"I'm thinking." Achmed's voice bristled with urgency.

"Father!"

"OK. We'll take him to the medical center at Tatvan."

"Tatvan? That's the wrong direction," Matthias protested. Tatvan was due east. However, they lived in the outskirts of Diyarbakir, the largest city in southeast Turkey, seventy miles to the southwest.

"Exactly," his father said. "If anyone comes looking for *him*, they won't find *us*. We can get there without having to pass through the lake region. And," he studied Roger's map with its prominent circle around Mount Ararat, "I believe the young man was headed in that direction." He pointed to the circled mountain. Scribbled drawings of Noah's Ark adorned the map's margins.

Roger remained unconscious while they loaded him onto the cart. At the last moment, Matthias placed the broken camera into the hip pouch attached to Roger's belt.

Matthias looked around at the moss banks of the pool. There was nothing to indicate that anyone had been there. They climbed into the front seat of the wagon and started their journey.

Two hours into the trip, Roger awoke babbling. "S-Stuart... E-E-Eden... E-e-earthquake... C-c-crater..." Matthias crawled into the back of the wagon and cradled the boy's head. Roger opened his eyes and stared up at him. "W-w-where are the goats?" he asked and then passed out again. Matthias climbed back onto the bench in the front, next to his father.

"He's American. I can tell by his accent."

Achmed grunted. Matthias knew his knowledge of English worried his father. His father reasoned that he had learned the language so thoroughly because he was planning to leave Turkey. This was only partly correct; Matthias would never shirk his familial obligations—although he'd gladly move to America if someone took the cross he was forced to bear by virtue of being in the direct lineage of Simon of Cyrene.

An hour later, reaching a well, they stopped to water the horse and have a drink. Matthias brought a cup of water back to Roger. He shook the American's shoulder, gently at first, proffering the cup of water—then firmly. There was no response. He lifted an arm. It was pale, limp. Suddenly anxious, Matthias felt the great vessels at the neck and lay his head on the stranger's chest. Dead!

He rushed to tell his father.

"Let us leave this place quickly," his father said.

"B-But—"

"*Abi*, NOW!" his father ordered, using the Turkish term that denoted Matthias as his eldest son and heir.

Achmed covered the body with a blanket, and soon they were on the road again. "This is a problem," he said to his son. "This is a big problem."

Matthias asked, "But surely the problem is not ours."

"Yes, it is! We are two Christians who are 120 miles from our home, and we have a dead body—an American—in our wagon and a kilo of gold beneath our seats. The settlement is under our protection. We cannot do anything that puts the settlers at risk."

Matthias had forgotten the gold the settlers had given them. Long ago, the settlers had discovered a rich vein of the precious metal while digging one of their hillside dwellings. Since then, they generously provided it to the Cyrene family to use when they needed it in the outside world as compensation for the ever increasing costs of their sustenance.

"Let's both think about this, and ask the Lord's guidance while we drive the rest of the way to Tatvan."

They continued in silence. It seemed to Matthias that his father was driving more slowly than before, as if to delay their arrival at the town for as long as possible.

Twenty minutes from town, Matthias motioned to his father to stop the wagon and said, "Why not simply proceed as planned?"

"What do you mean?" his father replied.

"Well, we were going to leave the boy at the medical center and then disappear, right?"

"*Tamam*, okay!"

"OK. Then that's what we'll do. We'll leave the boy outside the emergency room door and turn around and head back. He hasn't been dead long. The doctors will assume that he died right outside the door, trying to reach the medical center. They are more likely than anyone else in town to know what to do with a dead American boy. If God wants to keep the settlement hidden, He will protect us from discovery."

"So be it," Achmed conceded. "Let us pray that the Lord will accompany us every step of the way."

Both of them were well aware that the lives of more than two hundred people depended upon their secrecy.

The sun was setting when they deposited Roger's body at the foot of a ramp leading to the back door of the medical center. They were halfway back to the settlement before anyone noticed it.

◆ ◆ ◆

AN HOUR OUTSIDE THE TOWN, Achmed and Matthias pulled over for a nap. Matthias didn't relish sleeping in a wagon that had so recently contained a corpse. He mentioned that fact to his father, and they decided to sleep with their heads at the other end. Because of this, neither noticed the RBW (for Roger Bassett Warren) scratched into the side of the wagon by Roger during one of his final moments of lucidity.

NINE

WEDNESDAY, JUNE 22

BRAZIL

RICHARD ROEBUCK did not bring his personal helicopter pilot to Brazil; he'd had his own pilot's license since his late teens. The scruffy owner/pilot/receptionist of a small private chopper company on the edge of the Amazon rainforest received an unprecedented five thousand dollars for the use of his machine—no questions asked.

Richard used his personal GPS (Global Positioning System) device to pinpoint the campsite. Because he wanted to scrutinize the situation in advance, in secret, he set the helicopter down a mile from the research site, out of earshot. There had been no sign of civilization for three hours.

The overbearing odor—eucalyptus cough drops—reached Richard long before he reached the campsite. The Boalyptus tree— the object of their investigation—was huge, twenty-five feet in circumference. Seen up close, the resemblance to a Boab tree was undeniable, albeit with a bit of Banyan in its ancestry.

The majestic tree sat on the edge of a sinkhole that was ten feet deep and fifty feet in diameter; the overhanging section revealed a bizarre root system.

Richard recognized the tree from countless video transmissions. He scanned the sinkhole for the entrance of the tunnel leading to the main lab under the tree. Photos of the underground lab more often than not displayed a ceiling of hundreds of root tips—each terminating in a suction device with a tube connected to a workstation. The process was reminiscent of a dairy milking machine: *thwup-thwup-thwup*. Noisy, but Richard knew that with every *thwup*, the lab techs thanked their lucky stars that they didn't have to employ a distillation device like those used for the collection of maple syrup—that would have been like watching paint dry.

The sleeping quarters near the center of the sinkhole were crude, really nothing more than glorified tents. Next to those, two picnic tables beneath an awning abutted the kitchen shed. Opposite: supply bins, two small labs, a tap into an underground water source, a humming generator whose cables led to solar energy collectors on the forest canopy, two outhouses labeled *Adam* and *Eve*. The lush vegetation *did* inspire images of the Garden of Eden, until one noticed the fencing encircling the site.

What a job—two hundred thousand a year each, for camping in one of the most idyllic places in the world.

Plant life was missing from the floor of the sinkhole, as were the creepy-crawly things that lived close to the ground. The team had mixed an epoxy compound with the dirt removed from the tunnel to make a solid foundation. Standing on the fertile peat, looking down at the lifeless gray floor, he recalled the occasional and frustrating anomalies in the imaging software used by his satellite system—some regions appeared as empty gray circles no matter how extensive the tomographic data.

RICHARD CRAWLED closer to the edge of the pit. For all practical purposes, he was perched upon a natural canopy to the tunnel entrance as he strained to peer into the shadows. *Some of the roots are as thick as my legs!* Between two such tendons, a carefully excavated vent emitted light from the subterranean lab. He felt like Captain Hook spying on the Lost Boys.

Thwup-thwup-thwup went the suctioning tubes. Laughter emerged from the vent, then words and identifiable voices.

"Try this one."

"I'm wasted. Let Langford test it."

"Two volunteers please; one for the distillate and one for the synthetic."

"Gil's expendable; give him the synthetic." *(laughter)*

"...I'm...busy..." *(muffled)*

A female voice chuckled.

"Me too."

"Langford, what's the difference? We already have the formula."

Richard recognized Jed Bonham deferring to Dr. Langford Perkins, the research team leader—as usual. Suddenly, he realized what he'd just heard: They already had the formula! That fact hadn't been mentioned in their reports.

This sounds promising. He stopped, reconsidering his reservations. Maybe his reconnaissance trip had been unwarranted.

Two people emerged from the tunnel, hand in hand, sprinting to one of the tents. *My God! They're naked!* And giggling. Richard hid behind the tree, but the couple's backs were toward him; they were oblivious to their surroundings—apparently under the influence of something.

They're fiddling while Rome is burning. And I'm dying! He crawled forward, listening intently.

"I know we have the formula, but we have a dozen formulas. We need more control over the onset and rebound periods."

"I vote for the two-minute onset and five-minute rebound."

"Those numbers will be too low for some people."

"Let 'em call customer service!"

Richard felt confused. The conversation was not consistent with their reports. Sounds of lovemaking emerged from the tent, punctuating the fragments of sentences emanating from the air vent. Someone turned on a CD player in the lab and strains of heavy rock music obscured parts of the conversation.

"Listen. We have the perfect drug. This is going to make XTC extinct. *Ex*-tasy—*Ex*-tinct. Get it?"

"Langford, you're a...genius."

(Roaring laughter)

Yes, Dr. Perkins had been quite the overachiever, Richard recalled. The psych profile must have missed something though. His blood began to boil. Apparently, they'd succeeded in isolating the two components of the elixir, but they should be focusing on the healing ingredient. *They're not only using my money; they're making drugs.* As the discordant music grew louder, understanding the conversation became difficult.

"In the name of scientific—"

"...going to make billions."

"...still a breakthrough..."

"Absolutely..."

"...wipe out the XTC market...easily...an economic depression in the Netherlands. They make five billion a year selling *E*; they'll need a lot of wooden shoes to cover those losses."

(More laughter)

"Come to South America and learn to be a drug baron," two people chanted.

"But we have to string along the old man a few more months. Whose turn is it to give him the next report? I want that person clothed and coherent twenty-four hours in advance."

Richard had heard enough. He didn't need the adverse publicity that would result if he were to report them to the government— the buck stopped with him, anyway. But that was no problem. These people were expendable.

He drew two circles in the mud in front of him, one representing the subterranean lab under the Boalyptus, the other, the bivouacs. He picked eight seedpods from a branch, and placed two of these in the larger circle—those represented the couple still engaged in their arduous passion. Whenever he recognized a different voice coming from the lab, he placed a pod inside the larger circle. Soon, he had accounted for the whereabouts of all eight researchers.

He took two of the three grenades from his belt and placed them next to the circles. Sitting motionless, he pondered the situation and formulated a plan.

The lovebirds skipped from the tent to the tunnel. Richard moved the remaining two seedpods into the lab circle. They were all there—rats in a trap.

Idiots!

He quickly stood, armed a grenade, and tossed it over the rim to the far side of the exposed roots. He dropped the other one directly below his perch and ran.

Don't try this at home, kids.

When the grenades detonated, Richard was far from the tree. The majestic Boalyptus fell toward the sinkhole in slow motion with an ominous cracking. Screams cut through the noise. The tree jarred to an abrupt stop, its crown resting on the top of a tall palm. Now there was only screaming mixed with the blaring rock music. The Boalyptus settled at a 45-degree angle.

Richard returned to the site. The roots pushing downward formed a grating that cut off entry to the tunnel—now a rudimentary jail. On the other side, the back of the tree, the roots burst upward—another tangled barrier—many still attached to their extraction tubes. The tubes that had pulled free made grotesque sucking noises in time with the music: *thwup-thwup-thwup-chuka-boom-chuka.* Richard could see the lab some twenty feet below; jumbled bodies tried to escape through the tunnel, only to find it blocked. No one looked up.

He stepped out of sight and edged away, tracing a semi-circle around the camp and giving wide berth to a ten-foot army ant mound. When the kitchen was between him and the tree trunk, the tunnel entrance was visible from the rear window, through the screen door. The roots now barred all passage to the lab, but a hand hacked away at the bottom of one with a tiny dissecting knife.

After climbing in the kitchen window, he surveyed the provisions they had bought with his money. Sitting with a Perrier in one hand, and a plate of croissants on the table, the pitiful progress of the hand with the knife was, at least, entertaining.

Here's to stringing along the "old man." He raised his mineral water in a toast to the fallen tree.

Finishing his meal, he pocketed a mandarin orange ripening on the windowsill. Next, he climbed out the window and then reached back inside to retrieve two ten-gallon canisters of honey—organic; all eight crewmembers were vegetarians.

Back at the tree, another hand desperately sawed with another tiny lab tool.

The nozzles built into the side of the honey-cans were far too small for his purposes, but his pocketknife enabled him to peel back half of the upper lid of one canister. Shifting the container to block his face, he resisted the urge to heckle his captives; if they had any inkling of the source of their predicament, somehow it would come back to haunt him.

I own this honey. I paid for all this. I own these people!

He stepped to the spot where the hand frantically sawed on the roots. There was a startled "Hey! Who—" Richard began pouring; the honey flowed gracefully. Soon, the exclamations below revealed that everyone had assembled to see what was happening. Without trepidation, he fully upended the container, drenching their bodies with the sweet, sticky goop.

They hurled back obscenities. A few were so stoned they rolled around on the floor licking the honey off each other. The next part of his plan called for haste.

He kicked off the nozzle of the other can, and, starting at the former ceiling of the lab, slowly backed away pouring a thick trail of honey. It took twenty minutes to reach the army ant mound. Now nearly empty, the can was light; he ran as close as he dared, hurled it at the center of the mound, and rushed back to the kitchen shed.

RICHARD SAT in the kitchen inspecting the tunnel entrance through a pair of binoculars. No one was near the entrance. The sounds made it clear that everyone had decided to enjoy each other's honey-coated bodies. Outside the kitchen, he detached one of the tarpaulins, and holding it in front of him like a shield, approached the tunnel entrance. Unnoticed, he fastened the tarp to the wall of roots blocking the tunnel.

A hand grabbed his ankle.

"Hey man, whoever you are, help us out of here."

When Richard stomped on the wrist of the person clutching his leg, he both heard and felt bones splintering. The agonized expression on the face was easy to imagine.

Imbecile!

With the tunnel entrance covered, his plan proceeded unobserved. The army ants were only ten minutes away; their unmistakable crunching gradually overpowered the sound of rustling leaves.

First, he checked the researchers' "black box." It wasn't black, but orange: a ten-inch cube of almost solid steel with a handle, it contained a mirror backup of all the data from all the computers at the site. The inset LEDs indicated that it was synched up to the second. He ripped out the cords and ran it up to the edge of the sinkhole.

Then, he took a hammer to the computers, making certain to shatter the hard drives. Next, a strong tug on the cables leading to the rainforest canopy brought the solar-collectors and satellite dish crashing down, outside the sinkhole perimeter. Dragging them to the enclosure, he used them to pull down the fences, until everything converged at the center of the sinkhole.

He surveyed his work while eating one of the mandarin oranges. He spit the pits in an arc, toward the Boalyptus, trying to get them into the hole where he had poured the honey, succeeding with only three before giving up.

The first of the army ants came to the end of the honey trail. The trapped researchers were silent as they absorbed what was happening. Then, while thousands of hungry ants dropped upon them, they began to cry. Their desperate wailing was irritating, and when they started to scream, Richard picked up an iPod, inserted the ear buds, and pressed the Play button. Instantly, Barber's "Adagio for Strings" replaced the gruesome racket.

He smiled. *So much for health food.*

He took a box of explosives from one of the storage bins, and gently climbed out of the sinkhole. A steady two-lane highway of army ants surged behind the tree. It fit perfectly with the music. Within the departing dark mass, one area was incongruously white. He tiptoed closer to investigate. A miniature motorcade of particularly large ants struggled under the weight of five eyeballs. As he watched, the last two members of the procession paused and turned toward Richard.

He flinched, but then he saluted. *Here's lookin' at you, kid.*

The "Adagio for Strings" reached its final cadence as he lifted the explosives. The atmosphere was oppressive—no more sounds came from the captives, yet the crunching of ants continued. He threw the iPod into the center of the camp, and carried the explosives to the tree obstructing the cockeyed Boalyptus.

Attaching a cord to the grenade pin, he packed the grenade and the explosives at the base of the obstacle. After unwinding the cord, then backing away to a distance of thirty yards, he gave it a yank, pulling the pin from the grenade.

The explosion blew away the bottom of the supporting tree, and the Boalyptus continued its fall into the sinkhole. On impact, the epoxy foundation split. The sinkhole collapsed inward. A branch penetrated the quagmire, liberating the underground stream. The churning morass made a sucking sound as all traces of the camp folded under the fallen tree. Soon, the forest was still again.

The stillness brought to mind the ticking clock inside his body. There wasn't another human being within a hundred miles. Alone, he screamed at the top of his lungs: "I need a cure for cancer, not a drug to replace XTC!"

Nonetheless, Richard picked up the black box; he knew exactly where to sell the data it contained: the cartels that would bring its misery to every ghetto in the world long before legislation could be passed against it. This project hadn't been a total loss; at least he'd see some ROI—*Billions? Probably not. Hundreds of millions? Guaranteed!* — If he lived long enough.

Richard returned to the helicopter; he didn't look back.

Twelve hours later, he stepped onto the tarmac at the airport in Seattle.

TEN

TURKEY

MATTHIAS AND HIS FATHER were back at the pool the next morning; they traveled quickly through the hidden gorge. Neither could recall an occasion that had called for one of the Cyrene caretakers to return this quickly, for any reason. Nonetheless, Achmed had decided that this possible security breach warranted a break in procedure.

They walked quickly to the cloister. Barnabas sat at a desk perusing the newspapers and magazines that had arrived yesterday.

"Why, Achmed, what a pleasant surprise. I didn't expect to see you again for a month," he exclaimed.

"Brother Barnabas, dear friend, something terrible has happened." His father could barely contain himself. "We found a boy near the entrance...seriously injured, possibly from a fall off the rocks."

"And then what happened?"

"We transported him to a medical center, but he died on the way. From bleeding inside, I presume. There may be an investigation."

Barnabas listened attentively to the whole story. Then, with a mischievous grin that Matthias found to be out of place, considering the circumstances, he said, "We have a visitor, too."

Matthias could see that Achmed did not attempt to hide that he was appalled Barnabas paid him such little heed. The descendants of the apostles could give the impression of complete naiveté. They studied newspapers and magazines, yet they had no idea what it was like outside in the real world. Even more disturbing was their failure to understand the effect that death had on the rest of the world. Sometimes, caring for the settlers was like having two hundred children.

Matthias perceived his father's frustration growing and checked himself. At moments of aggravation like this, they both tried to remember that, with very few exceptions, none of the settlers had left this place since the founding of the settlement, two thousand years ago. Everyone present, except him and his father, had been born here and would die here.

Achmed tried to share Barnabas' excitement. "Oh really?" he said.

"Yes!" Barnabas' enthusiasm was evident. "He arrived yesterday after that little earthquake. I believe he fell from the rim of the crater. Some children brought him to me right in the library. He's injured, too. Maybe this is no coincidence."

"Is it serious? The other boy died."

"He can't walk...Sister Abigail is tending to him. She speaks English, and he does, too." He laughed, "So do I, of course." Brother Barnabas had a reputation as the linguist of the settlement; he often reminded others of that fact. "I understand that he's been sleeping quite a lot. He hit his head a few times rolling down the side of the crater."

"Can we see him?" Matthias asked. "The other one spoke English, too. Considering that they both turned up on the same day, I suspect there is a connection between them."

BROTHER BARNABAS led them through a hall and up some stairs. Stuart slept on a bed in a room overlooking the garden. Sister Abigail sat by him. They studied the boy for some minutes, and then returned to the hall to discuss the matter.

Matthias whispered, "The skin is the same color. The boys are approximately the same age. They both speak English." He glanced at the clothes on the table next to Sister Abigail. "The clothes and boots are similar."

He waited for Barnabas to digest the information, but the older man said nothing.

Matthias continued, "I conclude that the two boys were traveling together and somehow became separated by yesterday's tremor. Is it possible that they were on the rim and one fell in while the other fell out?" He used both hands to draw the trajectories in the air.

Barnabas admitted that it was.

"If that's the case," Achmed said, "then we must decide what to do with this one—"

"Stuart."

"—When he recovers."

"Naturally," Barnabas said. "Brother Philios has called a meeting of the elders for tomorrow at noon. Maybe you should stay over tonight in case you're needed."

"That will be fine with us," Achmed answered for both of them. Everyone present knew that Matthias yearned to spend some time in the library he loved so much.

THE LOW MURMUR of the powwow in the hall drifted into Stuart's room. It reminded him of the whispering—*Yes. Come to me.*—of his childhood, and his eyes flickered open with the memory. He raised his head and stared out the window. He saw the tops of trees with purple blooms on them. They were beautiful. He wanted to see more and raised himself onto his elbows. The trees were evenly spaced in curved rows.

The centerpiece of the garden seemed to be a large vine plant, also adorned with flowers, though crimson. The vines, if that's what they were, reached to the sky, then gracefully arched outward and downward as they plunged into the earth, thickening. The effect was like a cascade of water, as if a strong underground stream were bursting through the surface of a lake, straight up. The reddish flowers drooped off the vines like tears, reminding Stuart of a weeping willow tree. Unlike a weeping willow, this plant had no trunk and branches for support.

Or did it?

He looked closer and thought he could almost make out that, beneath everything, supporting the massive eruption of vines, was a trellis. Or was it? Straining his eyes to see closer, he suddenly realized it was a cross. Again, he thought he heard the whispered *Yes. Come to me...* but no; it was a warm breeze rustling the leaves.

An extraordinary feeling of peace overwhelmed him, and he closed his eyes again, drifting off to sleep.

◆ ◆ ◆

STUART DREAMED OF MEREDITH as he often did. They were walking by the sea in Santa Monica. They stopped to embrace, Meredith with her back to the setting sun. Her hair smelled of jasmine... and the sun shining through it made little rainbows. The effect was enchanting.

Maybe it was because Meredith's hair was different. It was special. She had more than her share of hair. Cascading down below the middle of her back, it swelled out with gentle waves until it was bigger than any other part of her body. They often joked that because of Meredith's mass of hair, forty men had to go prematurely bald, to maintain the balance of nature. Its thickness gave it a soft resilience that allowed it to move in opposition to the laws of gravity when she walked. When they embraced, he could feel hair cascade like silk over his arms; it was like a down comforter folding and molding around him.

He awoke thinking of her.

He missed Meredith acutely. He always did when she wasn't around, but she was usually around. At school, they were constantly together. He walked her to classes; she walked him to classes. They studied together in the library; they ate meals together in the cafeteria. They lounged in the student lounge together.

"You have it bad," Roger had said.

Stuart admitted that he was right.

"When are you going to show Meredith the true meaning of life?" Roger held the opinion *if it feels good, do it*. Whenever he saw an opportunity, he urged Stuart to take Meredith to bed. It had become more of an issue between them than it was between him and Meredith.

Stuart knew that Roger was proud of his sophomore sexual conquests, even more so than of his freshman victories. Thankfully, Roger didn't spend as much time bragging about them as some people he had encountered.

Actually, Stuart had assumed he would lose his virginity at college. It hadn't happened in freshman year. There was a great deal of physical attraction between him and Meredith. The touch of her skin against his sent a frisson of electricity to his heart and left him breathless. He sensed she felt the same way. Yet, the first time the heat of the moment threatened to overtake them, she had started crying. Stuart was taken aback.

"What's wrong?"

Her tears turned to giggles. "Let's save *that* for when we're married."

"Wait until we're married?" Stuart had replied. "I haven't even asked you yet!"

They laughed until they were gasping for breath. It broke the sexual tension of the moment, and the two of them ended up having a deep conversation about the matter.

Meredith had seemed embarrassed. "Everyone's experimenting—it's like they're riding a roller coaster in an amusement park dedicated to experimental behavior. They're stretching out, but the momentum driving them forward is forcing them to make life decisions without stopping to consider the consequences."

"Have you noticed people doing things just to demonstrate their free will—not because it was right or wrong? I have."

"Exactly!" Meredith relaxed. "Even where one path is indisputably the *right* one, they choose the other one. They say to themselves, 'If I were to do the *right* thing at this juncture, I would be doing so for no other reason than because it's right. But, if I do the *wrong* thing, I will be exercising my freedom to choose.'"

"They don't care about consequences."

"Especially the ones who say," she put on whiny voice, *"it wasn't my intention that such-and-such happened—"*

"—Their consciences are damaged."

Even before they had met each other, they both had felt detached from their contemporaries, a feeling that bordered on being outsiders. Their mutual decision for abstinence became another bond emphasizing the rarity of what they found together. When they talked about it, they found they were much more in love with each other than when they began the conversation. It became one of their inside jokes. Standing in front of a movie poster or a restaurant, one of them would say to the other, "I haven't even asked you yet," and they would both burst out laughing as hard as they had on that day.

The young couple had many inside jokes. And pet names. Meredith would put on her heaviest Yiddish accent, mimicking her uncle, and call Stuart "Schtoodles," at which point he would reply, "Meredith, Schmeredith." They had such fun together it practically hurt to think about her when she wasn't there. And she wasn't there now.

Stuart had been writing a letter to Meredith on the night before he and Roger climbed to the rim of the crater. Roger asked him what he was doing."

"I'm writing to Meredith."

"Can I read it?"

"Out of the question."

"Why not?"

"It's a love letter."

"If you can write it down, it isn't love."

Stuart thought about that. After a while, he concluded it was the wisest thing Roger had ever said. He threw away the letter and wrote a postcard to Meredith instead. He saw a corner of it sticking out of his pants pocket—his clothes lay folded on the table next to Sister Abigail.

Stuart realized he would not be able to reach the card. *Are my legs paralyzed? Will I ever walk again?* His heart began to thunder in his ears.

What would Roger do in this situation? Stuart was aware that much of Roger's fortitude was a façade; he suspected that his friend might have broken down whining by now. In fact, he found that his own stoic reaction to the situation surprised himself.

I'm in the middle of nowhere. I don't even know where I am, can't speak the language, and likely won't ever walk again; so why am I feeling optimistic?

Debating how to phrase a question to Sister Abigail, how to ask her whether there had been any news about Roger, he slipped back into unconsciousness.

◆ ◆ ◆

WHEN STUART AWOKE, a strange young man was sitting where Sister Abigail had been.

"I'm Matthias." The stranger said, stretching out his hand.

Shaking it, Stuart felt a lifetime of manual labor in its roughness. "Stuart Pierce."

"How do you feel?"

"My legs seem to be paralyzed, but other than that, I can't complain."

"Do you know where you are?"

"In the crater?"

"Yes. In the infirmary."

Stuart glanced out the window, remembering the cross. "Is this a monastery?"

"Something like that."

"I thought so."

"Why?"

Stuart nodded in the direction of the cross. Matthias looked out the window and seemed surprised that the cross was visible from Stuart's bed.

"Are you a believer?" Matthias asked.

"A what?"

"A believer. Do you believe in God?"

"I think there is a God. Of course, I'm not one-hundred percent sure."

Matthias looked puzzled. "I believe in God with all my heart. Thus, I can understand there might be people with the opposite belief. However, I cannot comprehend being uncertain." He waited for Stuart to continue.

"I've tried to find God." Stuart surprised himself by pouring out the story of his lifelong spiritual quest to Matthias, a perfect stranger. Ten minutes later, he concluded, "I suppose even this trip to find Noah's Ark ties in with that search."

"Noah's Ark?"

"That's why we're in Turkey."

Matthias sighed. "You're American, aren't you?"

"Yes. From Los Angeles."

"I'd like to go there some time."

"Roger and I just completed our sophomore year at college in L.A. —Hey! Where is Roger, anyway? Hasn't he found a way down yet? Is it possible to climb into the crater from the rim?"

Matthias stood up.

"I'll try to get some information about him," he said, and quickly stepped into the hall.

Sister Abigail returned. She was pretty and that made Stuart yearn for Meredith. With a sudden shock he felt himself wondering, *Will Meredith still love me if I'm a cripple?* He forced the thought from his mind.

Stuart stared out the window again. The cross-shaped trellis brought to mind a paper he had written for his "Comparative Religions" course. Inspired by Father Romero's sermon, Stuart's essay had compared his and Meredith's decision concerning sexual abstinence, with the story of Calvary—Golgotha, the Hill of Skulls—the three crosses, Jesus in the middle, one criminal crucified next to Him— mocking him, another on His other side—repenting moments before death; everything came down to two choices. Stuart's speculations on the symbolism of an absolute standard of good versus evil had annoyed the professor who had been a staunch advocate of relativism.

He found the strength of his conviction growing. *Am I changing?* He asked himself the question repeatedly. *Is it because of my legs? Will I ever walk again? Moreover, if I can't walk, how will I get out of here?*

He soon drifted off to sleep.

ELEVEN

THURSDAY, JUNE 23

DAWN

THE THREE GUARDIANS sat around a circular table, upon which rested a diorama. Three miniature towers were equally spaced on the model; lines drawn between them would have created an equilateral triangle. Each man sat behind one of the towers—behind the particular tower that was his responsibility. They stared, they prayed, and they stared some more. They deduced, they discussed, they debated, they disagreed, they stood and paced, and then they returned; the cycle repeated; the order wasn't always the same; neither were the players.

"Thirty-three years."

"But only eleven remain."

"And then what?"

"Will the long-awaited Day begin?"

"Let's look to the earth." They walked in silence to a place where a small fence encircled a barren spot of ground, twelve feet in diameter. Out of habit, they assumed equidistant positions around its circumference mirroring their earlier positions around the diorama. They stared at the ground.

"Nothing."

"Which, in itself means nothing."

"Or it means that we are nearing the end—"

"Are we to believe that tree number one-hundred-and-sixty-two is the last one?"

"I do."

"And the earthquake yesterday…is that connected?"

"I believe it is."

"Then how?"

"It's a sign from God; most earthquakes are."

"Will there be a bigger one? Should we sound the alarm?"

"Not yet. Not yet."

"That young man who fell into the crater, is he part of it?"

"I believe the events have now commenced. I think the young man is part of what's going to happen."

"But what role does he play?"

They turned to look at the garden, at all the blooming trees that had mystified them for nearly a year. Slowly they walked the course, passing by each one, stopping, counting, memorizing, comparing.

They would do the same tomorrow—and the day after that, and the day after that…

NOON

INSIDE THE CHURCH, Philios and the other elders met around a long table in the gallery—the one above the aisle on the north side of the nave. Philios, statuesque, with classical proportions, sat at one end of the table—Achmed at the other. Matthias, who normally didn't attend elder meetings, sat on a chair a bit removed from the table but closer to his father than to any of the other elders. Barnabas was also there, similarly placed; he wasn't officially an elder either.

Philios took inventory around the table: Achmed—the provider; Jared, Boaz, Simeon—guardians; Pius, Gregory, Theophilus—scholars; Micah, Nathanael, Gamaliel—from the Hall of Names; Zebediah—the farmer. They were all good men.

"Brothers, we have a problem," Philios said in the deepest part of his already deep voice.

"But before we speak of that, I want to clarify that Barnabas and Matthias are here at my invitation. They are free to join the discussion whenever they have anything to contribute.

"Maybe Barnabas should start."

Barnabas moved closer to the table.

"Esteemed colleagues. I think all of you know we have a visitor. This is a rare event."

"It has never happened before," Jared interrupted.

"As the Lord is my witness, it has," Gamaliel said.

"Saint John the Divine," Pius added.

"Actually, it has happened at least eight times in the last two millennia, not counting John," Philios interjected. "Let us allow Barnabas to present a summary, please?"

Barnabas described everything involving Stuart that had transpired in the past forty-eight hours.

When he finished, Micah said, "Brother Philios, you stated that this has happened before?"

"Yes. On five of those occasions, the *visitor*, so to speak, did not survive the fall into the crater; three others went on to live out their lives with us. None of those three married; their bloodlines ended."

"And don't forget the three women," Achmed added. "Once, my great, great grandfather came upon the bodies of three young women as he turned the corner in the ravine. No one ever discovered who they were, how they had died, or how they had ended up there. We don't even know whether they had been all the way into the crater."

"So you are saying that throughout the past two thousand years, we have had twelve visitors total, excluding John, but the effect is as if there had never been any. Is that correct?" Gamaliel asked.

"Essentially that is correct."

"Then what makes this one special?"

"Perhaps I can shed some light on that," Achmed said. "The boy Stuart was not alone. During the earthquake on Tuesday, he was on the rim with a friend. He fell into the crater, but his traveling companion fell onto the boulders outside the gorge. The other boy died while Matthias and I were taking him to a medical center. There will be inquiries. Both boys are American; an investigation is likely. Surely, the parents of the boy who survived will demand that local authorities undertake a search. In fact, a search may already be underway."

The issues surrounding a search provoked a good deal of concerned murmuring around the table.

"That this comes during our watch is no coincidence," Philios said. "Consider the developing situation in the garden."

"Yes," said Jared. "We are considering that situation. You know that is what we do all day, every day. We are no closer to determining the meaning of the concurrent flowering of the trees than we were when it began, a year ago."

"And the bearing of fruit remains an even greater mystery," Simeon added.

"You said that three visitors remained with the settlement in the past," Nathanael asked. "What is to prevent this one from staying?"

Matthias raised his hand. "Maybe I can answer that."

"Go on."

"Stuart is a seeker. I've talked to him. He hasn't found the Lord yet, but I do believe he is close. Secondly, I agree with my father's concerns; we need to talk seriously about the likelihood of an investigation."

"So what can we do?" Boaz asked.

"Brothers," Philios said, "I believe as always, there is one solution, and only one solution. We can pray."

The rest nodded.

"God is doing something with the garden and with the visitors. And maybe, with the people who will come seeking him. Who are we to understand the ways of the Lord? The Lord has been faithful to us in the past. Let us not forget who brought us here in the first place. The Angel of the Lord said, what our ancestors did has been done in Heaven, 'For this place is here, though it is also in Heaven.' Moreover, that we 'have nothing to fear. No evil will befall' us."

Everyone around the table joined him in saying, "The King of Kings has need of this place when he returns."

"My considered opinion is that we do nothing but pray. God is in control of this situation, and He will show us what His plans are, if it is necessary that we know."

Matthias added, "And let us also pray for the soul of the boy Stuart. The Holy Spirit is working intensely in him. That is evident in everything he says. Pray for his salvation; I believe that will resolve all our other concerns."

"Do not let the boy leave our village until there is a resolution," Jared said.

"Of course not."

The fourteen men prayed until the middle of the afternoon. Everyone at the dining hall noted their absence.

TWELVE

LOS ANGELES

AFTERNOON (GMT-7)

WALTER AND KATHY WARREN waited in a rarely used office at LAX—Los Angeles International Airport. Less than 24 hours ago, they had received the call from the American Consulate in Turkey. Their only child Roger: killed in a climbing accident. His body would arrive today, at three o'clock in the afternoon.

Walter couldn't stop the words of Arlo Guthrie's song from replaying in his brain, like a broken record. *Be the first one on your block to have your boy come home in a box.* Once he had shouted aloud, "Stop!" but it had had no effect.

Between sobs, Kathy Warren mumbled "Why God? Why God?" The words ran together until they sounded like, "God Why? God Why?" Then she would burst into tears and start all over again.

The two pitiable parents stared into the empty space between the window and the clouds. Nothing had prepared them for this. Nothing had prepared them for anything like this.

Brad and Margaret Pierce rushed into the office. "We came as soon as we heard," Brad said.

Walter glanced up. Brad had a developing potbelly that, depending on what he had been eating, sometimes managed to force open the space between his two lower shirt buttons for a peek at the world. Right now, it seemed to be staring Walter in the face.

The disarray of Margaret's straight, light-brown, shoulder-length hair disclosed her state of mind. She sat down next to Kathy and pulled the weeping woman's head to her shoulder. It was an awkward moment. Roger's fate was known, yet there had been no word about Stuart.

Brad had the rough, five-o'clock-shadowed face of a blue-collar worker, a practical man. His expression conveyed a no-news-is-good-news attitude that Walter found utterly inappropriate.

An airline official stepped abruptly in front of their seats. "Please come with me," he said flatly, as the couple looked up at him with eyes of despair.

◆ ◆ ◆

A MAN FROM THE MORTUARY stood next to the aluminum coffin.

Coffin!

The word exploded in Walter's mind and took on a completely new meaning. Kathy had thrown herself on the thing, wailing, pounding on it, as if destroying the cursed box could "take back" all that had happened, all that had led to their standing there now. All that had resulted in the death of their child.

Their only child.

The mortician's cleanly pressed suit and smooth glazed shoes contrasted sharply with Walter's wrinkled sports coat, matted white shirt, and wingtips in desperate need of polish. Walter's horn-rimmed glasses completed the picture of a professor's professor. He lifted them when curious, and used them to punctuate his remarks when excited.

Looking around, Walter lost track of reality for a moment. *Where's Roger? We're supposed to be meeting Roger and Stuart here after their trip abroad. Where are they?*

Everything else was a dream: the casket in front of him, his sobbing wife. It wasn't real. Neither was the man in the suit handing him a brown cardboard package.

"Here are his personal effects," the man said. "I'm sorry. The manifest says his boots were stolen."

Personal effects!

There's nothing *personal* about a brown cardboard box with the name of his dead son written in magic marker on its side.

He began to break down, to stumble. The package started to fall from his hands.

"Mr. Warren," repeated the man, catching the box and forcing it back into Walter's reluctant grip.

Their eyes locked.

Walter could see that the mortician understood his pain. But his eyes were saying something, too: *You're the father. You're the man. Be the man. Be strong.*

Walter straightened his back and looked at the stranger with gratitude. Without opening the package, he kneeled down to comfort his wife. It was an instant in time, frozen forever. Seared into their minds was an agony that would often return, whether they liked it or not.

◆ ◆ ◆

WHEN THEY GOT HOME, Walter tossed the package onto the kitchen table and rummaged in a drawer for the box-cutter.

Kathy came to life. "You're not going to open that now, are you?"

"If I can find the box-cutter, I am."

"Those are Roger's personal effects," she continued. "There might be something…you know…personal, in there."

"You mean 'personal' like the day you found that packet of letters under Roger's bed—letters between him and the Pierce girl, Cynthia?"

Roger had discovered Kathy reading the letters and shouted, "Mom. Those are personal!" Indeed, they were; Walter had read a few of them, too. He saw his wife blushing at the memory.

"It didn't seem to change your attitude toward Roger at the time," he continued. Nevertheless, Walter knew it had made her wonder why he never sent such graphic letters to her. She mentioned the incident now and then. He suspected that the question was going through her mind again right now.

Walter stared her in the face. "Do you think we will find something that will change our feelings for our son? I wouldn't worry about that."

He cut open the box. There wasn't much inside: Roger's Swiss Army knife, a cheap wristwatch, his belt pouch (empty), his new digital camera (smashed), his dilapidated world map, and a map of Turkey. He laid everything out on the kitchen table and discarded the box.

They stared at the items in front of them. Walter remembered giving the camera to his son for his birthday a mere three weeks ago. It had set him back a pretty penny. Roger had been so happy with it. Now, here it was, smashed!

Kathy pointed at the camera, "We should get the pictures developed." She straightened her curly, blond hair. It was permanently in a permanent. Walter realized he couldn't remember what it looked like when he met her.

He didn't feel like wasting any more time explaining to her that this camera was a digital camera and didn't use film. She hadn't grasped his prior explanations of that fact.

He wondered if it would be possible to retrieve the pictures from the device. Picking it up, he pressed an oval button next to the view-screen in the rear of the camera. The words "Low Bat" appeared on the screen and it sputtered out.

"I'll take this to someone in the digital imaging department tomorrow; maybe they can salvage the photos."

They went back to staring at the items on the table. Neither moved; there was nothing more to say.

The ring of the telephone broke the stillness. Kathy answered it.

"Oh. Hello Father Romero…"

"…Yes. We're holding up…"

"…We have Roger's camera and may be able to see where he was at least—" She choked on her words.

There was a long pause, and Walter surmised that Father Romero was consoling her. His wife responded without emotion, "Yes, tomorrow afternoon will be fine. Come by anytime. And don't forget, we want to have the service the day after tomorrow. On Saturday... Goodbye."

"What was that all about?"

"Father Romero wants to meet with us tomorrow afternoon. We have to make some decisions about the service and so forth."

"And so forth?"

"You know: the burial, the religious aspects. That type of thing."

Walter harrumphed. He considered the campus chaplain to be a buffoon. He had given up on the church long ago. Oh, he still went to services; Kathy would have worried too much about his immortal soul if he stopped attending. Further, he had many friends among the parishioners. Yet, if he hadn't lost his faith when his parents died, the death of Roger would have killed it. Better this way, he reasoned. Otherwise, he might be in Kathy's position now, questioning God every moment. For that matter, if there really were a God, why *would* he let such a terrible thing happen? Walter didn't get it. That's why he didn't ask himself those kinds of questions anymore.

He placed the camera in his briefcase. Delicately, he set the briefcase down next to the front door, and went upstairs. He lay in bed for hours, staring at the ceiling.

THIRTEEN

EVENING

BRAD AND MARGARET PIERCE had trouble sleeping. Not knowing whether Stuart was alive made it feel like time had stopped.

Brad retreated into himself, running through potential scenarios until they had enough detail to piece together a plausible reality. When that happened he would speak aloud.

"This has got to be those Kurdish Separatists. Somehow, the boys were mixed up in that conflict over there. Roger must have mouthed off at them—he's done that to me you know—so they killed him. Now, they're holding Stu hostage. Probably the consulate already has the ransom demand but isn't telling us for reasons of national security."

(Ten minutes passed)

"No. It's gotta be the Shiite Muslims. Islamic Jihad. They beat up Roger because he's a Christian. Probably caught him praying. I've heard they kill Christians. Maybe they didn't mean to kill him, but they beat too hard on the boy. Thank God this family's atheist. It probably saved Stu's life."

Brad had no idea what Shiite Muslims or Islamic Jihad meant, or Kurdish Separatists, for that matter. Nevertheless, he had heard these terms on the radio and deduced they were definitely the bad guys.

(Another ten minutes)

"Well, they were right next to the Russian border, weren't they? What do they expect from those commies. Two red-blooded American boys. Don't we have NATO bases in that part of the world? You'd think that with what we pay in taxes, they'd at least be able to protect our kids."

(Ten minutes)

The litany was like a wave. Whenever it crested, Brad broke out his latest theory. When there was no response, it subsided, only to build to a peak again.

MARGARET WARREN had a different way of dealing with the situation. She never stopped talking. It didn't matter whether Brad was listening or not. She kept rambling on and on.

"If only the boys had stayed home this summer. Last summer was enough.

"We should never have let them go abroad again. What were we thinking?

"This wouldn't have happened if they hadn't gone to that primitive country…*Where is Turkey anyway?*

"We could've had just as much fun going to the beach here…and Disneyland…*I've never been out of California. It's not necessary.*

"They would both be alive now if only I had been stronger. I should have put my foot down and forbidden it. All this exploration, expedition—it's all guy-stuff. Dangerous. Something was bound to go wrong."

Margaret had forgotten her therapist's advice not to say *could've, would've, should've,* or *if only.* Moreover, there was a good reason for that. She was rolling a growing snowball of subjunctives that threatened to burst apart when it collided with the wall of present tense reality at the bottom of the hill.

This might have gone on all night if Brad hadn't suddenly sat up in bed and shouted, "We've got to do something! We have to go over there and find our boy and bring him home."

"Brad. What can *we* do? The authorities say they're handling it. They said they'd find him."

"That's not good enough, Margie. They might not find him in time. Whatever happens, we're not accomplishing anything here. I'm going to Turkey after the funeral. You can come or not." He turned over with an air of finality.

For some reason, Brad was able to fall asleep after this outburst. It was as if, now that there was a plan of action, everything was going to turn out all right. Margaret lay awake, her eyes filled with apprehension.

◆ ◆ ◆

SHORTLY AFTER MIDNIGHT, Margaret heard Brad whispering, "Margie. Are you awake?"

She turned to him.

He fumbled the light switch on his night table and sat, cross-legged, facing her.

"We've got to start planning this now."

"Oh Brad. I don't know. Do you really need me to come too?" *If only I had gone with my roommates that summer in college when Suzie and Lorraine went to Italy; it might not seem so foreign now...* "Don't you think I'm a bit old to be traipsing off to Turkey on a moment's notice?"

"Of course not. I've never been out of America either. Nevertheless, we have to do this. Nobody's as motivated as I am. Come on Margie. I'm sure we can find him. Let's go look at some maps and call the airport. We're wasting time."

Reluctantly, Margaret got out of bed and followed Brad. They tiptoed to Stuart's room, careful not to awaken Cynthia. There was a world map pinned to Stuart's wall, and a globe next to his desk.

Looking at the map in Stuart's room, they realized that Turkey *was* quite far from California. They checked it on the globe; it was practically on the other side of the planet.

Margaret looked around her son's room. Nineteen years of memories. She saw her old lava lamp that she had given him when he was nine. His bulletin board still displayed his high school swimming certificates. A pair of running shoes lay next to his bed, as if he had kicked them off moments ago. The telescope that he had won in the science fair pointed out the window, ready for him to walk in any moment and look through it.

This may well be all that I have left of my boy, forever—for the rest of my life.

She put her hand inside Brad's and said, "Count me in."

She used to say that a lot when they were sweethearts in high school. Brad stared into her eyes, feeling as if they were teenagers again. Margaret realized she hadn't used that expression once since she returned from college. She wondered whether Brad had guessed what happened there on that one weekend that had so drastically changed her personality.

"You're on, baby," he said, just as he used to say in high school.

FOURTEEN

FRIDAY, JUNE 24

MORNING

B RYCE BRINKMAN was checking the satellite readings
from the previous night when she heard an urgent knock at
her office door. *That's a man,* she said to herself. *No woman
knocks like that.*

"It's open," she hollered.

Walter Warren came in puffing. "Professor Brinkman?"

"You are?"

"Walter Warren from the history department."

He looked familiar. She assumed she had seen him at the fac-
ulty club. At least he wasn't one of the ones who persisted in hitting
on her incessantly. She knew she was a knockout, but that didn't
give them a license to come sniffing around her office, prowling for
cake.

"Come in. By all means, come in." She made a sweeping gesture that involved her whole arm and took in the whole office.
"How can I help you?"

"Professor Brinkman, I was wondering…"

"Bryce," she said.

Walter held up the broken camera. Bryce made a show of looking offended. *Do they think this is a camera repair shop?*

"Bryce," he hesitated. "My son had a fatal accident in Turkey earlier this week. They sent his body back yesterday." Walter's voice was cracking. "His camera was with it. I thought maybe…"

Bryce softened. "I'm so sorry. I don't know what to say. Have a seat. Let me see what I can do."

"It doesn't use film; it's digital," said Walter.

Bryce saw him glance at the words "Department of Digital Imaging" under her name on the smoked glass of the office door. "Oh well then. We're all 'digital' in here. You've come to the right place."

She smiled as she took the camera from Walter's outstretched hand. Their fingers touched as he handed it to her. In that moment, she knew what he was thinking: too pretty to be so scientific.

Bryce fiddled with the camera for a moment. "The battery's dead."

"I know," said Walter.

Apparently, he's not a complete techno-illiterate.

Bryce's office was spartan. The absence of books seemed incongruous to the university environment. An immense flat-screen monitor on her desk dominated the room. On one wall, a series of plaques arranged vertically, proclaimed Bryce—some with and some without the Department of Digital Imaging—as the recipient of this or that research grant. At the bottom of each were the words, "Richard Roebuck Research." There were no gaps between the dates.

Bryce noticed his furtive glance to her vacant ring finger. She also knew that rings didn't stop most men. When he looked up, their eyes met. He blushed. "This is a very nice camera," she said. "It takes professional memory cards, like mine."

She opened the drawer to her desk and took out a similar camera that Walter recognized as the top of the line from his shopping experiences of last month. She slid out her camera's memory card and inserted the one from Roger's. Pressing some buttons on the back, she showed Walter the view-screen.

"The pictures are all intact. Do you want me to print them?"

"Please," Walter answered.

Bryce transferred the card to a slot on the printer behind her. After a minute or two, she handed the memory card back to Walter.

"The images are on the printer's flash drive now. It will take only a few minutes to print them." She fiddled with the printer.

The machine warmed up with sounds of incomprehensible internal mechanics. It made a sudden click-clack, and a large glossy photo slid into the printer's tray with a whirr. It was a picture of an old man in the front of a goat wagon. Obviously, someone standing in the wagon had tried to capture the goat's point of view in the photo. Bryce handed it to him. There were a dozen similar shots.

She stood and straightened her skirt. Bryce always wore light-colored suits with skirts above her knees. She came around her desk to look at the photos with Walter.

"Your son is a good photographer." She winced. "I'm sorry. I forgot."

Walter attempted to smile, unsuccessfully.

The next photo was different. Bryce and Walter studied it to-gether. It revealed a small village within a crescent-shaped mountain range. In the center, they saw a sizeable church with a round golden dome. Beyond the church were several smaller buildings, perhaps a monastery. The pillars of all the structures were gold as well. The mountainous crescent in front of the church was dotted with dwellings that seemed to extend into the rock. There were additional cave-like openings on the wall behind the church. In the foreground, they saw a farm, and what looked like the beginning of a grove of fruit trees. In the background, in front of the far wall, was a garden unlike anything they had ever seen.

"That's the last photo," announced Bryce. "Where is that place, anyway?"

"We don't know," admitted Walter. "My son didn't regain consciousness after he reached the emergency room. The doctors said that his internal injuries were consistent with those of a mountaineering fall. Maybe this is where he was climbing. They were searching for Noah's Ark in Turkey."

Bryce checked something in the display of the printer. "That picture was taken at 11:47 p.m. on June 20."

"It looks extremely sunny for midnight," Walter said.

"Right. Your son probably still had the camera's clock set to California time." Her eyes glazed for a moment while she calculated. "That would make it 8:47 a.m. on June 21, in Turkey."

"Time of death." A shadow passed over Walter's face.

Bryce shifted uncomfortably. She didn't know what to say.

Grasping the stack of photos, Walter said, "I don't want to take up any more of your time. Thank you very much for this. You've been a great help." Walter clutched the photos as he left Bryce's office.

◆ ◆ ◆

BRYCE BRINKMAN locked her office door and entered her lab by her personal entrance next to the desk.

My lab, she thought smugly as she closed the door. She surveyed the spacious laboratory. Four graduate assistants concentrated intensely at separate workstations. Earl, her primary research assistant, was sitting in an open cubicle that commanded a view of the whole lab.

Earl Cole had been her assistant since her M.I.T. days. In fact, he was the one who had urged her to apply for the Triple-R post-doctoral fellowship. It was only right that she brought him with her when she moved to California; his salary was well within her budget. Still, she felt that there was something weasel-like about him. Worse, he smoked cigars—big fat Cohibas that someone smuggled in from Cuba. She didn't completely trust the man. What's more, he had a tendency to sweat when he was nervous, frustrated, or afraid.

In spite of this, Earl possessed a relationship to "edges" that Bryce was still trying to fathom. She knew his type. She suspected that in his teens Earl had been like one of the boys who sat by her in sixth grade—the ones who doodled pictures of airplanes firing small projectiles out the front of their nose cones. Their missiles traced a trajectory defined by endless repetitions of themselves, each painstakingly hand-copied along the imaginary flight path.

She was probably the only girl in the class to realize that those missiles had targets outside the edges of the paper. Had they been real, their paths would have annihilated certain other class members, usually those who were tormenting the boys during recess, but often the teacher. With a quick rotation of the paper, the ones drawing the missiles could disavow any criminal intent.

Earl wasn't as good a programmer as Bryce was—she often reflected that references to her work were the first time in history the words "woman" and "programmer" had been used in the same sentence in a positive sense—nonetheless, he had managed to develop his childish game into an adult art form.

Bryce used great subterfuge to discover this secret weapon.

Earl's program allowed him to enter the three-dimensional co-ordinates, with a precision in millimeters, of any other person in the lab. Then he could type text on the side of a virtual missile displayed on his laptop, and aim the screen at that person, silently performing a countdown. A press of the ENTER key launched the projectile at its target. Stunning visual effects occurred as it gathered momentum and seemed to pass through the edge of the screen, into the imaginary space between Earl's laptop and the victim's head. His eyes tracked the progress of the invisible weapon at every stage of its journey. An assortment of sound effects accompanied the impact, debris and occasional body parts being flung as far back as Earl's screen and appearing there at the appro-priate moment, a convincing illusion created by computer animation: never twice the same.

It had take Bryce years to discover what Earl typed on the pro-jectiles he sent whizzing around the office. When she had, her opinion of him fell yet another notch. The payload delivered by his creations revealed much about his inner personality. All the virtual ICBMs he aimed at the cute female graduate assistants were labeled according to the theme, "I strongly desire to sleep with Earl Cole," whereas those bearing Bryce's own name often simply stated, "drop dead." Yet, even this knowledge stimulated Bryce's theories about thinking beyond the edges. Earl was definitely outside the edges; on the other hand, he had never known what it meant to live on the inside of them.

EARL'S CURIOSITY often bordered on suspicion. "What was all that about?" he asked.

"Not much," Bryce said. "A prof from the history department had a problem with his son's camera. That's all."

"Anything *interesting*?"

"Maybe."

The word "interesting" held special connotations for both of them. Richard Roebuck, Bryce's billionaire benefactor, was interested in *interesting* phenomena—the type of things that the magazine *Skeptical Inquirer* was always trying to discredit.

Six years ago, Roebuck had read Andrew Carnegie's "Gospel of Wealth" in which the once king-of-robber-barons declared the end of the iron age and the beginning of the steel age on the first day of the twentieth century with the words, "The man who dies rich, dies disgraced."

Carnegie boasted 400 million dollars when he retired, a vast sum for his era. Declaring that "a kept dollar is like a stinking fish," he turned his efforts to philanthropy. He gave away 350 million of his fortune to causes, often offbeat: 7,000 pipe organs to churches, for example. Thirty million went to old friends and tenants. Much of the rest went to establishing funds some of which shamed the government for not having thought of them first. Notable among these was a pension fund for presidential widows.

The man detested the concept of family trust funds, saying, "I'd sooner leave my children a curse than a dollar." Carnegie left his wife and daughters only enough to carry them through one generation.

Intrigued, Roebuck had made inquiries about recent recipients of Carnegie's charity.

Roebuck came upon the name Bryce Brinkman. Digging further, he ended up spending an afternoon studying Bryce's dissertation on "Very-Long-Distance Non-optical Imaging." He ordered a clandestine background check, including a discreet psychological profile. He could recite it from memory.

SEX: FEMALE.
AGE: 34.
IQ: 200+.
PHYSICAL HEALTH: EXCELLENT.
MENTAL HEALTH: OVER-ACHIEVER.

```
SPIRITUAL FACTORS: NONE.
HISTORY: MIDDLE CHILD OF 5, RURAL
          PENNSYLVANIA.
ECONOMIC SCALE: ±57.
ATTACHMENTS: STRONG ATTACHMENT TO
          FATHER, (NOW DECEASED).
RELATIONSHIPS: NONE.
EVALUATION: SELF-AWARE, SELF-STARTER,
          EGOTISTICAL, INVENTIVE, GOAL-
          DRIVEN, SPORADICALLY
          ARROGANT, POSSIBLY A FAÇADE
          FOR DEEPENING LONELINESS.
SKILLS: UPPER-MANAGERIAL, PROJECT
          LEADER, DISCOVERER.
FIELD: SCIENTIST, VERY LONG DISTANCE NON-
          OPTICAL IMAGING.
CLASSIFICATION: UNATTACHED TYPE—A
          WORKAHOLIC.
```

Roebuck told Earl, whom he secretly paid to "prospect for minds" at M.I.T., to make certain that Bryce applied for the next Triple-R grant. Bryce was completely unaware of the behind-the-scenes aspects to her good fortune.

AFTER TWO YEARS of successfully applying Bryce's revolutionary imaging techniques to Roebuck's own satellite network, Richard invited her and Earl to his palatial home outside Seattle for a week.

Bryce had been surprised to find him so charismatic. He possessed an honest-looking, baby face, with dirty-blond hair that looked as though it had just been ruffled by someone's hand. Wire-rimmed glasses completed the picture of innocence.

The purpose of their visit was not rest and relaxation. Throughout the week, they met with doctors, a few scientists from the private industry sector, and professors from other universities funded by RRR.

They learned that Richard Roebuck was dying. It was a rare form of cancer. Its progress was slow, but the outcome was inevitable and medically irreversible.

"I've applied much of my wealth to genetic engineering corporations and other institutes conducting DNA research."

"I've heard," Bryce said.

"So far, these aren't moving quickly enough. I suppose I'm an impatient patient."

Bryce smiled.

"Several years ago, I decided to explore more esoteric possibilities. One of my funding recipients compiled a list of *interesting* phenomena: areas of research that offer some chance of reversing this ghastly disease that is determined to bring about my early demise."

"What type of areas?"

"Here are some examples—now don't laugh—the Fountain of Youth, the Fruit of Immortality, Magnetic Resonance…We found a whole sub-category of healers in various third-world countries. Roswell, and other similar unexplained phenomena are on the list."

He pointed to the bookshelves behind his desk.

"My teams of scientists have produced volumes upon volumes containing all existing credible research on those topics."

Bryce saw applications for her personal work in many of these explorations.

They sat in the billionaire's living room, the lakeside of which was entirely glass. Bryce listened as Richard described his goals while they shared a glass of wine from a bottle that cost more than she earned in a month—a fact she was unaware of at the time.

Richard stood in front of his living room window that provided a 240-degree panorama of pine trees and shoreline. His house was the only visible structure for as far as the eye could see. The natural beauty outdoors framed his silhouette.

"The world will be a different place when we pin down the 'Y-factor'."

"The Y-factor?"

"We use the term Y-factor to mean the cure for disease and old age. Think of 'Y' as representing 'Youth.' Or, imagine 'Y' to be one step beyond 'X,' the letter associated with claims of the paranormal."

Richard made a feeble attempt to portray the altruism of Andrew Carnegie's "Gospel of Wealth."

"The press has accused me of devoting an inordinate amount of resources to the Y-factor out of purely selfish motives—"

"*Time Magazine?*"

"—'A dying billionaire's self-centered grasping at straws,' I believe is how they put it in *Time*."

"I read that."

"I want you to understand that such claims are not true. Naturally, I want to live. Every human wants to live. We all have a built-in sense of self-preservation. But think of what harnessing the Y-factor will do for humankind. Bryce, I vow to you that the results of our labors will be available to every member of the human race. This is not going to be an elixir of the rich and famous."

Bryce was impressed.

Much later, she would discover that Roebuck's decision to market the youth serum was far from noble; it stemmed from financial considerations alone. He had long since worked out the numbers relating to selling a longevity product to a small group of the wealthy, versus selling the product to the population as a whole. The figures were undeniable and inescapable. He would make much more money in the end, by wide-scale sales to John Q. Public, than he would ever make by selling the product to the one percent of the people who controlled ninety percent of the world's riches.

Bryce noticed that throughout all their conversations, the success of the mission was never in question. That was understood. It was always "when" we achieve the Y-factor, never "if" we achieve it.

Roebuck was clearly accustomed to having everything go his way. So was Bryce for that matter. Had she known the truth about her own indomitable successes, she might have conceded that her career represented nothing more than another one of Roebuck's achievements.

WHEN THEY RETURNED to Southern California, the focus of her lab shifted. While the graduate assistants continued to work on collecting data and honing Bryce's imaging software, Bryce and Earl sifted through terabytes of satellite input looking for Roebuck's Fountain of Youth. Only the two of them, and Roebuck, were aware of the true nature of their work.

After Bryce's initial reports, Roebuck arranged for the expansion of her lab and an expense account that was, for all practical purposes, bottomless.

Now, six years later, the wellspring of research money showed no signs of running dry. Bryce's technical resources had expanded to cover the globe. From both her desk in the outer office and her console in the lab, she had access to more information about the surface of the planet than anyone else in the world, excluding Richard who owned the whole system. She firmly believed the old adage; knowledge is power. But wielding that power, well, that's what complicated matters.

FIFTEEN

AFTERNOON

WALTER AND KATHY sat on the couch across from Father Romero. He was sitting in the most comfortable armchair in their house. The grieving father paid little attention to the conversation. *Let Kathy handle this*, he said to himself. *She's the religious one*. Besides, he wasn't convinced that Father Romero's effusive commiseration was fully genuine.

Walter wanted to go upstairs and lie down again. It was only 4 p.m. but he felt as though he had put in a full day. Maybe when he awoke everything would be back to normal.

"Are you sure you won't have another cup of tea?" Kathy asked, and Walter realized that Father Romero was standing, ready to leave.

In the midst of Walter's misery, standing up was like rising through clotted cream that had gone sour. *Am I expexcted to say something?*

"Father Romero," he said, taking the photographs out of his briefcase, "I wonder if you've ever run across a church like this." He handed Roger's last photo to the priest.

"Certainly." Father Romero glanced at the photo, and then studied it closely. "This is a Byzantine church. I wrote my thesis at Boston College about Byzantine churches."

"Boston?"

"I tried to get as far from Mexico as possible when I chose a college; in those days, some of us were ashamed of coming from south of the border."

Walter nodded, knowingly.

"Before I came back to Los Angeles, I spent three years abroad on a T-REX grant—that's the Theological Research Exchange—continuing my research. When I returned, I published my findings as "Byzantine Churches of the Holy Land and Bordering Regions." You probably haven't read it—it's somewhat of a coffee-table book for the clergy."

Walter tried to conceal his surprise. Father Romero didn't seem like the type to have written a thesis for an advanced degree in any field. He felt a twinge of shame for falling victim to the Mexican stereotype portrayed by the media. The idea of a "coffee-table book for the clergy" threw him a curve. He didn't know whether Father Romero was making a joke, or maybe the clergy did have their own demographic these days, including a backlist of clergy-oriented coffee-table books.

Father Romero had deflected the original question so master-fully that Walter couldn't think of any safe way to respond. He simply kept his mouth shut as he took back the photo.

ROGER'S PHOTO had made a deeper impression on Father Romero than the bereaved couple grasped. Shocked that he couldn't immediately identify the church in the picture, he resolved to check his book for it when he returned to the rectory. Surely, a church with such extensive gold embellishment would be easy to spot among the nearly one thousand photographs he had assembled and annotated in his book.

But he already knew there was no such golden church in his book, and that fact sincerely disturbed him. His book contended to be complete in its coverage of the subject.

He tried not to display the extent to which the photo had stirred up his curiosity. This was clearly not the time for that. He should be focusing on the grieving couple that had lost their son.

◆ ◆ ◆

BRYCE SAT DOWN at the largest console in her facility, the one in the center of the lab that faced the private door to her office. She accessed her office printer on the network, and copied the files she had saved from Roger's memory card. She launched a proprietary software program she had written that was one of the backbones of her research, and initiated an analysis of the photo of the mysterious monastery.

The photograph appeared on her monitor as a flat image covering most of the screen. She clicked a button on a virtual palette, and slowly the image began to shift its angle. The top rotated backwards while the bottom seemed to rise. An imaginary line bisecting the photo horizontally was the axis of this rotation. As the picture rotated, the various objects within the photo extruded in three-dimensions. Before thirty seconds had elapsed, a 3D projection of the image filled her screen, and she could view it from any angle.

What the government wouldn't give for this software.

And that was essentially the problem; Roebuck could afford to pay her far more than the government.

She loaded the software model she had created into the WCD—the World Contour Database—as a search entity. In less than a minute, the words "NO MATCH FOUND" appeared on her screen. *That's odd.* Roebuck had long ago mapped the contour of the entire globe with his satellites. Those mappings were all contained in her database.

She tweaked a few software controls and executed the search a second time.

Still no match.

Then she remembered that she knew the exact time of the photo, 8:47 a.m. local time in Turkey—5:47 GMT. She studied the shadows cast by the church in the center of the photo. There was only one place in the world where the shadows were like that at 5:47 GMT on June 21. *That was the solstice too*, she recalled. *That should make it easier.*

She extracted the shadow patterns and, using the archives from earlier in the week, she ran a shadow pattern search on Turkey, based on the known time and date. Again, the computer failed to find a match.

This was starting to become a challenge. Bryce liked challenges. Pattern matching was not the solution; she turned to mathematics.

Again, starting with the shadows, she figured that calculating the length of the shadows in the photograph, at that precise time, in that particular country, should allow her to pinpoint the location. Bryce searched for a frame of reference to use for measuring the shadows. She decided that the doorways of the church were probably a good place to start.

"Cole," she shouted across the room. "Would you get me the dimensions of a collection of representative church doors in Turkey, please?"

"Any particular region?" Earl Cole was accustomed to Bryce's bizarre requests and was unfazed; he immediately commenced perusing the net for information.

"Give me the doors of six, typical, domed churches equidistantly spaced and located as close as possible to a line bisecting Turkey from west to east."

"No problem."

Half an hour later, Earl strolled over to Bryce's workstation with a printout of the information.

"What's up?" he asked.

"I'm trying to pinpoint the location of this church, and it's not in the WCD, so I'm triangulating using the shadows from this projection. I need the door as a known reference. I already have the exact time and date."

"I'm sorry, but Byzantine church doors—and that is a Byzantine church, look at the shape—range from 2.1 meters to 4.8 meters. That's a wide range."

"But it will help."

Bryce entered the constraints into her program, and selected an item from one of its menus. Seconds later, a map of Turkey appeared with a box superimposed upon it. The box designated a rectangular area from 38 to 40 degrees latitude and 40 to 43 degrees longitude.

"That narrows it down."

"Have you tried the heat signature?"

"We're still trying to reduce the search area to something manageable—"

"Biological chromatography?"

"Not yet. How about you run the heat signature and I'll check chromatography."

"OK. That dome is brass, I presume."

"Nope. Real gold. That's one of the first things I checked. The secondary reflections and tarnish pattern gave it away."

"Well, that quantity of gold in one place should have an entry in the metallurgy profile for the region. I'll look into it." Earl went back to his desk.

Bryce used an on-screen eyedropper to take a sample of the predominant color of the flowers in the garden behind the church. Purple. She noticed a tiny area of red showing through between some of the flowers, and sampled that as well.

When Earl came back, she was staring at the screen, deep in thought. "According to all the mineral data for the region, that place doesn't exist. How did *you* do, Bryce?"

Bryce jerked back to reality. "See that little blotch of red? That's a one hundred percent match with the color of human blood. Then again, many known flowers are that color.

"Now, look at the surrounding purple vegetation. There's no match anywhere on the planet for that shade of purple. I ran it through every comparison I could think of. It does not occur in nature."

"Those are plants of some kind," Earl snapped. "That's obvious."

"Yes. I can see that. This has to be a singularity. These plants are one of a kind. I should call Richard immediately. Cole, can you copy this image to him? I'm going to need to refer to it."

◆ ◆ ◆

TALKING TO RICHARD ROEBUCK always made Bryce nervous. The man was dying after all, and she couldn't forget that he pulled the strings controlling her financial future.

"Richard, it's Bryce Brinkman," she said shyly.

"Bryce! You're the only Bryce I know so you can drop the Brinkman."

She blushed and heard him chuckling.

"I've just received a remarkable image from Cole. It has the caption, 'Bryce wants you to see this.' What's it all about?"

"Yes sir. I'm phoning about that image. It's definitely somewhere in Turkey. I rendered it, but I couldn't find the model in the WCD. There's a good deal of gold in the region, but our metallurgy concentration maps are drawing a blank. Also, I shadow-triangulated the region using the heights of doorframes of existing churches as a reference point. Now, I've narrowed down the field to an area of 320 by 240 kilometers."

"Byzantine churches," Richard interjected.

"Yes," Bryce continued. "All the similar churches that Earl found were Byzantine."

"And?"

"I noticed an *interesting* factor when I ran the spectral chromatography on that garden in the background of the picture. That plant, whatever it is, doesn't exist anywhere else in the world."

"The purple might be grapes."

"Why do you say that?"

"You're talking about the region where Noah's Ark reportedly set down. There are many indications that the first fruit Noah planted after the Flood was a grape. There's even an ancient town around there whose name translates to 'Where Noah Planted the Vine.'"

"Anything else?"

"Is the town of Van in your target field?"

She checked.

"It is. Why?"

"Because unique to that region, is the Van Cat. It's a protected breed: a bushy white cat with one blue and one green eye. It doesn't exist anywhere else in the world either. Strange, eh?"

Bryce deflated a notch. Sometimes she got the feeling that Richard knew everything.

"Exact coordinates?"

Bryce recited them; she could hear Richard typing over the phone.

"Did you notice the region had an earthquake on Tuesday?"

Bryce quickly checked the information in a small box at the lower left of the map on her screen.

ACTIVITY: 21:06—05:48 GMT LATEST
SEISMOLOGICAL (6.7 RICHTER).

The time indicated was one minute after the photo had been snapped.

How could I have missed that?

"That's one minute, possibly less, after the photo was taken."

"Yes." Bryce's parachute was losing wind by the second.

"If this crater were the earthquake's epicenter, that church may have been reduced to a pile of rubble."

Bryce was searching the net for that information.

"The epicenter wasn't close enough to any of the three craters we're looking at. It is unlikely that the church sustained damage."

"I know."

He had already checked, of course.

"Why do *you* think it's not in the WCD?" Richard asked, as if sensing her discouragement.

"We haven't got every inch of this planet in the WCD yet," Bryce answered, "as you well know. And as you know, many larger meteor craters are not included because their residual magnetism clouds our sensors. Remember, we're the ones who aren't using any optical techniques in compiling the database. Computer programs based on optics combined with expert systems are subject to optical illusions just like people, and our system tries to eliminate that possibility. There are several craters in Eastern Turkey; at least three are in our target region."

"Judging from the characteristics and curvature of the mountain range in the photo, I suspect this is a view from the rim of a crater. The problem is, which one?"

Inside she cringed. Craters bothered Bryce because the SAT-Net allowed her to see only their edges. It was like a trip back to the blurry parts of her childhood. She was five-years-old, looking up at the large wooden bowl on her father's desk; the one she was too short to see into; the one from which her father pulled coins and candies, keys and cards, and once a kaleidoscope that had changed her dreams. By the time she was tall enough to peek into it, she had misplaced its mystery. Richard's satellites and her computer programs provided her with access to the entire planet. However, when it came to meteor craters—thankfully, not all of them—she was able to map only their edges, nothing within those boundaries.

"Bryce."

"Yes?"

"Were you aware that some early churches in what is now Turkey contain meteorites? Venerated objects…"

Bryce's gasp was audible in Washington State.

(silence)

"You know who took the photo don't you?"

"Yes, the son of a professor in the history department. But the boy is dead; his body came back in a box. There's no information on where he was hiking. Someone dropped him outside an emergency room in Tatvan, roughly equidistant from all three craters. He said he was going to find Noah's Ark; therefore, I'd vote for the crater near—"

"—Mount Ararat, of course." Richard finished her sentence. "This *is* interesting. Let me think about this for awhile and get back to you."

◆ ◆ ◆

EARL COLE WATCHED Bryce's mood swings with amusement while she talked to Richard on the phone. During the conversation, his email icon started flashing and he checked his inbox. There was a message from Richard. *He must be typing to me while he's talking to her*, Earl realized.

RR: Cole, if you receive this while I'm still talking to Bryce, open your chat-window.

Cole opened an IM session immediately, and began typing.

Cole: Here I am boss :-).

RR: Is Bryce onto something?

Cole: I did the metallurgy scans myself. We both worked on the triangulation. And I've double-checked the chromatography. She might be.

RR: Should we pursue this?

Cole: You're the boss ;-).

```
RR:        You know I'm paying you more than
           her to watch her so you can advise me
           on this type of decision. What's your
           advice?!?!?!
Cole:      I say go with it. It's more promising
           than anything else we've had for the
           past three years.
```

Earl noticed that Richard had logged off without saying thanks or goodbye.

Typical.

Nevertheless, he did appreciate the vote of confidence in his advice…nearly as much as he appreciated knowing that his salary was nearly double that of Bryce. And knowing that she didn't know it had sustained him through many confrontations with the stuck-up ice-queen over the past eight years.

Of course, it was also true that Richard Roebuck "owned" him—had owned him ever since the first time he met him that night in the *Bois de Boulogne* on the western edge of Paris, thirteen years ago. The scarf had been too tight; the girl had died in the bushes. Girl? A *poule*, a *cocotte*, a streetwalker. He assumed they were alone—it was 3 a.m.—but Richard had been sitting in a parked car, watching, filming, and scheming. Richard had called it "a classic case of Desert Island Defense Syndrome"—two people are on a desert island, a mountaintop, or alone in the wilderness; one suddenly has an irrepressible urge to kill the other just because there are no witnesses, just because he can get away with it; most don't act on the urge. Most who do are never caught. The syndrome had been used as a defense in murder trials since the 1950s and had resulted in acquittals, but never in France. Earl argued that it had been an accident—in fact, it had been, though no one would believe him. Richard said not to worry; he wouldn't say a thing, but he might need a favor sometime. The newspapers reported that the woman was a single mother supporting three children under the age of six, now orphaned. Four years later, Richard phoned and demanded payment, just like the devil.

Sixteen

Seattle

OUTSIDE SEATTLE, in a room more voluminous than most houses, Richard Roebuck sat staring at the three computer monitors on his desk. Behind the monitors, he could see the lake and vast forest. He was alone.

The first monitor provided a real-time display of his wealth in the upper half of the screen. Below that were up-to-the-minute graphs of all the major stock markets in the world.

The second monitor displayed the projections of six doctors about how much longer he had to live. These ranged from two months, to two years.

Two of the doctors, his personal doctors, lived on the premises of his estate. The other four comprised 'outside opinions.' Three of these 'outside opinions' were human, the fourth was an expert system called MEDEX running on a super-computer in Berkeley, California.

The graph displayed time on its horizontal axis, with today's date at the far left. The vertical axis measured confidence, on a scale of zero to one hundred. All the doctors updated their estimates daily. The computerized doctor updated its opinion continuously.

The doctors could do this because Richard Roebuck had a monitoring device implanted in his body—in fact, several. These tiny devices continuously transmitted his physical profile to the doctors' computers. For MEDEX, the intermediary wasn't needed. Richard's implants communicated a stream of information about his blood, as well as other bodily fluids, and processes. By pressing one key on the keyboard, he could bring the entire data stream up on the screen if he wanted to, but he didn't. He avoided scrutinizing his situation that closely.

The software running on Richard's computer examined the ever-varying opinions that it received and plotted them on the temporal graph. Then, based upon the inside and outside estimates of his mortality, combined with the latest cancer survival statistics for the world, the computer defined an average region of days and confidence about when Richard would die.

It was terrible.

The shape changed continuously, and he couldn't stop himself from looking at it. It contracted and expanded on both the temporal and confidence axes—almost billowing. Right now, the far left border of the highlighted region edged past the two-months boundary, bringing his earliest possible expiration date closer to the current date. Death never had been this close. Granted, where it crossed the boundary was only at a forty-two percent confidence level, still, the other end of the region, at fourteen months, was only at a fifty-nine percent confidence level. Five months along the graph, the confidence region reached eighty-three percent. Richard didn't like to see that.

Bryce would say I'm only looking at the edges.

He tried to look at it her way, without success.

The display on the far right monitor was roughly a twin of the one on the middle monitor. Instead of doctors, it displayed the opinions of the various astrologers, healers, shamans, herbalists, and holistic medicine men that he consulted, and who were on retainer.

Richard had become surprisingly superstitious, making certain to isolate the two sets of opinions from one another. He kept their data and programs on different computers that weren't even on the same network, as if one might infect the other.

He found it amusing that the New Age practitioners were consistently more confident than the ones who had graduated from medical school. Their mortality estimates were usually two months better than their counterparts. Richard suspected that they merely wanted to prolong their paychecks.

He usually took an average of the two figures, two and four months, in this case.

Three months to live…That's not fair!

He looked around at the spoils of his vast empire and, for the umpteenth time, tried to understand how the richest man on the planet could be condemned to die in three months; how something that was too small to be seen with the naked eye, was nonetheless determined to kill him. And how it could be that no amount of his money could change that fact.

Money had no value if what you wanted to buy wasn't for sale.

He didn't like to think about what would happen if he were unable to solve this *problem*, as he called it. There was no denying that his efforts had thus far yielded precious little.

◆ ◆ ◆

RICHARD HAD NEVER been interested in spiritual matters before he became ill. His only spiritual experience to date, the memorization of one hundred Bible verses to win two baseball tickets, had left no lasting impression, although the verses remained inscribed within his photographic memory to this day: *He that hath no money; come ye, buy, and eat; yea, come, buy wine and milk without money and without price.* They made no sense at the time, and still confounded him. Attending that baseball game, at which Justin Robinson had proclaimed that Richard was going to Hell for being an atheist, was the last time he had thought about God.

Until recently, that is.

Because he was funding research into so-called *interesting* phenomena, he found himself brought into contact with many people who were spiritually oriented. The word "God" had been spoken more times in his house, than ever before, and certainly with greater reverence.

At first, he considered "God" to be merely something else to search for, something that could be found by applying a well-funded research group or scientific expedition to the task. So far, it hadn't turned out that way.

Three months!

He stared at the graphs again. He knew he was only looking at the edges, and one edge in particular. He was relying on Bryce's ability to look between the lines.

Three months!

It was getting close, whatever it was. He needed a solution quickly.

◆ ◆ ◆

FIVE MINUTES AFTER BRYCE hung up the phone, she slowly strolled to Earl's cubicle, stopping briefly at each grad-student's workstation along the way.

The phone rang again. Earl answered it, then said, "For you."

Naturally, it was Richard. "Let's go for it, Bryce."

"That was quick."

"Well, you know I'm a bit pressed for time. How soon can you and Earl be ready?"

"Give us 24 hours."

Earl started to sweat.

SEVENTEEN

SATURDAY, JUNE 25

TURKEY

AFTERNOON (GMT+3)

STUART AND MATTHIAS talked together in the library. Stuart was still in a daze from the church service. "That was wonderful," Stuart said to Matthias. "All those songs...in so many languages."

"I noticed English, French, German, Latin, and Hebrew," said Matthias.

"I think there were more—"

"Maybe."

"—And the sound was heavenly."

"Practically everyone was singing...except the babies."

"How many do you think there were?"

"As a matter of fact, I know the exact number. There were 211 in church today, counting the three of us visitors: you, my father, and me.

"And when Philios preached..."

STUART HADN'T CONSIDERED that Philios preaching in English was anything out of the ordinary. Had he known English was being spoken in deference to his own linguistic non-abilities, he might have been embarrassed. Everyone he met since he had arrived spoke flawless, though heavily accented, English.

Sitting in a wheelchair near the back of the church, Stuart felt completely at home. He didn't question the feeling. He reached beside him to touch the smooth coolness of the stone pew next to him, polished by more than a thousand years of use.

Philios told the story of the crucifixion. Stuart had read the story before, although he didn't recall that the version he had read included all the details Philios was mentioning. He found it particularly odd that Philios used the words "our ancestors" so often. Then he remembered where he was and chalked it up to the likelihood that some of these people could trace their lineage to the Jews of Jesus' time. Nonetheless, the large bushy-haired preacher spoke as if the events had happened yesterday.

Much of what he said began with the words "John has written..." and occasionally Stuart recognized fragments of what followed as being from the Book of John in the Bible. He remembered comparing several translations of that text for a course at school.

Interspersed with these quotes, he heard much description, evidently passed down through generations by word-of-mouth. "James son of Alphaeus said..." or "Bartholomew observed..." or "Thaddaeus told us..." or "Simon the Zealot saw..." and so forth.

"Joseph Justus called Barsabbas kept watch over the Roman soldiers through a crevice between two large rocks. *Our Lord is in there...in the tomb of Joseph of Arimathaea.* Barsabbas wasn't there to steal the body, as some had suggested. He only wanted to stay as close to Jesus as possible. All of them did. From my grandfather Philip's vantage point, when the stone rolled from the tomb..."

Stuart got the impression of an elaborate network of scouts recording the proceedings from many positions.

At every name Philios mentioned, one or more people in the congregation stood.

"Those are their descendants," Matthias whispered.

Philios continued. "It was essential that they remain hidden. Simon of Cyrene had received a vision from God when he carried the cross to Golgotha for our Savior. God revealed to him what would happen unless important steps were taken."

When Stuart heard the words, "Simon of Cyrene," he was surprised to see Matthias and his father stand.

Now, everyone was standing except Stuart.

Well, I have a good excuse. He looked down at his useless legs in the wheelchair. He hadn't thought about his legs since arriving at the cloister. Somehow, such afflictions didn't matter here. He wondered why he was unable to work himself into a frenzy over the loss of the use of his legs. Surely, he would be acting differently if he were back in California.

Philios began to lead a prayer.

Everyone standing raised their arms in the air, as if to reach up and touch God in the Heavens. Stuart had never seen such a thing. He bowed his head in respect.

The prayer went on and on and on. Stuart worried that he might doze off. Much of what he had experienced since his fall from the crater rim was like a dream. He wondered if he were having a lucid dream right now. According to an article he'd read, one could be conscious in the dream state, observing, or even controlling the flow of the dream.

His wheel chair started moving. He became aware of hands on his legs, touching every inch of them.

The praying became more intense, a language Stuart couldn't understand, had never heard before, and soon Stuart detected warmth permeating every atom of his body. A pleasurable humming, an almost electrical energy tickled his legs everywhere. He felt his soul being rolled into a perfect sphere of beingness, and he was gently cradled in loving hands and lifted up.

He pushed away his instinct to flee, and gave himself over to what was happening. It was like floating in liquid light.

Suddenly, the voices of the congregation stopped, replaced by a rustling, a wind that seemed to whisper *Yes. Come to me.* Stuart opened his eyes to discover that he was in the front of the church, and nearly all the men stood around him. The whole thing hadn't been a dream.

Philios was directly in front of him.

"Stand and walk," Philios commanded.

Dazed, Stuart obeyed.

Everyone hugged him, but he was only vaguely aware that he had been healed. Something far greater was happening within him.

EIGHTEEN

BARNABAS APPROACHED the two young men. He loved to explain how the library was organized. "We're standing in the Recent Reading room," he said, gesturing enthusiastically. To Stuart, he resembled Friar Tuck from Robin Hood: jolly, plump, and apparently gentle.

"In this room, we keep reading materials from the past ten years. The wall farthest from the door shelves the items that are ready, or nearly ready, to be transferred to the main collection. When I was very young, this room contained twelve years of material instead of ten. In my father's day, it contained fifteen years of books and journals."

He led them over to the leftmost of three doors on the western wall.

Looking through the door, Stuart saw a room with another door opposite to the one they were standing at; through that was another room with a door at its opposite—and then another and another.

On the outside wall of the room they were looking into, to the south—to their left—were windows. Another door was centered on the inside wall, to the right. This pattern too repeated through many rooms. In fact, from east to west there were three rooms across—corresponding to the three exits from the reading room—and there were seven rows of three rooms extending away from the Recent Reading Room.

"The seven rows of rooms correspond to the seven ages of history," Barnabas explained. "Originally, a single group of three rooms was attached to the Recent Reading Room. The remaining ranks were added when they were required. Thus, as we walk farther from the reading room, we walk through time, passing through 2,000 years of history along the way."

Barnabas pointed down the southerly row of rooms.

"This file of seven rooms contains writings that are godly, writings about God and about our Lord and Savior—or writings that were undeniably created to glorify Jesus and lead people to Him."

He led them to the far right door and pointed down its row of rooms.

"The north file of seven rooms contains writings of an opposite nature. Books on this side are written by those who deny Christ or who attempt to mislead people and turn them away from the Light."

"And the center rooms?" Stuart was becoming very interested.

"Those are classrooms. Children spend their first seven student years—ages eight through fourteen—studying the holy books in the south-side rooms. During that part of their education, they aren't allowed to enter the rooms on the north side, and they must do all their reading in the center classrooms—and under the supervision of their teacher."

Guiding them back to the far left door, Barnabas elaborated.

"The students commence their studies in the next room, with the oldest writings, and gradually move toward the present in the farthest room—one room per year. In this way, they collapse the entire history of mankind into a seven-year course of study."

"And then?"

"From the age of fifteen to twenty-one they are called novices, and as such, they study the books in the north row of rooms. They learn the manner through which 'he who rules this world' works to destroy God's creation."

"He who rules the world?" Stuart asked.

"Referring to Satan."

"Satan rules the world?"

"Let's come back to that."

Barnabas continued. "During this period—the teenage years—they study the more advanced holy books in the south file, too. They have their classes in the stacks along the north side or the south side so as not to disturb the younger pupils."

Stuart realized that the system needed to accommodate all levels of students simultaneously.

"At the age of twenty-one, they must decide whether to become scholars or not. Those who choose the scholarly vocation spend another seven years studying the books on the north and south walls of the classrooms. These books are corrupt in some way or another. The tainted books are like an apple with a worm in it; the ungodly parts are clearly delineated from the godly parts. The books on the north walls of the classrooms are more adulterated. They are like a cup of water with a drop of lemon juice; the lemon taste permeates the whole liquid, no matter how faintly."

Stuart recalled the bowl of lemon-water on the bus to Batman. This made him think of Roger. *Where was Roger? He's really missing something.*

Barnabas interrupted his thoughts. "Journals and newspapers are found on the rear (east) walls of every room, every room within a period that such writings existed, that is." They peered into the classroom. "As you can see, the front (west) walls of each classroom display maps and charts."

The layout looked surprisingly like a typical American classroom to Stuart.

"The walls separating us from the fourteen outside rooms, seven to the south and seven to the north, are designated for specific topics. As I mentioned, the back wall of each contains periodicals. The inner wall—the other side of the classroom wall—is where the holiest books are kept. The western walls have books written by people from the settlement. None of the outer walls—by the windows—have shelves, but they do have study carrels and desks. It's a matter of the light, you see."

The lack of electricity wasn't a problem—things had been designed to make the most of the available natural light.

"The inside shelves in these fourteen rooms are organized into four quadrants each. Northeast is for the sciences, southeast for the arts, northwest is for history and biography, and southwest is for literature, poetry, and fiction."

They walked to the center of the reading room. Equidistant from the four walls stood a diorama of the library—a scale model, meticulous in detail. Stuart crouched and peeked inside; the roof was cut away to display the interior of the connected buildings. The accuracy was extreme, and he imagined that this is what a three-dimensional photograph might look like. He found himself turning back and forth from the reality of the reading room to check details in the diorama.

"It's more than a simple model," Barnabas explained. "We use dioramas to record history; every object in the diorama contributes to our historical record—the details *must* be accurate. There are six more of these in the museum—one for each of the stages the library building has gone through. It's the same for all our buildings: an exact replica of every stone and brick, and every tile."

The settlers had developed the practice of miniaturization to an art form. The detailed faces on the miniature figurines were uncanny. Looking through the roof of the diorama, he saw a tiny Barnabas standing in the reading room. Outside the main door, two people carried bundles of books.

"Isn't this you?" Stuart asked Matthias.

The young man nodded and beamed.

"Every month Matthias and his father bring us at least a dozen books and several hundred newspapers and journals. Their family has supplied our reading material for nearly two thousand years." Barnabas looked gratefully at Matthias. "And other things, of course."

"We are the only family of the town that lives outside the crater—we live near Diyarbakir; it has been like that for two millennia," Matthias said. "The new books start out against the south wall of the reading room—"

"—But after a scholar reads a new book, he never returns it to the south wall," Barnabas explained. "Instead, he shelves it somewhere along the western wall—assigning it a category by where he places it: godly, or godly but tainted. The next person who reads that book will return it to the shelves to the right of the southernmost door, or to the left of the center door, depending upon his or her decision regarding it's final disposition. Our readers have varying opinions; consequently, certain books move around a lot. It takes ten years for a book to be permanently assigned a place in the stacks; by then, any controversies are usually resolved."

To say that Stuart marveled at the library would be an understatement; he was in awe—and not only at the idea of having the freedom to spend ten years in determining a book's placement; his mind reeled at the implications of a learning process integrating the written words of knowledge with the layout of the rooms that housed them.

Stuart pointed to the shelves on the north wall of the reading room. "What about those books?" he asked.

Barnabas smiled. "Like all the books in the Recent Reading Room, those too are less than ten years old, but they were written by our own scholars."

"Oh really?" Stuart ambled in that direction.

Barnabas headed him off saying, "Yes. Perhaps Brother Philios will let you look at them sometime. For now, I believe they deal with topics that might confuse you. Paul once said, 'I have fed you with milk, and not with meat: for hitherto ye were not able to bear it, neither yet now are ye able.' Let us continue our tour in the stacks."

◆ ◆ ◆

THE "STACKS" as Barnabas called them, were unlike anything Stuart had ever seen. Entering the first room through the far left door in the reading room, he felt as if he was going back in time. Many of the shelves held scrolls—they resembled his mental image of the Dead Sea Scrolls; in fact, some were even older; the dry desert air has a way of preserving such things.

"This room is dedicated to materials concerning history that pre-dates the birth of the Messiah."

Stuart pointed to some shelves with books that were clearly modern day. "What are those doing here?" he asked.

"Throughout the ages, many erudite and godly people wrote about the times before Jesus," Barnabas explained.

As they entered the second room Barnabas said, "This is my favorite room. It covers the birth of Jesus through the death of John, the last Apostle, in 100." He paused, "A-D" he added. "As you probably know, 'AD' refers to the one event that was so profoundly significant to the world, that people renumbered the counting of years, starting from that point: His birth."

Barnabas looked knowingly at Matthias. "None of the Apostles outlived John." Stuart noticed some unspoken subtext pass between the two of them.

He looked around. The room was full, bursting at the seams.

"I know what you are thinking. This room is stuffed. We are planning an extension to the south, to divide this material into two parts. The room we stand in now will go through AD 33, and the new wing will cover the rest. Of course, we will have to build a new wing to the north as well. It's just as crowded as this. Adding the new wings will make the library take on the shape of the cross." His enthusiasm was contagious.

"This next room starts with the invention of paper, and ends right before the Byzantine period," Barnabas explained.

"Not really," he said, smiling. "The invention of paper has little to do with the reason this room starts at the year 100. Again, it begins at the point in history at which there were no living Apostles; what some people call the beginning of the 'Church Age.' We often call this room, the Roman room."

Quickly ushering them into the fourth room, Barnabas said, "This room includes the main part of the Byzantine period, starting with the Council of Nicaea in AD 325 and ending at 641. A joyous 316 years of expansion. Our church—where you attended services this morning—was built during this period."

They entered the fifth room.

"This room encompasses the Middle Ages, arbitrarily starting with the year 642, nineteen years after Mohammed founded the heresy of Islam. No one remembers why that date was chosen to begin this room. One opinion is that 642 was the year we received a large 'donation' of manuscripts rescued from the fire at the Library of Alexandria in 640; it was necessary to build a new room to spread out the new acquisitions. Or, 642 was the year the remains of the Second Temple were cleared from the Temple

Mount in Jerusalem—the year the first structure for Muslim worship was completed in its place. That structure became the Dome of the Rock fifty years later; now they call it the Haram esh-Sharif, the 'Noble Enclosure.'"

"The golden dome in Jerusalem reminds me of the dome on the church here. Is there any relationship?" Stuart asked.

Barnabas gave him a strange look and said flatly, "None whatsoever."

Stuart blushed.

"According to some people, the Middle Ages ended in 1453 with the fall of Constantinople—the city you call Istanbul—to the Muslims. Others claim it ended with the invention of movable type printing by Johan Gutenberg in 1454. Actually, there was a time when the Middle Ages, the Renaissance, and the Reformation were taking place simultaneously, in different parts of Europe. Here we consider the 'Age of Reason' to have begun in 1455, with the publication of the first Gutenberg Bible, that marked the beginning of the widespread availability of the Holy Scriptures."

Barnabas directed Stuart into the sixth room.

To Stuart, it looked like an antique library. The books he saw reflected the development of printing techniques. He noticed that the arts quadrant of the room was filled to capacity, as was the northwest, 'history and biography' area.

They arrived at the last room.

"We call this room, the 'Age of Invention,'" said Barnabas. "This one also has a problematic starting date. We chose 1896 rather arbitrarily. Actually, we moved the date back several times and will probably do so again in the future.

"It's hard to pinpoint an exact year to begin this period of history. Starting in 1890 with the first motion pictures, invention began to accelerate. In the next fifteen years, man invented the diesel engine, flashlights, thermos bottles, electric toasters, escalators, loudspeakers, paperclips, air conditioning, disc brakes, airplanes, vacuum tubes, and photoelectric cells. Simultaneously, scientists made many discoveries: viruses, electrons, X-rays, hormones, blood groups, and vaccines. Aspirin and silicone also date from that turn-of-the century period, as did both Max Planck's quantum theory and Einstein's theory of relativity. All this had a profound impact on society. You can tell by looking at the art, and listening to the music created then. It was definitely a fascinating time to be alive."

"So why pick 1896?" Stuart asked.

"Because 1896 was the year of the invention of the modern-day typewriter. That particular invention had a powerful effect upon our little community."

Stuart recalled seeing quite a few typewriters throughout his tour.

He peered around the room. It resembled a room in a typical library like those he had frquented all his life. He recognized one of the newer books: *Goedel, Escher, Bach* by Douglas Hofstedter; he wondered if Barnabas had read it.

Stuart realized he could easily spend hours—no, days—within this room, within any of the rooms he had seen, so far. But Barnabas was determined to show him the whole library.

They went into the adjacent center classroom. Turning around for a last look at the first familiar things he had seen in days, he noticed that over the doorways connecting the stacks with the classrooms, the names of the historical periods were inscribed in six languages. The heading over the doorway they had just come through proclaimed, "Age of Invention."

NINETEEN

UNGODLY BOOKS—Stuart looked through the opposite doorway, to the north, the side of the building that Barnabas said housed such things. Oddly, what he saw was reminiscent of a contemporary shopping mall bookstore: the colors, covers, titles, and typefaces. *The Seventh Way, Wicca—A Handbook for Novices, New Age Shamanism, Buddhism for Beginners, Enlightenment for Dummies.*

He read over the categories beginning with the letter "A" on one shelf: Ascended Masters, Acupuncture, Akashic Records, Alchemy, Alphabiotics, Altered States of Consciousness, Alternative Medicine, Animism, Anthroposophy, Aquarian Age, Aromatherapy, Astral Projection, Astrology, Atheism, Atlantis, Auras, Avatars, and Ayurvedic Medicine. It went on and on. And those were just the A's.

Stuart shuddered. Those topics didn't do anything for him. He lumped them all together with UFOs. Substance? Nil, nix, nada. He couldn't understand why people fell for such things. Obviously, it was a big business. In the context of this quiet dreamy monastery, an edifice that he would have described as *holy*, such books seemed even more out of place.

Yet, Stuart had to admit that in some strange way, the gaudy covers and large titles were beckoning him, as they had in bookstores in the past—daring him to touch them, to open their covers and drink in their hidden knowledge, promising to divulge secrets that were essential to true happiness if he would only take that first step.

Not a chance!

Stuart turned back to face Barnabas.

Maps, charts, and timelines covered the front wall. The doorway in the middle actually had a door installed in its frame because it led to the outside. Otherwise, the room resembled a normal classroom.

Barnabas directed Stuart's attention to the right side of the wall.

"We may be isolated, but we do keep track of the world." Barnabas motioned to the topological maps, geopolitical maps, and statistical maps that displayed population density, climate, and religion. Many maps had arrows with dates beside them showing the movement of peoples, power, or ideas.

Stuart recognized most as Mercator projections, but he also saw several other types of projections that he had learned of during his last semester at college. There were several Lambert projections with the lines of longitude plotted at double their distance from the equator, their prime-meridian being half the length of the center line, giving the earth an elliptical shape.

Stuart turned to the left front side classroom. Two maps dominated the wall. Beneath them, a large strip of paper, three feet wide, extended the length of the wall on that side of the door. The bottom edges of the maps touched the top of the strip of paper. In the center of it, was a meticulously drawn picture of a cross. *Like the one that Jesus was crucified on*, Stuart presumed.

He suddenly realized that, excluding the one serving as a trellis in the garden, this was the first cross he had seen since arriving at the monastery. He found this astonishing. This was a monastery after all. *Or was it? Shouldn't there be crosses everywhere?*

He looked carefully at the picture of the cross. He saw lines originating from various parts of it, extending to its right under the map of the world. In due course, each line made a right-angle turn upward to the map. The lines continued onto the map and stopped at locations throughout the world. There appeared to be a pattern to it. Each line had compact text written along it, including dates corresponding to several different calendar systems.

His eyes followed one of the lines originating from a black dot upon the city of New York, down to the long sheet below the map. The line made a right turn to the cross. A red dot appeared on the point at which it intersected the cross. The line continued through the cross and farther along the lengthy strip of paper. It stretched to a chart consisting of a large spiral punctuated by green dots at regular intervals. The line he was following ended at the next-to-the-last green dot on the spiral. The number "161" was written next to it. Again, he saw text written along the line, but he was too far away to read it. He followed the spiral inward and saw that the center of the diagram bore a cross as well.

That makes three.

He walked closer.

"Let's see if we can find Matthias," Brother Barnabas said, maneuvering Stuart to the doorway at the back of the classroom.

Stuart wished he could look more closely at that cross but shrugged and followed the monk. He wanted to ask Barnabas why those were the only crosses he had seen in the monastery, but he quickly forgot the matter.

He saw newspapers and magazines on racks lining both sides of the doorway as they passed through it. Again, he felt as if he were in a library back home.

They found Matthias in the second room, sitting by a window with a book called *The Bible Jesus Never Read*, by Philip Yancy. Stuart realized he had never seen so many Bibles in his life. Matthias followed them back to the Recent Reading Room.

◆ ◆ ◆

THEY HAD KEPT their voices down throughout the tour of the library. As they returned to the reading room Stuart realized that they were alone. The paunchy librarian took the opportunity to shelve some books that were on the reading tables.

Stuart wandered over to Matthias. "Why isn't anyone else in the library?"

"It's the Sabbath," Matthias replied. "The people of the settlement take God's commandments to heart, rigorously. 'Remember the Sabbath day by keeping it holy. Six days you shall labor and do all your work, but the seventh day is a Sabbath to the LORD your God.' Wait until you see the hustle and bustle in the library tomorrow."

"I thought the Sabbath was Sunday."

"Not for us. Shabbat is from sundown on Friday until sundown on Saturday, as it has been for Jews since the days of Moses. Being Christians, the settlers don't observe all the contrivances about how to keep the Sabbath holy."

Barnabas was taking an interest in their conversation.

"Two of the Talmud treatises deal exclusively with how to observe the Sabbath," Barnabas commented. "But Jesus didn't tolerate such things. He said, 'And you experts in the law, woe to you, because you load people down with burdens they can hardly carry, and you yourselves will not lift one finger to help them'."

"In the Gospel of Luke," Matthias said.

"Right," Barnabas continued. "Jesus had many confrontations with the rabbis concerning the Sabbath. Whereas the rabbis focused on legalism, trying to make people follow their Sabbath rules as an end in itself, Jesus taught that God had created the Sabbath for the good of mankind. Therefore, man's needs must take priority over the laws contrived by the rabbis concerning the Sabbath. He even said, 'the Son of Man is Lord of the Sabbath,' and for this, a group of very legalistic Jews called Pharisees planned to kill him.

"Jesus, Himself, worshiped in the synagogue on the Sabbath. The Apostle Luke tells us: 'on the Sabbath day He went into the synagogue, as was His custom.'

"Most of the early Christians were Jews; they kept the seventh day, Saturday, as the Sabbath. However, the resurrection of Jesus happened on Sunday, and this is one of the cornerstones of Christian faith. So, they began to meet for worship on Sunday as well. They called it 'The Lord's Day.'

"In both Galatia and Corinth, Paul taught Christians to bring their weekly charitable offerings to the church on Sunday, the first day of the week.

"Then, during the Apostolic Age, the gap between Gentile converts and Jews grew. The Christians—the ones who didn't live here—gradually gave up their observance of the Jewish Sabbath on Saturday, and met for worship only on the Lord's Day.

"Here, we observe Shabbat, and we worship on both the Sabbath and the Lord's Day. Usually Philios preaches on only one of those days. Tomorrow, it will be one of the elders, although sometimes Philios surprises us. Moreover, on the Lord's Day, we partake in the Feast of the Lord—communion."

Stuart was fascinated. He could tell that Barnabas relished this opportunity to lecture him about the history of the people of the village. Matthias also appeared to be captivated, although he must have known much of what Barnabas was describing.

"In many ways, we have always resembled what the world now calls Messianic Jews. We never forgot that Jesus was a Jew, living among other Jews in a Jewish land. He kept the Torah. Being a Jew, He observed the Feasts set forth in Leviticus: Passover, Yom Kippur, Shabbat, and the rest. When Jesus referred to Scripture or said, 'It is written,' he was referring to what we now call the Old Testament."

"That makes sense," Stuart said. "The New Testament hadn't been written yet."

"In the Apostolic Age," Barnabas continued, "the question was not whether Jews could be Christians, it was whether Gentiles could be Christians. The Gospels were written not only to convince Jews that Jesus was the promised Messiah for them, but also to convince them that Jesus was the Messiah for the Gentiles as well as the Jews."

Stuart was beginning to realize that the settlement people had little contact, if any, with the outside world. He also realized that this was not the case with Matthias. Thinking of the outside world made him think of Roger, as he often had since awakening from his fall. Stuart had assumed that Roger would arrive at any moment. Now that four days had passed, he wasn't so sure.

"Matthias, a friend was with me up on the rim—right before I fell into the crater," Stuart said. "You know, Roger. Have any of the others mentioned him? He should have arrived by now. I'm worried."

Matthias winced. "Stuart," he said. "Maybe you better sit down."

Stuart felt himself being steered to a circular alcove on the north side of the reading room. Obviously, hiding his emotions was not one of Matthias' strong points. He was holding something back; his face at least, told that much. Yet, what story was he trying so hard to hide?

BROTHER BARNABAS hastily walked toward them, "Ah. You've discovered the Alcove of Saint John the Divine. Near the end of his life, he came to visit the settlement and he used to sit right where you are now. In fact, he's the last person to visit...officially that is.

"One of Matthias' own great, great grandfathers, Alexander, had heard that John was preaching in Ephesus and went there to tell him where the pilgrims had settled. John knew they had left the Holy City, but had not been able to get a message to them after the fall of Jerusalem in AD 70.

"John and Alexander showed up with a pack-mule loaded down with scrolls. We still have all those, in the first and second rooms on the left. John preached here for three months nearly every day. When I say 'here' I mean, right here. Right where you're sitting.

"Back in those days, the church hadn't been built yet. This was the main building. We gathered in this nook all the writings that were by, or about, John, including copies of the scrolls he brought with him, converted to traditionally bound books.

"Speaking of bound books, maybe you'd like to visit the scriptorium—the place where all the books are bound, printed, and restored? It's in that cluster of three buildings, next to the Museum—the same place they make the dioramas—and the Hall of Names." Barnabas pointed out the window, and then realized that Matthias and Stuart were in a serious discussion.

"Oh... excuse me for interrupting. Maybe another time." He backed away.

"You were saying you had something to tell me," Stuart looked questioningly into Matthias' eyes.

"Yes. I... er... don't know where to start." He hesitated, finally blurting out, "Stuart, I'm sorry to have to tell you this but your friend is dead. My father and I found him by the pond at the base of the crater. Apparently, he fell all the way down from the rim. When we found him, he was barely alive. He mentioned your name. He drifted in and out of consciousness. By the time we got to the medical center," he paused, "it was too late."

Stuart froze in mid-breath. He stared through the window at the crater wall. Slowly, each of his eyes glazed over with one large tear. He didn't blink. Neither boy moved. Matthias could practically feel the memories of Roger racing through Stuart's mind. His blurring tears hid the outside world only long enough to convey that every returning memory of his friend would be fainter than the last.

Stuart gripped Matthias' arm. "Matthias. Do you think Roger is in Heaven or Hell?"

TWENTY

A T THE SUGGESTION of Matthias, the two young men walked to the place where Stuart had fallen into the crater. They walked in silence until they were in the middle of the fruit orchard.

"So what's your answer?" Stuart asked.

"My answer to what?"

"Is Roger in Heaven or Hell?"

"Only God knows that."

"Last week I wouldn't have asked that question. I mean, I believe in God—I think I've always believed in God—but after being here I'm starting to believe in Heaven and Hell, too."

"And…"

"Well, is there some way to know whether Roger is in Heaven?"

"Did he believe in God?"

"I think so. He was a Catholic if that counts for anything."

"It doesn't. Did he accept Jesus as his Savior?"

"I don't know. He stopped going to church when we went to college."

"Jesus said, 'I am the resurrection, and the life: he that believeth in me, though he were dead, yet shall he live,' meaning in Heaven, for eternity."

"What is Heaven like?"

"No one except Jesus has ever been there and come back to tell us about it."

"Everyone here is a Christian, right? Doesn't anyone know what Heaven is like?"

"We do know that Jesus is there…And Satan isn't." Matthias said. "We also know there is no death in Heaven.

"We have indications that time flows differently there. Earthly concepts of time and space do not apply to God. For us, time has a beginning and an end. If God were *inside* time, undergoing it sequentially, then He must change—but God is changeless. It is likely that time is not linear for God, but that He is in some unfathomable manner aware of, or able to experience, all events of time simultaneously.

"God knows every aspect of our lives before we exist in our mother's womb. Moreover, he knows what will take place at the end of time because, from His perspective, these events have either already taken place, or are always taking place. We cannot understand what it is like to exist outside time, nor is it important that we understand such things."

"Why isn't it important? Aren't any of you curious?"

"If God wanted us to understand such things, He would have put them in the Bible." Matthias stopped walking and pointed to the shrubbery. "Do you see these flowers?"

"They're Morning Glories."

"Yes. They open in the morning when the sun rises. And they close at night when it sets. They don't need to understand why they open, and if they did, they wouldn't need to understand why or how the sun rises. Without the sun, they wouldn't open; they'd die."

"We could shine an electric light on them," Stuart suggested.

"Without the sun, there would be no electricity," Matthias said.

"Speaking of electricity, why aren't there any electric appliances here? I can't remember when I've seen so many mechanical typewriters. It's as though I've traveled back in time. Then I look on the library shelves and see the latest issue of the Economist. What's up with that?"

"Electricity doesn't work here."

"What do you mean, 'electricity doesn't work here?' That's impossible. What about batteries?"

"Batteries don't work here either. Believe me, I've tried. If the elders had some computers or even a cell phone, this would be a different place."

"Why doesn't electricity work here?"

"I believe it's because this is a meteor crater. Residual magnetic effect neutralizes electrical apparatuses."

Stuart considered the implications of having no electricity for a couple of minutes as they walked.

The Amish manage without electricity. But…

"You mean no one here has ever heard a compact disc? Seen a digital video?"

"Not exactly. Once Philios and Barnabas came with me to the end of the ravine and listened to Bach's "B-Minor Mass" on my iPod. They were reduced to tears. I offered to accompany them again to let them hear other music, but both declined. They didn't want anything to pollute the memory of that first experience."

"And the people here. What's with them? Every member of the congregation stood in church this morning. You said people stood when Philios mentioned an Apostle who was one of their ancestors. Really, what are the chances of two hundred descendents of the Apostles gathering all in one place?"

Matthias grinned. "You have good questions," he answered. "I don't suppose you would believe me if I said it was a family reunion."

"Na-uh."

They walked in silence again. Matthias picked a couple apricots and handed one to Stuart. Plainly, he wasn't going to comment further on that topic.

"Did Roger suffer?"

"What?"

"Did Roger suffer? You said he went in and out of consciousness; that you spoke with him. Did he suffer?"

"I have no way of knowing that. But judging from his injuries, I would hazard a guess that he did suffer."

"Why does God allow suffering? If there really is a God, why did he allow Roger to suffer? Why was I spared?"

"Let me tell you a story about my cat."

"Are you trying to change the subject?"

"No. I think this will help you understand why God allows suffering."

"OK. Go ahead."

"My cat expects me to feed her every day. I look at my watch and when it's six in the morning, or six at night, I feed her. She doesn't know that I check the time on my watch, and even if she did, she could never understand how to tell time. She listens to her stomach and her stomach has become synchronized to my schedule. Sometimes I'm late getting home. I usually have a good reason. And I'm definitely not late because I want her to suffer. All the same, when I return, clearly my cat is suffering. Her stomach is yearning for food. She'll never understand that I didn't make her suffer on purpose. She'll never understand what it was that made me late. The only thing that matters to her is that I'm faithful in feeding her every day, though sometimes it's according to my own schedule. Although she suffers, she knows that I never introduce trials in her life beyond what she can bear. Get the picture?"

"I think so," Stuart said. "But we're not cats. We're humans. The Bible says God made us in His image. Why can't we understand the *why's* of human suffering?"

"We may have been created in God's image in many respects, but our intelligence and our other capacities don't come close to those of God. The gulf between God and us is wider than the gulf between a human and an ant.

"Recently, I saw an ant crawling along the cloth covering one of my loudspeakers. I inserted an audio disc and when I pressed Play, the speaker was vibrating so much that the ant was quivering. That ant had no idea why the surface it was walking upon suddenly started shaking. Ants don't have ears so it could not experience the music. Even if they could, this one would never be able to understand how inserting a disc into my player had anything to do with his situation, or why it was necessary to press the 'Play' button. We're like that ant when we try to understand the workings of God."

"OK. OK. I'm starting to get the picture."

They reached the spot where Stuart had fallen into the crater, and they stared up at the rim.

"That was a long fall," Stuart observed.

"Yes. It's a miracle that you're alive."

"A miracle?"

"Well, maybe not a *miracle* miracle…but who knows?"

"That reminds me of another question."

"Be my guest."

"People are praying throughout the world for miracles. Especially in churches like the one we attended today. And on Sunday mornings. How can God be there for everyone at the same time? Can He split himself into billions of pieces? Is *all* of God *everywhere*, or just pieces of Him?"

They watched a bird fly over the rim of the crater.

Matthias said, "Do you see that bird?"

"Yes."

"Your question reminds me of the boy who lives next to me. He is a television addict, and he asked me the same question."

"I'm listening."

"I told him this story: Once upon a time, a baby bird was flying down a street. Because the day was warm, the windows of all the houses were open. It was evening, and most people were watching television. When the bird flew by, there was a matter of national importance; all the networks switched to cover the ensuing presidential announcement. The small bird noticed this and saw the same man on the TV screens in every house she passed. Finally, her curiosity got the better of her and she flew through the window of one of the houses. She flew around the TV, and she flew under it. Then she flew back to her mother. 'Mama,' she said. 'I saw a man in all the houses. It looked like the same man, and it spoke with the same voice, but he was in all the houses at the same time. How is this possible?'

"That baby bird had no more likelihood of understanding how the president could be on many televisions simultaneously, than we have of understanding how God can be in many places simultaneously."

THE MEADOW was quiet where they were sitting—on the lush green grass at the spot where Stuart had landed—and the breeze was warm. A sudden volume swell called attention to a persistent drone of buzzing bees. He looked at Matthias questioningly.

"There are twelve beehives in the northwest of the crater." Matthias said.

"They produce more than three thousand pounds of honey every year. The families each receive two pounds a month."

"What do they do with the rest?"

"The farmer mixes some in with the food for the animals. But that leaves nearly 2,000 pounds, more than 2,500 twelve-ounce bottles, for my family to take out with us. We usually return with honey. Most people in the outskirts of Diyarbakir where we live assume that we are keeping bees somewhere in the hills. They're convinced that we keep the location secret because it's the sweetest honey in the region, and this region is already famous for its honey. It's a great cover story."

"Why would you need a cover story?"

Matthias grinned. "Because my family lives in Diyarbakir. I just said that. We come here once a month to deliver provisions," as if that explained everything.

Stuart was confused. He leaned back and tried to follow the path of one of the bees with his eyes. There were more: a *bike* of bees. *What had possessed him to memorize that list of animal groups?*

He noticed that the bees made a crescendo when they came close, a diminuendo when they retreated. It was like the tremolos of a viola section. In the pianissimo moments, he detected the sound of the stream. It suggested the purity of a glass harmonica—not a harmonica that one blows into, but the nineteenth century instrument designed to produce a tone through the same principles as stroking the rim of a wineglass with a moist finger. Occasionally, the running water dislodged some pebbles that interjected staccato notes recalling a marimba. The sporadic plopping of a seedpod falling into the still water at the banks provided punctuating accents. Less frequently, an orange would drop from one of the trees and roll to the ground, rustling the leaves as it did, and ending with a thud like a tom-tom. Some birds abandoned themselves in spontaneous song. It was a symphony of God's creation.

"Do you believe that God created everything?" Stuart asked.

"With all my heart."

"Don't you think that someday man will unlock the secrets of life? Scientists have already created a virus, a polio virus I think, back in 2002."

"Yes, man may be able to create a reasonable facsimile of life. However, man will always need to start with something. You see, God doesn't need to start with anything when he creates. He does it all *ex nihilo*, out of nothing…"

"I think I'm beginning to understand," Stuart said. "Yes, I am beginning to understand."

They sat quietly until the dinner bell rang.

◆ ◆ ◆

WHEN THEY WALKED back to the dining hall, it crossed Stuart's mind that if Roger had died, Roger's parents would soon be on their way to retrieve the body. Maybe they had already done so. Or, maybe the body had been shipped back to them, in which case, his own parents would be on their way, looking for him. They might be in transit right now. Something pushed those thoughts from his mind. That "something" was the denial that Roger was dead, and the inexplicable joy that had filled Stuart's being since he first came to the crater.

Something was happening, but he didn't know what it was. If only the outside world would not intrude until whatever was happening had actually taken place; something inside him told him that it was going to be good.

◆ ◆ ◆

PHILIOS AND BARNABAS met, as was their custom, in the north gallery for an hour of prayer, before breaking their fast on Saturday evening. Matthias accompanied them as he often did when he happened to be in the crater on a Saturday.

Before they got down to business, Philios asked the men, "What are we going to do about Stuart?"

"He's making progress," Matthias answered. "We had a great conversation this afternoon."

"Your report?" Philios asked Barnabas.

"I took him on a tour of the library, but I kept him away from the garden charts in the seventh classroom. Naturally, those stirred his curiosity."

"Did he say anything, or ask anything?"

"Well," Barnabas blushed, "I did most of the talking."

Barnabas saw Philios and Matthias glance at each other, tellingly.

"It isn't often that I have a chance to give someone a tour of the library."

"I guess I've spent more time talking to him," Matthias said.

"And…"

"He's a seeker. He won't stop until he finds what he's looking for."

"Do you think he's looking for Jesus?"

"I do. He believes in God, and he asks all the right questions. He's making a sincere effort to work things out in his mind."

"Praise the Lord that it is happening here where he is less likely to be misled."

Barnabas interrupted. "Surely that's no coincidence. And it was no coincidence that the children brought him first to the library."

"Is he aware that no amount of 'working things out in his mind' as you call it, will succeed?"

"I'm not sure."

"My worry is that he will return to the world, knowing we exist," Philios said.

"An unbeliever, loose in the world, knowing about Stauros…That's never happened before," Barnabas said.

"Couldn't he be trusted?" Matthias asked.

"Even Jesus said 'he who is not with me is against me'," Barnabas said. "Unless one decides for Christ, one is by definition in opposition to him."

"But would he rather die before disclosing our secret?" Philios asked. "Any Christian would." His eyes met those of Matthias, "You're the expert on the outside world. What do you think?"

"I tend to side with Brother Barnabas," Matthias replied. "Stuart is honest and moral. He's close to meeting the Lord, but he hasn't yet. I believe it will be better if he stayed until he did."

"Maybe you should take him on a tour of the garden," Barnabas suggested.

"God shall deal with Stuart in his own time. There's nothing we can do to speed up the situation. You know that," Philios said.

"That's true," Matthias said, "but I have seen Stuart gazing at the garden, longing to see it—"

Again, Barnabas interrupted. "Maybe it's part of God's plan that you show it to him."

"I'll decide that—with God's leading—*after* I've had a chance to speak with the young man." Philios made it clear that the discussion was over. "Let us lift up the matter in prayer right now."

The three men prayed together until dinner.

TWENTY-ONE

LOS ANGELES

AFTERNOON (GMT-7)

KATHY WARREN whimpered at the funeral. When she wasn't crying, she was staring at the large crucifix behind the pulpit.

How could you do this Lord? she shouted inside. *There are plenty of families with two, three, four, even more children. If you needed a child, why didn't you take one from a family that could spare one?* Roger was our only child! *I'm too old to have another.*

I've been a good girl. I haven't missed church in years. No, make that decades. OK, maybe I didn't understand much until they switched from Latin to English, but I'm sure I wasn't the only one.

I've tried and tried to love my neighbor though there's no denying she's a lying, mean old biddy.

"Alice McAllister." She mouthed the words.

What a stupid name. What had possessed her parents to take her first name out of her last name like that? No matter how much you said it, it sounded like Alice Mc-Alice-ter. It's like Butros Butros Gali. Probably that's where her parents got the idea.

Alice and her precious Irish heritage. As if she's a better Catholic because her father came from Ireland.

How many Hail Mary's have I said in my life, Lord? A million? Didn't they count for anything? Weren't you listening to me Lord?

Or do you listen only to Irish-Catholics like Alice McAllister?

I've always kept the Ten Commandments. As best I could. Everyone tells a white lie at some point. Eventually, everyone does the laundry on Sunday after a little-league game.

But not everyone has an affair with her son's boy-scout leader; Kathy Warren's conscience shouted.

That was ten years ago she silently screamed back. *I confessed that sin at three different churches, for extra measure. Naturally, I didn't want to confess it to Father Romero, but they were Catholic churches.*

WALTER had been out of town at the annual four-day conference for the American Society of Medieval Historians. Roger's scout leader had driven her son home from a nature hike. Patrick Gordon was a strong, outdoorsy man. For some reason, she was very turned on by his scouting uniform, it looked like Roger's only ten sizes bigger. The Bermuda shorts had been the last straw. He mentioned that Roger was the final boy to be dropped off, so she offered him some lemonade.

"I'd rather have a beer," Patrick said.

They were sitting on the porch having a drink when Roger rushed across the porch and announced, "I'm sleeping over at Stuart's house tonight."

As soon as he was out of sight, Kathy said, "The sunset is much prettier from the deck in the back."

So they retired to the secluded deck that Walter insisted they add the year before. One thing led to another, and then she was letting Patrick out the front door at 7 a.m. the next morning. As she did so, she saw Alice McAllister jogging by with her two poodles. Alice had seen Patrick leaving. The look she gave Kathy spoke volumes about her suspicions. And Kathy had read every word of them.

If only she had waited ten minutes.

ARE YOU punishing me for that Lord? I never did anything like that again. That was ten years ago, Lord! If you are, this punishment is way out of line, isn't it?

He's punishing me for that sin. Kathy had long since ascertained that some type of prejudgment had taken place for this particular transgression.

And I suppose now I'm going to end up in Hell, too!

"Well, if God wants me to go to Hell, I can't do anything to prevent that," she spoke aloud.

What about my son's graduation…what about his wedding…what about my grandchildren.

Did you have to take all of that away too?

She burst into tears again.

◆ ◆ ◆

FRIENDS, FAMILY, AND RELATIVES gathered at the Warren's house after Roger's funeral. The Pierces were there; so was Meredith. To everyone's relief, Kathy had finally stopped crying, but tears had etched her agony onto her face, a constant reminder to all present.

Walter couldn't bear to witness his wife's anguish, but he didn't look at his feet; he never did that. Still, he didn't want to raise his head and meet the eyes of the people in his house, so he looked in between. What he saw were sleeve cuffs and jacket bottoms, so many that he became even more claustrophobic than when he had been shut accidentally in a coat closet as a boy.

Feeling powerless, Walter observed Father Romero's attempts to comfort Kathy, as if a hand on his wife's shoulder and a priestly pronouncement had any hope of bringing a smile to the face of the mourning mother.

He saw Brad's daughter, Cindy, talking with a girl he didn't recognize. Walter supposed it was one of Roger's friends, maybe a classmate from school. Maybe he should go introduce himself.

He decided no introductions were called for.

After a while, he felt that people were glancing in his direction now and then. Was there some protocol? Maybe they expected him to give a speech. He wasn't up to that again—recalling the opening of the eulogy he had delivered at the church, "There are words to describe a husband or wife who has lost his or her spouse. We call them widows. There are words to describe a child who has lost his or her parents. We call them orphans. No words exist to describe a parent who has lost a child. I have lost my only child, and it is something so terrible that our language has no word for it. I'm not a widow. I'm not an orphan. I don't know what I am..." He might have relived the excruciating eulogy in his mind, were it not for the merciful interruption of his mother-in-law raising her voice and announcing, "Attention everyone. There are sandwiches and snacks on the table in the dining room."

Why do people always eat after a funeral?

He followed everyone into the dining room and found he was not the least bit hungry. The others appeared to be. He stood off to the side and watched, wondering how all this food had come to be on his dining room table. He surveyed the scene in the mirror over the mantelpiece, and discovered that the perspective it offered made the event less real; it was as if he were watching a movie.

Everyone who hadn't already approached him to say that they were "truly sorry for his loss" came up to him now and offered their condolences. He noticed a large chunk of chicken salad on the corner of his colleague Reed Osgood's mouth, and suppressed a desire to eject the man from the premises, or at the very least to shout out, "I will not stand for that. This man is dishonoring the memory of my boy!"

Instead, he shifted his gaze to his golf trophies in the glass case in the corner. They didn't mean anything anymore. He wished that every hour he had spent playing golf, had been spent with Roger instead.

He felt as though he couldn't breathe, as if he had no air.

It's true. I can't breathe because I have no heir.

The phrase echoed in his mind. He chuckled.

I can't breathe because I have no heir.

He was on the verge of bursting into hysterical laughter.

I can't breathe because I have no heir.

Then the nightmare relented. Throughout that day, the unspoken words of the undertaker had rescued him repeatedly. *"You're the father. You're the man. Be the man. Be strong."*

TWENTY-TWO

MEREDITH MADE A BEELINE to the Pierces the moment she saw them alone on the terrace overlooking the Warren's back yard. As she walked, her pants clung like spandex. She always wore stylish jeans that were never blue, but usually tight—tight because she imagined herself heavy below her waist, and she didn't trust mirrors.

Meredith had the wild, copper-colored hair of a woman whose veins contained the pure blood of one of the original Judaic tribes. It stretched down below the middle of her back. "Thick" or "full-bodied" didn't do her hair justice; "voluminous" was only a contender for its description. She always kept it tied, clipped, or otherwise gathered together at a point slightly below her shoulders, where it gave the impression that she was wearing a hood, as it billowed out behind her. Meredith knew her hair was unique. She often imagined it was the headgear an Israeli princess would have worn to keep the sand off, thousands of years ago. And that it was made of plush velvet bedecked with royal jewels and small golden tokens signifying all the rights and privileges afforded to its owner by birth. As she approached the Pierces, the wind lifted the massive calash of hair, magnificently.

Her hair was undeniably pure bred—even her eyelashes were naturally long—but Meredith had not been born with the perfect nose she had now. Similarly, the flawless alignment of her teeth had been purchased in her early teens, although the price was much dearer: three long years wearing a retainer. The two cosmetic enhancements worked in concert as she gave the Pierces a big smile.

"Mr. and Mrs. Pierce," she said. "I want to come with you."

"Come with us. Where?"

"To Turkey. To find Stuart."

"Child, whatever gave you the idea we're going to Turkey?"

"You are, aren't you?"

The look that Brad and Margaret gave each other said it all.

"But we hardly know you."

Stuart had brought her around to the house a couple times throughout the past year. No, they didn't know her. But she knew them, and much of what she knew, she had learned last March when the five of them—including Cindy—had sat around the dinner table at the Pierce's house. Stuart's father overheard her say to Stuart, "Schtoodles, this was great. You have to come home with me for dinner over Spring break. We're having a Seder." Mr. Pierce interrupted, "A *satyr*? One of those things that is half horse and half human?" That's when she realized that they didn't have any Jewish friends. Stuart had jumped in to rescue her, "No dad. A Seder is a special meal that commemorates the Exodus of the Jews from Egypt." His father had responded, "A Jew eh? Well, pass over the cream, will you. Get it? Passover—pass over."

What a nebbish!

In Meredith's experience, although the "Jesus killer" belief caused some Christians to become anti-Semites, many atheists were anti-Semites, too. She knew that Brad Pierce was an atheist.

Nonetheless, his motivation made sense to her. Atheists had decided they didn't need God. By denying the existence of God, they were elevating themselves to the position at which they imagined they were the most important beings in the universe, when actually God is more important than anything. For an atheist to envisage God picking a certain race of people as His *chosen* people was an affront to their sense of status in the overall scheme of things. It produced a knee-jerk reaction, and that reaction was anti-Semitism.

Thankfully, Stuart was not an atheist. He was seeking something, just like she was.

"But Stuart and I know each other very well. We've been dating since last summer. And, I've had experience with that part of the world."

She had spent the previous summer at a kibbutz in Israel. On the flight home, she changed planes in Lisbon, where Stuart and Roger boarded. Her seat was beside Stuart's and they ended up talking for the next ten hours.

When her father had arrived at the edge of the airport causeway to pick her up, she ran back to Stuart and kissed him on the cheek, pressing a piece of paper into his hand with her phone number on it and the words "You're a real *mensch*. Call me!" He telephoned her the next day. Since then, they had been inseparable.

The atheist is considering it, she thought, watching for Mr. Pierce's reaction.

Meredith was no atheist. She was sure God existed, and she feared him dutifully. The part she didn't understand was what it meant to be Jewish. She knew she had another name, "Maytal," that meant, "Dew water." But so what? She had played "hide the matzo" when she was young; she had timed things perfectly to assure the bandages were removed from her nose enough in advance of her sweet sixteen party to allow the bruises to heal; she had even managed to keep her virginity; and she had watched "Schindler's List" three times and cried each time.

Nonetheless, she was sure that being Jewish was more than that, and she didn't fully understand what it meant. That's what led her to the Kibbutz last summer; the experience had turned out to be much more than she had expected.

The Kibbutz had provided her with the roots she lacked in L.A. She knew more about being a Jew now. Maybe not everything, but she believed it would be enough to get her through the next few years.

In Israel the previous summer, she arose six days a week at 5:30 a.m., and worked knee deep in steamy mud, clearing weeds to make way for new banana fields.

She loved it.

Friday's work ended at noon on Shabbat. She learned to like Vodka Balalaika punch at the volunteer pub on Friday evenings.

She also sampled strawberry tobacco through a water pipe, and she hadn't liked the licorice aftertaste.

She made friends for life with others her age: Swedes, Danes, Estonians, South Africans, Australians, Koreans, Brits, and other Americans. Many were not even Jewish.

On their days off, they took trips to Massada, the Dead Sea, the Red Sea, the Negev desert, the Golan Heights, Tiberius, Lake Kinneret, and of course, Jerusalem, several times.

In Jerusalem, she had been surprised to find herself moved by the holy places of Christianity, particularly the depictions of Mary Magdalene, whose hair rivaled Meredith's own, a similarity that gave rise to many remarks from her companions. Along the way, she learned about Messianic Jews—something she hadn't heard of before—Jews who believed Jesus was the Messiah.

The Messianic Jews called Jesus by His Hebrew name, Yeshua, often ate kosher, kept the feasts of Leviticus, and followed all the commandments in both the Old and New Testaments; in other words, they kept the Torah. She knew she wasn't supposed to believe in Jesus, but the more she thought about it, the more she discovered she didn't know why.

The final two-and-a-half weeks of the summer, she spent traveling with a girl from New Zealand who had been her roommate at the kibbutz. The two nineteen-year-olds bussed from youth hostel to youth hostel.

The first five days they snorkeled off the coast of Egypt, and visited the pyramids. Next, they took twelve days to make their way to Nice, France, where they parted company, Meredith flying on to Lisbon.

She felt the entire summer had been an irrefutable rite of passage into adulthood, and the final wonderful episode of that three-month experience had been getting to know Stuart on the plane ride home from Lisbon to Los Angeles.

BRAD PIERCE needed less than one second to make up his mind. "Out of the question," he retorted.

"Mr. Pierce. Please!" Meredith put on her half-worried, half-pleading face, the one that always worked when she wanted to get her way with her own father.

"You're still a child. We can't be responsible for you over there."

She could tell he was grasping at straws.

"We may be dealing with Shiite Muslims," he whispered.

"I can speak a little Hebrew."

Margaret Pierce, who wore the pants in the family and who hadn't considered whether a knowledge of Hebrew would be useful on the expedition, suddenly spoke. "Can you read the words in the window of Bornstein's Bakery?"

"Of course."

"That's where we buy our bagels on Saturdays. Twenty years and I still don't have a clue what it says."

"It says 'Bornstein's Bakery Featuring Bornstein's Bagels, The Best Baked Bagels since Barzillai.' Barzillai was the one who brought provisions (bagels?) to David and his army when the king fled from Absalom."

"You're hired!" Margaret said. "We're leaving tomorrow. Can you be ready?"

"You bet!"

◆ ◆ ◆

FATHER ROMERO approached Walter after all the guests left.

"I wonder if I might have another look at that photo you showed me yesterday," he said, as gently as possible.

"Sure. We can look at it on Roger's computer."

Oh great! Now I'm responsible for reviving all the memories that being in his son's room will bring back.

"Are you sure it's OK?"

"Follow me."

The two men ascended the stairs unnoticed by Kathy and her mother who were clearing away the dishes from the dining room.

Father Romero had never liked entering the rooms of the recently deceased. He hesitated slightly at the threshold. Then his eyes saw the black emptiness of the computer screen and visions of the golden church dominated his mind.

Walter switched on the computer. "This will take a minute."

Father Romero looked around the room while they waited for the computer to start up. The room was filled with Batman memorabilia: posters, figures, trinkets, videos, and games—it was everywhere. On one shelf he saw Batmobile models in various sizes, although to Father Romero's eyes, they were simply models of cars. On another shelf stood figurines of many of Batman's nefarious adversaries. However, Father Romero failed to make any connection between them and the superhero; instead, he focused on one particular grouping of three figures—the caped wonder in the center. It brought the crucifixion to mind, the three crosses on Calvary hill, the guards casting lots for the purple robe.

Whenever Father Romero saw a group of three of anything, he imagined the crucifixion. Ten years ago, when he was fresh out of seminary, God often revealed Himself to him through such groupings—triplicities, he called them. A flood of memories returned; temptation had very nearly gotten the best of him, a woman had been trying to seduce him, but he looked up and saw three trees standing starkly like the three crosses on Calvary hill. One of the trees was dead. Like the criminals crucified with Jesus, one had chosen death, the other, eternal life. The message of the motif was clear. He had promptly disengaged himself from the woman and prayed for forgiveness. Even earlier, when he left home to go to the seminary, his Spanish-speaking father had stood there, solidly flanked on either side by his brothers: Juan-Carlos, who would end up disgraced in prison, and Pedro, who would follow in his father's footsteps and bring joy to the whole family. Again, the crucifixion archetype had played out in his life.

The computer made a sound that startled him.

"The photos are on this memory card," Walter said as he slipped the card in a small device next to the monitor.

Father Romero watched eagerly as a checkerboard of photos, each the size of a postage stamp, appeared on the screen. Walter moved the pointer to the one in the lower right corner and clicked.

There it was again—that mysterious church. Father Romero studied at it carefully. A long structure extended behind the main building. A monastery? A library? Classrooms? He wondered...

There was no doubt about it; he had never seen this one before.

An enthusiastic reverence swelled inside him with a passion that he hadn't experienced since right after seminary—that direct involvement in God's plan that he had known then, without reservation or question, during those years in the Holy Land, traveling from church to church, steeped in history. His spirit was being renewed, and the effect upon his faith was noticeable, if only to him.

Why, I'm actually thinking of going there.

The idea startled him. Except to preach and minister to his flock, he hadn't left the confines of the rectory in a decade, much less the state of California. He felt safe there, insulated from the outside world, protected in some way.

Father Romero noticed the printer next to the computer.

"I wonder if I could have a print of that," he asked.

"I can try."

Walter saw a tiny image of a printer on a bar of icons running across the bottom of the screen. He clicked on it with the pointer. Nothing happened. He clicked again. Still nothing.

"Maybe we better turn the printer on," Father Romero said, as he pressed the clearly labeled power button on top of the device.

Walter blushed.

This time when he clicked, a whirring began, and the sound of the printer comforted him. A soft clackety-clack followed as a sheet of paper disappeared inside the printer, only to re-emerge a moment later with a full-color copy of the image on the screen.

Father Romero snatched it eagerly.

"Thank you," he said without taking his eyes off the picture. "Now I must be going. I know you and your wife have things to do."

WALTER COULDN'T IMAGINE what Father Romero meant by having "things to do." What does a father do after burying his only son? Again, the ominous *I can't breathe because I have no heir* taunted him. Would life ever return to normal?

TWENTY-THREE

ANTARCTICA

C AM WAS HAVING TROUBLE sleeping. He knew that his earthquake prediction system had one major flaw: if either a mainshock-aftershock or pre-shock-mainshock pattern occurred within the second half of the lunar cycle—from the midpoint between lunar perigee and apogee, until apogee itself—he had no way of identifying it. Actually, that wasn't completely true; he could identify it at the precise moment of apogee, but by then it would usually be too late.

The possible pre-shock they were considering at present was the six-point-seven of June 21; it had occurred well within the window of uncertainty. He suspected that Richard Roebuck's group had found a solution to the uncertainty period problem. Their telecommunications data conveniently captured by the government's monitoring system called Echelon made it clear that the Triple-R researchers didn't have to wait for lunar apogee to interpret the SLUGS. Apparently, their group had a filtering algorithm for background seismic noise—one capable of discarding the moon's gravitational influence.

He knew that he could easily tap into their research with Echelon again; enough probing, and eventually he would discover their secret.

In spite of this, Cam considered himself an ethical man. He wasn't religious. He didn't believe in God, nor did he disbelieve. He was agnostic. Nonetheless, he had a strong sense of morality. The facts gnawed at him; he couldn't erase the knowledge that he had received the crucial "nudge" to examine the directional fluctuations of the magnetotactic bacteria, from a Triple-R Lab transmission—surreptitiously—by way of the Echelon global eavesdropping system. He rationalized this by telling himself that he had not ordered the intercept, nor had he requested it. The data had simply appeared in his email box tagged with the subject line, "This might interest you." It was from the Echelon team.

The attached file had been a "nudge," nothing more. It had pointed him in a direction. If he requested a follow up, he would compromise his personal moral code. He wouldn't be able to live with himself.

Already, the guilt he felt toward his work—work that was now based upon someone else's discovery—was eating away at his heart and soul. Every day his conscience condemned him with greater conviction.

He stared at the MDTs—the Magnetosomic Deviation Trajectories—day in and day out. He told himself that he would have made the connection without help, eventually. He ran the data through every seismological noise filter in his repertoire. Computers crunched away at the numbers around the clock, without any sign that the breakthrough he needed was any closer.

There was no way to tell whether he was looking at an asynchronous pre-echo—meaning a temporally-displaced predictor: data he could use to foretell a future megathrust or major aftershock; or an authentic synchronous echo—meaning the quake on the June 21st solstice was inarguably a pre-shock, and a mainshock would likely occur before the lunar apogee, or maybe, concurrently.

Chester "Cam" Morgenstern looked at the clock—the one that was counting down to the apogee: 84 hours and counting. When the countdown reached zero, all the MDTs would become crystal clear. Would he be able to sleep in the meantime?

TWENTY-FOUR

LOS ANGELES

EVENING (GMT-7)

FATHER ROMERO got to the rectory at 8:20 p.m. The smell of old leather mixed with incense made him feel at home. He laid the photograph that Walter Warren had given him, carefully, on his desk. He turned on his desk lamp and stared at the photo for a half hour. Through the open window, he heard wisps of music and remembered that the chancel choir was rehearsing in the sanctuary. In his mind, he sang along. One phrase fit perfectly with all the melodies: "I have to go and find that church."

A copy of his book, "Byzantine Churches of the Holy Land and Bordering Regions—A Complete Compendium," lay on his desk next to the photograph. He hadn't thought about his book much after it came out in print, but now, the words, "Complete Compendium," appeared to jump off the cover at him.

I guess it's not complete if it doesn't include this one.

Had he missed any other churches?

The gold of the dome and columns was puzzling. Certainly, many people he had interviewed would have known of a church of this splendor. Clearly, it was in use. Had it been built since his return to America?

He considered the possibility that the gold and the extra wing had been added to an existing church since he had done his research. He went through his book again, meticulously examining each photograph to see whether the mysterious church might be nothing more than a newly gold-plated version of one that he had previously researched. Then he noticed the garden in the background. It was marvelous, phenomenal, and obviously well over ten years old.

No, they must have kept this a secret deliberately. That's what disturbed him.

He debated phoning Dobro Suleyman, the Prefect of the Department for the Preservation of Turkish Antiquities—the D.P.T.A.

Dobro had helped him extensively when he was writing his book, ten years ago. The man was a Muslim; nonetheless, he respected Father Romero's faith in a way that the priest found difficult to reciprocate. When he left Turkey, Dobro had urged him to come back and write a similar book featuring Islamic mosques.

Father Romero sent him an autographed copy of his book, graciously acknowledging Dobro's assistance in the frontal matter. Dobro sent him a couple postcards the first few years after he returned to America, but they hadn't been in contact for nearly seven years.

Finally, he decided to phone his old friend. If anyone knew about a church covered with this much gold, it would be Dobro. On the other hand, the quantity of gold in question was exactly the type of historical site the D.P.T.A. was likely to cloak in secrecy. He tried to think of a way to bluff the information out of Dobro without raising the man's suspicions, but he could not come up with a plan.

At 9:15 p.m. (11:15 a.m. Turkey time), he dialed Dobro's home number, hoping the Prefect hadn't moved.

"*Efendim.*" (Hello).

"*Suleyman bey lüften.*" (Mr. Suleyman, please).

"*Bir Dakika.*" (One minute).

A male voice came on. "*Allo?*" (Hello?).

"Dobro my old friend. It's me. Rafael Romero."

"Ah. Father Romero, my friend, this is an honor. So much time has passed. I hope all is well with you and yours."

"Please, Dobro. *Serefinize.*" (This is in your honor).

"But no. I protest. It is I who am honored by your call."

Father Romero knew this could go back and forth all night if he let it. He decided to get to the point.

"Dobro, you remember my book…"

"But of course."

"I'm thinking of making an update. Someone suspects that the book is not as complete as the title claims." The "someone" he referred to was Father Romero himself; that fact was best left unsaid at this moment.

"But how can this be?"

"That's why I'm phoning. To ask you whether any new Byzantine sites have been reported."

"Well. It is unlikely. No one has registered any new sites at my Department since you were here. You know better than anyone that the people who built those churches died more than a thousand years ago. What are you thinking?" Dobro sounded suspicious.

"It's probably nothing. I'm due for a vacation and might turn up in your neighborhood sometime this summer."

"It would be a privilege to meet with you again. Please phone me the moment you arrive. If I am not here, I am at my office in the Department. You have the number, correct?"

"Yes," Father Romero replied.

"It's been a pleasure to talk to you again, my friend."

"No, the pleasure was all mine."

"I beg you to the contrary, but my joy to hear from you surpasses the imagination."

Again, Father Romero realized they were getting into a loop. He knew only one way to end it.

"*Güle Güle*" (Good Bye), he said, and quickly put down the telephone.

At 9:30 p.m., he called the bishop. After the obligatory chitchat, Father Romero said, "You know that vacation you've been trying to get me to take for the past five years? Well, I think I'm ready to take it." He explained the situation.

The bishop seemed pleased, "I have a fresh young graduate from Loyola Seminary who'd love a chance to get his feet wet."

"Don't forget that most of our parishioners—more than seventy-five percent, actually—are gone for the summer holidays."

"That's perfect. He needs to build his confidence slowly. But he's eager. So eager that when I tell him about this opportunity, he might jump on a plane and show up in time for noon mass tomorrow."

Hanging up, Father Romero was pleased that the conversation had gone so well. Maybe he could get on his way sooner than he expected.

He lay in bed thinking of what the discovery of such a church would mean, particularly if it were a secret. He pictured himself lecturing about it to his colleagues, maybe to the Council of Bishops. Maybe he'd even get a bona fide church—not that the University Chapel wasn't a real church, but he knew that things were different outside the walls of academia. The golden church was beginning to resemble the Holy Grail in his imagination.

Then, out of the blue, he recalled the words he had often repeated ten years ago while he was researching his book, "The glory of this latter house shall be greater than of the former, saith the LORD of hosts: and in this place will I give peace..." And "...whatsoever ye do, do all to the glory of God."

And Father Romero was ashamed.

TWENTY-FIVE

SUNDAY, JUNE 26

TURKEY

AFTERNOON (GMT+3)

AFTER THE SUNDAY SERVICE, at which Philios had preached, everyone went to the dining room for a hearty communal meal. Bowls of pomegranates, figs, and olives were on the tables.

Stuart felt the furtive glances of the other residents. For some reason, it didn't bother him. He sat with Philios, Barnabas, and Matthias. When all two hundred were seated, women served a steaming dish made of brown beans, seasoned with garlic, mint, and oil.

Philios stood and said a blessing, ending with the words, "And bless this food to our bodies, in the name of our Lord and Savior, Jesus Christ. Amen."

Barnabas pressed Philios to elaborate on some topics from his earlier sermon. Stuart listened intently. The sermon described the power of the cross.

Philios told of Joan of Arc, and how the nineteen-year-old martyr asked to see a cross, level with her eyes, as she was being burned at the stake for heresy. Centuries later, the church rewarded her with sainthood. Saint Joan.

Stuart found the story captivating. His questions were many, and he became increasingly engrossed as he weighed each answer.

"What did you mean by 'whatever is bound on earth is bound in Heaven,' and 'whatever is loosed on earth is loosed in Heaven?'" Stuart asked.

"Jesus said *that* after he told the Apostle Peter he was to be the 'rock' of the church, and gave him the keys to the Kingdom of Heaven—not 'keys' in the physical sense of the word, of course. Matthew 16:18-19 recounts the report.

"It reminds us that there are two realms, the physical world on earth, and the spiritual world in Heaven, and that while separate and distinct from one another, they are still strongly connected. The two dominions are so interrelated that much of what we do in the earthly world, also happens in Heaven, and vice-versa. God directed Paul when he wrote to the Hebrews about the earthly sanctuary being 'a copy and shadow of what is in Heaven.' Often, there is a direct correspondence of things or events."

"Such as?"

"One good example is the great rebellion against the authority of God. The apostasy of Satan and the angels who followed him— one-third of the angels—resulted in their expulsion from Heaven. In the End Times here on earth, we expect a comparable rebellion against the authority of God. This will accelerate when the Rapture removes believers from the earth, because then the Holy Spirit, who is now restraining the state of lawlessness, and who lives in true believers, will also be removed.

"Because time flows differently in Heaven than it does on earth, these events have likely already occurred from God's perspective, or perhaps are always occurring. Even the words that Jesus uses in this passage point us to that conclusion; the literal translation is not 'will be bound' and not 'will be loosed,' but rather, the future perfect: 'will have been bound' and 'will have been loosed' (*estai dedemenon* and *estai lelymenon*).

"Abraham's offering of his son Isaac as a sacrifice in the earthly realm—in which God intervened—is seen by some people to mirror God's offering of His Son Jesus as a sacrifice from the Heavenly realm.

"Similarly, things on earth may correspond to utterly different things in Heaven. Revelation 5:8 tells us that earthly prayers are like incense in Heaven.

"Rivers that flow with water here on earth might be shadows of rivers that flow with the water of life in Heaven. Similarly, Jesus' blood, although it resembles normal blood when seen on earth and might stain our robes red here, is something beautiful and cleansing in the spiritual realm, and when the tribulation saints wash their robes in His blood, they become white.

"Even minor things on earth might have major counterparts in Heaven. The song of a bird that comforts us in a moment of sorrow might be a choir of angels in Heaven. The painful crown of thorns placed upon Jesus at the crucifixion could have had another Heavenly aspect, maybe a fiery crown of gold adorned with jewels that are life-giving stars. And when Joan of Arc beheld that crucifix while she was burning at the stake, angels in Heaven might have been caressing her soul."

"Are you implying two interdependent spheres of existence?" Stuart asked.

"Most assuredly. God in Heaven is separate from His creation. Our eyes are of earth, designed to observe things in the physical world. But sometimes, our eyes can discern spiritual occurrences or the effects of activities that happen in the spiritual realm: blessings, judgments of God, schemes of the adversary, even miracles."

This discussion enthralled Stuart. He found Philios' explanations thought provoking. The idea that God could use the tense of a verb in the Bible to disclose aspects of His divinity was overwhelming. Nevertheless, at the same time, he was surprised to find it comforting, as if the pieces of the puzzle were finally arranging themselves in their proper places. He felt a longing growing inside him; a desire to learn all he could about God.

They finished the main course and started on dessert—a recipe that Barnabas pointed out was from the days of King Solomon—crushed red lentils, mixed with honey and flour, and then fried in olive oil. Delicious!

All of a sudden, Philios asked him a question, "Tell us, Stuart, how do you feel about the cross?"

Stuart was self-conscious. "Do you mean the cross as a symbol, the one on church steeples, or the actual cross used to crucify Jesus?"

"You pick."

"OK. Well, the symbol of the cross reminds us that Jesus was persecuted to the point of death for what he believed in. At college, we learned that this represents a level of personal conviction demonstrating how strong our wills could become if we truly believe in ourselves.

"Our professor claimed that the Catholics depict the cross with Jesus suffering on it to maintain control over their followers by way of the threat of Hell and Purgatory through fear: the crown of thorns, the nails, the blood—all conjure up terrifying images—whereas Protestants depict the cross without Jesus to reinforce a belief in the mystery of the resurrection. The empty cross, like the empty tomb, symbolizes the fact that Jesus is no longer on earth, but has returned to where he came from. The hope of an afterlife becomes a bargaining chip."

Philios and Barnabas looked at each other.

"Do you believe what you've been taught?"

Stuart hesitated. "I've never given it much thought" He saw the surprise in their faces.

"I mean, I memorized it, took the exams, and passed," he explained. "But as to sitting down and thinking it through—whether my teachers are right or wrong—I haven't really done that."

"When were you planning to do that?"

"Well sir, since I got here I've been doing a lot of thinking. Not about the cross specifically, but about religion—spiritual things. The way people talk about Jesus here, it's as if they know Him personally. They speak of their ancestors being at events that supposedly involved Jesus himself."

"Supposedly?"

"My Comp-Rel teacher—Comparative Religions—said the Bible is nothing more than a group of stories fabricated by the disciples to further the teachings of Jesus. He did admit that Jesus was the greatest moral teacher of them all, though."

An uncomfortable silence hung between them.

Stuart fidgeted. *What drew me to take that course in the first place?* he wondered.

A dove started cooing. Then another, breaking the tension.

Philios stood and gazed out the window, looking long and hard at the garden to the northwest. He said, "Stuart, I'd like to show you something."

Stuart followed Philios' gaze with anticipation.

Twenty-Six

PHILIOS LED STUART through the door of the dining hall. They walked to the right, to the arching bridge that crossed the babbling stream directly in front of the church. The curvature of the bridge was extreme, and standing in its middle offered one a fabulous panorama of the surroundings.

Philios swept his arm around the crater valley, and said, "I'm sure you have many questions."

Stuart nodded.

He motioned to the church. "Our forefathers finished building that church in the year 610. Oh, it wasn't this elaborate then; they added the gold embellishments more than a hundred years later. Still, they had the foresight to place the dome of the church at the precise center of the crater.

"It helps to imagine the layout of Stauros as the face of a clock with the church spire as the axis of the clock hands."

"Stauros?"

"Oh yes, our little village has a name. And this bridge is the Constantinople Bridge. It was an achievement without precedence for its builders.

"Standing on the bridge, we are on an imaginary line that runs from three o'clock to nine o'clock. It runs along our little road. It's no coincidence that three o'clock is due east and nine o'clock is due west, another fact for which we thank our founding settlers.

"The line runs through the center of the church, and through the middle of the classrooms in the library. All you can see of the library from this vantage point is the edge of Saint John's Alcove…there, peeking out from behind the church."

Philios pointed south. "You entered the crater at six o'clock—not six o'clock in the evening, but six o'clock on the imaginary clock face. The stream takes a bend here under the bridge. To the south, it follows a course along an imaginary line between half-past one down to half-past six. After this bend, it runs on a line from four o'clock to eleven o'clock, straight into the garden. It doesn't run through the garden; the stream stops halfway in. Or, I should say it starts there. That's where the source spring bubbles out of the ground."

Looking up the stream toward the garden made Stuart's heart leap. On the right side of the stream and extending in the direction of the crater wall, was the dining hall they had just left. Windows next to the veranda on this side of the dining hall afforded a soothing view of the stream and the church.

Directly across from the center of the dining hall, on the left side of the stream, was a house. Philios saw him looking at it.

"That's my house," he said. "The pastor and his family always live in that house."

"The head farmer also has a separate house." He pointed east.

Stuart turned and saw the road continuing to the crater wall. On the right side of the road was the farm. It consisted of several small buildings, a large barn, two silos, and finally, a house noticeably bigger than the pastor's.

"The farmer usually has many children to help him in the fields," Philios grinned. "That farm has to support more than 200 people. That's why it occupies the entire southern half of the crater."

Stuart recalled the fruit orchard he had walked through on his first day in the crater, and again with Matthias. From the bridge, he saw that it covered an area from the stream to the crater wall, bounded by an imaginary line drawn between five o'clock and ten o'clock, to use Philios' terminology. The area between the orchard and the farm buildings consisted of vegetable fields and grain fields.

The region extending south of the church to the crater's western wall, and bounded by the stream on its east side, was given over to grazing. Dozens of sheep and horses meandered in the pasture. Stuart could see the stables against the crater wall between eight o'clock and half-past eight.

Looking in the other direction, between eight and seven-thirty, there was vegetation. He asked Philios about it.

"Those are grape arbors. We drink many forms of grape beverages here, unfermented wine, and more. Our ancestors used to use the grapes to make grape sugar too, but now Achmed and Matthias bring us all the refined sugar that we could want.

"Behind the grape arbors is a small grove of trees; beside that, a promontory of rock, facing west like a hook, or the claw of a bird. Within the hook is what we call the 'honeymoon house.' When people marry in Stauros, they usually spend their honeymoon secluded there. The rock formation and the grove of trees behind the grape arbor provide total privacy."

Memories seemed to flood his mind. "Years ago, I spent my honeymoon there."

Stuart was on the verge of asking where the stream went. It appeared to flow right into the crater wall. Then, to Stuart's disappointment, Philios started walking back over the bridge away from the church. Stuart had hoped they would head in the other direction, to the garden. Even the stream's rushing water seemed to be whispering, *Yes. Come to me.*

The road dead-ended at the crater's east wall. The community woodworking shop stood directly in front of them, and a pleasing smell of sawdust permeated the air.

Keeping the farm to their right, Philios led them to the corner of a block of houses. To the north, was another block. Both had four houses on all sides; each block consisted of twelve houses.

A row of eight houses hugged the bottom of the crater wall to the east. Stuart saw another dozen houses carved out of the wall of the crater and continuing upward to the rim, until there were three rows of houses attached to the crater wall, six in the first row, four above that, and two just beneath the top. He could see more houses built into the wall farther to the north.

"This is where most of the people now live," Philios said, "although, when Stauros was founded, there were only thirty-three people in all, counting men, women, and children. By the fourth generation, the number of residents had increased to thirty-three couples and 132 others, mainly children. We've limited the population to that number ever since; our resources cannot support a larger group of people. Theoretically, each couple should have two children. In practice, it's not so exact; some have three or four, others have one or none. There are fifty-two residences in total, forty-eight in the village proper, plus my house, the head farmer's house, the honeymoon house, and the cool-down house."

"The cool-down house?"

"Yes. That's behind the garden at twenty-past eleven on the clock face. Internal family conflicts happen; someone needs to get away for a while—to cool down. That's what the cool-down house is all about. Most of the time, it's used for other purposes. When two weddings happen within several days, it doubles as a second honeymoon house."

"That's understandable."

They continued walking along the street beside the crater wall. The houses on their left stopped after the second block. At the base of the crater wall to their right, were four more houses, each next one farther from the last.

When they got out of town, they were at one-forty on the clock face.

Stuart gazed across the canyon at the library. Between the library and the place where they were standing, he saw a large fenced-off playground full of children. This extended from the northwest wall of the dining hall, halfway back to the northeast wall of the crater.

They walked to the corner of the playground, and listened to the laughter of the children.

To the north, Stuart saw a pond, nearly two hundred yards in diameter. Steam drifted from its surface, and Stuart realized it must be fed by a hot spring. There was an elegant tiled bathhouse curving around the edge of the pond closest to them. Philios led them around the back of the baths.

Standing on the edge of the pond to the north of the bath-house, Stuart breathed in a lungful of damp steam. He squatted down to test the temperature of the water. It was very hot. He took another deep breath as he bent over it. So close to the surface, the steam burned in his throat. For a moment, he felt as if he hadn't breathed in air, it was so full of moisture—the sensation was the opposite of what a fish out of water must feel.

After a few minutes, they both spontaneously started walking to the wall. A channel originating at a small waterfall due north of them fed the pool. Alongside that channel, they passed two buildings, the first, a textile mill, then, at the foot of the wall, the laundry.

As they neared the waterfall, Stuart began to sweat. The heat was unbearable. Philios led him up ten steps carved in the rock. At the top, Stuart saw the source of the heat, a semicircular trough, five yards in length and two yards wide at its widest point. It was like a tear in the earth, filled with lava. He stared at it, mesmerized.

Philios broke the spell. "Centuries ago, an attempt to redirect the hot waterfall feeding the pool opened this fissure of molten rock."

Stuart realized the lava was flowing, slowly, but flowing none-theless. It smelled like rotten eggs.

"The magma helps us in many ways. It heats the water of the pond and the bathhouse, and the steam maintains a comfortable humidity throughout the crater while creating an updraft that pushes away any clouds above the crater. It also facilitates the laundry. The lava even carries away some of our waste. Eventually we'll find other uses for it."

A walkway paralleled the perimeter of the lava trough.

Philios and Stuart moved along it hastily. The hot waterfall originated from a crack beneath the center of the path. The rushing of the water increased in volume as they stepped over it. They left by way of a stairway at the far end; it was identical to the one they had ascended.

The heat diminished with each step away from the lava. Soon, they were crossing the bridge again.

"Would you care for something to drink?"

Stuart, genuinely thirsty, accepted the offer gladly.

After they stepped off the bridge, Philios led him to the right, in the direction of his house next to the stream, due north on the church side of the bridge.

The pastor's house had decks on all sides, and they sat on the side facing the church and library. To the northwest was the garden. Philios' wife brought out a large clay jar full of pomegranate juice mixed with orange juice. The three of them relaxed on the deck, until their cups were empty.

Philios spoke a few words to his wife in a language Stuart didn't understand. He motioned Stuart to the church. For the second time, Stuart was frustrated that they walked in the opposite direction from the garden.

Philios led him along the covered portico that hugged the boundary of the church. Soon, they reached the fifty-foot, covered walkway that connected the back of the church to the library.

Instead of entering the library, they followed another stone walkway to the stream, traveling in the direction of half-past one o'clock. On their left, midway to the stream, Philios pointed out the scriptorium, the diorama museum, and the Hall of Names— three low triangular buildings that almost touched at their apexes; from the air, they would have resembled a pie with every other piece removed. He touched Stuart's shoulder and pointed.

"You saw the diorama in the library; dozens more exist in this building. We use them to keep a visual historical record."

The museum tugged at Stuart, but he longed to explore the garden. Philios gave a look of approval.

"And the Hall of Names, that's an experience in itself—with all their tangled charts and graphs. We have to keep close watch over the gene pool of our little colony. Often, the marriages must be 'arranged' as you call it. With less than fifty families to draw upon—*ever*— we have no room for error. Our ancestors learned early, the effects of inbreeding; from AD 700 to 1000, the Cyrene family provided untainted genes, to get Stauros back on track. Inside this building are diagrams of all our interconnecting family trees; after two thousand years, these schematics practically cover all the walls; it's amazing."

At the mention of the word "tree," Stuart again stared long-ingly at the garden. Philios smiled, as if the young man had passed a test.

When they reached the rushing water, the path ended at the vertex of a stylized "T"—northwest, the stream flowed out of the garden, and southeast it gushed under the bridge.

At that corner was a tower. Philios beckoned Stuart to follow him up its central spiral staircase to the platform at a height of nearly five meters. A low wall encircled the platform. The roof added another two meters to the tower. The tower platform accommodated three comfortable lounge chairs.

They rested.

"These observation towers are often manned for days on end."

Philios pointed. "There are two other towers." One was due north of them, close to the wall; the third stood at half-past ten, equidistant from the other two. Connecting them would form an equilateral triangle. The three towers had domed roofs—gold, like the church dome.

To the west behind the library, Stuart saw tombs carved into the crater wall, a metal shop, and a mine. North of that were rows of beehives. He didn't want to know about those things; he wanted to know about the garden.

Stuart stared out at the garden. He did some mental calculations. The garden was circular, centered in the northwest region of the crater. Stuart estimated it to be more than 1,600 feet in diameter, maybe 2,000.

From this vantage point, the layout of the garden was apparent. A sea of purple flowers encircled a large bushy plant—the one with the crimson flowers and spectacular vines that he had seen from his infirmary window. From here, its shape brought to mind angels he had made as a child by laying on his back in pristine snow, flailing his arms, and getting up ever so carefully, then leaping away from the impressions of his feet. Extending such a snow angel into three dimensions, and standing it on end, approximated the profile of the extraordinary plant at center of the garden. At first, the surrounding trees appeared to be arranged in concentric circles, then the light changed—a passing cloud uncovered the sun—and the shadows of the treetops revealed that they traced a spiral. The red plant, the spiral's point of origin, was a third again taller than the ones surrounding it.

Stuart longed to enter the garden.

His wish was granted. Philios turned, pointed, and led him down the stairway. They headed along the path next to the stream; both the path and the stream disappeared into the garden. With each step that brought them closer, Stuart's heart beat faster until he felt dizzy with excitement; he placed his hand on the older man's shoulder for support. Something too wonderful for words was just beyond the entrance.

TWENTY-SEVEN

A S THEY ENTERED THE GARDEN, Stuart marveled at the trees creating the spiral. They were undeniably all the same type. Almost a cross between a giant dandelion and the Pollard Willows that he recalled from the large book of Van Gogh's art his mother kept on their coffee table in the parlor.

The trunks were thick—as thick as a man's thigh. They were cylindrical, without an apparent root system. None of the trunks had any branches, and on inspection, Stuart determined that this was not due to pruning, rather, it was their apparent natural state.

The bark was golden brown, indistinguishable from the color of people's skin in this part of the world.

On the top of each trunk, at a height of approximately nine feet, straight branches literally burst out in all directions, to form a sphere three to four feet in diameter; this was what recalled the top of a dandelion.

At the end of each branch, a single flower bloomed. The lower blooms hung six feet from the ground. Stuart imagined that if a giant plucked one of these trees and blew upon it, all the flowers would scatter like the spores of a dandelion at the breath of a child.

Maybe God was that big.

Standing in their midst, Stuart realized that the trees were not evenly spaced along the spiral. Drawing a straight line from any tree to the center would not intersect any other tree.

"It's beautiful," he said.

"Yes, most assuredly," Philios responded.

They stood still again, drinking in the fragrance of the blossoms, listening to the buzzing of the bees—*from the beehives he had seen earlier*, Stuart realized.

Just as he thought he might pass out from the loveliness of it all, Philios said, "Come."

They walked to the center of the garden.

As Stuart had seen from his window, the central tree was different from the others. The blooms were crimson, the color of blood. At fifteen feet in height, this one was taller than the rest. And not only did it have roots, it seemed to consist entirely of roots. The cascading effect of the vines, reaching upward and then curving outward, downward, and finally inward, was more pronounced up close. Again, he recalled a willow tree, this time a weeping willow, as if an invisible giant hand had closed upon the bottom of the tree, encompassing all the flexible willow branches in its grip.

The crimson flowers were intricate, complicated, elaborate, and...he couldn't think of a word that was suitable to describe the complexity of their beauty.

Then, Stuart noticed the cross beneath everything, supporting the plant. Upon closer examination, he saw that each vine originated from the wood of the cross. Initially, they were a quarter inch in diameter; this expanded to one-and-a-half inches at the apex of their upward journey, and reached a diameter of nearly four inches by the time they plunged into the earth at the foot of the cross.

"Awesome!" Stuart said.

"These vines are not what they seem," Philios explained. "Each of these vines extends out into the garden and becomes first the root, and then the trunk of one of the trees with the purple flowers.

"With several exceptions, the first twelve roots broke ground exactly thirty-three years before the death of each of the original Apostles. On the day of that Apostle's actual death, the corresponding tree blossomed with the flowers that you now see in abundance. Afterwards, each tree bloomed for a week every third year on the anniversary of that Apostle's death.

"Originally, a central ring of twelve trees grew around the cross, augmented by three outside that circle; those outer three began to define the spiral. One of those sprouted two years after the founding of this settlement, the other, two years after that. Another eighteen years elapsed before the sprouting of the last of those three.

"The thirteenth tree bloomed upon the death of Paul, and the fourteenth in AD 70 upon the destruction of Jerusalem. The fifteenth bloomed when God revealed the end times to John and he transcribed them in the Book of Revelation. A year later, the twelfth tree bloomed, on the day of John's entering Heaven. All the other trees bloomed in chronological order."

"If this group bloomed out of order, how did they determine what was actually taking place?"

"They didn't figure it out right away. Because the roots sprang from drops of Jesus' blood at the base of the cross, and these were underground, no one realized that the trees and the cross were connected until the second century AD."

"Wait a minute. You don't mean this is the cross that Jesus was crucified on, do you?" Stuart asked incredulously.

"None other." Philios' voice was reverent. "Fashioned from the tree planted by Seth on his father Adam's grave.

"But I thought the crucifixion happened in Jerusalem."

"And so it did. Our ancestors brought the cross to this place nearly two thousand years ago."

He studied Stuart's face. "If you've heard legends of the discovery of the cross by Saint Helen, the mother of Constantine the Great, and how it was subsequently divided into thousands of pieces, I can tell you there is a grain of truth to that story. Although, it wasn't the Holy Cross of Christ, nonetheless, it had been used to execute an innocent Christian for his faith. The blood was in all the right places, both figuratively and literally. The only thing it lacked was the epigraph nailed to the top, the board that said in Greek, Latin, and Hebrew, 'The King of the Jews.' Saint Helen attributed its absence to vandals."

Philios pointed to the cross in the center of the garden.

"Look between the vines, you can see the epigraph at the top."

Stuart felt light-headed. He stepped over to the spring, six feet from the base of the cross—the source of the stream that ran through the crater—and he splashed water on his face. It was cool and refreshing, the perfect temperature. He would have expected no less from a spring in front of the cross of Jesus' crucifixion.

PHILIOS LED Stuart around the spiral from the inside out. It was a humbling experience. As they passed each tree, he mentioned its initial year of blossoming. "103, 117, 132, 141, 149, 150."

At the twenty-first tree, he stopped for a moment. "This one bloomed on the day that Polycarp was martyred in 160, not far from here. The Romans tried to burn him at the stake, but God was protecting him, and the flames wouldn't touch him. Finally, they stabbed him to death."

Stuart shuddered.

They continued to walk. "165, 200, 202, 236, 250." Philios paused.

"This one bloomed in 254, on the day that the Lord revealed to Origen that Jesus and God were one substance.

"303, 311, 313." He stopped again.

"This tree bloomed in 325, during the first Nicene Council. More than three hundred bishops attended and established the Nicene Creed."

"We studied that in Comparative Religions last semester. We didn't have to memorize it, but for some reason, after I read it twice, it turned out I had it memorized. It's the weirdest thing."

Stuart recited. "I believe in one God, the Father Almighty, Maker of heaven and earth, and of all things visible and invisible.

"And in one Lord Jesus Christ, the only-begotten Son of God, begotten of the Father before all worlds; God of God, Light of Light, very God of very God; begotten, not made, being of one substance with the Father, by whom all things were made. Who, for us men for our salvation, came down from heaven, and was incarnate by the Holy Spirit of the virgin Mary, and was made man; and was crucified also for us under Pontius Pilate; He suffered and was buried; and on the third day He rose again, according to the Scriptures; and ascended into heaven, and sits on the right hand of the Father; and He shall come again, with glory, to judge the quick and the dead; whose kingdom shall have no end.

"And I believe in the Holy Ghost, the Lord and Giver of Life; who proceeds from the Father; who with the Father and the Son together is worshipped and glorified; who spoke by the prophets. And I believe in one holy catholic and apostolic Church. I acknowledge one baptism for the remission of sins; and I look for the resurrection of the dead, and the life of the world to come. Amen."

Stuart saw that Philios was both surprised and impressed.

Philios continued, "At least that's one of the theories. The other theory holds that this tree bloomed when Saint Helen discovered the other cross on Golgotha. To understand this theory, we have to go back to 311. You see, right before the last battle during the Great Persecution of Diocletian, the Battle of the Milvian Bridge, Constantine had a vision of the cross above the battlefield. Beneath it were the words, '*En Touto Nika*,' meaning 'in this sign conquer.'

"The vision of the cross moved Constantine to order his soldiers to put crosses on their armor before the battle that ended in Constantine's unconditional victory over Maxentius. It made such a profound impact on him that he asked his mother to travel to the Holy Land to find the true cross of Christ. Helen and her soldiers found what they believed to be the Holy Cross on September 14, 325, buried in the earth at the original site of Golgotha. The cult of holy relics was born.

"A fragrant Vasiliko flower—Basil—was growing on the spot where Helen found the cross, and since then the Orthodox Christian Church has revered that flower.

"Constantine managed to obtain other holy relics too: the bones of Andrew, Luke, and Timothy. He tried to get them all, and even built a Church of the Apostles, where he planned to have twelve niches containing the Apostles' bones with his own body lying in their midst as the 'thirteenth Apostle'."

"Amazing!"

"There's more. In 614, Persians captured Jerusalem and stole the alleged cross of Christ. The Byzantine Emperor Heraclius and his army of Christian soldiers recaptured the city after fifteen years of war. Heraclius returned the cross to the Church of the Holy Sepulcher, where legend has it, shortly thereafter it was cut into pieces and distributed to other centers of Christianity: Alexandria, Antioch, Constantinople, Corinth, Ephesus, and Rome. In those days holy relics were believed to have magical properties so it was common to distribute fragments—such as bones of the Apostles, shreds of their garments, splinters from the crosses upon which they were crucified—as widely as possible."

"But you said that the cross Saint Helen found was not the true cross of Christ, didn't you? It seems to me that a good deal of fuss is being made over a mistaken identity."

"That's one way to look at it. Then again, God can use anything to further his Kingdom. By the time Saint Helen found the cross she thought belonged to Jesus, execution by crucifixion had long been discontinued. Of all the crosses buried in the hill of Golgotha, many of them had been used to execute men whose only crime was their faith in Jesus. Had it been the true cross, the result would have very likely validated the outcome that Simon of Cyrene saw in his vision when he carried the patibulum—the crossbar. Good did come from Helen's mistake.

"But it wasn't the true cross, and it wasn't the blood of Christ on that cross, so the legend never took hold. Personally, I don't believe that God would have allowed the true cross to be chopped into thousands of splinters. And it turns out, He didn't."

Stuart felt his heart leap whenever Philios said the words "true cross."

They continued along the spiral of trees, and he was able to examine the cross from every angle. He found it difficult to take his eyes off it.

"339... The next four trees are among my favorites. No one disputes them.

"367: Athanasias, the Bishop of Alexandria listed the 27 books of The New Testament that comprised the modern canon. Twenty-six years later, Augustine's Councils cited the same 27 books.

"380: Gregory of Nazianzus explained the 'three-in-oneness' of God—the Trinity.

"381: Jesus is declared to have a true human soul by the Council of Theodosius at Constantinople.

"390: God reveals to Apollinaris of Laodicea that Jesus had a human body but a divine spirit.

"397, 407, 420, 430. Saint Augustine enters into Heaven."

"431, 432, 451, 476, 484, 496, 519, 526, 529, 537, 539, 541...The Plague."

"Wait a minute," Stuart said. Some of these things seem..." he searched for the right word, "...positive, and others seem negative. How can that be?"

"A good question. Over the centuries, we have determined at least three reasons a tree sprouts around the cross. First, the arrival in Heaven of any of God's saints, and I don't mean saints in the Catholic sense. Second, to commemorate an outpouring of God's blessing, grace, mercy, or protection; or God revealing something about Himself. Although, what we believe to be a revelation may be something that has been there all along, so it might be more precise to acknowledge such things as discoveries of earlier unacknow-ledged disclosures. All blessings show something about God to us if we can understand them. Finally, a tree may sprout at the com-mencement or culmination of a demonstration of God's wrath, which, I should add, often results in a large number of souls entering Heaven—and we're back to the first reason.

"Here in the crater, when we verbalize these reasons, we use the terms 'rejoicing, revelation, and wrath,' although 'wrath' could be the wrong word. Our scholars argue whether such things represent 'wrath' from God's point of view, or whether the designation of 'God's wrath' is simply placing a human emotion upon something we cannot understand—viewing an act of God from within our limited human frame of reference. On the other hand, the Bible does quote God expressing what seem to be human emotions; for example, God says, 'I hate divorce,' in Malachi 2:16.

"I've been skipping some trees. You've noticed. It's not that we don't know the associations of those trees, although some are under debate, and some for which we have no idea what their connection is."

"Why is that?"

"Even the smallest of the small can accomplish great work for God's Kingdom. It's possible that some of the trees about which we have no information concern cases like that. You probably know Jesus' parable of the mustard seed.

"When asked what the Kingdom of God is like, what it could be compared to, he replied, 'It is like a mustard seed, which is the smallest seed you plant in the ground. Yet when planted, it grows and becomes the largest of all garden plants, with such big branches that the birds of the air can perch in its shade.'"

Stuart said, "I think someone arranged for a few mustard seeds to be planted in my life, and I feel as if they are beginning to take root."

Philios smiled.

"547, 553, 581, 590, 614, 630, 637, 640, 678, 680, 718, 732, 787, 800, 856. Well, that takes us through the first millennium. Seventy trees around the cross. Seventy drops of the blood of the Lamb of God.

"Seven is the Lord's number." He laughed. "Oh, the theories that some of our ancestors have proposed about some of these first seventy trees."

The trees were closer together now. Stuart followed Philios between two trees so close to one another that their leaves inter-mingled. The younger man closed his eyes when he pushed his way through; the leaves brushed against his arms, and he felt a surge of energy. For a moment, it was as if they'd mirrored the contour of his body, forming a cloak that pressed him lovingly then relaxed, returning to their former state.

Stuart looked at his arms. The scratches from his slide into the crater wall were gone, even the scabs. He pulled up his shirt. All the bruises from his fall had disappeared! He was sure the leaves were responsible, and he was planning to mention it, but his companion clearly thought it to be nothing out of the ordinary.

They continued around the spiral, Philios reciting dates and stopping, as if randomly, at various trees.

"1096. The Crusades begin here...

"1334. Wrath. The Black Death.

"1431. Rejoicing. The martyrdom of Joan of Arc. The eighty-ninth to bloom."

Stuart recalled Philios mentioning her in his sermon.

The explanations became briefer.

"Revelation. Luther..."

A couple trees farther he stopped, "This is the ninety-ninth tree. It blossomed in 1536 when Tyndale was put to death. He translated the Bible into English. Believing it to be part of the

Lutheran reform, Ecclesiastical authorities ordered his Bible burned."

He started walking again. "Rejoicing, Rejoicing, Wrath, Wrath, Wrath, Wrath. Rejoicing, Revelation, Revelation…

"And here the twentieth century starts. 1901. Revelation. The outpouring of God's blessing upon the Pentecostal Church in Topeka, Kansas.

"Another ten, and then the founding of the State of Israel in 1948—tree number 150. Finally, the last twelve. The second and third from the end bloomed close after one another—upon the evidence of God revealed by decoding the human genome in 2000, and the change in the collective world attitude that commenced on September 11, 2001.

"Throughout the final years of the twentieth century, we thought those two trees were the last; we couldn't find any more drops of blood on the cross that had not already sprouted a vine. Yet, at least one more drop must have been underground, because a new tree sprouted in 2000, and it hasn't bloomed yet. Remember, it takes thirty-three years until they first blossom."

THE TREES ended in front of the north observation tower. This one had a second, lower circular building attached to it. Philios led them into the tower. Stuart saw spiral stairs, the same as he had seen in the tower they had entered earlier. Here, a door abutted the point where the stairs neared the second building. Directly beneath that door, on the ground floor, was another door.

"I think you're going to like this," Philios said.

Stuart followed him up the stairs to the doorway into the ad-joining building.

They stepped onto a walkway three feet wide; it encircled the inside of the smaller building next to the tower. The walkway had a metal railing and by holding onto the rail, one could lean out far into the space in the middle of the building.

Below them, in the center of the ground floor, was a circular pedestal, five feet high, upon which was a scale model of the garden. It was lovely! Nearly ten feet across.

On the wall encircling the model below them, was a map of the world. It started three feet from the ground floor, and ended nine feet farther up, at the walkway that Stuart and Philios stood on.

Beneath the map, and encircling the model, were shelves of books and papers.

A piece of thread was attached to nearly every one of the trees of the model garden. These threads stretched to the surrounding map. When Stuart saw the next to the last tree connected to the city of New York by such a thread, he realized that these threads were indicators of the locations associated with the events in history marked by the trees. It all fit; now he understood the map and the cross-chart in the seventh classroom.

Philios and Stuart continued around the walkway staring at the model below them.

"It's impressive, isn't it?"

Stuart nodded. Speechless.

When they returned to the doorway leading back to the observation tower, Philios said, "Come up to the top of the tower. Now that you've been through the garden, you will see it with different eyes."

They stood without a sound, for many minutes, their attention fixed upon the garden.

"Any questions?"

Stuart had hundreds. He didn't know which to ask first.

"I saw fruit at the base of each flower. Are those edible?" he asked, wishing he had asked the question when one of the pieces of fruit had been in reach.

"We don't know. We've studied the garden for nearly 2,000 years. The trees have never borne fruit before. This is a new development. We have learned that each tree has 144 pieces of fruit on it, 23,328 in all—at least that will be the number when the final tree blooms.

"Each piece of fruit is bigger than a cherry, yet smaller than an apricot, and conveniently the size of a single mouthful. All the fruit is the color of white gold, and so far, none of them has fallen to the ground. Beyond this, we don't know anything about the fruit. There was another time when fruit on a tree of God played a big part in the future of the human race. We don't want to repeat that mistake, so no one has tasted the fruit."

A chill enveloped Stuart's body as he remembered how close he had come to picking one of the inviting golden orbs.

"You said that the trees bloomed triennially, upon the anniversary of their original bloom. From what you've told me, that would create a staggered pattern of blooming. Despite that, excluding that last one, all the trees are now in bloom. How do you explain that?"

"I can't. The scholars haven't stopped debating that since it happened less than a year ago. For the first time in history, the trees are all in bloom together, and moreover, they are bearing fruit for the first time. Some of our people have pointed out that we are rapidly approaching the year 2033, the two thousandth anniversary of the crucifixion and resurrection of Jesus Christ."

TWENTY-EIGHT

LOS ANGELES

AFTERNOON (GMT-7)

DURING MASS, FATHER ROMERO thought of nothing but the golden church. In his mind, he checked and rechecked a list of things he needed to bring with him to Turkey. He could scarcely contain his eagerness to start packing.

His sub, Father Dominicus Jordan, had arrived, courtesy of the Bishop, ten minutes before Mass. An attractive, clean-shaven young man with shiny black hair, there was even a pious texture to his skin.

He looks like the young priest from that old Exorcist movie, Father Romero noticed. *He'll do well in this town.*

There was time to introduce themselves to each other, but little else.

During Mass, Father Jordan sat near the pulpit but slightly behind Father Romero, an appropriate position of subordination. The young priest dutifully stood and smiled when Father Romero introduced him. The older priest perceived a ripple of edgy anticipation run through the female members of the congregation right before the handsome young man sat down again. He hoped there wouldn't be any *incidents* while he was away.

Calculating how long it would take him to pack and adding in travel time to the airport, Father Romero realized with some frustration that he had neglected to include at least an hour or two for showing the young priest around, making him comfortable, and getting him settled in the rectory. He suspected a number of the "good Catholic ladies" would wait around after mass for a personal introduction to his temporary replacement; they could give Father Jordan the tour.

He chuckled, forgetting that his microphone was still on.

THINGS PROCEEDED the way Father Romero had envisioned after the service. He arrived back in his office at 3 p.m., having finally extricated himself from the young priest. Miss Pamela Parker and Enid Fitzsimmons generously agreed to take Father Jordan to tea. He knew that Enid wouldn't leave until Father Jordan gave her a blessing, while Pamela would remark that priests were sinners like everyone else in the world—the finale of a miniature passion play.

Father Romero packed a small case with two changes of clothes, his trusty binoculars—dating from the last time he had been in the Holy Land—and his Bible.

He tried to decide whether to bring a copy of his book; it would add so much weight. Finally, he concluded it might be useful as a tangible credential for places from which he might be turned away otherwise. He tossed a copy of it into his suitcase, watching the heavy book compress the contents. *Well, at least I won't need an iron*, he thought as he snapped it closed.

◆ ◆ ◆

BRYCE BRINKMAN studied the photograph, and shouted to Earl, "I need information about Byzantine churches." Earl raised his head slowly. She was ordering him around again. He silently swore. Again, the money Roebuck paid into his offshore account for him to keep track of her, consoled him.

"Be a dear and try to dig something up at the library, will you, Cole?"

Earl didn't mind when Roebuck called him "Cole," but he detested it when Bryce did.

"At your service." He added an unspoken obscenity.

Twenty minutes later, Earl was standing in front of the reference counter at the university library. The reference librarian was sitting at a desk behind the counter busily shuffling papers. She bore the pallid look of a protein-deficient vegetarian. He had seen it before; even dated a few. He cleared his throat a couple times.

Why was it so hard to get the attention of a librarian?

He coughed.

It's just as bad as trying to flag a waitress in a restaurant.

Finally, the woman came to life, and moseyed to the counter. She was wearing a silly T-shirt that said, "There are no stupid questions." He noticed her name tag: "Monika Kunsli, Reference Librarian."

Sounds foreign.

"I'm looking for something about Byzantine churches."

Clearly, she didn't have a clue what the word "Byzantine" meant; Earl loved stumping librarians, had enjoyed it all through his college studies. He hoped she would ask, "In what period would that be," so he could respond, "The Byzantine period"; that would wipe the smirk off her face.

The girl pretended to know where to find something useful. She said, "Just a moment," and walked over to one of the shelves. She returned with a book entitled, "Byzantine Churches in the Holy Land and Bordering Regions—A Complete Compendium," by Rafael Romero, S.J.

"Will this do?" she asked, intensifying her smirk. She handed it to him.

Thick and glossy, it was a coffee table book. Nonetheless, the cover maintained it was the "Complete Compendium."

Earl was impressed. The woman had actually found something.

"This'll do, just fine," he said, and taking the book, he retired to one of the study carrels.

He sat down and perused the tome. It promised more than one thousand photographs of Byzantine churches. Drawing in a deep breath, he resigned himself to the task of comparing each one to the print that Bryce had given him. From experience, he knew that things would not go well if he returned without results.

He noticed Monika continuing to mess about with books in the same general area from which she had retrieved the one in his hands.

They were sponges, these reference librarians.

They started out knowing nothing, but then when you asked for something, after they found a little bit, then they kept on looking, and looking, and looking for more on the topic; even if you were perfectly content with what they had already given you.

Earl imagined a dry sponge near a puddle of water. If the sponge merely touched the tiniest edge of the puddle, it would suck up the whole thing. Conversely, if there were no contact, there would be no action, and the sponge would remain dry. Empty.

A sponge never planned ahead. Librarians were like that with knowledge.

From his jaundiced viewpoint, Earl believed that all women were like sponges sucking away the vital parts of men. Three wives had led him to the conclusion that they sponged either money, time, or emotional energy, giving little in return.

He saw the librarian walking toward him with an armful of materials: oversized folders, probably containing architectural drawings of Byzantine churches. Apparently, she's sopped up some more information, he mused.

She arrived at his study carrel, and said, "I found these folios on churches of that period."

Earl realized that he had been searching for that term for years. *Reference librarians had a 'folio-er than thou' attitude*; he said to himself.

He burst out laughing. "Folios! Thank you, but I think this volume will be quite enough." He put it under his arm and started walking to the check-out desk by the door.

On the way back to the lab, he convinced himself that, although he hadn't identified the church in the photo, he wasn't returning empty-handed. The big book was under his arm, after all.

Earl had a love-hate relationship with Bryce. He knew that were their positions reversed, if he were the head research scientist, and she the assistant, he would be madly in love with her. The way things stood now, he hated her for being in the limelight.

Bryce had no idea that Earl's feelings toward her were anything but professional.

"This is the standard reference," Earl said, attempting to hand Bryce the book.

"Did you find the one we're looking for in it?" she asked, avoiding taking the heavy volume from him.

"There was this pesky librarian, who was trying to be so helpful that I couldn't hear myself think. You know what I mean?"

"No," Bryce said flatly, looking at Earl as if he were from another culture.

Reluctantly, she flipped through the book and skimmed a page near its beginning.

> Emperor Constantine legalized Christianity in the Roman Empire in 313, thus putting an end to the persecution of Christians. The name of Byzantium was changed to Constantinople, and later to Istanbul. One result of the freedom for Christians to worship without persecution was the construction of many churches.
>
> Byzantine churches often employed cruciform floor plans (in the shape of a cross), and domed roofs were typical. To emphasize the Holy Trinity, many architectural forms were repeated in triplicate: three-tiered domes, triply-arched entranceways, tri-segmented semicircular windows, and later, triple buttresses used to prevent walls from buckling outward due to...

Blah, blah, blah...

> ...The transept represents the crossbar (patibulum) of the cruciform design.
>
> In the Byzantine era, churches sought to bring in natural light because there was no electricity...Glass and ceramic mosaics reflected natural light entering the church through clerestory-rows of horizontal windows...Gold was a favored adornment; besides being highly re-

> flective of light, it highlighted the splendor of
> God. ...such mosaics were favored on additional
> grounds: three-dimensional art works were be-
> lieved to lead to the worship of idols and
> therefore, were barred...

Bryce skimmed on.

> ...Iconoclastic controversy 726-843. The Old
> Testament warns against idolatry, and... In 730,
> the Emperor Leo enforced a decree ordering the
> removal of figural images from all churches—
> excluding the holy cross as specified in Scripture
> (Galatians 6:14). In spite of this, icons were rein-
> troduced in 843.

Bryce closed the book. She chuckled. "Well Cole, I guess you
have your work cut out for your then, eh?"

Earl turned quickly toward his desk in an unsuccessful attempt
to hide his grimace.

TWO HOURS LATER, he approached Bryce. "It isn't in here,"
he said triumphantly.

"Are you sure?"

"Positive. Unless, they plated one of these churches with gold
since the time this book was written."

Bryce grabbed the book and examined the publication date.

"Ten years," she said, half to herself. "That's unlikely. These
embellishments look like they're centuries old."

She got worried. What if she had miscalculated the location?
What if it weren't even in Turkey at all? Roebuck would have her
head. He didn't like mistakes. It wasn't that he couldn't afford
slipups; he didn't have the time...literally.

"Cole, go back and check through all those photographs again,
keeping in mind that the gold might be a recent addition. While
you do that, I'll run all the imaging checks again as a precaution to
confirm we have the correct location. It's essential for us to wrap
this up tonight; I've booked us on a flight to Turkey tomorrow
evening."

"Anything you say, Professor."

Bryce postulated other frames of reference to triangulate the crater's location from the shadows in the photo. The result was always the same region in Turkey.

For a moment, she considered the idea that it wasn't a crater. She studied the photo with a magnifying glass. There was no doubt about it; the church was higher than all the other buildings. Obviously, it stood upon the central peak, a small mound characteristic of larger craters, formed by the rebound of the meteorite at the point of impact.

BOTH HAD TAKEN Melatonin and stayed awake all night to reset their internal clocks to the EET—Eastern European Time. By 2 o'clock the following afternoon, they were exhausted. Earl had found nothing, and all Bryce's calculations had been triple-checked.

"Maybe this 'Complete Compendium' isn't so complete after all," Bryce said in a way that was intended to give the impression that Earl was to blame for the problem, if only for having supplied a faulty reference.

"I'm going to bring the thing with us on the plane, to check it myself," Bryce continued, implying that Earl wasn't even capable of adequately checking the book, "…in case you missed something. It will give me something to do on the flight."

Earl consoled himself with Richard's promise to share with him, the profits of commercializing the "Y-factor." No matter how many times he calculated and recalculated his percentage, it came to billions; the longevity market would yield trillions.

TWENTY-NINE

THE TELEPHONE GLOWED, and the name "Richard" appeared. Bryce pressed the speaker button.

"Are you two ready?" he asked.

Bryce and Earl looked at each other and then at the book that had occupied so much of their time.

"Ready as we ever will be," Bryce said.

"Still haven't nailed down the precise location of that church, have you?" It was uncanny how, from a single sentence, Richard could deduce the progress of their whole day. "Here's a tidbit that will put the matter in a slightly different perspective."

"Go on."

"While you two were taking a crash course in Byzantine Churches, I've been running projections from the data we collected about Tuesday's earthquake."

"It was a mere six-point-seven."

"You're right, Bryce—but it's looking more and more like a pre-shock."

"Pre-shocks are never anywhere near that high on the Richter scale."

"Not in recorded history, you mean. But eighty percent of the simulations I ran today ended in an eight-point-six or greater primary quake within seventy-six hours."

"There's no way to predict earthquakes."

Roebuck hesitated. "That's not entirely true. Predictive seismology is a new science, but when you use data gathered near one of the earth's magnetic poles, it starts to become accurate. This comes from my team in Antarctica. They are years ahead of the Department of Defense group working a mere thirty miles away from my group. The DOD doesn't have a clue that my team is even monitoring seismology; my team's main mission is to study micro-organisms embedded in the permafrost—magnetotactic bacteria that have been frozen for thousands of years."

"Magneto-what?"

"Magnetotactic bacteria—bacteria that orient themselves according to the earth's magnetic field. Like miniature, motorized compass needles, they swim in the direction of the North Pole when they are in the Northern Hemisphere, and the South Pole when they are in the Southern Hemisphere. Actually, they will swim toward any moderately strong magnet. Their cells contain magnetite particles and magnetosomes."

"Magnetosomes?"

"Perfect magnetic crystals—often chains of crystals—created through biomineralization bounded by a cellular membrane; these bacteria are part metal—they each contain their own little magnet factory, and they use the magnets they manufacture for navigation."

As usual, Bryce cringed at the thought of Richard being so far ahead of everyone else in the field—including her. With no apparent effort, he integrated vast quantities of incongruent information and made inferences in irrelevant areas.

"I was originally attracted to magnetism—"

"Very funny."

"Completely unintentional, I assure you."

"Go on."

"After the now-debunked 'Baylor experiment' in 1997—a double-blind study at Baylor College of Medicine that claimed to prove the effectiveness of magnets in pain reduction—one of the researchers approached me. His theory proposed a cancer treatment using biomagnetics, particularly magnetotactic bacteria. But the human body is non-magnetic—otherwise your body would explode during an MRI; and water, the main constituent of the body, is diamagnetic—meaning it is slightly repelled by magnetic fields. But if magnetotactic bacteria could be trained to bind with cancer cells…Think of this: relocating inoperable cancers simply by moving a magnet; perhaps coercing them to swim to a place where the human body could expel them naturally. His proposal called for studying, *in situ*, bacteria that had already navigated to their goal, instead of those simply headed in the right direction. That's how the lab at the South Pole came about."

"I was a teenager then…just putting away my dollhouses…" Bryce said.

Richard continued. "I visited the Antarctic project in September of 1999. The camp is between the Mertz Glacier and the Commonwealth bay, on the edge of a dry valley. It's as close as we can get to the magnetic South Pole; the pole is gradually moving in the direction of Australia, and it's offshore now. The French have long maintained a meteorological station on a nearby island: *Dumont d'Urville* Station. *D'Urville's* the explorer who discovered the Venus de Milo, the one at the *Louvre*."

"Dry valleys in Antarctica?"

"Bryce, you must visit the place. It's spectacular. There are many small 'dry valleys' on the continent—most run four miles wide and twenty miles long. These are the driest places on earth, with no rainfall for millions of years."

"Your point?"

"Sorry. I was telling you about my visit to the Antarctic base in September of 1999. The week before that, I had been bombarded with images, seismographs and more, of the August seventeenth Izmit quake—the one on the North Anatolian Fault Zone, the NAFZ, where the Arabian and Eurasian plates meet; the one that killed seventeen thousand people. That's in your target region, by the way. By then, I had the quake's PMA profile (Pre-shock—Mainshock—Aftershock profile) memorized. When I got to the base, I saw the same seismographs everywhere. I got angry; I mean, I wasn't paying them to study earthquakes—right?"

"Right."

"Well—now listen to this Bryce, this is how major discoveries are made—they claimed that the data on their monitors represented tiny fluctuations in the swimming direction of the magnetotactic bacteria; they have quite a colony of the living bacteria with them to use as a control population for the frozen specimens. Nevertheless, there was no denying that these momentary 'blips'—little corrective movements—spiked the graphs in a pattern identical to the Izmit earthquake signature. After filtering out the effect of the moon's gravitational field—fortunately, we had an audio engineer with experience in noise-reduction algorithms from his previous job for a synthesizer company—we assumed that the bacteria had been reacting to magnetic field distortions caused by the quake. But no such distortions were recorded. Then we studied the dates. The bacterial record was from twenty-nine days before the quake. Even so, these minute directional fillips all pointed precisely to the hypocenter of the Izmit quake on the Anatolian fault. And each little bump on the bacterial record corresponded to a magnitude five or greater shock, twenty-nine days later—to the second."

"Hypocenter?"

"That's an earthquake's point of origin within the earth—the focal point where the quake actually begins; the epicenter is merely the point on the earth's surface directly above the hypocenter."

"Are you saying that the motion of microscopic bacteria in Antarctic caused an earthquake in Turkey, the way some say the fluttering of a butterfly's wings in China can cause a tidal wave in Tierra Del Fuego?"

"Not at all. You're missing my point. I don't buy into that garbage."

Bryce wasn't sure about that.

"I'm merely saying that somehow, the magnetotactic bacteria exhibit ripples in the earth's magnetic field in advance of when those little field distortions manifest as earthquakes. Call it a 'pre-echo' if you like. These little slugs, invisible to the naked eye, are a perfect earthquake prediction mechanism. Many other animals have magnetosomes in or near major sensory organisms—this could explain why pets often seem precognitive about quakes. All their magnetosomes suddenly reorienting to the hypocenter would produce an alarming sensation."

"Yes. I've heard that some seismologists monitor the 'Missing Pets' pages of newspapers; the number of disappearances usually rises right before a major quake."

"Well, keep in mind what I just told you—and keep it confidential—and get ready to receive the quake-projection sim-data."

BRYCE AND EARL watched the three-dimensional animation of their 320 by 240 kilometer search window with the time element accelerated by a factor of sixty times sixty—each second equivalent to one hour. Waves of rainbow colors rippled out from the epicenter with increasing complexity and intensity, each burst of energy ranging farther than the one before. Bryce remembered the small pools of oil reflecting the sun in the crystal clearness of the stream behind her house. As kids, they had called it "poison water."

In simulation after simulation, she and Earl saw the total demolition of two—and often all three—of their candidate craters.

EVENING

FATHER ROMERO stood at the international check-in counter of LAX—Los Angeles International Airport—at 5:30 that evening. The flight to Rome was direct, but there, he would change for a flight to Ankara. He would change planes again for Dogubayazit close to the base of Mount Ararat.

He glanced to the counter at his right and saw a strikingly beautiful woman with a small, rough-looking man. Something about the woman caused him to stare. To his surprise, she was carrying a photo of him. Within moments of Father Romero realizing that it actually was a photo of him, he remembered that it was the one on the back of his book.

The woman was carrying a copy of his book!

How odd…yet somehow…exciting.

Puffed up with pride, he had decided to try to catch her attention when the airline agent behind the counter said, "May I see your passport please?"

Father Romero complied, and there was some paperwork to complete, some questions to answer. When he looked back to the other counter, the woman with his book was gone. She hadn't noticed Father Romero.

THIRTY

MONDAY, JUNE 27

MEREDITH WAITED FOR BRAD and Margaret Pierce at LAX. Father Romero was already airborne, on his way to Turkey, while Bryce Brinkman and Earl Cole sat on another plane bound for Amsterdam; there they too would switch to one destined for Turkey.

Meredith had had no problem convincing her parents to let her go back to the Holy Land. Her mother had been delighted. The elder Mrs. Montgomery hadn't even had time to complete a full circuit of bragging to all her friends about her daughter's previous summer working on a kibbutz. And, Meredith's passport was still good.

The problem had been with the Pierces. Neither of them had a passport, but their flight was scheduled to depart on Monday afternoon.

On Monday morning, they went to the consulate with Walter Warren, and met with the man who had helped arrange for the return of his son's body less than a week ago. They explained their plans to search for Stuart. Walter's contact had sympathy for them. He asked them whether they had considered the possibility that the boys had taken a side trip somewhere. Tatvan, where Roger's body had been deposited, was close enough to Mount Ararat, the traditional location of Noah's Ark, but it was also equidistant from the borders of Iraq and Syria.

The man was well informed. "I know that the consular assistant over there, Tommy Dorfler, is doing everything he can. He has been scouring the Ararat region already. He has had a photo of your son since last Wednesday."

Brad and Margaret were surprised to hear that an investigation was already underway.

"A photo?" Brad asked.

"Yes. With the new digital passports, we transfer the image file for them to print out at their location, instead of a hard copy. It's much more efficient. Your son's passport was only a year old, so we decided not to bother you with an official photo request."

He took out a card and scribbled a name and number on the back of it. "This is Tommy Dorfler's mobile-phone number."

In the end, the consular officer managed to expedite their applications, although they hadn't walked out of the building with passports. The man had promised that someone would meet them at the airport that afternoon and deliver their passports, and someone did just that.

◆ ◆ ◆

MEREDITH'S PARENTS, along with Roger's parents, were at the airport to see the three travelers off. Her parents had a privileged lifestyle; her father owned a successful delicatessen in Sherman Oaks; her mother was a professional busybody.

Mrs. Warren, eyes still red from the aftermath of Roger's funeral, promised to pray for the expedition. Roger's father, Meredith noted, was still *not all there.*

Cindy Pierce was standing close by, apprehensive at the thought of having both her parents leave the country at the same time. Cindy had a Panda bear purse designed to appear as if it were hugging her hip. She gripped one of the arms of the Panda like a child looking for security.

Meredith sincerely believed that Cindy would continue to surround herself with teddy bears long into her adult life, and she looked for one whenever Stuart's sister was around. Cindy had a vast repertoire of methods to assure a teddy bear was always close by. Meredith was privileged to know that the lifeless body of Cindy's stillborn twin sister had clung to her side at birth, similar to the Panda purse; only Cindy's parents, she, and one other person knew that.

Meredith overheard Brad tell Cindy, "You keep the Monk safe." She knew that "Monk" was the name of the family beagle. More than once, she had heard Stuart's father say, "What do we need a priest for—we have our own monk right here!" And then burst out laughing at his own joke.

"Don't come back without my brother," Cindy said.

Meredith hugged her. The prospect that Stuart might be dead, or worse, had never entered Meredith's mind.

She kissed her father goodbye, and watched as her mother zoomed in on Mrs. Warren. She suspected that her mother intended to comfort Roger's mother by recounting the story of every one of her friends who had ever lost a child. She knew her mother had good intentions, even if they often backfired.

No matter. We're off. Meredith could barely contain her excitement.

Next stop Turkey!

THE SECOND WEEK

And the LORD God said, "The man has now become like one of us, knowing good and evil. He must not be allowed to reach out his hand and take also from the tree of life and eat, and live forever." (Genesis 3:22)

THIRTY-ONE

MONDAY, JUNE 27, PRESENT DAY

TURKEY

MORNING (GMT+3)

B RYCE AND EARL stood in the airport at Dogubayazit. It was the standard point of entry for seekers of Noah's ark. Bryce had been to London, Paris, even Monte Carlo, but from her point of view, those places were no more than imperfect replicas of New York, the only difference being that many people spoke unintelligibly, and she couldn't understand any of the magazine covers. Turkey was a completely new world. Here, she couldn't begin to imagine what was between the edges.

We're not in Kansas anymore.

During the flight, she had compared Roger's photograph with every picture in Father Romero's book. After going through the book once, as quickly as possible and to no avail, she had gone back and examined every one of the nearly one thousand photos meticulously. That church was the key to finding the singularity in the garden behind it., She was starting to feel like an expert on Byzantine churches by the time she fell asleep over the Atlantic, although she still hadn't found a match to the one in the dead boy's photograph.

Most of the flight, Earl had been unconscious. He'd taken a couple pills right before the plane took off, Bryce noted with contempt. Whenever he wasn't snoring by her side, during the rare moments he was awake, he played games on his PalmPad while waiting for another pill to kick in.

During the last hour of the flight, Earl drank coffee and read pamphlets graciously provided by the airlines and the Office of Turkish Tourism.

"You're wasting your time reading that stuff," Bryce said.

Earl pointed at a paragraph in red letters on one of the flyers. It stated that permits were required of all people climbing Mount Ararat in search of Noah's Ark.

"But we're not looking for Noah's Ark," Bryce countered.

"We still need permits."

"We're going to check out the crater on the Armenian side of the mountain."

"We're going to need permits just to hike through the Ark area."

"If you say so." Bryce resigned from the dispute.

"And, what if we find Noah's Ark? The mere wood used to build it is probably holy. Probably something Richard would be interested in. He might think it had healing properties." Earl chuckled.

"What are you getting at? Do you actually believe there would be something special about the wood of a 4,300 year-old boat?"

"Richard does."

"Well, what about you?"

"I was raised in the church."

"What's that supposed to mean? You haven't been to a church for years."

"It's imprinted in me."

"Uh huh. Didn't you once say that religion had a lot in common with Las Vegas?"

"It does—a Las Vegas magic show on a grand scale—both call for suspension of disbelief."

"You mean you believe it when you see it, but afterwards you know it was a trick?"

"That's right. It's like that with the church and me. When I'm in church, I believe it, but for the rest of the time, the whole thing seems like a trick."

"As if there's a hidden, sort of 'Wizard of Oz' pulling the strings?" Bryce remembered playing Dorothy in the drama club as a teen.

"It's confusing; that's why I never think about it."

"So, back to my question…"

"I can't explain why, but I have no doubt that the wood from Noah's Ark would be mystical. And being so, it would *have* to possess supernatural properties."

Bryce wasn't sure about that. Nevertheless, she was sure that Earl was correct in his assumptions about Richard: that he would believe it to be special, and that the strength of those beliefs might exercise a psychosomatic effect upon his body. *Wasn't that the principle behind voodoo?*

BRYCE SLOWLY SCANNED the airport. The smells hit her first. It was like being in a spice factory. Even if a McDonald's had been there, the traditional odor of potatoes in near-rancid cooking oil would never have cut through what was floating into her nose. The aromas came from the wares of loud vendors: *manti* (dumplings), *boreck* (filled pastries), and of course, lamb *kebab* with rice pilaf. She recognized mint and dill mixed with frying onions as a waft of yet another unidentifiable fragrance drifted by.

Stopping to inspect one of the stands selling sweets, she saw English translations on the menu-board: "Twisted Turban," "Lady's Navel," "Lips of the Beloved," "Nightingale's Nest," and other bizarre names. What could they possibly be?

The large number of people selling carpets caught her attention.

Not something you'd expect at an airport.

All the carpets were Turkish, of course. These were hand-woven with sun-dried wool and depicted patterns from times long forgotten. She knew women had made them, although only men were involved in their sale. There was one such carpet in her living room, and she had learned something about both their history and their quality control. Finer carpets had a double knot on the back, assuring their durability and longevity. Vegetable dyes instead of synthetics would have been used in their coloring, and it was important to view the carpets in natural light to assure they hadn't faded. The airport, Bryce observed, afforded little natural light.

The roar of people talking, shouting, hawking their wares, competed with the culinary delights and tapestries for dominance over the senses: hearing versus a coalition of smelling and sight. The delicious aromas and colorful woven mosaics almost drowned in the ocean of sound. And this sea of noise organized itself into periodic waves. These were defined by their loudness, growing to crests and then breaking, as often happens when a party of chattering humans all pause for breath at the same time, creating that moment of awkward silence reflected in red faces upon its departure. But here, Bryce saw, there was a mediator: an ancient and enormous parrot, obviously the lifelong companion of one wrinkled carpet salesman. The royal blue bird with its scarlet plume, allowed the silence to continue only so long, while its eyes scanned the crowd searching the faces for a predator that had stolen its family in the jungle. Then, upon finding nothing but more of the same, the parrot would issue an earsplitting squawk. The human throng seemed to take this as an "all clear" signal to carry on their conversations where they had left off.

Bryce noted that within the background rumble, borrowed words from English—cognates, as they're called among the cognoscenti—were nonexistent, particularly when compared to her experiences at the airports of Paris and Monte Carlo. The sense of security afforded by periodic English utterances was also missing. The reason for this, she surmised, owed to the absence of a continuous stream of American tourists. Her blond hair and short skirt stood out like a giraffe in a cow pasture.

Bryce's initial discomfort at stepping forth into this foreign culture abated when she realized that men were glancing at her, just as they did in America, coveting her. Again, knowing the extent of her beauty comforted her. She *was* beautiful, and she appreciated that. In addition, she relished the idea that the letter 'B' defined the left edge of the word "beautiful," as it did with her own name. She secretly wished that the practice of bestowing honorific titles upon people hadn't died out—titles based upon the synchronicity of their leading edge letters with those of the names of the people bearing them: cognomens. She would be "Bryce the Beautiful." Earl would be "Cole the Corrupt." What she didn't want to admit to herself was that the upbringing of most of the males—Moslem—in her immediate vicinity caused them to assume she was a prostitute.

AFTER FIGHTING their way to the airport doors, a journey that included wrestling their luggage from a Faginesque gang of street urchins—would-be baggage porters looking for a quick twenty-thousand Turkish Lira—they finally succumbed to one of the taxi drivers who were bickering over them, and squeezed into his cab. Immediately, Bryce smelled pizza; she realized that Cole had somehow managed to procure a flat, round piece of bread covered with minced meat, onions, and tomatoes. It wasn't pizza in any sense of the word, but Cole was eating it with unbridled pleasure, tiny bits falling into his lap.

◆ ◆ ◆

TWO HOURS after stepping off the plane, Bryce finally sat in her hotel room, catching her breath. Mount Ararat dominated the view from her window. There was a soft knock at the door, and Earl entered, carrying the Transmogrifier.

"Transmogrifier" was a word they used between themselves, sort of an in-joke—the only one they had. To the rest of their colleagues, the conglomeration of scientific equipment was known by its official name: the "Field Research Model" or "FRM" for short. It was something they had been working on for years—literally a field lab in a box.

The name "Transmogrifier" originated during a lunch break at the café near the student union at the university. Eavesdropping on two students at the next table, they determined that the young men were self-taught guitarists, discussing the use of computers in their musical endeavors. One kept saying, "Man, all you have to do is transmogrify it. I've been telling you that. Remember, transmog-rify, transmogrify!" Bryce and Earl looked at each other as if they had been transported into a cartoon, and somehow the real world had become what television showed children on Saturday mornings. Bryce had suppressed an urge to stand up in the name of scientific reason and say, "I beg your pardon."

When they returned to the lab, both looked at the box they were assembling. Then, pretending to be Sherlock Holmes, Earl said, "Ah. The Transmogrifier. I knew we'd find it sooner or later. Watson, bring me my magnifying glass." That had been one of the few times they had laughed together, and they did so for the rest of the day. Whenever they stopped laughing, one of them would use the word Transmogrifier in a sentence to bring on a new episode of mirth. The name had stuck.

Earl put the Transmogrifier on Bryce's bed in the hotel room. It resembled a leather briefcase, only larger. Grade "A" Titanium reinforced the outer leather shell. This was the first time they were going to put it to the test in legitimate field research; Bryce could hardly contain her excitement.

Thanks to the generous funding of Richard Roebuck Research, they had two FRMs. The one sitting on the bed periodically backed itself up to the other one, which they had shipped to an office in Athens. It was another advantage of having one's own personal satellite network. In the event of damage to, or theft of, the primary unit, the fully up-to-date backup was less than two hours away.

The computer inside the FRM had four ten-gigahertz dual-core processors, operating in parallel. Should one of the processors fail, its work would be offloaded to the remaining three, in an instant. If the current task called for four processors, the other three would generate a virtual processor in RAM, with only a twenty-five percent hit on power. It was similar to a starfish losing a leg and regenerating a new one. In fact, during lab trials, everyone referred to the procedure by saying, "the FRM just starfished."

The processors used cutting-edge architecture: Multi-State-Computing, or MSC, pronounced "messy," for short. Designed by Apple, MSC was at the core of the generation of computers following on the heels of RISC—Reduced-Instruction-Set-Computing. Whereas all previous computers, including RISC computers, used binary states to represent numbers as ones or zeroes, the heart of MSC architecture consisted of molecules that could denote twelve states. Instead of employing a base-12 numbering system, these twelve states were assigned to the digits zero through nine, with the remaining two states representing True and False. Whereas earlier computers represented *False* with *zero* and *True* with *one*, the new MSC approach of isolating the true-false aspects from the numeric aspects prompted a quantum leap in processor logic, opening whole new worlds of computing.

The rest of the world had standardized on dual, five-gigahertz processors, but Richard had connections, and when it came to technology, he could obtain the latest and the greatest.

Earl unlocked and opened the case, and Bryce again saw the vast array of miniature devices in little pockets inside the lid. These included tiny wireless video cameras, listening devices, motion-detectors, and GPS-tracking locators. It typified standard-issue spy paraphernalia. When the computer monitor swung open, the screen hid most of the miniature electronics. Besides the main monitor, a smaller screen on the right side of the case swiveled out for video links and communications. It also served as a receiver for the wireless mini-V-cams.

There had been problems taking the FRM through customs, and they suspected they hadn't experienced the last of the difficulties it was likely to cause for them with the authorities. According to their cover story, they were seismologists. Everybody liked seismologists in Turkey because of the nerve-wracking unpredictable earthquake activity. The Turks knew that seismologists had complex, incomprehensible equipment. The recent earthquake made their story all the more plausible.

Bryce watched Earl check all the components of the FRM.

"Here's a cool feature I added right before we left," he said.

Earl typed a few commands and a schematic of the lab in Los Angeles appeared on the screen; a 3-D photo-accurate icon—a *picon*— represented each physical device in the lab.

"Click on any of the computers or other devices, and you can run them from here." Earl chuckled with pride.

Bryce used the track pad to position the cursor over the tiny picture of her workstation computer in the center of the screen. She clicked. Her virtual desktop appeared upon the FRM's monitor. She ran one of her programs.

"I'm impressed," she said, but inside she vowed to discover how and for how long Earl had had her password.

THIRTY-TWO

EARLY AFTERNOON (GMT+3)

B Y TWO O'CLOCK, they were at the Office of Tourism, trying to obtain climbing permits for the Mount Ararat region. Earl's bad manners didn't help the situation. Bryce purposely concealed any intentions to travel to the other side of the mountain.

"You understand that permits are necessary because so many have died up there," said the man behind the counter. His English was perfect, with only a touch of accent. "The last one who died, Sertac Tumerdem, was climbing illegally to take photos for his girlfriend. He fell to his death on July 18, 2001 near the summit. This is for your own protection."

The man possessed a wealth of information concerning the Ark, a fact established beyond question by his endless rambling about the relic.

"You call the mountain Ararat. Moses called it Urartu. We call it Agri. It is 16,945 feet high, higher than any point in Europe. Above 14,000 feet, you will find a permanent seventeen square-mile ice cap, three hundred feet deep. One reason it is so beautiful is that we're on level plain—and so is Agri—less than 3,500 feet above sea level. The mountain towers above everything, dominating one's field of vision, for as far as the eye can see.

"It is that ice-cap that most people believe preserved Noah's Ark. Nearly all eyewitnesses in the past century claim to have seen it sticking out of the ice.

"Maybe you recall 'Ararat-300'—the three-hundredth anniversary of the scaling of Mount Ararat by the French nobleman Pitton de Tournefort. Even your American astronaut James Irwin attempted to find Noah's Ark several times.

"Was there a flood?" he asked no one in particular.

Bryce hadn't asked; the question wasn't on her mind.

"Scientists find fossils throughout the world, but animals fossilize only when they are buried quickly by mud—the quantities of mud that would be created by a forty-day rainstorm followed by a year of immersion.

"If other animals find a dead carcass, there will be no fossil. If a carcass lies exposed to the weather, there will not be a fossil either. If a carcass has time to decay, likewise: no fossil. The only event that could have simultaneously caused that many fossils around the world is a global flood.

"The pressure of the water on the earth's surface caused earthquakes. These, in turn produced tsunamis—massive tidal waves—that reshaped the contours of the planet, killing all living things in the process. Only eight people survived."

"If the flood created that many fossils, why weren't any human fossils found?" Earl asked with a smirk.

"A mere one quarter of one percent of the fossil record consists of vertebrates," Bryce interjected.

"Yes. And ninety-nine percent of those are of only a single bone or tooth."

"Meaning less than one quarter of one-hundredth of one percent of all fossils consists of more than one bone of an amphibian, bird, fish, reptile, or mammal."

The Turk tried to take over the conversation again. "Don't forget that few humans inhabited the planet before the flood, compared with the billions we have now, although there might have been more than a million. Nonetheless, those who were present weren't stupid. Unlike the animals, they were capable of trying to rescue themselves by seeking higher ground.

"The fury of the flood waters and tidal waves was tremendous. Boulders as big as houses were tossed around like pebbles. Humans exposed to that deluge would have been torn apart like tissue paper in a washing machine.

"And remember, those that weren't ripped to shreds, would have been among the last to die. They would have ended up closer to the top of the sediment where their bodies would have been exposed to oxidation from ground water, oxidation that would have totally obliterated any trace of them."

"Human corpses tend to bloat," Bryce explained, "turning them into floating carrion for birds desperate to find a place to land and something to eat. Whatever was left would have been a feast for sharks and other carnivorous fish. So you see, the absence of human fossils would be expectable."

The matter settled, Earl and the man behind the counter filled in forms for permits to climb Mount Ararat.

Bryce became bored and read one of the plaques on the wall. There was a statement from a volunteer at the Smithsonian Institution claiming to have witnessed the arrival of Ark artifacts after the 1968 expedition, and in a wooden frame, a faded 1948 clipping about an unseasonable thaw having revealed part of the Ark for a summer.

She noticed a display of photos, drawings, and a few artifacts in a large case.

This is quite a cash cow for them.

Interspersed among the items in the display were parts of the "Statement of Ed Davis, 363rd Army Corps of Engineers. Hamadan, Turkey." She read a few of them—those that were beneath photos that caught her attention.

> ...Inside the broken end of the biggest piece, I can see at least three floors and Abas says there's a living space near the top with forty-eight rooms. He says there are cages inside as small as my hand, others big enough to hold a family of elephants.
>
> I can see what looks like remains of partitions and walkways inside the bigger piece. I really want to touch it — it's hard to explain the

feeling. Abas says we can go down on ropes in the morning. It begins to rain and we go back to the cave...

Next morning when we get up, it's snowing. It had snowed all night and it's at least belt deep on me. I can't see anything down in the canyon. The Ark is no longer visible. Abas says, 'We have to leave, it's too dangerous.'

It takes five days to get off the mountain and back to my base. I smell so bad when I get back, they burn my clothes. And no one seems interested in what I saw, so I quit talking about it. But I dream about it every night for twenty years.

There's something up there..."

"Hey, Earl. This guy says 'I really want to touch it—it's hard to explain the feeling...' He dreamed about it for twenty years. 'There's something up there...'" Bryce quoted mockingly. She taunted him with an impression of the "Twilight Zone" theme: *Doo-dee-doo-dah, doo-dee-doo-dah.*

Enough of that. Bryce studied the laminated map covering one of the walls. She saw the well-known meteor crater near the Iranian border. Her satellites had imaged that particular crater without a hitch.

She searched the map to the north of the Ararat summit, halfway to the small village of Godekli, to find the WCD "blind spot" that was their destination. Although a finger of Turkey divided Iran from Armenia at that point, it was equidistant from the two countries. She was happy to see that the official map also displayed nothing in that region.

They're sitting right on top of it, and they can't see any more than I can. The thought reassured her.

She glanced over her shoulder. Earl was showing the photograph to the man behind the counter.

Was he out of his mind?

She tried to slow her rapidly increasing pulse rate. She heard Earl ask the man if he had seen the church in the photo before. The man said he hadn't, but Bryce saw a look of surprise pass through the man's eyes.

Another thought crossed Bryce's mind: *What if someone is deliberately concealing the existence of the crater?*

◆ ◆ ◆

AT THE DEPARTMENT for the Preservation of Turkish Antiquities in Ankara, Dobro Suleyman was gazing out his window, half-asleep. He answered his phone on the first ring.

"Suleyman."

"Mr. Suleyman, I'm calling from the Office of Mountain Guides in Dogubayazit."

"And."

"An American couple left my office just minutes ago."

"So."

"They had a photo of a church I've never seen before. They were convinced that it was in this region."

"So."

"I know you are the one who helped that American Priest write his book about those churches, and I thought—"

"—That I might be interested? There are many Byzantine churches."

"Not like this one."

"How so?"

"It was covered with gold."

"Are you sure?"

"Positively. And I know if anyone would like to smuggle gold out of our country, it is the English speakers—"

"—And it is my job to stop them."

"Exactly."

"I'll leave this afternoon on the last shuttle flight. Would you wait in your office for me? Even if it runs overtime?"

"With pleasure. I await your imminent arrival."

THIRTY-THREE

MID-AFTERNOON (GMT+3)

BRYCE AND EARL walked along the sidewalk to the front door of the hotel at three o'clock. They passed a priest who was paying a taxi driver. The man acknowledged Bryce with a puzzled expression, as if he had seen her before.

Bryce returned his stare. She smiled. *You're a long way from Rome, Father*, she said to herself, seeing his clerical collar. She recognized his face, but couldn't put a name with it. It always troubled her when she couldn't remember where she had met a man, or whether she had ever actually met him.

Stepping off the elevator, they walked down the hall. Bryce noted that the "Maid Service" sign was gone from her door, and smiled; her room would be clean. Knowing that their climbing permits were in order gave her a secure feeling. Things were falling into place.

"I'm going to take a nap," Earl said when she stopped to unlock her door. His room was at the end of the hall. "I suggest you do the same. We're going to need all our strength tomorrow when we're climbing around the mountain."

She walked through the door; the maid had tidied her desk; her copy of "Byzantine Churches of the Holy Land..." now stood between two bookends on the desk. The back cover faced Bryce— the photograph of the author was the man on the steps of the hotel!

Bryce did an about-face and called down the hall as Earl fumbled with the key to his room. "Cole, get back here. Quick."

With an exasperated look, Earl pocketed his keys and walked back to Bryce. She led him into her room, grabbing the book as she sat down.

"Look," she said. "This is the guy who smiled at me outside the hotel."

"Right." His sarcasm was irritating.

"I'm not kidding. Didn't you get a look at him?"

"I don't memorize the faces of everyone who gives you the once-over."

"Very funny."

"Really, I don't."

"Listen Cole, this can't be a coincidence that he's in this town at the same time we are."

"Why not?"

"Because he wrote the book. He's the authority on Byzantine churches. If anyone knows where that gold-plated church is, he does."

"I get it."

"Do you? Let's look at what we have." She started making a list.

"One. While searching for Noah's Ark, Walter Warren's son dies mysteriously.

"Two. The last photo he took was of a gold-covered Byzantine church, with a garden containing plants growing nowhere else on earth.

"Three. No one knows precisely where Walter Warren's son died, thus, no one knows the location of that church.

"Four. *The Complete Compendium of Byzantine Churches* also has no record of such a church.

"Five. The crater containing the church and garden does *not* appear in the WCD. We were unable to pinpoint its location with the SAT-Net.

"And six. The author of the 'Byzantine Churches' book just happens to appear at our hotel."

Bryce held her hands out in a gesture meant to say, *Should I draw you a picture?*

"OK. OK," Earl said. "Let's pretend it isn't a coincidence. What's the point?"

"I'm not sure. Wait a minute." Bryce read the bio next to Father Romero's photo on the back of the book.

"Hey. This guy's from the university, too. He's the head chaplain."

"Well, that *is* a coincidence," Earl admitted.

"Cole. Use your brain. I made a print of that photo for Walter Warren. His son's body had just been transported from here to Los Angeles. Do you think that this Father Romero might have seen that photo? Perhaps become interested precisely *because* it's not in his book?"

"I suppose it's possible."

"Maybe the boy's funeral was held at the university chapel?"

"Bryce, you're a genius." His sarcasm was effusive. "But what does it all mean?"

"I don't know, but I'm going to find out. We're going to have dinner with the Father…tonight."

"OK." Earl said. "It's 3:30 now. Let's try to arrange it for 7:30. You still need a rest. And I have some things to do."

◆ ◆ ◆

BRYCE RETURNED to the hotel lobby carrying Father Romero's book. He still stood at the reception desk. From a distance, she double-checked the photo on the book's back cover. Then, clutching his book to her chest, she walked confidently toward him as he turned from the counter.

"Excuse me."

"Yes."

Father Romero did a double take as he saw the copy of his book, and realized that this was the woman he had seen standing in the check-in line at LAX.

"You're Rafael Romero, right?"

"That is correct."

Bryce introduced herself and stammered. "I was wondering…if…if you would autograph my book."

"It appears to be a library copy."

"Uh. You're right."

Bryce blushed.

"Actually, I wanted to ask you some questions about Byzantine churches, and—" She paused for effect. "May I invite you to dinner?"

Father Romero considered the invitation. Bryce saw him trying to make up his mind.

"My colleague Earl Cole will escort me."

"Ah. In that case, I accept."

"He's tied up until seven. Would 7:30 be all right?"

"Perfect." Father Romero's smile didn't quite conceal his yawn. "I wanted to take a nap before dinner anyway. Jet lag, you know."

"We'll see you then."

◆ ◆ ◆

EARL PHONED Richard Roebuck from his room immediately after parting with Bryce.

"Something's going on here."

"Details?"

"The priest who wrote the book about Byzantine churches just checked into the hotel."

"I doubt that is a coincidence."

"Exactly."

"You should take steps to know where that priest is at all times."

"I'm on top of it," Earl said, readying the Transmogrifier.

"And don't forget, we're looking at an 89% probability of a major earthquake in your area within forty-eight hours."

"I know." Earl was sweating bullets.

"We have to be in and out before that earthquake hits." Richard broke the connection without saying goodbye.

THIRTY-FOUR

OUTSIDE THE HOTEL, Earl flagged a taxi and said to the driver, "Take me to a church."

The driver stared blankly at him.

"A church. You know." Earl raised his right arm and made a cross by placing his left forearm perpendicular to it. The driver didn't understand. Earl was becoming frustrated. He started to sweat.

Looking around him, Earl realized he hadn't seen any churches, only mosques, and they wouldn't have what he was looking for.

"Church. God. Jesus."

Earl pointed upward and then made the sign of the cross in the only other way he could think of, briefly touching his forehead and then his shoulders.

The cabby still didn't get it. Earl made the sign again, and again. Thick beads of sweat began dripping from his forehead.

He pulled out his PalmPad and stylus. Flipping it open, he quickly drew a picture of a church, one that resembled the Byzantine churches he had seen in Father Romero's book.

Something seemed to be dawning on the cab driver.

Finally, Earl drew a cross at the top of the dome, and the man's eyes sparkled with recognition.

"Ah Ya. Ah Ya. Kreestus. Kreestus." The taxi driver had finally understood. Earl wiped his brow.

"Na. Na. You Amayreekan."

They drove off.

Thirty minutes later, Earl stepped out in front of an ancient Byzantine church.

Turkey: where the old meets the older.

He asked the taxi to wait—another communication challenge.

Earl needed a cross for his plan, and so far, he hadn't found one in the whole country—what little of it he had seen up to now.

He stepped into the church and looked around. It wasn't empty. A small group of people prayed near the front of the building.

He felt as if he were literally stepping into a page of Father Romero's book. A rare peacefulness endeavored to caress the thick exterior of his psyche, but that passed in a moment.

He searched the premises for a suitable cross to "borrow." The only ones he saw were on the top of what looked like a balustrade: the icon screen directly in front of where the people were praying; thanks to Father Romero's book, he now knew this was called the "iconostas." He strolled toward it, pretending to be a tourist.

Well, I am a tourist, after all.

Clearly, the praying women didn't intend to leave soon; Earl had to devise an alternate plan.

Walking around the inside of the church again, he came to the end of the icon screen, the end with the cross extending from it. A small ring projected from the back of the cross, probably to facilitate the attachment of a velvet rope.

Without warning, Earl pretended to trip, flailing his arms in the air for some support. He grasped the wooden cross on the iconostas, and heard it snap off as he hit the floor, cross in hand. The people rushed to his aid, but by the time they got to him, he had slipped the object into his pocket.

He stood, brushed himself off, and staggered a bit for effect. He apologized profusely for any disturbance he had caused. Two minutes later, he was in the taxi rushing back to the hotel.

WHEN EARL walked down the hall on their floor of the hotel, he noticed a "Do Not Disturb" sign hanging outside Bryce's room. He hoped she was sleeping.

Back in his own room, he took the cross from his pocket. It was perfect—a flawless carving of Jesus on the cross. There were some rough edges at the bottom where he had snapped it off, but he would soon take care of those.

Using his trusty Swiss Army knife, he filed the bottom smooth. The post was hollow. That would save time.

From the top of the Transmogrifier case, he retrieved a GPS-tracking module the shape of a fountain pen but smaller. He slid it into the hollow end of the cross. The fit was snug, and he had to slam it down on the desktop to drive it home. Immediately after doing so, he tested it on the screen of the Transmogrifier. Nothing damaged.

He peered into the bottom of the cross. There was no way to get the thing out now, but holding it under the light, the grey metal of the tracker was visible, and that was unacceptable.

Earl went downstairs to the small tourist shop in the lobby of the hotel. There, he purchased an ornate bottle of perfume, without sampling it. He also acquired a pendant consisting of a flat, molded steel soccer ball with the words, "Turkish Champs" built into the relief, and painted red. It was on a chain designed to wear around the neck, made to resemble a gold medal.

Back in his room, Earl took the lid off the perfume bottle. *Pity*, he thought, as he discarded the bottle and its contents. Hesitating, he sniffed the scent on the stopper. *Ugh!* No major loss.

He took some Super Glue out of a utility compartment in the Transmogrifier case. The multifaceted crystal stopper from the perfume bottle fit perfectly into the base of the cross. The Super Glue dried in seconds, assuring that the GPS-tracker remained hidden.

He pried the chain off the soccer-ball pendant, fed it through the brass ring on the back of the cross, and examined his handi-work. The crystal stopper at the bottom of the cross could have been created expressly for its current purpose. Moreover, the gold chain and reddish wooden cross fit together as if made for each other—an appropriate gift for a priest.

Earl looked at his watch: 5 o'clock. He still had time to take a nap.

♦ ♦ ♦

FATHER ROMERO was having trouble sleeping so he decided to phone his old friend Dobro Suleyman.

"*Efendim.*" (Hello)

"*Suleyman bey lüften.*" (Mr. Suleyman please)

"*Bir Dakika.*" (One minute)

A male voice came on. "*Allo?*" (Hello?).

"Dobro. It's me, Rafael."

"Ah. Father Romero, my friend. Again, you honor me. It seems like only yesterday that we were talking."

"We were, Dobro. And please: *Serefinize.*" (This is in your honor).

"Have you made up your mind about coming to Turkey?"

"Dobro, I'm already here."

"This is a pleasant surprise. What a coincidence."

"A coincidence—how so?"

"Earlier today I received a call from an associate in Doguba-yazit—"

"But that's where I am, in Dogubayazit!"

"—Concerning an American couple who were looking for a Byzantine church covered with gold. I recall that you asked me about the discovery of any new sites. If you're in Dogubayazit, were you the one making inquiries today?"

"Not a chance. I got off the plane, went directly to the hotel, and straight to bed for a nap."

"Are you sure?"

"Of course I'm sure."

"Well, I'm coming to Dogubayazit this evening to follow up on the call from the Office of Mountain Guides. Perhaps we can meet and compare notes?"

"I have a dinner engagement tonight, but I'd be happy to meet you for a nightcap, or tomorrow. I'm staying at the same old hotel. It's become quite fashionable."

"This feels like old times, eh?"

"Yes it does."

"But remember what happened after the publication of your book—the pilfering of the ruins; if this golden church exists, we must proceed carefully."

"Dobro, do thy duty."

The two men chuckled.

Dobro gave Father Romero his mobile phone number, and the priest reciprocated with his hotel number.

Father Romero lay in bed trying to begin his afternoon nap. He found it all the more difficult to fall asleep now that he had talked to Dobro. He hadn't mentioned the American woman because he suspected that she and her companion were the ones that Dobro was looking for. If there were a new site, particularly the golden one in the photograph, he didn't want Dobro's department putting a cloak of secrecy on it before he had done more research.

THIRTY-FIVE

S TUART SPENT MUCH of the day in the library, specifically, the seventh room, studying the maps that correlated the trees surrounding the cross to historical events and geopolitical locations. It was fascinating. If the days and dates were accurate, and of that he had no reason to question, then this represented a phenomenon far beyond any natural explanation.

Why should trees, in a remote part of Turkey, sprout from the ground exactly thirty-three years to the day before events of such historical magnitude?

And what about the cross at the center of it all? Not to mention, the vines issuing forth from its wood. The cross posed additional questions. He didn't want his thoughts to go there. Yet.

The vines, after billowing upwards, plunged into the ground. A spirit of doubt crept into his mind.

How could he be certain that those vines became the roots of the trees?

Or that the vines originated at what were supposed to be drops of blood. That made it more peculiar. First, he would have to accept that those were drops of blood.

Jesus' blood!

Maybe blood mixing with the sap of the wood—wood from a rare tree—would cause a chemical reaction. That might explain the thirty-three-year pattern.

But that didn't explain the interrelationship of the blooming trees with the historical events that shaped the world. There were so many variables.

Or was the blood of Jesus special?

Something inside him tried to push that thought from his mind…Unsuccessfully.

If Jesus truly had come for all mankind, past, present, and future, mightn't it be that the DNA in His blood contained a program of the coming events of the human race? Or that all DNA contained such a program?

That's impossible! Something inside him shouted. That goes beyond the laws of nature. That requires a leap of faith. Faith in Jesus. Faith in God. *Yes. Come to me.*

At that moment, Matthias entered the classroom, and, for some reason, Stuart felt glad that he now had an excuse to postpone thinking about the implications of such a faith.

"It's amazing, isn't it?" Matthias said.

"That's a fact. But I've been wondering: once they figured out what was happening with the trees—I mean, how they were linked to historical events—why didn't the people use that information to predict what would take place?"

"In most cases, the events that eventually coincide with any individual blooming could not have been predicted at the time of the tree's sprouting.

"Take the vine that sprouted in the year 127. Who could have known that thirty-three years later this would bloom on the day of Polycarp's martyrdom?

"Or the thirty-first tree, the vine for which sprouted in the year 292. No one could have predicted that would bloom on the day of the establishment of the Nicene Creed in 325. Yet, the Nicene Creed has provided countless Christians with a way to formalize—internally—the basic elements of their faith, ever since.

"Or tree number 49: the Antioch earthquake that killed 250,000."

"Are you saying that if God needs a large number of souls up in Heaven for some unfathomable project of His, like a war in the spiritual realms or something, that he sends an earthquake or a plague to retrieve them?"

"Not exactly, but that is an interesting image. God surely views death in a different way than we humans."

"Well, no one can predict or prophesy earthquakes."

"It's like that with all prophecy. One normally doesn't know a prophecy has been fulfilled except in retrospect."

"But these aren't human prophets. These are trees. They are undeniably connected with some stream of knowledge outside time."

"Yes, as were the prophets. God is that Being outside time. God is the God of all knowledge."

"It must be different. A tree is not a person."

"Right. But think of the prophecies fulfilled by Jesus."

"Umm. Would you refresh my memory please?" Stuart asked sheepishly. He couldn't think of even one.

"It depends on whom you listen to. The number of prophecies is 25, 36, 52, 61, 300, 425, 456, 1817, or even 2500."

"How so?"

"It depends upon the strictness of a scholar's definition of prophecy, and other factors: for example, whether they include New Testament prophecies.

"Many Messianic prophecies—meaning those dealing with the Messiah Jesus—were stated in three parts: the first part concerned the prophet's own time period and thus authenticates his role as a prophet; the next had to do with Jesus' first coming; while the third part deals with Jesus' second coming. It is difficult to distinguish the second and third parts from each other until the fulfillment of the prophecies.

"More than eight thousand of the Bible's thirty-two thousand verses concern prophecy."

"But couldn't the fulfillment of all those prophecies—at least the ones in the Old Testament—have been *arranged* or contrived after the fact?"

"The discovery of the Dead Sea Scrolls proved this was not the case. The eight hundred scrolls at Qumran predated Jesus by more than a century, but their texts are nearly identical to those of the Masoretic version of the Hebrew Old Testament, the Hebrew text approved for general use in Judaism. Every book of the Old Testament except 'Esther' is present in the scrolls."

He put his hand on Stuart's shoulder.

"Come back to the second row of rooms for a moment, I have something to show you."

The two young men walked through the central doors until they reached the rooms devoted to the time of Jesus and His Apostles. Matthias pointed to a chart on the wall at the front of the room.

"This is in Aramaic. I'll translate." Matthias proceeded to read the forty-nine prophecies on the chart, starting with *He will be born in Bethlehem (Micah 5:2)*, through *He will begin his ministry in Galilee (Isaiah 9:1)*, to the very end: *At his death His hands and feet will be pierced (Psalm 22:16)*. "Those forty-nine prophecies about Jesus were fulfilled. Forty-nine at the very least.

"At Westmont College, Peter Stoner, Professor Emeritus of Science, calculated the probability of one man fulfilling even a small number of prophecies. Six hundred of his students helped him.

"They examined eight prophecies and estimated that the chance of one man fulfilling all eight was one out of ten to the seventeenth power, or one with seventeen zeroes after it. And that's only for the fulfillment of eight prophecies."

"How could they do that?"

"Here's an example. Chapter five of the book of Micah, verse two, says that the Messiah would be born in Bethlehem Ephrathah and not another town that also had the name Bethlehem. Micah wrote it seven hundred years before the birth of Jesus. Professor Stoner and his students divided the average population of Bethlehem during those seven hundred years by the average population of the earth. They determined the odds to be one in 280,000, for that single prophecy. [Roger Stoner, *Science Speaks*, Chicago: Moody Press, 1969]

"One with seventeen zeroes after it is a very large number. Stoner used this illustration to help us conceive of it: 'suppose that we take ten to the seventeenth power silver dollars and lay them on the face of Texas. They will cover all of the state two feet deep. Now mark one of these silver dollars and stir the whole mass thoroughly, all over the state. Blindfold a man and tell him that he can travel as far as he wishes, but he must pick up one silver dollar and say that this is the right one. What chance would he have of getting the right one? Just the same chance that the prophets would have had of writing these eight prophecies and having them all come true in any one man, from their day to the present time, providing they wrote them in their own wisdom.' [Ibid. 106-107]

"Stoner concluded, 'Any man who rejects Christ as the Son of God is rejecting a fact proved perhaps more absolutely than any other fact in the world [Ibid. 112] '. Remember, that's only when you consider eight prophecies. There are many more in the Scriptures."

"That's impressive."

They both paused to reflect upon the matter.

"Couldn't the people who live here tell anything from the cycles of the trees?"

"Consider this. When a bee flies from flower to flower, gathering the ingredients to make honey, that bee has no idea that his actions also transport pollen from anthers to stigmas helping the plants to reproduce. The bee doesn't need to know this, and if he did, what would it matter? Would it change the situation?

"The trees around the cross have no more direct effect upon us than the pollen sticking onto bees' bodies has upon them. The trees could be operating in concert with the history of this world, but on some far-removed plane of existence, they are like an echo of a sound that happens too far away for the person making that sound to hear it."

"But," Stuart interrupted, "the bees could not exist without the flowers. And this little side effect caused by their traveling from flower to flower—meaning the fertilization of the flowers themselves—serves as a vital function in their ability to sustain their own lives. Speaking of echoes, don't forget that an echo can cause an avalanche far away from, and unseen by, the person who made the original sound."

"Yes. God is great, isn't He?"

Stuart was quiet. He found Matthias likable, but sometimes the guy reminded him of a fanatic.

"You're absolutely right," Matthias continued. "The cross and its surrounding trees will undoubtedly play some role in the future events of the world. We don't know what that is. We only know that something might be about to happen—"

"Because all the trees are blooming, bearing fruit for the first time in history?"

"Yes. Some incredible, maybe inconceivable, event is taking place in the spiritual realm."

Stuart closed his eyes, trying to imagine.

THIRTY-SIX

ANTARCTICA

1700 GMT

SCHEDULES AT THE CENTER for Predictive Seismology tended to be cyclical; Cam found himself alone in the control room with the first officer and the new recruit again.

"How are the SLUGS doing?" Cam asked.

"The slugs?"

"Sensors for Lateral Underground Geomagnetic Slippage," interjected the first officer. "The S-L-U-G-S's."

"The SLUGS are magnetotactic bacteria, each a mere ten-millionths of a meter in length—they look like slugs—and in most parts of the world they swim toward the South Pole at a speed of 150 nanometers per second; here, they swim downwards," Cam explained to the new recruit.

"And they sense lateral magnetic slippage?"

"They appear to. They are always swimming, but they exhibit tiny directional changes—ever so briefly—that correspond to the seismic patterns of forthcoming earthquakes. The problem is that unless the moon is at apogee—as far as it can be from the earth—the signal contains too much 'background noise.' The moon's gravity confuses the little buggers."

"Can't you filter out the noise, use pattern-recognition with a notch-filter or something?"

"We're working on it."

"How did you make the connection?"

Cam looked at the first officer. They came to a silent agreement about something, and the first officer returned to his computer.

"Have you heard of Echelon?"

"You mean the network of spy satellites that examine all communications—"

"—Except fiber-optic," interrupted the first officer.

"Yes, that's exactly what I mean."

"I know what I've read."

"Well, I'm authorized to access Echelon from time to time."

"Am I supposed to be impressed?"

"We intercepted something from the base about thirty miles from here that is funded by Richard Roebuck."

"And?"

"And it wasn't sushi." The first officer roared with laughter. The Roebuck Research lab was rumored to receive regular deliveries catering to any whim of the scientists they employed—most were spoiled brats from Silicon Valley—no matter how outrageous.

Cam rolled his eyes. "They had documented the magnetotaxis connection; they are funded by a grant to study the SLUGS...medical applications or something."

"So you incorporated the SLUGS into the prediction equation?"

"It was relatively easy. We were already studying the little guys so we had the equipment in place. You see, because of the excitement over ALH84001 at the time I set up the lab, there has always been a group of exobioligists on staff—specialists in extraterrestrial life."

"You lost me after ALH."

"ALH84001 is a meteorite found in the Allen Hills of Antarctica, hence, the 'ALH,' in 1984, hence, the '84.' It was the first meteorite found that year, hence, the '001.' ALH84001 was grouped with eleven other meteors as having originated on Mars because each contained traces of Martian atmosphere. Scientists have known the composition of the Martian atmosphere ever since the Viking Lander reported from Mars in 1976. The bombshell laid by ALH84001 at the beginning of the nineties was that it contained fossils—magnetofossils—of magnetotactic bacteria; thus, life on Mars. I'm surprised you haven't heard of it."

"1984? I was two years old."

"Then you were a teenager by the time ALH84001 was found to contain evidence of extraterrestrial life."

The first officer stood, pushing his chair under the desk. "Still no change in the prediction. We're at fifty percent and holding."

Cam groaned. "Can't we do better than that?"

"Thirty-six hours until apogee."

THIRTY-SEVEN

TURKEY

SITTING IN THE HOTEL restaurant, Bryce and Earl presented Father Romero with a somewhat edited explanation of their purpose for being in Turkey. Father Romero was pleasantly surprised to find that ultimately, the three of them worked for the same university; that fact offered many topics for conversation, all of which allowed them to gracefully sidestep the issue of the gold-covered church. Nevertheless, as soon as the busboy cleared their dinner dishes and the waiter took their orders for coffee, Bryce put Father Romero's book upon the table.

"Your book is sub-titled, 'A Complete Compendium,'" she said. "Are you sure that you have tracked down all the Byzantine churches in the region?"

The question startled Father Romero; he could not mask the emotion it provoked.

"Until recently I would have responded with an emphatic 'Yes' to that question."

"And now?"

"I'm not entirely sure."

Father Romero gazed at the mirrored wall of the dining room. Their reflections stood out like an Italian fresco: his own large frame dominating the center; the scruff, sleazy Mr. Cole to his left; the statuesque, angelic blonde on his right. His nervous rumination about the crucifixion was accompanied by a pulsing tic on his temple. He gritted his teeth and scrubbed his hands with a towelette unconsciously plucked from a bowl near the condiments.

Bryce reached into her bag and withdrew the photograph of the mysterious church. She laid it dramatically on top of Father Romero's book. A pregnant silence followed.

Father Romero wondered how many people now possessed the photograph that Professor Warren's son had snapped last week.

"Ah. I see you know Professor Warren. I don't think I saw you at the funeral."

Bryce said nothing.

"Such a tragedy about the boys," the priest continued.

At the word "boys," Bryce caught her breath and looked at Earl. His expression indicated he had heard it, too. She decided to lay more of her cards upon the table.

"Boys? I'm not sure what you mean. Walter didn't mention that any other boys had been killed."

"No one knows whether the other boy, Stuart, is dead or injured or simply being restrained from communicating with the outside world. No one knows where he is."

Again, she locked eyes with Earl. She decided to take a chance.

"Isn't it likely that he's here?" She thrust her finger down upon the church in the photograph.

"That is definitely a possibility."

"And where is this church?"

"I haven't the faintest idea," Father Romero said with obvious discomfort.

There was an awkward stillness.

Father Romero continued. "May I ask what is your interest in this matter?"

"As I said, we're conducting research on recent seismological activities. There was a minor earthquake here a week ago, and we're working on the predictive capabilities of the satellite network we use." Bryce decided there was no reason to bring Richard Roebuck into the picture.

"Because the satellites we use employ non-optical methods for constructing images, sometimes their data contains holes. Usually, those holes are at places where anomalies occur in the earth's magnetic field. From the satellite's point of view, most of these are meteor craters. When they are large enough, we don't have anything more than a blank circular area in our WCD—World Contour Database."

"Go on."

"This church is obviously in a crater."

Father Romero studied the background closely and admitted that might be true.

"We can tell the general area of this location by the shadows, because we have the exact time of the photograph. But we can't resolve it to an area smaller than 320 by 240 kilometers. There are three blank spots in that area; three that we assume are craters. Professor Warren mentioned that his son was looking for Noah's Ark. So… *Voila!*"

"I see. But your interest in the church?"

"We couldn't find the church in your book. There are no churches with anywhere near that quantity of gold on it in your book. Because it is unique, we took it for granted that the locals would be able to identify it. This turned out not to be the case."

"Oh. Did it?"

"Yes. We inquired at the office of guides today. Did you know that you need a permit and a guide to do any climbing or hiking around Mount Ararat?"

"No."

"Well, those are easy to come by. Ararat, or *Agri* as they call it, is a gentle mountain. But be prepared to hear an earful about the Noah's Ark leg—" She started to say "legend" and then remembered he was a priest.

"—Event." She said.

"When I was writing my book, they were quite forthcoming with information pertaining to churches from the Byzantine era. I wonder if they might be shielding this one, because of all the gold. You may have already encountered the 'Department for the Preservation of Turkish Antiquities,' whose main job is to prevent people from taking historical artifacts out of the country. Because so many of their relics are now sitting in museums outside Turkey."

"That's certainly possible. The gold would make it all the more attractive to fortune hunters."

Earl put down the final stub of his cigar, and spoke. "So you have absolutely no knowledge of the location of this church." He measured his words and pointed at the photograph.

"None whatsoever."

"And the other boy has made no contact since this mess started."

"Not to my knowledge."

"Well, I suppose we've given each other all the help we can," Earl said with a finality that implied it was time to move on.

"I suppose."

Earl pretended he had suddenly remembered something. He reached into his pocket, and said, "While inspecting one of the local churches, I managed to obtain this little trinket."

He pulled out the crucifix containing the GPS tracking device.

"I'd like to give you this as a token of our appreciation for all you've told us."

"But I couldn't...I mean...I didn't."

"I insist."

Father Romero reluctantly accepted the gift.

"Try it on."

The priest put it around his neck.

"Perfect," Earl said. "Maybe it will give you luck."

"*Luck* does not exist, Mister Cole. God is in control."

"Right." Earl grinned.

They were standing now, and Bryce shook Father Romero's hand enthusiastically, defusing the tension that had arisen at Earl's use of the word "luck."

"We'll be off early in the morning so I doubt our paths will cross again until we're back in California."

"You're probably right. Well, I'm going to spend the day making inquiries in town, and then I'll go get that permit you mentioned."

◆ ◆ ◆

BRYCE COULD BARELY WAIT until they were back upstairs to ask, "What on earth was that all about?"

"That crucifix has one of our GPS-trackers embedded in it. I believe it will be to our advantage to keep track of the location of Father Rafael Romero at all times."

"Oh really?"

"Richard agrees."

Bryce didn't like it when Earl contacted Richard behind her back.

Earl opened the Transmogrifier and initialized the tracking system.

"See. It's working. He's right below us. Look at the difference between his signal and the location of our computer."

"Great thinking, Cole."

"Wait, there's something else."

Earl popped a mini-disk from his pocket recorder, and inserted it into a slot on the Transmogrifier. He launched a program on the computer.

Scanning forward, he clicked an onscreen button. They heard the question, "You have absolutely no knowledge of the location of this church?" followed by Father Romero's answer: "None whatsoever."

"I recorded our whole conversation."

"Whatever for?"

"I'm running it through a voice-stress analyzer to confirm he was telling us the truth."

Bryce noted a highlighted region scrolling across the on-screen representation of the sound waves of their chat.

"He's telling the truth," Earl said triumphantly.

"Of course he's telling the truth, you nitwit." Bryce replied. "He's a priest."

"Oh? I'm not so sure that the those two things are as intrinsically related as you imagine."

She scowled at him.

THIRTY-EIGHT

A FTER DINNER, MATTHIAS suggested a stroll around the perimeter of the crater. The evening was unusually cool, although it was still light.

"There are paths most of the way," he said.

They walked due east, to the woodshop. Stuart enjoyed shuffling through the sawdust as Matthias led him to the back of the building. There, a narrow path proceeded clockwise along the base of the crater wall.

They walked in silence until they passed the farm buildings and saw the grain fields to their right.

"We were discussing the prophecies Jesus fulfilled," Stuart said. "Are there any prophecies that he didn't fulfill?"

"Oh yes. Many," Matthias replied. "So far, we've only mentioned prophecies concerned with His first coming. Many others refer to His second coming and the times immediately preceding it."

"Such as?"

"There are prophecies describing the division of Israel and the fall of the enemies of the Jews, about Jerusalem becoming the most important religious place on the earth and it becoming an international problem, and about Jesus' gathering up believers, his return to conquer evil and rule His Kingdom, and the global witnessing of these events. Much of the book of Revelation is prophecy."

"And when is all this supposed to happen?"

"Jesus said, 'But of that day or of that hour no one knows, neither the angels who are in Heaven, nor the Son, but only the Father.' So, it will undoubtedly arrive 'as a thief in the night,' in other words, totally unexpectedly."

They were passing the vegetable fields. The orchard of fruit trees began where the vegetables ended.

"Most of the fulfilled prophecies relate to Jesus' death."

"That's right."

"Why didn't the period between his birth and death receive equal coverage?"

"You'll have to ask God that."

"It's as if there is a fascination with the morbid details of His crucifixion."

"The crucifixion was the spiritual mechanism through which God bestowed his greatest gift to humankind."

"Spiritual mechanism?"

"An earthly process with Heavenly consequences."

"For example?"

"Jesus' crucifixion had spiritual corollaries for all mankind. It cleared them of their sins by serving as atonement for Adam's fall from grace. It required a second perfect man, Jesus, to redeem humankind's sinful nature; the sinful nature that Adam, the first perfect man, introduced into the world.

"We can't understand how the process works, because it's a spiritual mechanism. But it had an unfathomable effect in Heaven and upon earth. The skies became dark, there was an earthquake, and the curtain in the temple was torn in two."

"Curtain?"

"A curtain separated the "Most Holy Place" from the rest of the temple. This "Holy of Holies" is the heart of the temple. Only the high priest was allowed to enter that sacred place, and only upon one day of the year, the Day of Atonement: Yom Kippur. Even the earliest tabernacles were divided into two such compartments by a curtain. The curtain had cherubim embroidered on it in red, purple, and blue.

"Once a year, on Yom Kippur, the high priest tied a red woolen cord between the horns of a goat called the scapegoat and the neck of another goat. Later, they cut the cord in half. Jesus became the sacrificial lamb for humankind, and His sacrifice was permanent—for all people, past, present, and future."

"OK. Are there any more?"

"Any more what?"

"Any more spiritual mechanisms?"

"Quite a few. The more we fast, the more we are able to deny the distractions of the flesh and commune with God. It takes a good deal of discipline, but the way it works is a spiritual process.

"The more we pray, the more He sees our prayers are earnest. The more we read the Bible, the more He will show us how it applies to our own lives. The Bible is one of the ways that God talks to us. The more we walk in Jesus' steps, so to speak, the less temptation, worry, doubt, and fear can influence us.

"The more we reflect the light of his love and forgiveness, the more he forgives us. Do you remember, 'Forgive us our trespasses as we forgive those who trespass against us?'"

"From the Lord's Prayer?"

"Yes. The word 'as' in that context means 'only as much as' or 'only so far as'."

"I see...I never thought of it that way."

"The more we trust in Him, the more He protects us with His blessings.

"The more we praise Him, the more the man of lawlessness—the Antichrist—is restrained in the world.

"Imagine that the earth is the center of a dandelion. When we praise God, our praise shoots to the Heavens like the dandelion's stamen, or like one of those grand-finale fireworks. It makes an even larger sphere. God is the target of all those rays of praise. From His perspective, being outside our own notions of time and space, He can turn his viewpoint around so that he is at the center, and all the praise reaches Him as if the whole world surrounded Him."

"That's quite an image."

They were through the fruit orchard and standing by a stream that headed into a ravine.

"Where does this stream go?" Stuart asked.

"To the outside world."

There was silence. Matthias tried to hide the worried look upon his face.

Stuart had a fleeting image of walking down the gorge, and wondered whether Matthias would try to stop him.

"You mean I could walk through that ravine, all the way back to Batman?"

"Yes. It's how my father and I travel in and out of this place. Do you want to?"

Stuart didn't answer immediately. He turned and gazed over the floor of the crater, his eyes coming to rest upon the little bit of garden that was visible from where they stood—a patch of purple beyond the golden dome of the church.

"No. Not yet anyway. It's so peaceful here; I want to stay. I have a strong feeling that something important is going to happen."

Then again, the thought of contact with the outside world reminded him that there might be a search party, people looking for him, to take him away from all this. He found himself wishing that if there were a search party, that it would be delayed until this 'something important' that he felt was going to happen, had actually taken place.

Matthias, who had been holding his breath, exhaled with relief. He led them up the stream a few yards to a place where rocks arranged like stepping stones allowed them to cross the water.

Again the sound of the rushing water seemed to mask a thousand voices murmuring, *Yes. Come to me.*

They continued quietly, the sheer crater wall at their left, and soon found themselves beneath a grape arbor. Matthias stopped and picked a bunch of grapes for Stuart.

"If you look back at the wall," Matthias whispered, "you can see part of the honeymoon house. Glance at it quickly; it's not polite to stare and the custom is 'Do not disturb' when that house is in use."

Stuart was surprised he hadn't noticed it. He looked over his shoulder. Where the grape arbor ended stood a grove of trees, and then an opening into a small canyon extending east-southeastwards within the crater wall. They had been walking next to the promontory that was the northern wall to this smaller canyon.

Ivy hid the walls of the narrow canyon; halfway in, Stuart saw a wonderful colorful house. Facing southwesterly, it was ringed with flowers.

"There's a hot-spring pool right behind it," Matthias said.

"Looks cozy."

"I've heard that it is."

Emerging from the grape arbor at eight o'clock on the imaginary clock dial, they came upon the stables. The smell of horses and straw was something that Stuart liked almost as much as the smell of sap and sawdust.

The majestic Arabian horses nuzzled them; Stuart and Matthias fed the last of their grapes to the first ones they encountered. The stables were clean as new hay, and Stuart saw several foals.

Matthias bent over and picked up two brushes; he handed one to Stuart.

"Know how to do this?"

"Not really."

"Follow my lead. Brush with that soft brush everywhere I loosen the dirt with the hard brush."

Their brushing made the horses noticeably happy. It was obvious that these horses were well cared-for, and Matthias knew them all by name: Mirene, Dilano, Suneval; they were all Arabian. He explained some of the names. "In English, this would be Fire-Dancer, this one is Equine-Fairy, and here is Wind-Drinker."

Because it 'drinks' the wind while it runs, Stuart imagined.

"What's America like?" Matthias asked while brushing the legs of one of the larger horses.

"What?" Stuart was kneeling down following in his brush tracks.

"What's America like? I mean, where you live…in California. I've always wanted to go there."

"Well," Stuart didn't know where to begin, "everything in California is very new. California isn't much more than 100 years old—nowhere close to the age of this little village. I guess that's why everything is so clean. The skies are so blue and the grass so green; the colors of flowers are brighter than anywhere else. It's probably because of the angle of the sun or something.

"Where I live, in the valley outside Los Angeles, the weather is always perfect. Warm in the day, and cool at night. It practically never rains. As you've probably heard, it never snows in the winter; it's just a slightly cooler version of the summer. If you do want snow, you can usually drive up the mountains on the north side of the valley and be in the thick of it in less than an hour.

"Often, you'll be standing somewhere, and out of the blue you'll feel as though you've seen the place before. And you have. In a movie! The sheer number of movies made in the area means there's a good chance of walking into a place you've seen in a movie.

"Likewise with people. Half the population has appeared as an extra in a movie at one time or another, so you feel as though you've seen everyone you meet, somewhere before. And in fact, you have. It can be confusing."

Matthias laughed. "I'd love to see it sometime."

"Well you should come for a visit."

"I can't," he said longingly. "Our family has taken care of the settlers here ever since Stauros was founded. It's our responsibility, and it passes from father to eldest son. I'm the eldest."

Coming out the other end of the stables, they soon were walking parallel to the back of the seventh rank of rooms of the library.

Stuart stared at the crater wall. There was a network of caves dug into the rock. It looked primitive. He asked Matthias about them.

"Those are the tombs. They go deep into the side of the crater. The bones of everyone who has lived here for the past two thousand years are in those caves. Some of my ancestors bones as well..."

...including great grandpa Simon, whose ideas brought our family to this place!

"That one too?" Stuart asked, pointing to a larger, reinforced opening that showed signs of recent work.

"No. That's the gold mine. Centuries ago, the settlers were expanding the tombs to the north and came upon a vein of precious metal. Since then, they've used it to finance the growth of the settlement to the current 208 people—the optimal sustainable state of equilibrium for the farm.

"They've also had extra gold for other things," he said, pointing at the gold-covered church.

"It must have taken a long time."

"Yes. Unlike those in the outside world, here in Stauros some people work on a single project their whole lives, like the decoration of a doorframe. Others work on a project that they know won't be completed in their lifetime."

They came upon a small building, the size of the woodshop.

"This is the metal shop," Matthias explained, "although it would make more sense to call it the gold shop."

They paused to peer inside, and then headed to the observation tower to the west of the garden. The path swung inward by the stream, briefly making a detour around the cluster of twelve buzzing beehives.

THIRTY-NINE

S TUART WAS GLAD they were going to climb the north-west tower; it was the only one he hadn't been in, and he longed to view the garden from all three vantage points.

When they were sitting on the observation deck at the top of the third tower, the beauty of order within chaos again fascinated Stuart—randomly spaced trees arranged in a perfectly non-random spiral.

"What do you think is the meaning of that?" he asked, pointing at the spiral of purple trees.

"I believe it has something to do with the second coming of Jesus. Angels told the original settlers that Jesus would need this place when he returned."

"Do you really believe He will return? It's been a long time."

"Definitely. Some of our scholars believe it will happen in the year 2033. That's when the final tree will bloom—if it is the final tree. They have no way of determining that for sure, but, in 2033, exactly two millennia will have passed since Jesus left the earth. It seems logical to me. But Jesus said, 'no one knows the day or hour when these things will happen, not even the angels in heaven or the Son himself…'"

"Could the garden have something to do with the spiritual mechanisms you were describing earlier?"

"Positively. As Christians, we accept that many earthly phenomena correspond to Heavenly phenomena that are beyond our comprehension, at least until we arrive in Heaven."

"Are there any other spiritual processes that you can be sure of?"

Matthias paused to think.

He slapped his head, as if remembering something obvious. "Of course! The most important one. We don't think much about it here, because everyone is saved."

"Saved?"

"Salvation. That's the most important spiritual process of all. God has arranged things so that we can have a relationship with Jesus to ensure our place in His eternal Kingdom. All you have to do is ask.

"It's like turning a switch on that has been set to the 'off' position all one's life. The first part of the act of turning on this "light switch" is to genuinely repent of our wrongdoings, sincerely ask Him for forgiveness, and honestly promise—with His help—to turn away from sin. The other part of it is to believe, without reservation, that God loves us so much that He sent His only begotten Son Jesus to die for our sins, and that Jesus was physically resurrected from the dead. And that through this event, by way of a spiritual process that is far beyond human comprehension, we are given the opportunity to be saved from spending an eternity cut off from Him, and instead, to have an everlasting spiritual life in His presence."

"That's all there is to it?"

"For some people it's not as easy as it sounds."

He looked Stuart in the eyes.

"Taking those steps allows the Holy Spirit to come to rest in our heart, the core of our spiritual being. As quickly as a light turning on, our minds become reconfigured, radically changing how we think, and thus, how we live. Moreover, the Holy Spirit gives the believer gifts, and plants seeds that grow into the "fruit of the Spirit": love, joy, peace, patience, kindness, goodness, faithfulness, gentleness and self-control.

"This potential to be saved and host God's empowering Holy Spirit within us is built into every human being—God designed us that way—but it's up to each individual to make the choice to bring about the transformation."

"Are you saying that it's biological, neurological, or—?"

"To visualize the change that occurs, consider this: crucial stages of childhood development also recalculate the passageways of our brain—the branching and connections of thoughts themselves. When a baby no longer remembers the birth experience, or when a child realizes that they are not the center of the universe, both trigger a change of awareness, reconfiguring the way the child thinks. You can probably remember the point at which you became able to observe your own behavior, an observation that usually results in a loss of spontaneity and increased embarrassment. No one can return to an earlier state of being."

"I know, 'childhood's end.'" He thought back to the day that he learned there was no Easter bunny, trying to recall the trauma that knowledge had produced in him. Trying to remember the rationale behind thoughts he'd had before that day. He couldn't.

"When one takes the step to receive the gift of salvation, asking for forgiveness and believing in Jesus, it introduces an even more overwhelming realignment of mental processes, forming what is, for all practical purposes, a new mind; a new will, a new awareness and appreciation of God's creation. That's why people refer to it as being *born again*. It feels like that."

"You're starting to lose me with that. Do you mean you relive the birth experience?"

"No. Not that. Think more along the lines of reprogramming the stimulus-response patterns, activating new modes of under-standing, and triggering the comprehension of true morality. Before the experience of spiritual rebirth, when a person was wronged, his or her first thought might have been of revenge. Now, because of the person's new mind, that reaction is automatically routed to another place, one of forgiveness instead. Imagine a person who comes upon a wallet full of money on the ground, and formerly would have said, 'Wow. I can have a party.' Now, their first concern would be locating its owner. From this respect, the degree of change depends upon how entrenched one was in the worldly scheme of evil. But the end result is the same, thoughts will now travel on routes mapped out by spiritual guideposts, instead of worldly ones."

"You mean they're not even tempted to keep the money?"

"Well, temptations presented by the world no longer have a hold upon a person in the same way they did before being born again. You will, in many ways, have great control over the power exerted by a situation or object that tempts you to make a detrimental decision, or to take a counterproductive course of action."

"So Christians are pillars of morality? That doesn't jive with some of the things I read in the newspapers."

"I'm not saying that Christians are perfect, or that they are immune to temptation, because, as we know, everyone continues to sin. *Oh wretched man that I am! Who will deliver me from this body of death!* It is a process through which God helps us to become more like Christ."

"God helps you through sin?"

"Sin is very tempting. But fulfillment of that temptation is no longer the first thought of a Christian, and often it isn't their second or third thought either; such backsliding is usually temporary and happens in a vulnerable moment. There are forces that wait for those moments; they leap upon a person at every opportunity. And those forces are much more concerned with Christians, people they can try to turn away from Christ, than with people who are already facing the wrong direction."

"So only Christians stand a chance at having morals?"

"I didn't say that either. Although one of your most famous presidents said, 'You can't have national morality apart from religious principle.' George Washington, I think."

"In his farewell address." Stuart was impressed with Matthias' knowledge of American history.

"Right."

"And all you have to do is just believe and ask?"

"Yes. There's nothing else—no tasks, no works or deeds, no rituals, no catechisms or Sunday schools. Salvation is by the underserved favor of God alone—what we refer to as "grace." If one could *do* something that obligated God to give us salvation that would imply that we could *control* God. And no one can control God. He is above everything."

"That makes sense. I can certainly believe that God is all-powerful, too powerful to be controlled by humans."

"God arranged the crucifixion to stress this. There were three crosses on Golgotha that day. Jesus was crucified between two criminals. The two choices were blatantly displayed. One of the criminals chose to believe in Jesus; the other rejected him. To the one who recognized Jesus as the King of Kings, he said, 'today you will be with me in paradise.' That man, facing death, nailed to a cross, had no hope of being able to *do* anything to assure his salvation. Yet, Jesus saved him through his faith, not his deeds."

"So all those people with their 'holier-than-thou' attitude aren't accomplishing anything?"

"Nothing that will get them into Heaven; although Jesus' brother James tells us that for anyone who *has* received salvation, faith without action is dead."

"Good deeds won't get a person to Heaven?"

"Paul captures the most important idea when he says, 'it is by grace you have been saved, through faith—and this not from yourselves, it is the gift of God—not by works, so that no one can boast.' So that none can boast that they are going to Heaven by virtue of all the wonderful things they've done. You see, all that's necessary is to love the Lord. When we love and trust Him, He gives us the faith to continue. Faith isn't something we *do*, it's a gift from God."

Stuart found himself looking for holes in Matthias' reasoning.

"If God is all-powerful, then why didn't he design people to love him automatically?"

"Love has to be a conscious decision, or it means nothing. God could have created us to love him, of course. But what kind of love would that be? When you are presented with the choice—to love or not to love—then questions about whether love is real and uncon-ditional disappear. It becomes an act of free will—all the more priceless.

"God had already created sinless beings that worship him. They're called Angels. Although it's a choice for them too, but maybe an easier choice because they are always in His presence."

"Whew! That's quite a proposition. I'm going to have to think that over for a while." He wasn't stalling; he really was thinking about it, and thinking hard.

"I know, but don't put it off long. When Jesus comes back, it will be too late to make that choice."

"I'll keep that in mind. I feel like I'm on the verge of finding something, something I have searched for my whole life."

"That's ironic."

"Why?"

"That I have the faith you have been seeking; but you have what I want."

"What's that?"

"A normal life in a country like America."

"America's the only country like America."

Matthias made a quick gesture with his hands that Stuart interpreted to mean "Bingo!"

At that moment, sounds of laughter interrupted their conversation. They were coming from the cool-down house to the northwest of the garden. Stuart and Matthias turned just in time to see a happy young couple running into the house.

"Looks like they're having fun."

"Yes. I don't think they are there to cool down. I imagine they are taking a vacation. You know, the cool-down house is available as a vacation getaway when it's not being used for cooling down."

"That reminds me of Meredith."

"Meredith?"

"That's my girlfriend. I really miss her right now."

He stopped talking, replaying one of his daydreams about Meredith. He found himself wishing that she could see the garden, share this experience with him. That whatever work this place was doing in him, would also be accomplished in her. That they could go through this together.

"Where does she stand on matters of faith?" Matthias asked.

"She's Jewish," Stuart said. "At least, she claims to be. She doesn't attend synagogue, but she did spend last summer working on a kibbutz in Israel. We met on the plane going home to L.A. She has amazing hair. I can't describe it, but it's huge. I think it's from her Jewish roots. Do you have a girlfriend?"

"I'm married," Matthias replied.

"Married? You're very young to be married."

"In my family, we get married at the age of eighteen. All the marriages are arranged."

Matthias saw the look on Stuart's face.

"Oh. It's not as bad as you think," Matthias said. "Ilana and I love each other. My parents were extremely careful when they arranged our marriage. They spent years considering the choices, and Ilana's parents were involved in the process from the start to finish. I doubt that I could have found anyone as perfect for me as Ilana if I had tried to do it myself. I know I would have wasted a lot my life looking."

"It sounds so foreign to me. Unnatural."

"It's not unnatural in this part of the world. In Stauros it's even more important; all the marriages have to be arranged for obvious reasons: with only two hundred people, our gene pool is very limited."

"I can understand that."

"Do you have any brothers or sisters?"

"I have one sister," Stuart replied. "Her name is Cynthia, but we call her Cindy. I suspect she is quite upset by what has happened."

FORTY

LOS ANGELES

NIGHT (GMT-7)

C INDY COULDN'T SLEEP. She was lonely being the only one in the house, and she was sad about Roger. Although they had broken up more than a year ago, he was the first person of her own age, someone she had actually known, who had died.

After tossing and turning for what seemed like hours, she finally got out of bed and stumbled to the kitchen for a glass of milk. Monk was sleeping on the floor by his bowl and opened one eye to assure she was all right.

Sitting at the kitchen table, she starred at the map of Turkey on the wall. Her father had tacked it up the day Roger's body had been returned. The map completely covered the display of her drawings that had been there since first grade, as long as she could remember anyway.

Is Stuart's problem covering up my life?

She tried to imagine where her parents and Meredith were right now. She did some quick calculations and realized that they were still in the air.

So, they aren't in Turkey yet.

Her eyes scanned the map, reading the strange names of the cities and trying to pronounce them. She finished her milk, but didn't feel any sleepier.

She wished that Roger hadn't died. The house felt stuffy, and she gazed out into the back yard. The moon was bright, and she had no trouble seeing every detail. Opening the door, she stood on the deck and savored the coolness of the night. She saw the barbecue grill and remembered how often Roger had eaten with her family, even before they had started dating.

I need to take a walk.

She went upstairs to get dressed.

Back in the kitchen, she paused and held up Monk's leash, but he wasn't interested; she had taken him for a walk right before she went to bed.

Cindy didn't have any particular destination in mind when she started walking. However, ten minutes later, she found herself outside the Warren's house. Mrs. Warren was sitting on the front porch, staring at the moon.

"Is that you, Cynthia?" Roger's mother called from the porch. Her voice was as flat as the lid on Roger's coffin.

Cindy walked toward the house. "I was thinking about Roger," she said when she was standing on the porch.

"So was I," Mrs. Warren replied.

"You know, we used to date."

"I remember."

"It would be nice…I mean, I wonder…Could I just stand in Roger's room, one last time? If you're going to clean it out or something, I'd like to have a good picture of it in my mind."

"You poor girl. You need some sort of closure as much as I do," Mrs. Warren said.

Cindy blushed.

"Come right in. I'm sure it's all right with Walter. He's already in bed." She didn't say "asleep" because she knew that Walter was just lying there, staring at the ceiling, looking for the same thing she was looking for in the moon.

They went upstairs. Mrs. Warren switched on the light as they stepped into Roger's room. Cindy froze, remembering her child-hood with Roger.

Because Roger had been her older brother's best friend—forever it seemed—she had tagged along with them since she was eight years old. Roger had even invited her to his tenth birthday party. There had been Batman figures on the cake and Batman balloons. She remembered Roger unwrapping a yellow Batman wallet. Her present to him was a "Paint-by-Numbers Batman" book. The word "Authorized" appeared on the cover and she asked her mother what it meant.

When Roger unwrapped her present, she said, "It's authorized."

"By whom?"

"Batman," she guessed.

After that, she was an official member of the club. Whenever they needed Batgirl, she was available.

The following year, Roger had a Batman Piñata. Everyone had to pull a string; the winning string released the Piñata's treasures.

She couldn't invite him to her birthday parties. They were for girls only. Nevertheless, he privately gave her a Batgirl book with a picture of Batgirl on the cover, kicking so high that the heel of her right foot was actually higher than her head. Cindy had attempted to reproduce the position and discovered, to her dismay that she couldn't. She had prayed that Roger wouldn't uncover this flaw.

She walked around the room.

On the shelves were Batmobiles of various sizes, 1/32, 1/50, 1/64, Batcycles, Batwings, and Batman on a Zoomcycle. She remembered Roger's Green Batman bicycle helmet.

Another shelf held action figures, including some of Batman's nefarious enemies and associates: Penguin, Riddler, Joker, and Catwoman. Then there was Robin. Her brother Stuart had always been Robin.

A Batplane model hung from the ceiling.

For her tenth birthday, he'd given her a Batman Kaleidoscope. She still had it.

Her eyes started to water when she saw that he still had his Bandai Batman Walkie-Talkie. She had been fifteen when they actually started dating. Roger was sixteen. That summer, they bought the walkie-talkie set. Sometimes they stayed up into the wee hours of the night, talking to each other on the walkie-talkies in the dark. "Batman calling Batgirl…Come in, Batgirl."

After they had been going steady for two and a half years, Roger started college; and that had been the beginning of the end. One day Cindy had to go the orthodontist in Brentwood, and on the way home, she and her father had stopped at an ice-cream parlor. Roger had walked by the window with his arm around another girl, obviously a college girl. As they waited for the stoplight to turn green, she saw him pull the girl close and kiss her.

Fortunately, her father had been with her, otherwise, she didn't know what she would have done—seventeen years old, at an ice cream parlor somewhere on Santa Monica Boulevard, her heart breaking. Her dad had followed her eyes and realized what was happening, and somehow, he had managed to get her home before she broke down in tears.

She'd never spoken with Roger after that.

Now, she was about to cry again.

Mrs. Warren was saying something about having to box up everything, and did she want to take anything as a memento.

Cindy's tears welled up, and she stammered, "I'll think about it," as she rushed from the room, down the stairs, out the door, and practically ran all the way back to her house.

THE MOMENT CINDY was back home again, she went to the kitchen and poured herself another glass of milk.

Maybe I need a drink.

She sat down at the kitchen table. It was midnight. Her parents were supposed to telephone before 2:00 a.m., to tell her that they had arrived safely.

She stared at the map of Turkey on the wall, wondering if their plane had landed yet. Red pushpins on the map marked each location they were sure the boys had visited, usually places from which they had received a postcard. Arrows were drawn in various directions, connecting the "dots" of the pushpins in an effort to deduce Stuart's current location. Cindy reread the notes scribbled in the map's margins.

She saw the word "Batman" written on the map.

I must be losing my mind.

She stood, walked to the map, and focused on the details. Sure enough, there was a town called Batman on the map. On the way to Mount Ararat—her parents had circled that—it appeared to be no more than a couple of hours from Dogubayazit, where they were going to stay. That was circled, too.

Cindy felt an unexpected and tremendous certainty that Roger and Stuart would not have passed up the chance to visit Batman on their way to find Noah's Ark. The more she stared at the name, the more she became convinced of that fact.

She went into the living room and waited for the telephone to ring.

FORTY-ONE

TUESDAY, JUNE 28

TURKEY

MORNING (GMT+3)

MEREDITH, BRAD, AND MARGARET negotiated the journey from the airport to the hotel without difficulty, thanks to the man from Cairo who sat next to Meredith on the final leg of the flight. The man was a Messianic Jew and had talked her ear off about Christian holy spots in Turkey; not that she had minded.

Did you arrange for that, God?

He continued his chronicle for hours, without seeming to take a breath. Meredith recalled learning about circular breathing in a music appreciation course—oboists had to learn to breathe that way—and she supposed the small round Egyptian used a similar technique to allow this uninterrupted monologue, breathing in through his nose without once breaking the speech issuing from his mouth.

He described the tombs of the Apostles Peter and John, the landing place of Noah's Ark, the Garden of Eden, and the seven churches of the Book of Revelation. Ephesus was now called Efes, Smyrna was Izmir, Pergamon was Bergama, Sardis—Sart,

Thyatira—Akhisar, Philadelphia—Alasehir, and Laodicea—
Eskihisar.

Meredith hadn't realized that so many landmarks of the Christian faith were in Turkey; she had assumed that everything was in Israel, within walking distance of Jerusalem.

When he found out that Meredith's interest in Messianic Judaism had been stirred up the previous summer, he said, "When I first read the Gospels, I realized that they were written by Jews with a predominately Jewish readership in mind. The genealogies and Old Testament quotations were the giveaway. These things would have had no significance to Gentiles alive at that time, although, even putting aside that level of analysis, it was clear to me that they were written to convince both Jews and Gentiles that Jesus was, in fact, the Messiah."

He continued his litany all the way to the hotel, with a steadiness and conviction that forced the three Americans into complete silence as they watched history pass by outside the taxi window.

When he parted with them at the hotel, they felt as if a heavy weight had been lifted from their shoulders.

Meredith pointed to a restaurant across the street. "Look at that: Noah's Pudding." The rest of the sign proclaimed in English, "Asure—Original Recipe of Noah's Wife."

"I read about that in the brochure they gave us on the plane," Margaret said.

"Me too."

"And?" Brad asked.

"And the ingredients include only items that were on the Ark when the flood waters subsided. Wheat berries, dried legumes, rice, raisins, currants, dried figs, dates, and nuts."

"Well it sounds like commercialization to me."

A man stood by a clapboard with a painting of Noah's Ark on it offering "Maps of the Holy Land." To Meredith, he resembled one of the people who sell "Maps to the Stars" on Sunset Boulevard in Beverly Hills.

At approximately 9:15 a.m., after checking in, Brad picked up the copies of Roger's photos and a blowup of Stuart's passport photo. "I'm going out to do some investigation; anyone who wants to accompany me is welcome."

"I will." Margaret grabbed her purse.

"I saw an internet terminal in the lobby," Meredith said. "I'm going to stay and check my email."

The three of them went to the lobby together. When the Pierces had left the building, Meredith bought a token from the concierge to use with the computer terminal. All that was necessary was to provide her room number; her Internet usage would be added to their hotel bill.

She sat down and logged onto her email account. Since Stuart's disappearance, she'd been checking it much more than usual, hoping for a message from him.

There was nothing from Stu, but there was an email from Grandma Miriam. It always amazed Meredith how her grandmother had embraced technology—email, at least—while her own parents remained computer illiterate; neither had ever had an internet account. Then again, Meredith knew that her grandmother had a mind of her own, just as she did.

The octogenarian often told her the story of how she had walked away from the Hasidic community in Antwerp upon learning of the boy designated to become her husband—the parents of the two families had arranged the marriage. Somehow, she'd made it to Amsterdam where she'd caught a plane to California. Even then, California had beckoned young people worldwide, with a lure approaching that of the Promised Land.

> Dear Maytal,
> *(Grandma Miriam always used Meredith's Hebrew name.)*
> I suspect you are in Turkey by now. How proud I am that you have such interest in our roots in the Holy Land—even more proud than I was last year when you went to the Kibbutz. By now, our people are scattered throughout the region.
> Look how far away I am. But don't forget that the ones who built their shrine to Mohammed on the place of our Temple have no love for our people.

> Don't wear any short skirts. I have seen
> a documentary about Eastern Turkey
> lamenting that 15% of the population is
> now comprised of prostitutes from Rus-
> sia. These "Natashas" are responsible for
> the collapse of family values in that part
> of the country, and now the native Turks
> tend to react to all foreign women with
> animosity.
> Keep your eyes open. I am praying for
> your safety.
> Mazel,
> Miriam
> P.S. If you meet any of our relatives,
> please greet them for me.

Short but sweet. Meredith knew that her grandmother was much more worried about this trip to Turkey than she let on.

She typed a brief reply, intended to reassure her grandmother, and recount the story of the Messianic Jew she had met on the plane. As she typed, it struck her that she mustn't divulge her growing fascination with Messianic Judaism. That would be too much for Grandma Miriam. But even as she had that thought, she sensed a tugging inside, and she knew her curiosity about the Messiah was far from quenched.

The email made Meredith examine her surroundings; she realized that, although she was in the Holy Land, she wasn't in Israel. Still, she felt close, in the same way that an American wandering through Canada felt close to the USA, while physically distant.

Thoughts of being far from America didn't capture Margaret's current culture shock. She had gone straight through the edge of culture shock and emerged on the other side, floating in a sea of the strange and unfamiliar, as if the very air had become thicker.

In at least one respect, it was thicker. Everyone was smoking! You didn't see that anymore in the United States.

Everywhere she turned, small groups of men sat chain-smoking and drinking thick Turkish tea from cups so small, they bordered on the ridiculous, and needed constant refilling.

The men were connected in some way, probably to the businesses they were sitting in front of. Their responsibilities appeared to rotate, with men taking shifts according to an unwritten schedule. But, in every small flock of men, as she preferred to think of them, one man appeared to be responsible only for moving the conversation along. He never took a turn at the real work. Or was he the one making the tea?

Finding so many ready-made groups made it easy for them to query a large number of people about the photographs. Brad and Margaret went from group to group showing the photos of Stuart and Roger, and the pictures of the 'goat man' as they called him (Hassan). They also showed the photo of the golden church. Sometimes a heated conversation ensued, and such outbursts gave the couple a glimmer of hope. But always, the final answer was the same: "Not here."

After an hour of this, Margaret asked whether she could use the "facilities" at the last café on a large boulevard. Moments later she came running out of the building with a look of horror on her face.

She grabbed Brad's arm and said, "We're going back to the hotel."

"Now?"

"Yes now."

"OK. But why?"

"That toilet was nothing more than a hole in the floor with two foot pads etched beside it for traction."

Brad chuckled. He'd seen one earlier but assumed they were only for men.

MEREDITH HEARD them coming before they actually entered the hotel. Mrs. Pierce rushed up the stairs and Brad walked over to the computer where she was sitting.

"No luck," he said. "No one we questioned will admit to having seen Stuart, Roger, or the goat man." He described how they had gone from business to business, speaking with the groups of men drinking black tea.

Mrs. Pierce rejoined them. Before she had finished her story about the Turkish toilets, a wiry man with a five-o'clock shadow approached them.

"Tommy Dorfler, United States Consular Department" he said, stretching out his hand and grinning. He gave Meredith a look that she didn't like at all, and she slightly moved to increase the distance between them.

The Pierces quickly recounted their lack of success to Mr. Dorfler while Meredith watched the man's eyes.

"I'm not surprised," he said. "I've been questioning the people in this region for nearly a week. In fact, I have the cooperation of the police force." He pulled a stack of flyers from his briefcase, all bearing an enlargement of Stuart's passport photograph.

"Many people said 'not here.' What did they mean by that?"

"I'm not sure. What were you showing them?"

Brad handed him their photos. Tommy leafed through them.

"I think I understand what they meant," he said, pulling out a photo of the goat man.

"The clothes this man is wearing, and the type of cart he's driving is not found in this region of Turkey. The man is Turkish, but he's not from around here. In other words: 'Not here.'"

"You mean Stuart and Roger might never have reached this area?"

"Exactly. I'm sure you know that the consulate has still been unable to determine where the Warren boy was coming from when he showed up outside the emergency room in Tatvan. That situation remains the same. It's a dead end…Oops, sorry." He noticed Margaret's distress.

"Tatvan is roughly equidistant from Iran, Iraq, Syria, and Armenia. We don't know for sure that they were really in this country." He seemed to relish that the picture he was painting was a bleak one.

"We do," Meredith interjected. "They were on their way to find Noah's Ark."

"OK. Even taking that as a given, how do we know that they made it farther than Lake Van?"

No one could answer that question, and no one could think of anything else to say.

Looking at the clock, Margaret broke the silence. "It's eleven o'clock, we must call Cindy immediately and tell her we got here safely."

Mr. Pierce said, "Excuse us for a moment."

"I'll wait down here," Tommy said, holding onto Brad's photos. "Shall I find a table for lunch at the restaurant?"

Everyone agreed that was a fine idea. They hadn't eaten since the 6 a.m. snack aboard the airplane.

"Want to help me pick out the table?" he asked Meredith.

"I think I'll go to my room and freshen up," she said.

◆ ◆ ◆

BACK IN THEIR HOTEL ROOM, it took Brad and Margaret five minutes to figure out how to place a long distance call. When Margaret finally got through to Cindy, she could tell her daughter had been crying. She started crying, too.

"Cindy, we haven't been able to find out anything."

"You've only been there, what, three or four hours or something?"

"Yes, but Mr. Dorfler has shown Stuart's picture around town for days, and no one has seen him. It's possible that they never made it this far. Tatvan is to the west you know, and they were coming from that direction, from Ankara."

"Listen Mom, I think I've figured something out. I have an idea where they might be."

"Have you heard from Stu?" Margaret squealed.

"You'd better put Dad on."

Brad came to the phone.

"Daddy, I think I know where Roger and Stuart were."

"Go on."

"Have you got a map of Turkey handy?"

"Yes."

"Open it."

"Done."

"You can see Ankara where they flew in. Right?"

"Check."

"And you can see Mount Ararat."

"Ditto."

"Remember how Roger and Stuart were always playing Batman and Robin? Stuart was always Robin; Roger was always Batman."

"How could I forget? I was once the Joker."

Cindy had to laugh. "Follow the road to Elazig. That's the name of the town on the postmark of the last postcard."

"I remember."

"There are two main routes from Elazig to Tatvan. The northern road goes through Bingol. But the southern route goes through Diyarbakir and then," she paused, Batman!" Her voice italicized the word.

"You could be onto something."

"I have a strong feeling about this, Dad. When I was in Roger's room last night—"

"What were…"

"—With Mrs. Warren. I was lonely. Anyway, he was still just as much into Batman as ever. I don't believe he would have passed up a chance to visit the town of Batman for anything. Plus, it explains why his body ended up where it did, instead of closer to Mount Ararat."

"It certainly does. It also explains why the goat photos were not taken in this region. Wait a minute." Brad quickly explained Cindy's news to Margaret.

"Cindy. Your call is a godsend. That Dorfler guy had nearly made us abandon hope. We're going to check out Batman first."

"Well, be careful. I've been watching the news. E.U. seismologists claim that last Tuesday's quake was only a preshock—a bigger one is coming any day now."

"We're earthquake veterans; you know that."

"Call me and keep me posted, will you?"

"You bet I will Cindy-rella," Brad said, using the nickname he had called Cindy all through her childhood.

"Love you!"

"You too."

Brad put down the phone. "Let's get going," he said to Margaret.

She stared at him as if trying to decide whether the immediate change of plans prompted by Cindy's call was a good idea, or whether her husband's resolve was simply another manifestation of the primordial bond between daughters and fathers, sons and mothers.

FORTY-TWO

TOMMY DORFLER SAT at the table in the hotel restaurant staring at the picture of the golden church.

That's a lot of gold…If I could get my hands on that… His scruples were few, and he was not beyond making a fast buck.

When he'd arrived in Turkey three years ago, the staff had called him "Miss Muffet." They made him sit at the visa window that they called, "The Tuffet." It came from their localized adaptation of the nursery rhyme.

Little Miss Muffet,
Sat at the Tuffet,
Keeping the Kurds away.

Essentially that was his job: to keep the Kurds—the Turks from southeast Turkey—out of America.

The United States had long studied the results of open immigration policies such as those in The Netherlands and Sweden. Much to the dismay of their immigration authorities, both countries now had negative population growth rates of their indigenous peoples, unlike those of their Islamic immigrants.

Tommy had discovered that a comfortable second income could be made in the black-marketeering of US Visas. When a wealthy, intelligent Turk who was fluent in English came to his window, he'd note the person's particulars before routinely denying his visa application. In the coming weeks, he'd play detective and gather a file of 'intelligence' on the person. If the person seemed suitably corrupt, Tommy would contact him anonymously, suggesting that a visa could be arranged upon the transfer of a certain sum of money to a numbered bank account in Switzerland. When the funds appeared on his bank statement, he'd contact the person again with instructions to resubmit the visa application on a specific day. The "mark" would come to the Consulate on a day that Tommy was Miss Muffet on the Tuffet, and he'd issue the visa, no questions asked. They never knew that Tommy was the anonymous called, so the never suspected that he had anything to do with the transaction.

Most of all, Tommy liked the "playing detective" part of the swindle. He fancied himself as agent "double-oh-seven" each time. He owned a copy of "The World is Not Enough," the 1998 James Bond movie set in Turkey, and sometimes he suspected that the NATO troops northeast of Mount Ararat actually were there to guard secret oil pipelines connecting Western Europe with China, via Turkey—just like in the movie. Naturally, the Department of Defense would never let on if that were the case.

He used his secret income to fund his womanizing habits. What a pleasant surprise it had been to discover that an ugly man could have the most glamorous women of Turkey, provided his bankroll was big enough and he was American. Generally, Tommy was enjoying his life abroad.

Oblivious to the outside world, he was eating marinated pistachios and trying to figure out how he would find the golden church, when the Pierces and Meredith returned.

"Mr. Dorfler," Brad said.

Tommy was lost in a daydream. He had remembered that King Midas was a real person from Turkey; he might have had a church like the one in the picture.

"Mr. Dorfler," Brad repeated.

Tommy turned with a start and acknowledged him.

"We've had news from our daughter that leads us to believe that Stuart is in or around the town of Batman. Have you heard of it?"

"Of course. It's the country's most important oil center. It's on the edge of the Kurdistan region. It's 185 miles from here— less than four hours by car."

"We want to leave immediately."

Tommy had to think fast. He needed to pump these people for information about the golden church.

"Have you packed your luggage?"

"We never unpacked it."

"Then I suggest we relax and I'll treat you to a pleasant lunch in the restaurant, courtesy of the United States government. You have plenty of time to catch the next bus. I happen to know that it leaves at 2:30 every afternoon and takes seven hours to reach Diyarbakir—but you're not going that far—you'll be in Batman by 8 p.m.

"I'd offer you a ride, but my car seats only two people. I could bring one of you along with me," he said, eyeing Meredith. "It's a Porsche." The car was another one of the benefits Tommy reaped through his under-the-counter visa deals.

"No thanks," Meredith said, clearly suppressing an urge to use stronger language.

"So. How about lunch?" Tommy said, unfazed.

Brad looked at his wife.

"If you're sure we have enough time."

"Good."

Tommy motioned to the waiter, and soon they were studying the menus.

"Again Noah's Pudding," Mrs. Pierce said.

"Last summer I saw plenty of dishes like that," Meredith said. "When I was at the Kibbutz: Stew of Abraham, Eggplant Isaiah. Usually, the ones with names like that are delicious."

Before they ordered, the waiter told them the traditional Turkish story of the chickpea. How it complains to the woman cooking it while it is boiling in the water. The woman explains the necessity of becoming soft enough to be eaten by human beings, and thus to become part of human life, through which the tiny chickpea can be elevated to a higher form. It symbolized the suffering of a soul before coming into the presence of Divine Love.

Such went the many stories of Turkish cuisine. Tommy thought he had heard them all. The sensual fables about food intrigued him in particular, along with the various culinary aphrodisiacs each region had to offer. Aphrodisia, after all, was a town in Turkey.

They were never able to determine how it happened, but it did. Mrs. Pierce had ordered the *Beyin Salata*, thinking it was "bean salad." She said, "I can't very well order chickpeas if I'm going to imagine them talking to me. When the waiter placed a sheep's brain—in one piece—on a bed of lettuce in front of her, she nearly fainted.

Tommy saved the day. He offered to switch plates with her. Organ meats were something he'd had to develop a taste for, because they were often in aphrodisiac recipes—the ones that weren't based on a combination of honey and thistles. Mrs. Pierce gladly accepted his *Coban Salata*, a "shepherd's salad" made by mixing tomatoes, cucumber, olives, parsley, and peppers. They shared the *Hydari*, a thick yoghurt blended with garlic, olive oil, and mint.

He tried to change the subject and bring the conversation around to the golden church. It became clear that Brad couldn't pronounce the names "Diyarbakir" or "Dogubayazit," so Tommy said, "You know, we all find it difficult pronouncing some of these Turkish words. Most of us call the first one, "Y'r Baker," and the other one, 'dog zit.' You know? Like a pimple on a dog. 'Dog zit.'"

"Hey! I have a dog," Meredith said.

Tommy soon realized that the three newcomers had no idea whatsoever about the location of the golden church, other than that it was likely to be near wherever the Pierce's son was—at the very least, the Pierce boy would know where it could be found. Tommy pointed out that it was getting late and he should help them arrange tickets for the bus to Batman.

"Are you sure you want to do this?"

"Well…" Margaret still had some doubts.

"Margie, I agree with Cindy. Don't worry." Brad put his arm around his wife.

"OK," Tommy said. "I'll make sure you're settled on the bus, and then I'll catch up to you by car in a few hours." Sizing up Meredith one last time he added, "I'll be driving alone." He paused, but there was no reaction. "I have some business to do here in 'Dog zit.' I have to tell the local police to wind down their investigation because we're moving it to Batman."

Actually, Tommy had other plans as well. This region was known for its potent aphrodisiacs, and he wanted to stock up before he left. Each town had its own recipes, carefully guarded secrets. By far the most famous was from Manisa. Using forty-one spices, the town rulers, who had passed the recipe down from generation to generation for 500 years, produced fifty tons of a paste called *Mesur Macunu* every year. During the annual festival devoted to its production, hundreds of kilos of the paste were thrown from the top of the mosque in the town's main square.

"Likely I'll be in Batman before you. But just in case, give me a call on my cell phone when you arrive." He handed them each a business card. "Oh, and by the way. The State Department has issued an earthquake watch for this region. Usually, nothing comes of their warnings, but I'm required to inform you."

"Consider us informed," Brad said, trying to hide his anxiety. Thankfully, Margaret had missed Dorfler's last remark; she would become hysterical if she suspected they were traveling into a fault zone that was getting ready to explode.

FORTY-THREE

STUART AND PHILIOS RELAXED on the veranda of the dining hall and looked in the direction of the garden.

"You said your ancestors brought the cross here nearly two thousand years ago," Stuart said.

"That is correct."

"Well, how did they get it here?"

"It's not a short story. But then again, it's not such a long story either. Do you want to hear it?"

"I'd love to."

Philios made himself comfortable and began.

"On the sixtieth day, shortly before dawn, three men rushed up the hill and took the cross: James, son of Alphaeus, Thaddaeus, and Simon the Zealot. Three Apostles of the Son of Man.

"They didn't stop running until the sun had fully risen..."

Twenty minutes later, he ended the story with the words, "Hail King Jesus. Righteous is the Son of Man. Worthy is the Lamb of God. Holy is the Lord of Hosts."

"That's fantastic," Stuart exclaimed. "Do you think that's what really happened?"

Philios peered at him. "I believe it with all my heart."

"Including the part with the angel at the end?"

"Definitely! The Bible tells us that we each have angels—note the plural—assigned to watch over us."

"So why don't they appear more often."

"When an angel of the Lord manifests itself into the physical realm of our world, it's no small event. Although they do make their presence felt daily, in many other ways."

"Aren't angels the spirits of people who have died and gone to Heaven?"

"Absolutely not. Angels are created beings just as we are. The difference is that God created us to live in the physical world, but He created angels to live in the Heavenly realms. They are even organized in a hierarchy: archangels, cherubim, seraphim, 'elect' angels, Heavenly Hosts, angels of judgment, and the like. Probably there are ranks of angels that we know nothing about.

"So many accounts of 'guardian angels' exist that, for all we know, they are a separate class of spiritual beings. Saint Jerome maintained that unrepented sin stopped such angels from aiding the wicked. Others believe that God has appointed both a good and evil angel for each of us. That could explain why good people experience bad things, but the Bible never refers to such a system. Instead, it cautions us not to worship angels, but to give all the glory to the Lord."

"How long have angels existed?"

"God created angels before He created us. He created them to serve in the Heavenly realm. After the creation of mankind, God has used angels to minister to us in many ways. The first angels we know about were sent to guard the gates of the Garden of Eden. Since then, they have appeared as mediators or messengers between humankind and God, in all matters except salvation—Jesus is the sole mediator for that."

Stuart considered the story of the settlement. "Each of the original settlers heard the angel?"

"I believe so. The story has passed down through the generations, exactly as I told it to you."

"So some of the people who founded Stauros were Jesus' original Apostles?"

"Yes. Philip, James the Lesser (meaning he was shorter than James the Greater, Bartholomew, Thaddeus (also called Jude), and Simon the Zealot (to distinguish him from Simon-Peter).

"All of them returned to the world once they had verified that everything was functioning smoothly at the settlement. After all,

Jesus had given them the Great Commission: 'Go into all the world and preach the good news to all creation.'

"My ancestor, Philip, and Thaddaeus were the first to leave. Philip was the first to be martyred. Thaddaeus came back and wrote the Book of Jude. He left again with Simon the Zealot in AD 44. Both were martyred. But before that happened, Simon returned briefly with many scrolls and much news from the outside world; and this may have sparked the settlers' hunger to keep abreast of current events. Bartholomew and Matthias left several years later. They were martyred, too."

"What did they do after they left?"

"Not much is known about any of the original twelve Apostles after Jesus ascended into Heaven. One thing is certain; they spent much of their time spreading the Gospel—the "good news"—as Jesus had commissioned them to do, so much that every one of the Twelve, except John, was martyred, brutally killed for their faith.

"Another thing we do know about the five who left: They never breathed a word about Stauros."

"I can believe that. Otherwise, this place would be on the cover of every magazine in the world."

Philios started to say something and stopped.

"I find it amazing that so many were killed. How can that be? And the five who left; didn't they know when they were going to die by studying the trees?"

Philios looked at Stuart with fatherly eyes, as if he were patiently explaining something to a child, something obvious to an adult, with moments of exasperation stifled by the joy of passing on the truth.

"It wasn't until Polycarp that the settlers began to contemplate a connection between the trees and outside events. That's when they started to look at the dates. Stauros was in its fourth generation, although several people who had met Alexander Cyrene and Bartholomew as infants were still alive.

"Once the relationship between the trees and the world had been established, the inhabitants of Stauros took upon themselves the task of studying the trees and documenting, as best they could, the events connected with them. So began the expansion of the library, the establishment of the *scholars*, the building of the observation towers, and finally, the building of the study center next to the northeast tower."

"And the martyrs? Why were they killed?"

"The world is set up to allow people to make a choice. Before Jesus, people had to choose to follow God's laws or not. Some, starting with Eve, chose to disobey the Lord. Jesus' crucifixion added another twist: people could undergo spiritual rebirth by choosing to believe in Him and the redeeming power of what happened on the cross. Jesus put it very simply when he said, whoever is not *with* Him is *against* Him. Sitting on the fence is not an option.

"Those who choose not to believe, try to thwart the truth whenever they can. Among them exists a wide spectrum of people, from those who impede the truth through inaction, to those who take a more active role in hindering the spread of the Gospel. You see, as much as Christians try to behave as Jesus would, those who are against us act to the contrary, just because it is contrary. Even when they are aware that a certain thing is *right* from any perspective, they will choose the *wrong*, simply to confirm to themselves that they are acting of their own free will."

"I can relate to that," Stuart said, recalling his and Meredith's similar conclusion regarding abstinence.

"The Apostles were living proof that Jesus is the way. Their spiritual gifts were fine-tuned to establish this fact beyond any reasonable doubt. Merely having an Apostle's shadow fall upon a person often resulted in healing. Throughout history, non-believers have imagined that they could stop the spread of the truth by killing its proponents. They don't understand that the more they try to stop our mission, the more we grow with opposition.

"Non-believers devised the most terrifying deaths for the Apostles, hoping to scare people into submission. Bartholomew was beaten, skinned, crucified, and beheaded. Matthias was beheaded. So was James the Greater. The other James was beaten, stoned, and had his brains clubbed out. Matthew was burnt in Ethiopia; Thomas was speared in India. The rest of them were crucified, Peter upside-down. Another favorite way to kill Christians was sawing them in half. Nero used to dip Christians in pitch and use them as lights in his gardens. The Apostle Peter's interpreter Mark was dragged to pieces.

"The reason so many are martyred is that they refuse to recant their belief in Jesus as the Messiah. People aren't often willing to give up their life for something, unless it is the truth. Have you ever heard of so many people willing to die for anyone else?"

"There have been many deaths in wars throughout the last century."

"I'm glad you mentioned that. Of all the periods of history, the twentieth century saw more Christian martyrs than any other period. A full sixty-five percent of the seventy million who have given their lives for their faith in Christ, were killed in the twentieth century."

"More than forty-five million people?"

"Yes. Mainly in Bangladesh, China, India, Indonesia, Nigeria, and Saudi Arabia and the rest of the Arab world. Muslim fundamentalism is the source of most of the killings. Sudan and the former Soviet republics are also hot-spots."

"I had no idea."

"Most people don't. It's not in the interest of those who persecute Christians to seek wide publicity. Jesus told us we should expect to be persecuted in His name. And that we would be blessed for it: 'Blessed are you when people insult you, persecute you, and falsely say all kinds of evil against you because of me.'"

"Then there must not be many happy Christians."

"Persecution for what is right, for the truth, never has the sting of the miseries justly inflicted upon evildoers. Remember, Jesus paid the ultimate price to achieve our redemption.

"See the metal shop?" Philios pointed to the crater wall.

"Yes."

"Well, just as gold has to be put through the fire to become pure, our hearts must be put through fires of hardship and persecution; that makes us pure."

"That makes sense."

"And when Gold is pure, the goldsmith can see his reflection in it; likewise, our Refiner should be able to see His reflection in us."

Suddenly, a puff of smoke arose from the chimney of the metal shop.

"That explains why some would choose evil over goodness, doesn't it?" Stuart said.

"For some, yes. It's a good deal less *hot* for them to be the persecutors than to be among the persecuted. But they will end up in a very hot place, if you know what I mean."

"Yes."

"For others, the battle for their souls is not as simple. We spoke earlier of angels, but fallen angels exist, too. Remember that one-third of the angels followed Lucifer when he rebelled against God and was cast out of Heaven. They became the demonic beings that continue to work to destroy God's Kingdom. Because scripture says Lucifer's fallen angels are already chained in Hell, some favor the notion that demons are a separate type of spiritual being, maybe the progeny of fallen angels with humans. Still, scripture often refers to events of the future as if they have already taken place. Remember?"

"Yes... We talked about God's perspective of time before. I understand that, as much as I can."

"Whichever is the truth, one thing is certain: demons are tireless in their attack upon believers and unbelievers alike, tormenting us to turn away from knowing and serving Christ. They work upon our thoughts and feelings with as much ease as we interact with each other in conversation. They entice and harass, they enslave and compel, they deceive and defile. They cause addictions and illnesses.

"When any thoughts are contrary to your conscience, or you find yourself having done something you wish you hadn't, when irrational fears and compulsions overcome you, or you engage in destructive behavior and self degradation, you can be sure that these feelings are not of God. On the contrary, they are the deceptions of spiritual beings that would have you lose your soul.

"Worry, Fear, and Doubt are some of their nicknames. Deceit, Hate, and Rage are others. Guilt, Confusion, Lust, Complacency, Hopelessness, Unforgiveness...They have many names; their numbers are vast."

"Are you saying those are names of spiritual beings?"

"Those are the names we know them by. They have other names as well: Appollyon, Asklepios, Baal, Basilisk, Moloch…and ranks too: powers, dominions, and principalities."

"But here, in Stauros, I truly feel the absence of things like worry, fear, and doubt; hate, rage, and confusion; and all those things you mentioned." Stuart said.

"This place is, in some respects, holy. It is a stronghold against such powers. Nonetheless, they attack us, even here."

Stuart remembered the doubts that had assailed him in the library on the previous day.

"If you do something evil, maybe by mistake, does it ever trouble your sleep?" Philios asked.

Stuart answered immediately. "Surely it would, it has. It would for anyone. Why do you ask?"

"Because it's not true that 'it would for anyone' as you said. There are many people in the world who cannot fall asleep until they do something evil. King Solomon pointed this out more than 900 years before the birth of Jesus: 'they cannot sleep till they do evil; they are robbed of slumber till they make someone fall.' (Proverbs 4:16)"

Stuart found that thought troubling, that there were people who couldn't sleep until they had committed some evil act. But the more he thought about it, the more he realized it was true.

◆◆◆

FATHER ROMERO walked back to the hotel. After spending the morning at the Department of Antiquities speaking with minor officials, he was shaken by their adamant refusal to acknowledge the existence of the golden church in the photograph. He wished Dobro had been there.

After lunch, he planned to go to the Office of Tourism to get a permit for Ararat and hire a guide. He'd just have to see for himself.

He went to the service counter to check for messages from Dobro.

There weren't any.

The clerk called to him before he reached the stairs.

"Mr. Romero. I almost forgot. You're from Los Angeles, are you not?"

"Yes."

"There were some people here from Los Angeles. You just missed them."

"I know. Ms. Brinkman and Mr. Cole. I had dinner with them last night."

"No. I mean three others: an older couple and a younger girl. They checked in and then checked out three hours later." As he spoke, he was searching through the guest register. "Ah yes. Mr. and Mrs. Pierce, traveling with a Miss Meredith Montgomery."

Very interesting.

"Did they mention where they were headed?"

"No. But they were met by another American who spoke some Turkish."

"Thank you."

Father Romero was becoming flustered as he tried to put together the pieces: he could understand the presence of the Pierces, but Brinkman and Cole...*what were they doing here?* He grasped the cross around his neck by the cut-glass ball at its base. Holding it up to the light created rainbows. *I wonder what this crystal is supposed to mean.* Was it intended to symbolize a mystical bond between the cross and the world where the two connected—at the base? Or did the small vitreous ball represent the earth, transformed into a precious jewel by the crucifixion, yet dwarfed in importance beneath the shadow of the simple wooden cross?

Lost in contemplation, he instinctively walked to the bicycle-rental service next to the train station. He rented a motorcycle—much newer than the ones he had rented more than a decade ago, when he had traveled around the country researching his book.

Riding the motorcycle to Mount Ararat took his mind off the dilemma. In less than a half hour, he was at the Office of Tourism, asking about a permit and a guide.

The man behind the counter double-checked his permission form, and Father Romero studied the big map on the wall of the office, looking for any reasonable candidates for the location of the golden church.

His eyes came to rest on the word "Batman" near the lower left of the map. He stared at it, trying to bring something to the front of his memory.

Why is that significant?

He suddenly remembered everything. Roger at age twelve coming to Sunday School costume parties dressed as Batman; Roger and his friend dressed as Batman and Robin at the church picnic; even the details of Roger's room, where he had stood just days ago watching the photo slowly emerge from the deceased boy's printer. The background came into focus. The room had been a museum of Batman memorabilia.

Father Romero stepped quickly to the counter.

"I've decided to cancel my exploration of Ararat," he said. "I hope this will not cause any inconvenience."

"Not to worry. The guide still hasn't returned from lunch."

The clerk refunded the money for his climbing permit and Father Romero rushed out the door. His luggage fit in the saddlebags of the motorcycle with room to spare. He could leave right away— one of the advantages to traveling light. And this is exactly what he did.

In little over an hour, he was speeding along the shores of Lake Van, feeling that he was getting somewhere at last.

FORTY-FOUR

BRYCE LOOKED AT EARL as he walked in front of her. He wasn't his usual sneeringly cynical self. He was having a blast. And he was happy being paid for it. She was, too. Hiking on the side of Mount Ararat was exhilarating. They could not help feel a rush of excitement at the possibility that the crazy Ark story might be true.

Earl and their guide, a member of the Mountaineering Federation of Turkey, headed for an outcropping of rock that formed a natural bench. Bryce followed. Sitting on the bench, they gazed out across the plateau toward the smaller of the two Ararat peaks. Scarcely a mile away, ice and snow covered its top, similar to the main mountain.

"That's the *Serdarbulak* plateau," the guide said.

Looking to the south, the plains appeared to continue forever. The absence of trees was noticeable. In the far distance, they saw some nomadic Kurds grazing a herd of sheep in a pasture.

"I'm going to boot up the Transmogrifier," Earl said. He opened his knapsack, and removed the silver-colored case that occupied most of the space inside it.

"Good. I'll use the facilities," Bryce said, heading for a large boulder.

On her way back, she reached down and picked up a peculiar rock. She carried it to the bench.

"Hey Cole," she said. "This looks like a chunk of pillow lava. How's that possible at this height?"

Earl studied the rock.

"That's pillow lava all right. Pillow lava has been found as high as 13,000 feet and 15,000 feet."

"Ararat is an inactive volcano," the guide said. "There has never been an eruption in recorded history; the volcano has no crater."

At the word crater, Bryce and Earl looked at each other.

"What about other craters?"

"You mean the meteor crater at the foot of the mountain near the Iranian border?"

"No. We've seen photos of that one. It's much too small."

"Too small for what?"

Bryce sensed it was time to change the subject.

"But pillow lava is formed only under water."

"Yes. At this level, some people might hold that as an argument in favor of the Biblical flood." Earl couldn't hide his sarcasm.

Bryce made some calculations. "Water at a depth of 15,000 feet would have submerged most of Europe and Africa."

"And if it had gone still higher? Let's say, until Ararat were completely covered…17,000 feet." Earl gazed at the top of Mount Ararat.

"Where could all that water have come from?" Bryce asked.

"I've been doing research on that." *It was true; he had—so had many of the members of the department—ever since he'd received that 'creation/evolution' letter from the chairman at the beginning of the summer.* "There are many theories. One insists a 'water vapor canopy' surrounded the Earth in ancient times. This canopy served to shield the pre-Flood peoples of the world from the harmful effects of radiation. It would explain the absence of cancer and the genetic mutations that have resulted in disease. Biblical longevity meets science."

"That wouldn't work," Bryce argued. "Any vapor canopy thick enough to cause the Flood would have raised the temperature of the Earth's surface to a level that could not support human life."

"But a thinner vapor canopy would have caused a greenhouse effect and maintained the Earth at subtropical temperatures, resulting in lush plant-life everywhere…The Eden theory."

"That wouldn't have been thick enough to bring the water to the level we're at now."

They were both caught up in mimicking the reasoning of what they considered "wacky science"—pretending to be snake-oil salesmen.

"You're right," Earl continued, "but picture this: a ring of mammoth ice crystals encircling the Earth before the Flood. There are ice crystals in Saturn's rings, you know.

"Plate tectonics collapsing the ocean floor to release the waters beneath the Earth's crust, coupled with underwater volcanic activity would have dispersed enough dust upon the vapor canopy to 'seed' the clouds the same way farmers do today. Add to this, some of the steam condensing into rain upon reaching a certain height, and the rest of it melting the ice-crystal ring; it's a recipe for the rainstorm of all rainstorms, with enough water to inundate the whole planet."

"The people on the ground would have interpreted the removal of the water vapor canopy to be opening of the 'windows of Heaven' referred to by the book of Genesis," Bryce explained. "It would have been the first time the ancient people saw stars."

"And here I have a bottle of hair-restorer to sell you." Earl said. "It will also cure your back ailments, and chilblains."

Bryce could barely restrain her laughter.

As if on cue, Earl pulled out—with a flourish—an appropriately sized widget from the silver case. They laughed; their guide was bewildered.

EARL HAD FINISHED preparing the Transmogrifier. The screen flickered to life.

"Let's see where our friend, Father Romero, is now."

Bryce looked over her assistant's shoulder. What they saw was discouraging. She noticed that Earl was starting to sweat—not a good sign.

"It looks like he's headed away from Ararat. How can that be?" she asked. "Are you sure this thing is working?"

"Positive."

"Maybe he's going to visit a friend."

"Not likely. Did you notice the look in his eyes when we mentioned the golden church? He's here for one reason, and one reason only."

"So what does this mean?"

"It means the man has information that we don't."

"And?"

"We've got to follow him." Earl swore.

"Follow him?"

"Yes. Follow him." He suppressed a string of obscenities.

"But your voice stress analysis showed he knew nothing of the location of the church."

"That was last night. We have no idea whom he's spoken with today, or what he's learned meanwhile. He's the authority on Byzantine churches; it's likely he has connections."

"Hmm." Bryce had been finding it altogether pleasant up above the rest of the world; the thought of racing back down the mountain was not appealing.

"Let's phone Richard for a second opinion."

◆ ◆ ◆

DOBRO SULEYMAN watched the scene through binoculars. So far, they were unaware that he had been trailing them all morning, always a half-mile behind.

He watched the short man become agitated and start gesticulating. Finally, the two had sat down again and peered intently into the silver case. Their motions showed that they were no longer upset, or at least they were not displaying any distress. He wished he could hear what they were saying. No matter, he'd question the guide later; all the guides knew much more English than they let on.

Maybe the Americans actually were *conducting seismological investigations.*

The man closed the case, packed it back into his knapsack, stood, and motioning to the guide, said something, and then pointed down the mountain. Quickly, the three of them turned and headed back the way they had come.

They headed right toward Dobro. He tried to find a place to hide. Climbing to a protruding rock ledge, he positioned himself so that he could follow their movements until the last moment. Soon, they reached the trail below and he flattened himself against the rock.

He caught a few words of their conversation.

"Richard says...the priest...at all costs... Byzantine church expert... assume... located the site."

The words "Byzantine church expert" rang in Dobro's ears. They couldn't be referring to anyone but his friend, Father Rafael Romero.

Was Rafael mixed up with these two characters? And where was Rafael?

When they got sufficiently beyond his hiding place, he climbed down and continued to follow them, closing the gap as they neared their rented automobile.

Fortunately, it took them a while to load the car and pay the guide. Otherwise, Dobro would have lost them when they left the parking lot. As it turned out, he had only moments to spare.

FORTY-FIVE

RICHARD ROEBUCK had signed off the video link with some misgivings. Telling Bryce and Earl to leave the Ararat region had been a tough decision, especially with them being so close.

Close? They were right on the mountain!

He now held a copy of Rafael Romero's book about Byzantine churches, and he was convinced that the priest would be the one to lead them to the site they were seeking, even if he didn't know that's what he was doing.

The situation had become urgent. His MEDEX mortality forecast showed a confidence rating of eighty-seven percent, and the peak probably of death—his—moved seventy-two hours closer with each passing day. His human doctors could find no grounds for the acceleration.

He was impatient. It was midnight in Seattle—the middle of the afternoon in Turkey. He knew he would never be able to fall asleep. Without realizing it, he was putting increasing hope in the outcome of Bryce's mission.

RICHARD REMEMBERED the last time he had felt this confident about a potential cure: the mistletoe fiasco. He'd lost eighteen months on that one, not to mention an investment running to eight figures.

The fiasco had started with genuine concerns about his niece and nephew. Using an annuity that Richard set up for them, his sister had enrolled her children in a costly private school. At first, that had seemed like a good thing. She'd chosen the Rudolf Steiner school system, called Waldorf schools in America—they went by other names in other countries. It wasn't difficult to find one—there were close to two hundred in North America and some six hundred in more than thirty countries worldwide.

Once, when he had been talking about science with his niece and nephew at a family cookout, they'd insisted that the heart is not a pump. According to Steiner education, "It is the feelings of the soul which gives rise to the movement of the blood; the soul drives the blood, and the heart moves because it is driven by the blood. Exactly the opposite of what materialistic science states." [Steiner, *Theosophy of the Rosicrucian*, Rudolf Steiner Press].

Further probing had revealed that the children were being taught even stranger ideas by the Waldorf School: colors can heal; there are not five senses, but rather twelve, and these correspond to the twelve signs of the Zodiac; the primary elements are earth, air, fire, and water; humans originated on the planet Saturn; and Atlantis actually existed.

"Joanne, this school you have your kids in—"

"What about it?"

"Have you heard of Rudolf Steiner?"

"Of course. He founded the system they use."

"Have you heard of Anthroposophy?"

"Maybe. Some of the parents and teachers mention it occasionally. So what?"

"It's a cult."

"A cult? What do you mean?"

"I mean it's a group of people who blindly follow the teachings of a religious leader claiming to possess esoteric wisdom—an authoritative and charismatic individual, who is at odds with the rest of the world. A wacko…Can I make it any clearer?"

"You mean Steiner?"

"He believed he was a prophet. He even wrote his own translation of the Bible."

"Well, we don't go to church. You know that."

"It's not as simple as that." He didn't want to upset Joanne. "I think you can find a better place for them."

"I'll consider it."

"Well, do something about it!"

"Please don't shout, Richard. I'm a grownup, not a child."

ALTHOUGH HE didn't want his niece and nephew attending the Waldorf School, Roebuck found himself drawn inexplicably to some of Steiner's extracurricular theories. While he acknowledged Steiner to be both one of the craziest charlatans of the twentieth century, and a proponent of pure junk science, he became convinced that the man's research might have come up with something practical, if only by accident.

Steiner's healing theories had intrigued Richard, and not the ones that called for children to lay on their backs with so-called "healing stones" distributed strategically on their bodies; the man had believed all rocks contained dormant highly-evolved spiritual beings.

Steiner had developed a system of Anthroposophical medical practices. Much of it could be thrown out immediately: the assertion that bacilli are demonic embodiments of lies; the Cabalistic view that reiterated speech sounds—in other words, chanting—had the power to cure illness.

All Steiner's quackery aside, one of his medical endeavors made sense to Richard: Mistletoe. Steiner had founded the Society for Cancer Research in Switzerland, to promote mistletoe extracts. The organization continues to this day.

Steiner became attracted to the mistletoe plant (*Viscum album*) after learning of its unique life cycle. Mistletoe is a semiparasitic plant producing a single pair of leaves each year and poisonous fruit that ripens in the winter. A tree without a trunk, some say its wood was used to fashion the cross of the crucifixion. Because of that, it was condemned to be a vine, just as the snake was condemned to crawl on its belly after tempting Eve.

Steiner noticed the similarity between the growth patterns of mistletoe and cancer. Mistletoe is a *saprophytic* plant, a parasite, growing in the bark of other trees instead of the soil. Cancer is also parasitic, relying on its host for nourishment. Both consist of undifferentiated cell types that develop into a ball of ever-increasing size, without regard to its host, surroundings, seasons, or even gravity; unlike most plants that grow upwards, mistletoe grows radially, in all directions, like cancer.

To this, he applied the homeopathic principle, *simila similibus curentur*, "like cures like." Steiner insisted that the lacto-fermented fresh mistletoe sap, one batch extracted in the summer and another in the winter, both obtained according to astrological principles on the solstices, must be combined to maximize its healing properties. He believed the resulting concoction would not only cure and prevent cancer, but would change a person's life decisively after death as well.

In September of 2001, Anthroposoph Robert Gorter explained this principle: "When you take a plant or mineral medication that has been prepared through an Anthroposophical pharmaceutical process, you link yourself to the being of that plant or mineral. After death, you meet this being very intimately. Mistletoe is a being of light. It assists with the expansion of the etheric body after death." [Joengel, Sebastian, and Michaela Spaar. "Thinking Strengthens Our Immunity: An Interview with Physician and Researcher Robert Gorter, MD, PhD." Anthroposophy World-wide, September 2001, Vol. 4 No. 1, p. 6].

The FDA turned out to be limiting dosages of mistletoe extract to homeopathic levels—one part per million—but in Europe, the laws allowed cancer patients to inject large quantities of it in undiluted form mixed with silver. Richard knew that business decisions were often based upon market analysis and profit considerations. Payoffs were common. He'd been involved in many, as both payer and payee. That the FDA, AMA, NIH, and drug companies appeared to be cooperating to suppress mistletoe therapies was no more than the expression of sound business practice. If a low cost, natural cure for cancer were to be found, those organizations and companies stood to lose billions.

Richard established a team extracting and combining mistletoe saps according to Steiner's principles. Much to his dismay, Steiner's theories about mistletoe turned out to be absolute garbage, like all of Steiner's other theories. Because Richard spent so much time studying the parasitic mistletoe, he found himself involved with similar notions. One that attracted him was the Hulda Clark theory. Her activities in the realm of medical quackery—the human intestinal fluke (*Faciolopsis buski*)—had long ago forced the move of her clinic to Tijuana, Mexico.

Although the medical community had disproved Clark's cures time and again, Richard became convinced that it was only her healing methods that were in error: black walnut hulls, wormwood, and cloves; he believed the parasite part of her theory was probably correct. He only needed to find the right antigen to neutralize the parasite.

That quest had led him to the rainforests of Brazil.

At the urging of Dr. Langford Perkins, one of his RRR grant recipients (now deceased), he had devoted far too much time, energy, and money to tracking down an anticancer agent to destroy the fluke.

Ultimately, it had all been an utter waste.

RICHARD ROEBUCK pictured the rainforest debacle—that hadn't been his "stairway to Heaven" either, but if anyone could afford the ticket price, it was he. He pressed a button on his desk, and his secretary appeared a moment later. "Have the jet cleared for an immediate flight to Turkey," he said. "And make sure they load the helicopter."

FORTY-SIX

LATE AFTERNOON

FATHER ROMERO came to the eastern shore of Lake Van less than two hours after leaving Mount Ararat. He paused at the intersection with the coastal road. Turning left to the north or right to the south, would have no effect upon his time of arrival—both were the same distance; both offered spectacular panoramas. He decided to take the northern route; on that side, the highway hugged the coast; it provided a lane—a buffer zone—between him and the cliffs that dropped sharply into the water, and this offered him security while his motorcycling confidence was shifting to higher gear.

Twenty minutes farther along the shore, he decided to stop for an early supper. The two sandwiches in his bag were made of the same olive paste and minced meat that had been his basic sustenance when he traveled around this region ten years ago.

He straddled the bike and gazed toward the opposite shore of the lake. He knew there was a Byzantine ruin behind the hills directly across from him—at least there had been ten years ago. Since he left Ararat, he'd passed several churches in varied states of disrepair. He longed to re-investigate each one of them, but resolved that his priority should be getting to Batman as soon as possible.

He gazed down at the water; three cats sunned themselves on a flat rock. They were asleep. When he turned off the motorcycle engine, the cats stretched their heads lazily in his direction as if the sudden silence had awakened them. They got up and made their way toward him, climbing the side of the hill along a narrow path; they gave the impression that they had all the time in the world.

The cats walked beside each other, and the one in the middle appeared drunk. Now and then, it veered off on a diagonal, bumping into the one on the right who would then bat it over toward the one on the left. It weaved back and forth, and shortly the one on the left would use its forehead to nudge it over to the one on the right again.

There was something odd about them. The cat on the left was calico and had only three legs, but that fact had no bearing upon its mobility. The orange cat on the right had four legs but only a stub of a tail.

They took their time approaching Father Romero, not because they were afraid, but because they were reacting to the lethargy produced by the afternoon sun. He suspected they wanted part of his sandwich. When they got closer, it was apparent that the middle one was blind. There wasn't a whole cat among them, although the sum of their parts was more than a cat and a half. He remembered the near-sacred Van Cat, common to the region yet forbidden to export, and he wondered if the middle one might be from that protected breed. Because the identifying trait of the Van Cat was one green eye and one blue eye, he would never know.

Sometimes, he asked himself why these triplicities always caused him to recall the three crosses of the crucifixion, and never the Trinity. Sometimes, he felt uneasy about that fact. He wondered if he were obsessed as he reached in his bag for one of his moistened towelettes.

More than five years had elapsed since God had showed him such a vivid sign. Oh, he had seen plenty of groups of three in the intervening period, however, the certainty that God was giving him a message hadn't been as prominent as it was today.

But what did it mean?

The cat in the center was blind. Usually, the central item in such communiqués was the pillar of strength. Should he spit on some dirt and rub it on the cat's eyes? He thought about what Jesus had done for the blind man near the pool of Siloam.

As he mulled over the situation, Tommy Dorfler's shiny red Porsche roared by. The three cats slowly shuffled back to their sunning rock, and Father Romero nervously scrubbed his hands with the towelette before sitting down to finish his meal.

◆ ◆ ◆

TOMMY DORFLER loved the precipitous hairpin turns of Lake Van's northern coastal road, the E-99. Speeding around the unexpected switchbacks fed his James Bond fantasy—the vast quantity of gold awaiting him, *really awaiting him this time,* completed the dream. It was a dangerous scenario.

Tommy considered his changing circumstances. Before seeing the photo of the golden church, he had always assumed that he would bottle up the most powerful Turkish aphrodisiac (once he had found it), take it back to America, and make millions. Now, getting his hands on the gold in the photo seemed a more promising venture.

Scarcely halfway around the lake, the sun began to set. As the water turned from blue to orange-magenta, it was difficult to take his eyes off the lake; therefore, he didn't see the large tent on the other side of the road. But he did notice three scantily clad women walking toward it—they cut between him and the lake. The exposed flesh prompted Tommy to check his rear-view mirror at the precise moment the sun fell below the horizon. At exactly that moment, the lights of the sign on the tent came on: *Cirk Bulgar.*

He slowed the car.

In the middle of the Turkish wasteland, in the middle of nowhere, the flashing lights of the tiny Bulgarian Circus rivaled Las Vegas in Tommy Dorfler's mind. In his fantasy of having enough money to travel anywhere, to visit all the casinos of the world, with their beckoning blinking patterns of bright lights, he imagined he was in Monte Carlo; the three girls show girls from the grand casino. He turned around and cruised back.

A circus!

After four days in Dogubayazit looking for Stuart, he deserved a vacation. There was no need to rush to Batman tonight; the others would be asleep by the time he got there. This was exactly what he needed; Tommy loved circuses.

As he parked the car, two of the girls entered the tent; the third busied herself with opening the ticket booth. Her back was to him—she was arranging things in the booth—and he studied the nape of her neck through the glass.

"Excuse me."

She turned. *Beautiful.*

He pointed to the front row on the seating diagram while proffering a bill.

Her fingers touched his when she handed him his ticket. Tommy suspected it was not an accident. He felt an energy pass between them.

No one else was around so he decided to chat her up. It turned out that she was also one of the performers—the rope act. He promised to give it special attention, and she smiled.

"The show starts at eight." Her English was perfect.

"What can I do until then? That's an hour and a half—"

"We have the animals fenced in around the back—for the children—you could see those."

"Will you take me on a tour?"

"I have to sell tickets."

"I'm starving. Can I at least get something to eat?"

She scribbled on a piece of paper and said, "Give this to the man in the purple trailer. It's the canteen for the performers. This says to give you my plate." She signed her name "Nishka."

"What man?"

"The cook. He's the one who taught me English. He used to work on a ship."

"But what will you eat, Nishka?"

"I never have time to eat when I work in the ticket booth."

Tommy walked around to the rear of the main tent. Sure enough, he saw a collection of fenced-in animals. Before he got to the fence, he passed an open-backed van. Inside was a young boy stretching a pole through thick bars, scrubbing the floor beneath a huge rhinoceros. The animal was bigger than an SUV; the nose horn alone was at least four feet long. Tommy noticed that the bars bent outward in places where the rhino had charged them. He realized he had never seen such a large animal.

"That's big."

The boy jumped in surprise.

"Yes. Big problem, too."

"Oh really?"

"Yes. Master trade all good animals for nose-horn two years before. One nose-horn, one llama, one yak, one zebra."

"So?"

"Master think he train anything. Llama, yak, zebra—they no train."

"And the rhino?"

"He stand on stool, and he make terrible big noise. But he no train. Just trick."

"That's the point, isn't it? To get them to do tricks."

"But this trick no trick. I hide under seats…wait signal. Shoot nose-horn with pellet gun. Shoot him in rear…he make terrible noise. That trick of trick." He went back to swabbing the floor beneath the rhino.

Tommy walked to the purple trailer. Most of the circus people had finished eating and were leaving. He struck up a conversation with the cook. From the cook, he learned that the rhino was eating them out of house and home. Everyone felt that it had been a bad business deal. Now they rented the beast out for parties.

"Parties?"

"Yes. A certain type of rich person likes to have a rhinoceros chained in their garden while they are having a party."

"Amazing."

Practically as amazing as the man's flawless British accent; it was humorously incongruous in the tiny chow-wagon surrounded by picnic tables. He stifled a laugh.

"And they feed him too," the cook added, clearly pleased by that fact. "Would you like to rent him?"

"No thank you."

"The owner and his wife *can* train any animal—circus animals that is. But we don't have any circus animals anymore." The cook pointed out the window.

Tommy followed the cook's gaze to a field behind the trailer; there he saw a woman with six cows— the black and white kind— Holsteins. The cows all had their front legs upon a pedestal. The pedestal was built to rotate, and the cows were slowly turning it by stepping sideways with their hind legs.

"Things were better before he traded the horses for the rhino," the cook said longingly, turning back to wash the dishes.

PART OF THE CIRCUS show featured a trained duck that quacked in time with the band—or rather, the single synthesizer player with a versatile drum machine. The music built to dramatic silences in which the duck let forth, right on the beat. Tommy convinced himself that a hidden assistant was shooting the duck with pellets to cause the metrical quacking.

During the intermission, various animals were brought around to sit on people's laps. A photographer snapped photos—available after the show for the equivalent of ten dollars, a hefty sum in that region. By far, the most striking of these was a baby lion the size of a Saint Bernard. The animal sat on people with such acquiescence that Tommy supposed it had been drugged. But the drug was wearing off; the baby lioness batted the cheek of a young girl with a force that provoked quite a commotion. Fortunately, the animal's claws had been removed.

Nishka made the rounds; now she sold popcorn.

A girl of many talents.

Nishka's act was in the middle of the second half. She was strong. Her arms stretched straight out over her head, locking her taut body at a right angle to the rope; she spun around in time with the music, thirty feet above the ground, without a net.

AFTER THE SHOW, he saw her again. This time she was selling the photos to the people who'd had them taken at intermission. Someone must have developed them during the second half of the show. He joined the end of the line.

"Can I see you after this?" He swept his arm around the area as he said "this," and hoped his meaning was clear.

Nishka looked at him with an expression he'd seen before in the eyes of women from Albania, Bulgaria, Romania, and other small countries where Gypsy blood still flowed in significant quantities—that desperate, hungry look that said: *take me to America…Please! I'll do anything.*

"Yes," she whispered.

THE OTHER CIRCUS PEOPLE slept while Tommy and Nishka finished several bottles of wine with her brother. Billed as "The Invincible Man," Nishka's brother would break bottles in a flat wooden box and then remove his shoes and crunch the shards with his bare feet, closing his act by jumping up and down in the box furiously, drums beating louder and louder, his feet remaining unscathed. At a hidden signal, the drumming would stop unexpectedly, leaving only the sharp, excruciating sounds of flesh against broken glass. He wore leather pants and a leather jacket; his open puffy shirt exposed his ample chest hair. Really only his feet were invincible, having attempted to shield themselves by building callous upon callous throughout many years of mistreatment. His act was his only talent, and his need for empty bottles as props prompted him to consume large quantities of cheap wine every night.

TO TOMMY'S SURPRISE, they ended up sleeping in the center of the ring. Nishka placed her sleeping mat there every night. "It's like sleeping in the middle of a big bubble," she said.

Their spot at the center of the tent dome brought into sharp focus the blend of smells that are unique to circuses: a delicate intermingling of straw and sawdust soaked in the effluence of large cats, combined with elephant droppings and horse sweat. Here, rhinoceros and cow replaced elephant and horse. The substitution was subtle but noticeable, especially at ground level. The odor wrapped around them like a second blanket, as they drifted to sleep in each other's arms.

In the morning, Tommy lay on his back and stared groggily at the top of the tent. The rising sun brightened the canvas, minute by minute. The tent's support beams resembled the hands of a clock. Through the haze of his hangover, the two main beams made it appear to be ten after nine. The twelve spotlights spaced equidistantly around the edges mimicked numbers on a giant clock face. He heard a loud ticking that he soon learned was the rhinoc-eros eating, its mammoth horn periodically hitting one of the cage bars while it chewed. As he passed from sleep to consciousness, he imagined that he was inside a huge inverted clock. Nishka was gone. He walked quietly to his car.

FORTY-SEVEN

ANTARCTICA

2100 GMT

CAM CHECKED AND RECHECKED the SLUGS. It was eighteen hours before lunar apogee, and the probability of a coming mainshock had risen to seventy-three percent. That was far too low in the realm of predictive seismology. He needed a reading of ninety-two percent or higher to call it. His pulse accelerated.

Forensic seismology had never been this stressful. Before coming to Antarctica, he had spent most of his time detecting whether an event on the other side of the planet was an earthquake or a violation of the CTBT—the Comprehensive Test Ban Treaty; it was a breeze in comparison. Although effective nuclear testing had been miniaturized so much that it was practically impossible to separate a test from normal background seismological activity, everything had already taken place before the forensic seismologists were involved. It was simply a matter of collecting and interpreting the data.

He remembered working on the *Kursk* project in 2000. The Russians had insisted that a foreign submarine had collided with theirs, causing its eventual demise and the horrible death of all aboard. Forensic seismologists had been able to discover the truth about the tragedy—that one of the *Kursk's* own torpedoes had set off the chain reaction resulting in the disaster.

Few people knew the true nature of his current research; fewer would have been able to understand it: generative seismology—the capability of creating an earthquake thousands of miles away through synchronized application of very strong magnetic pulses at the Earth's poles. The Department of Defense had given him *carte blanche* for this one. The mere thought of being able to press a button and liquefy the ground beneath a potential adversary without radiation, well, it was like a drug for the guys at the pentagon—those with the security clearance to know that such a thing might be possible.

"If you can predict an earthquake, you can figure out how to cause one; just reverse the process." they said.

It wasn't that easy.

Man had inadvertently caused earthquakes through under-ground explosions or pumping water into deep wells, but those weren't among the methods that the pentagon was considering. Cam had already concluded that their strategic dreams in this area weren't going to be accomplished by teaching magnetotactic bacteria to swim in formation. Nonetheless, the FOG project—for "Fist Of God"—plodded along. The way the money came in, it did seem as if it were growing on trees. Moreover, when Cam visited Washington, D.C., people he had never met would approach him and wink and say things like, "Can we FOG them yet or "When can we start FOG-ing those guys, professor?"

He didn't feel good about that.

No. He didn't like that at all. What they were doing was more like linear predictive coding combined with the same recursive and adaptive prediction used in speech recognition. Because of this, Cam preferred to think of generative seismology as a big shout, a *shout* through the earth—it wasn't a "Fist," it was a "Shout of God."

He glanced back at the monitor. The probability had edged upwards. Chief Science Officer Chester Aristotle Morgenstern decided to get some sleep.

It won't be long.

FORTY-EIGHT

WEDNESDAY, JUNE 29

TURKEY

MORNING (GMT+3)

STUART AWOKE BEFORE DAWN and couldn't get back to sleep. He made a valiant attempt for forty minutes, but his mind was racing with memories of the previous week. He needed to walk off this extra mental energy. No, he needed to think, to use it up.

He knew that the wall of the crater would shield the true sunrise until well after its occurrence. The crater wall also protected Stauros from the full force of the summer heat, and for this Stuart was thankful.

The soft predawn light penetrated the still air to create an ethereal tranquility. Not a single cricket chirped.

He saw no signs of any other early risers, but suspected that the farm was already coming to life, ever so quietly.

He grabbed a study Bible outside the door of the darkened library. A deep shelf beside the entrance held several compartments of Bibles in various languages; these were for anyone who wanted to study God's Word on one of the many secluded benches. He felt the weight of the Bible in his grip.

Have I changed? Is this place doing something to me?

Stuart hadn't planned to end up at the garden but that's where he found himself. He made his way to the center and sat on a stone bench facing the cross. There was an identical bench to his left. Between the two benches, the spring bubbled— the source of the stream flowing through the ravine by the orchard at the far end of the crater. It was still too early for anyone else to be there, and he could hear the sound of the water emerging from the depths of the earth, starting its long journey to the sea. It bubbled like a coffee maker in slow motion.

Stuart tried to imagine the events that had taken place upon the cross in front of him.

Had God actually become a man?

And if so, had He become flesh merely because all creative artists are compelled to paint themselves into the picture, or write themselves into the play? Or, was it for the spiritual reasons Matthias had described?

He pictured Barnabas, and how joyous the jolly little man seemed to be about Roger's death—or anyone's death for that matter—referring to it as "sleep" or "being in the presence of the Lord." He realized that none of the people in Stauros had ever met anyone who didn't share their beliefs concerning the afterlife.

Stuart asked himself whether he was afraid to leave because it would mean having to face the reality of Roger's death, or whether it was the peace he found inside the crater that kept his life on hold; he relished being cut off from all the spitefulness of the outside world.

The people of Stauros…Were they this nice because they were Christians, or because they were removed from any influence of the nastiness of twenty-first century reality?

If a loving mind remained untarnished by the viciousness of the world as long as it was not exposed to it, wasn't that an argument against man's innate immorality?

What about me? Will I be different when I return to the outside world? If I return to the outside world, that is…

He reflected on the way his thoughts characterized the outside world as filled with spitefulness, nastiness, and viciousness. And conversely, how he felt about Stauros: filled with peace, love, and kindness.

Was it that the people of the crater needed religion to sustain themselves in their isolation? They appear to be self-sufficient, but are they?

Do I need anything outside myself to feel secure? I've behaved all my life. I'm not a liar or a thief. I'm still a virgin. I'm getting great grades in college. Why do I need God?

Still, he sensed he did need something, that he had been seeking something for a long time. He realized coincidences had been intensifying around him; specifically, he was meeting more Christians. Strangely, on occasion, he felt compelled to turn and run from them. And this made him recall the other types that were popping into his life with increasingly regularity: the ones who urged him to avoid the light. Doubtless, they were evil, while the ones they shunned were the true "good guys."

Why did some people automatically react to Christians with mocking, smirking, and sneering?

Not believing in God is also a belief. It implies believing in the non-existence of the divine.

He began to discern that the noncommittal stance wasn't the safe hiding place some people assumed it to be.

How can I be certain, Lord?

The trees spiraling around him were a good argument for the existence of a spiritual dimension…That is, if what he'd been told about them were true. He thought about his walk with Philios in the garden, and then his study of the maps in the seventh classroom. Remembering the inscriptions he'd seen on the wall of the fourth classroom, he opened his Bible to the third chapter of the Book of John.

Before he could focus on the page in front of him, the words of his Comparative Religions teacher echoed in his mind: "The Bible was written to explain the unexplainable things in the world. Leaders invented God as an answer to the questions posed by uneducated nomads, or maybe as a means to control them, to keep the peace. But science can now answer all those questions, thus, the God myth is unnecessary. Consequently, the Bible is unnecessary."

It seemed to make sense.

Or did it?

He had never heard of desert nomads asking profound philosophical questions, nor had he heard that the Bible had created a peaceful society. Jesus and his Apostles died in horrifying ways. That surely didn't convey the impression that there had been any success in controlling the early Christians. Hence, the theory of his Comparative Religions teacher was wrong.

He was tempted to ask, *if it's true Lord, then show me a sign,* but something deep within him protested that to do so would not be right. If he were going to believe, he had to believe without seeing signs and miracles.

There it was. The possibility that he might *believe* had actually crossed his mind. As quickly as it had, his stomach growled and distracted him. It was nearly time for breakfast.

His hunger lured his eyes to the trees closest to him.

Maybe I should eat a piece of fruit, he thought, immediately wishing he could retract the idea. It seemed a dirty thing to do, holding a Bible in his hand.

He considered his options. His tacit assumption that he would head a company and make tons of money when he graduated from college still loomed foremost. Christianity didn't appear to be compatible with worldly success. Had there ever been any prosperous Christians? The news media seemed to limit their coverage to people who were either highly self-reliant, or who attributed their successes to some crazy Eastern philosophy or New Age hodgepodge of ideas.

He wavered.

If I avoid this whole issue, I can at least get somewhere in the world...Then I can make up my mind later, when I have a good deal of security to fall back upon.

But this position left him empty inside. The idea of a world without God evoked feelings that shocked him. Now was the time to make some decisions.

He read John 3:16. "For God so loved the world that he gave his only begotten son, that whosoever believes in him shall not perish but have eternal life."

Philios, Barnabas, and Matthias had all insisted that one needed only to believe, and God would hear. Could it be true? Could there really be only one way to God?

A light wind rustled through the branches of the trees, and this time, for the first time, Stuart could plainly distinguish the words it whispered: *Yes. Come to me.*

Stuart did something he'd never done before; he fell on his knees and prayed.

"Lord, forgive me for all the times I have not done the right thing, especially when I knew what it was. Please help me not to sin from now on. I believe that Jesus was your Son and that He died on this cross, even for my own redemption. I believe You raised Him from death. I want to be one of *Your* children, too. Heavenly Father, please have mercy upon me. Amen."

Stuart sensed something filling an empty spot in his heart; a place he hadn't known existed. A pure warm sensation around him brought forth memories of when he was a baby. For a second, his mind seemed to stop and start again. He wondered if he were going crazy. When the rhythm of his thinking returned, he couldn't recall the reasons he had ever doubted Jesus. He couldn't even remember the thought processes that had led to those doubts. He felt as though his mind were becoming aware for the first time, as it had when he was a baby.

Light was flooding the clearing in the center of the garden. The sun was rising over the rim of the crater.

God was giving him the gift of salvation.

FORTY-NINE

ANTARCTICA

0600 GMT

C AM CAME BACK to the control room after nine hours of tossing and turning in his bed, drifting in and out of fitful sleep. The place was crowded. The SLUGS had gone on parade less than an hour earlier, and the probability of a mainshock had risen to well over ninety-two percent. Cam knew it would hit one hundred percent when the moon reached full apogee. Now, came the worst part.

He went back to his office and drank a small bottle of antacid. He was getting too old for this.

Ultimately, it rested upon his shoulders to decide whether to issue a warning. But first he had to make the call—to verify the quake to the pentagon. If they learned of it through monitoring the remote backups, thirty-minute delayed, they wouldn't be happy with him. He weighed the various outcomes—anything to postpone the inevitable phone call. *Let others make the decision.* DOD would have a dozen people on the question within minutes. Even now, they were undoubtedly calculating projections about the effect of another megathrust along the NAFZ. He knew people were making simulations for economists, for politico-sociologists, for intermediaries and liaisons working for "men of power" throughout the world.

They would want to know whether the NATO bases could survive the quake, but mainly to draft a damage assessment.

They would want to know how many lives might be lost, but only among those whose lives they attempted to spare.

They would want to play God.

He suspected that they would never authorize a warning announcement. To do so was to admit that predictive seismology was a reality—and once people knew that, it was only a matter of time before others took the next logical step to generative seismology, and generative seismology would fall into the wrong hands; it had been the same with nuclear weapons.

Cam searched his cabinet for another bottle of antacid while he glanced repeatedly at the telephone. If he didn't phone them, they would phone him. He was very tired. Weary. He longed to take a slow walk in the forest; unfortunately, it was fifty degrees below zero outside and there wasn't a tree within a thousand miles.

What would happen if he didn't answer the telephone when rang? Over the next nine hours, he asked himself that question again and again.

FIFTY

TURKEY

IN THE MORNING, Brad, Margaret, and Meredith continued the task they had begun upon their arrival in Batman
twelve hours earlier: showing photos of Stuart all around town.
The dusk had deepened into darkness, and they had gone to sleep
discouraged.

Now, at the edge of town in the blaze of daylight, they came
upon a man coaxing goats into a wagon.

"Did you bring the photos of the 'goat man'?" Meredith asked.

"Of course." Brad flipped through the items in his folder, then
handed her a small stack.

The man in the photo!

She ran over to him and held up a photo of Stuart.

He pointed at the photo and laughed. Much to Meredith's
surprise, he started singing.

"Ah get bug drive-een up down de sum ole trip."

The mispronunciation stumped her for a moment, and then
she realized: *The Beach Boys!*

The man looked to be a hundred years old, but it was the first
solid lead they had. It broke the tension that had been squeezing
her tighter and tighter since their disappointments in Dogubayazit.
She hugged him, and he grinned.

"Hassan," he said, pointing at his chest.

"Meredith," she replied, "pleased to meet you."

Brad and Margaret stared at the two in astonishment.

With some difficulty, Hassan communicated that he could take them to the spot where he had last seen Stuart. He used sentences that were mainly single words: "Place...Ride...Boys go..."

Hassan pointed at the long flat cart full of goats and vegetables.

"I can't," Margaret whined.

"Yes you can, dear."

"Come on Mrs. Pierce." Meredith was already in the back of the cart.

Brad and Meredith each gripped one of Margaret's hands as they hoisted her into the wagon. At the same moment, Hassan said something in Turkish that must have meant 'giddy up' because the primitive vehicle promptly started moving, and Margaret plopped down with a thump.

Ten minutes later the older woman had arranged her seat to some degree of satisfaction; she eyed the goats with uneasiness while her companions stared out across the countryside, waiting for her to calm down.

AHEAD OF THEM, a cloud of dust appeared in the distance, growing larger by the second. Gradually, the incongruent sputtering of an engine broke through the periodic baying of goats. Then, to everyone's surprise, a booming baritone voice singing *Dona Nobis* burst through the cacophony.

"Doh-hoh-nah, Noh-hoh-bees, Pah-hah-hah-ahchem."

The wagon pulled over to let the vehicle pass by.

Instead of passing, the motorcycle slowed to a stop. Father Romero stared incredulously at the three Americans in the back of the wagon. The goats became silent.

Hassan looked on as the four stood chattering on the road between the wagon and the motorcycle.

After hearing their story, Father Romero asked if he could accompany them. They agreed without hesitation.

He turned the motorcycle around and then motioned Hassan to proceed.

"No... Scare goats...Motor scare...Sour milk." Hassan pointed back and forth between the goats and the motorcycle.

"I can't leave the motorcycle in the middle of nowhere...It's a rental." In all directions, the desert plain extended as far as they could see.

There appeared to be no solution.

"I have an idea," Father Romero said. He jumped on the motorcycle, waved goodbye, and sped off in the direction from which he'd come.

Twenty minutes later, they saw him, standing by the side of the road with his thumb sticking out. Hassan slowed the wagon and Father Romero jumped in.

"Where's the motorcycle?"

"I stashed it behind those rocks."

◆ ◆ ◆

HASSAN STOPPED THE WAGON at Cattakkopru on the west side of the arching Malabadi Bridge. He pointed across the bridge and said, "Boys." Then he pointed east and said, "Me." They got the message.

The four of them went around to the front of the wagon and shook the old farmer's hand.

"Licorice?" he asked.

Meredith recalled that Roger always managed to have some licorice with him, and the memory of Stuart's dead friend erased the smile from her face.

"He's asking for licorice," she said. "Anyone have any licorice?"

No one did.

The farmer looked disappointed.

Father Romero had an idea. Taking off the crucifix he'd received from Bryce and Earl, he placed it around Hassan's neck.

Hassan inspected it closely.

"Yayzoos Kreestoos," he said.

Father Romero gave him a blessing.

He grinned and waved goodbye.

The sound of the Turkish farmer trying to sing his Beach Boys tune receded in the distance.

"Well, what do we do now?" Father Romero's tone made it clear that he assumed the others knew where they were headed.

In the ensuing silence, the four of them realized they were very much alone. Margaret's breathing accelerated, and Meredith glanced worriedly at Brad.

"Calm down, Margie," He said. "Calm down."

AFTERNOON

MATTHIAS HAD LEFT for Batman before sunrise, with a cart of fresh honey. *I'll be able to sell all this before sunset.* If prior experience were any indication, his success was guaranteed.

Four tourists—Americans—huddled around a map as he crossed the Malabadi Bridge and Matthias recognized Meredith instantly. There was no mistaking that hair; Stuart's description had been perfect.

Their eyes met, and Matthias quickly focused farther ahead, his gaze continuing past the four out-of-place travelers. No one noticed the momentary hesitation of the cart.

Matthias surmised that these people must be looking for Stuart. The older couple was probably Stuart's parents; he had no idea who the priest might be.

The crunching of gravel became louder as the cart slowed.

They could have no idea of Stuart's whereabouts; they appeared to be hopelessly lost, even here at the bridge. *What would happen if the disoriented search party were left to their own devices?* Soldiers—or worse, the police—might pick them up. That might lead to a more serious investigation. The fate of Stauros was in his hands.

It's too early for me to be deciding such things. He hadn't officially assumed the responsibility for the settlers yet. His father had many more years left before it was time to pass the baton.

Matthias pulled the cart over, a quarter of a mile farther along. He prayed, "Heavenly Father, what should I do?"

Within minutes, the cart was headed back to the bridge.

The four were so engrossed in their map that they didn't notice him as he stepped down and walked to them.

"Meredith?"

Everyone turned and stared at him.

"Do I know you?" she asked. She searched his face.

"No," he answered. "But I know Stuart."

Immediately, they surrounded him, all speaking at once.

"Wait. Wait," Matthias said. "Don't worry, Stuart is fine. He's safe. I can take you to him."

"Will you?" Margaret wiped away tears.

Matthias led them to his cart. "Would you care for some honey? It's the best in the region." Twisting the top of one of the jars he added, "This one should be particularly tasty."

Brad squeezed in beside Matthias in the front; Father Romero, Margaret, and Meredith climbed into the back. They sat on jars of honey, between jars of honey, and surrounded by more jars of honey, dipping their fingers into the one open honey pot in the middle of the wagon.

From where he was sitting, Father Romero could see the initials "RBW" carved into the side of the wagon behind the women.

"What was Roger's middle name?"

"Bassett, I think."

"Ah." He didn't mention the carved initials, or the bloodstains beneath them.

FIFTY-ONE

TOMMY DORFLER got there late as usual. He had started at dawn, after his rollicking night twenty-five miles from Tatvan. *Just doing research on Turkish aphrodisiacs*, he said to himself.

The hotel clerk in Batman told him that the Pierces and Meredith had left early that morning. That was to be expected, but he had hoped they would have returned for lunch. No such luck.

Walking from the hotel, he saw a Western-looking couple getting out of a rental car—a Mercedes. Their clothes were American; probably they were, too.

The woman was a knockout. "This will only take a second," she said.

California! Her accent was a dead giveaway. He could even tell that it was acquired; she wasn't a native.

He put on his sunglasses as they walked by.

Adjusting his route to pass next to their car, he peered into the window. There, on the back seat, was a photo of the golden church.

Tommy's heart started racing.

"Bond... James Bond," he said to himself.

Within moments, he had moved his car around the corner to a spot that provided an unobstructed view of the Mercedes.

Across the street, a Turk—a Muslim—sat in a Renault Clio. He couldn't shake the feeling that the strange man appeared to be amused by his attempts at subterfuge.

FIVE MINUTES LATER, Bryce and Earl came out of the hotel in a huff.

They sat in the car for several minutes. Earl was setting up the Transmogrifier for Bryce to use as a guide while they followed the GPS-tracker embedded in Father Romero's crucifix.

The Mercedes roared to life and sped out of town. Moments later the Porsche followed.

Dobro, not far behind in the Clio, tried to make sense of the situation through his dust-coated windshield.

♦♦♦

BRYCE SAID, "This is easy," as she followed the little dot inching across the map on the screen of the FRM. The road was straight for twenty miles.

She watched as the tracking device stopped beyond Cattakko-pru, and then backtracked a bit before heading eastward.

Halfway to Kozluk, Earl slammed on the brakes, as Hassan's cart appeared to materialize out of the thick dust in front of them. The goat man had stopped to let them pass.

Earl and Bryce jumped out of the car and approached the wagon. It contained nothing but goats and vegetables.

"He's wearing the crucifix," Earl said.

"Where did you get that?" Bryce asked, pointing.

Hassan didn't understand.

She lifted the crucifix level with his eyes. "This!"

"Oh," he said, an expression of comprehension crossing his face.

"Ah wanna fine a new place where de keeds are heep," Hassan sang, trying to imitate the Beach Boys.

Earl turned back to the car in disgust.

"Let's go," he said.

"Round, roun, gateroun. Ah gate-around," Hassan sang.

◆ ◆ ◆

TOMMY DORFLER couldn't think of anything else to do except keep driving; slowly, he continued past the Mercedes. He tried to imagine what James Bond would have done in this situation.

Dobro followed, maintaining a safe distance.

There was a covered well a quarter of a mile farther, and Hassan stopped his cart to water the horse. Tommy pulled over to the side of the road.

Dobro kept going, but slowed as much as possible. He slowed to a stop a thousand feet farther, pulled out his binoculars, and focused on Tommy's Porsche. He saw that Tommy was watching the Mercedes; it still hadn't moved.

Why is everyone so interested in that goat cart?

◆ ◆ ◆

FATHER ROMERO had no idea of the confusion his gift to Hassan was causing at that moment. He looked at Margaret and Meredith. All four of them were dusty, stinking like goats, and covered with goat hairs.

"You were at the funeral," he said.

Meredith nodded.

"You're Jewish, aren't you?"

"So?"

"I was wondering what brought you to Turkey."

"I'm the girlfriend," she explained. "Meredith Montgomery."

"Pleased to meet you."

There hadn't been time for introductions in the goat cart. The goats had never stopped their noise, nor their constant butting of the unwelcome guests into new positions.

"And you?" Father Romero looked at Margaret.

"I think the question should be, why are *you* here?" she said.

"I spent three years researching Byzantine churches in this general region. Even wrote a book about it. It was a bestseller in monasteries."

The two women laughed.

"My book claims to be the 'Complete Compendium,' yet I don't recognize the church in this photograph." He pulled out the photo they all knew so well.

They stared at it, not knowing what to say.

"What's a Byzantine church?" Margaret asked.

"A church built during the Byzantine empire."

Father Romero responded to her blank stare. "Meaning from the beginning of the fifth century to 1453. The Golden Age of the Church Fathers overlaps with that, as do all seven crusades."

"And how do you come up with those dates?" Meredith asked.

"It's from the beginning of the early middle ages until the time when Constantinople fell to the Turks, the event that established the Ottoman Empire. Three of the seven ecumenical councils had already taken place to establish critical church doctrines: the Nicene Creed; then, the fact that Jesus had a true human soul; and finally, the fact that Jesus had a human body. Fully human and fully divine, the incarnation of God is a mystery that history has taught us to respect."

"I thought Byzantine referred to architecture," Meredith said.

"The architectural style we call Byzantine gathered momentum after the fall of Rome in AD 476. Byzantine churches have round arches, domes on top of pendentives, and foliage patterns in relief on moldings, as well as on the capitals of their columns—those ornamented ends that hold up the roof supports. Mosaics and frescoes decorate their interiors."

Father Romero pointed to parts of the church in the photograph as he spoke.

"Great. Well, we're trying to find Stuart."

"I understand. And I sincerely pray that he is at the village in this picture."

Meredith pointed to Matthias.

"He says Stuart's there."

"And so is the church."

◆ ◆ ◆

MEREDITH WONDERED what Grandma Miriam would say about her search for roots if she could see her now? Here she was, sitting with an anti-Semitic atheist, across from a priest, on her way to a Byzantine Christian church, where she hoped to find her *goyish* boyfriend. And all this, in a Muslim country. Without a doubt, she was heading in the opposite direction from Israel, in many ways.

At least this was a utility cart and not a wagon full of porkers.

FIFTY-TWO

BRAD PIERCE STUDIED Matthias during the trip.

"You're not one of those Kurdish Separatists, are you?"

Matthias smiled. "No."

"A Shiite Muslim?"

"I'm a Christian."

"Yes, but are you part of the Islamic Jihad?"

Matthias realized that Brad had no idea of the meaning of the terms he was using.

"That would be difficult. First, Kurdish Separatists are people from the Kurdistan region—the plateau encompassing Southeast Turkey, Northwest Iran, and Northern Iraq. They want to form an autonomous Kurdish state, hence, the name.

"Jihad" means "Holy War."

Islam is the religion of the Muslims. There are two main divisions of Islam, the Sunnis and the Shiites. The main Sunni sect is the Wahabis; the most important Shiite sects are the Fatimids and the Assassins."

"The Assassins, eh? Any chance they've assassinated my boy?"

"None whatsoever. I spoke with him last night."

"He isn't a prisoner is he?"

"No. He's not a prisoner."

"And you're sure they're not brainwashing him? I've heard all about Stockholm syndrome."

Matthias had, too. Stockholm syndrome was a defense mechanism of hostages who sympathized with their captors out of desperation; the name was a nod to a 1973 hostage situation at a bank in Stockholm; Patty Hearst and Elizabeth Smart were American examples. "No, he's not being brainwashed, but I do believe he is having some profound thoughts about God."

"Religion is a crutch for weak people," Brad retorted automatically. He turned to see whether Father Romero had overheard his remark, then he winked at Margaret and nodded to Meredith.

"Are you sure about that?"

"As sure as we're sitting here," Brad said.

"A crutch for weak people..." Matthias considered the idea. The concept was a new one for him. "Maybe everyone needs a crutch to survive in this world, but for some people that crutch is alcohol, drugs, cigarettes, a spouse, money, sex, or power. We're all weak, but not all crutches are negative. A crutch can give us strength. It can heal us, and it can allow us to function when we otherwise wouldn't be capable. Maybe the human condition is such that we naturally need some help—a crutch—to reach a higher spiritual level, like a mountain-climber needs a rope, or more; would you try to scale Everest without oxygen?"

"Hey, I'm an atheist. I don't believe in anything."

"That in itself is a belief. The word 'belief' means 'what you believe to be the truth.' If you believe atheism is true, that is your belief. And for many atheists, their atheistic belief is no more than a crutch to justify an immoral lifestyle."

"I mean I don't believe in God."

"Then you believe in the non-existence of God. Why do you think there are more than a billion Christians?"

Brad mulled over the question and looked toward the mountain in the distance. "How can you tell that the Christian God is the right one; what if it's the Muslim god, or the Hindu god? Or, what if the true God hasn't been found yet? Religions are a way of giving hope to the hopeless."

"Just a second sir. Give me a moment to answer some of those questions."

"What if I don't believe in a supernatural world? What if I believe this is all there is—that there is no such thing as a soul?"

"Is that what you believe?"

"I said I didn't believe in anything." Brad wiped his brow and thought for a minute. I'm not even superstitious. If I were superstitious and I fell into a manhole after a black cat crossed my path, I'd probably link the two events. Christians do the same thing when a fortunate coincidence happens—they assume it is a blessing from God. Can you tell me one miracle that can't be explained by science?"

"By their very nature, miracles cannot be explained by science. That's the definition of the word 'miracle,' something that can't be explained by science."

"That answer is a cop-out. If people were left alone, they wouldn't believe in anything. God is something that people try to add to a person. They've been trying to add God to me all my life."

Matthias smiled. "Maybe they care about you."

"Did God create evil and suffering? If He did, why? And if so, that means He's not so incredibly *good* as everyone makes Him out to be. If He didn't, then isn't it true that something more powerful than Him must have created it?"

Matthias was surprised at how well formulated Brad's questions were. He'd asked them before, if only to himself.

"Suffering can teach us things like patience and trust. In addition, it can cause others to offer us compassion and love. And, if we're the ones helping a suffering person, we can take away much from the experience."

"And if that doesn't apply?"

"Some suffering results from sin, but some suffering doesn't involve our *own* sin. Though, when it does, God has always given us a free choice whether to sin or not. Did you ever consider that maybe God values the free will to believe in Him, as more important than pain and suffering?"

"Even babies or children too young to sin, too young to choose?"

Matthias enjoyed defending his faith. "You've probably heard people say 'God needed him or her' or 'The Lord called her back.' Maybe that contains some truth. Heaven is a vast realm of existence about which we know little. So far, we have had to pass through death to get there. If God did need a soul for a purpose we can't possibly fathom, He can take what He wants. Or, if you accept the idea that many things and events in our world have corresponding but not necessarily similar aspects in Heaven, then such deaths and suffering don't need an earthly explanation."

Brad's expression showed that he believed he'd unearthed a fatal flaw in Matthias' reasoning. "You say that God wants us to make a free choice between sinning and loving Him, but if God knows everything in the past, present, and future, then how can free will exist? If he already knows I'm going to Hell, then how can I do anything to change the situation? Either God doesn't know the future, or I can't change my fate; they both can't be true."

Matthias knew they both *could* be true, but he didn't know how to get that across to Brad. "You seem to think that Christianity is so perfect, so transparent that you should be able to understand every facet of it. Everything in existence has some unexplained properties; why don't you allow Christianity the same freedom? Surely, you can't expect to understand the mind of God. If you could, you'd be God, yourself."

"I'm just not convinced that a God of Love as they call Him, would allow so many to end up in Hell."

"Why not? If the choice is to be genuine, people must have the option of totally rejecting God and God must respect that right. Still, if His love is authentic, He cannot permit his loved ones to do whatever they please—do you permit your own son to do everything he wants?"

"No. Certainly not." Brad paused, thinking of Stuart. "Is Stuart where he is because of his own free will?"

"At this point, I believe he is."

Matthias' answer placated him. Brad quickly returned to the theological debate. Matthias got the idea that these were questions he had pondered his whole life. For some reason, he trusted Matthias to give him the answers.

"How can you Christians say that the people of other religions are going to burn in Hell for eternity? What about God's chosen people, the Israelites...are they going to burn in Hell because they don't believe in Jesus?"

"I'm glad you mentioned burning in Hell. Here's an illustration: Suppose you were in a building that was on fire and someone came and told you there was only one way out, that all other routes would lead to your death. Would you question that person? I doubt it."

"It might depend on who was telling me. I don't want to believe in something purely out of fear."

"There's a big difference between legitimate warnings and scare tactics," Matthias replied.

"I've lived my life 'doing unto others as I would have them do unto me,' and I never needed God to tell me that such behavior was the right thing to do."

"Then maybe you could tell me *why* 'doing unto others as you would have them do unto you' is the right thing to do."

"It just is."

"There can't be a law without a lawmaker."

"It must be built into humans; the way preservation of the species is built into animals."

"Then does it hold true in *all* situations?"

"Well, maybe not all situations."

"That's the difference: morality based upon God is absolute; there are no exceptions."

Brad considered this. He turned to look at Margaret. The three in the back of the wagon had been attentively following the debate in the front seat.

"He has an answer for everything," Brad said to no one in particular.

◆ ◆ ◆

BRYCE AND EARL sat in the air-conditioned car looking at the screen of the FRM.

"Now what do we do?"

"We could go to both craters."

"Yeah. I suppose. But they're more than a hundred miles apart. It would be nice to know which one is more likely to be the right one. Plus, I'm not that interested in traveling any deeper into the area of Kurdish conflict."

"Richard's going to go ballistic if we aren't the first ones to reach the crater. Think what he's capable of—he might even kill the priest!"

Earl considered his position carefully.

"I think...I think...It could be possible to 'ping' Meredith's cell phone from one of our satellites, if she has it turned on," he said.

"You can do that?"

Earl knew very well that he could, but clearly was not sure whether he wanted to share that fact. "Yes. I thought it would be a good idea to monitor her calls."

"Uh huh," Bryce said, wondering what else Earl was monitoring.

"Let me have the Transmogrifier," he said.

"No. Show me how to do it."

"Please, Bryce."

"Really Cole. I can do it from here."

Earl reached over and typed some commands too quickly for Bryce to see. A list of phone numbers appeared on the screen.

"Hers is the second from the top. Just select it and press the ENTER key.

Bryce scanned the list and saw her private phone number near the middle of it. She grimaced at Earl. He smiled sheepishly.

I'll get to the bottom of this, Bryce silently vowed.

Meredith's information appeared on the screen: a list of conversations with times, dates, and durations, as well as the name and number of the other party. There was an on-screen button labeled "PING."

Bryce pressed the button. Immediately, the display changed. The map returned, and precise coordinates appeared across the bottom of the screen.

"That's it!" Earl exclaimed. "She's approaching the closer crater, the one to the northeast. He slammed the car into gear, and leaving a trail of dust, the Mercedes sped off back the way they'd come.

TOMMY WAS STANDING by the well, flirting with a young Turkish woman when he heard the Mercedes roar off. He ran back to his car and followed.

Unnoticed by anyone, Dobro stayed behind him all the way.

EARL SHOUTED, "Get Richard on the phone!"

"My, my. You're bossy," Bryce said.

"We have to tell him of the change in destination."

Minutes later, Richard's face appeared on the screen. The interior of his private jet was visible in the background.

"Progress," he demanded.

"Here comes the location." Bryce quickly transmitted him the map to the crater where Meredith's cell phone was heading.

"I'll be touching down in Diyarbakir in less than an hour."

"Good. Did you bring the chopper?"

"Of course."

"Well, we should be in the crater by the time you arrive. Let's hope there's a landing spot inside."

"Surely, in a crater of that size—"

"We have no data between the edges… except that photo."

"Bryce, one more thing."

"Shoot."

"The most recent simulations I ran on our earthquake problem… 97% verified a main thrust coming within the next six hours."

Late Afternoon

EARL DROVE the Mercedes as close as possible to the crater's rim. The road approached it from the northeast. He parked, and the two of them jumped out of the car.

Earl packed the Transmogrifier into his knapsack, and they both changed into climbing boots. He produced some cords, harnesses, and belays; he added some crampons just in case, and they headed to the side of the crater.

TOMMY DORFLER realized there was no way to get close without them seeing him, so he continued on, watching in his rear-view mirror. Evidently, they intended to scale the crater's outside wall.

I'll climb from the other side. He eyed the northwest rim.

DOBRO SLOWED the Clio as much as he could without arousing suspicions, and then stopped due north of the crater. He grabbed his binoculars. From where he parked, he could see both Bryce and Earl, as well as Tommy. Trying to appear incongruous, he got out, unfolded his map across the hood of his car, and pretended to study it, periodically raising the binoculars to his eyes.

◆ ◆ ◆

MATTHIAS LED the Pierces, Father Romero, and Meredith through the ravine. He worried what his father would say when they got to Stauros. More than that, he worried what Philios would say.

He avoided any mention of the cross as he fielded the traveler's questions concerning the history of their destination. Would he have the opportunity to get Stuart alone and convince him of the need for secrecy?

Stepping into the crater, they stopped and surveyed the sight before their eyes.

Father Romero leaned toward Matthias and said, "This place feels holy."

"It is, Father. It is."

Father Romero beamed. "Let us pray."

Brad turned away and picked an orange from one of the trees.

Margaret watched as Meredith moved closer to the priest.

She and Matthias bowed their heads, and Father Romero said a quick prayer. He thanked God for leading them safely to their goal.

Matthias led them to the church.

"Is Stuart in there?" Meredith asked him. She could barely contain herself.

Matthias nodded.

FIFTY-THREE

S TUART HAD SPENT the day elated and thankful. He'd looked for Matthias—he wanted to tell someone about his experience in the garden— but the young man had already left with a cart full of honey.

Stuart went to the library to return the Bible he'd borrowed. He saw Barnabas inside, straightening up the reading room.

"Barnabas. You'll never guess what's happened."

"Oh. I might."

"The most wonderful thing."

"Tell me."

Stuart described his early morning walk in the garden and how he had given himself to the Lord.

"Wonderful. A celebration of angels in Heaven is taking place."

"Really?"

"Yes, whenever a person is saved, the angels have a celebration. 'There is rejoicing in the presence of the angels of God over one sinner who repents.' (Luke 15:10)"

Barnabas paused for a moment.

"Let me give you a verse from scripture as a present. I'm sure you'll receive many similar gifts in your lifetime. This is from the second chapter of James, verse seventeen: 'Faith by itself, if it is not accompanied by action, is dead.'"

Stuart committed it to memory.

"Keep a watchful eye to everything you do. Let it be for the glory of the Lamb of God. And remember to share your faith at every opportunity."

"I wish I could share it with Meredith. I feel like telling everyone I know."

"God might arrange for that to happen sooner than you think."

Barnabas hugged Stuart.

"Let's go tell Philios."

They walked to the church.

◆ ◆ ◆

STUART AND BARNABAS rounded the corner of the church just as Matthias led Stuart's parents, Meredith, and Father Romero across the bridge.

Meredith's heart skipped a beat. "Stuart," she shouted as she ran to him. "You're alive." Tears streamed down her cheeks.

They embraced for longer and tighter than ever before. Meredith felt as if their bodies were melting into one; she hadn't realized how much she had been in denial about the possibility that Stuart might have been dead.

"Oh Meredith," he said, "something amazing has happened." Stuart took her hand and walked her toward Brad and Margaret Pierce.

He hugged his parents and said, "I want you to hear this, too."

There was so much to tell—so much about Jesus.

Philios had been walking toward them, but he stopped when he reached Matthias and Barnabas.

◆ ◆ ◆

BRYCE AND EARL made steady progress up the crater wall, and Bryce surveyed the land below them. As their elevation increased, she could see the rays of *ejecta* radiating from the crater, bits and pieces that had been hurled out at high speed when the meteor struck the earth, thousands, maybe millions, of years ago. She could also make out the *ejecta blanket*, material that had been tossed out at low speed after the impact, lying like a blanket around the crater.

They reached the top of the rim in less than an hour.

Pulling herself to the other edge of the crater rim, she got her first glimpse of the garden—it was lovely—the village, the church, the farm.

Standing on the northeast rim of the crater, she saw steam rising from the pond between her and the garden. The golden church drew her eyes to the middle of the crater; it was attached to some type of study center, she reasoned. Her gaze continued around in that direction—counterclockwise—and she saw, directly across from her, a field of grazing horses; it made her think of the stables of her parents' farm. A stream divided the horse field from the orchard and the vegetable fields from the farm. And between her and the farm, a tiny village stood: she estimated some forty houses.

Then she saw the people. Moving; going about their day-to-day activities; and it hit her: she was finally seeing between the edges!

Pretty as a picture. Bryce remembered Roger's photograph. It didn't capture the peaceful majesty before her eyes.

Thinking about the photo made her think about Roger's death. She realized the only possible cause: "Death by earthquake"—an earthquake-induced fall from the same crater rim upon which she now stood. He must have been standing over there, above the orchard, she guesstimated; instantly, she spun around and grasped the nearest boulder as if the earthquake Richard had predicted would happen in the next second.

When it didn't, she let her breath out and relaxed. She returned her gaze to the garden, this time taking the whole panorama into her field of vision.

There was no doubt in her mind: the garden was unique on the planet. Definitely a one-of-a-kind—it was beautiful.

She wondered how the Darwinists would explain such a phenomenon.

Darwin was under attack at the university again, and in the last week of classes, she had received a form requesting her signature. In so many words, the accompanying letter explained that all professors in the sciences were strongly urged to sign an attestation that they would not refer, in any way, to the Intelligent Design theory that was sweeping America.

Bryce did not put her signature on anything without adequate consideration. But her decision to explore the issue on the net was probably more a result of her exposure to some of the controversial hypotheses being researched by other recipients of RRR grants.

What she had found out about Darwin had troubled her. Java man, Peking man, Nebraska man, and Ramapithecus had all been revealed as hoaxes or apes. Even *Lucy*, a 3.6 million year old jawbone discovered in Ethiopia and assumed to be the missing link, had been reclassified as an extinct ape. All this had taken place so quietly that she realized the public was unaware of any such removal of authenticity, particularly if she, a scientist no less, was unaware of these goings on.

She'd learned that the dating of the "Mitochondrial Eve" was in question—the claim that global variation in mitochondrial DNA pointed to a single female ancestor of all humans was no longer a certainty.

Eve—the mitochondrial Eve—was purported to have lived one hundred thousand to one million years ago. Nonetheless, further study of the mutation rates in mitochondrial DNA placed Eve's life within the time-period suggested by the Bible. Again, the refutation of the original claims had taken place with little fanfare; Bryce suspected that few people were aware that the theory now supported a Biblical timeline.

The value of carbon dating had been called into question when a group of Christians in Texas buried a dead cat, and then dug up the skeleton two years later. They took it to lab in Houston for carbon dating. The scientists placed its age at six million years. The group who had originally buried the cat attempted to "go public" with the exposé of the evolutionists' favorite offensive tool, but the story had been reported only in Christian publications.

Bryce's whole belief foundation, the infallibility of science, was crumbling.

What started as an afternoon search for "Darwinism" on the net, consumed the first two weeks of summer vacation. She discovered that the scientific community was no closer to finding a missing link between apes and humans than they ever had been. In fact, they had never established a macro-evolutionary Darwinian transition between any species whatsoever, although everyone seemed to believe the contrary.

Bryce reread "The Origin of the Species" by Charles Darwin. She discovered that, although his theories of microevolution—those minor inter-species variations that are reinforced through natural selection and adaptation—had been firmly validated, the application of his macro-evolutionary claims, that the random mutation of genes produced a gradual, step-by-step progression from single-celled bacteria through fish to apes to humans, had never been proven.

Darwin himself stated, "If it could be demonstrated that any complex organism existed which could not possibly have been formed by numerous, successive, slight modifications, my theory would absolutely break down."

Michael Behe, William Dempski, and Jonathan Wells, all respectable scientists with doctorates, had raised a credible line of reasoning that helped to bring the Intelligent Design theory to the table. Essentially, Darwin and his colleagues had viewed anything they couldn't see or understand, as an impenetrable, and usually unquestionable, "black box"—cells, for example. As soon as scientists were able to look into those black boxes, it became clear that their workings could not have developed by chance.

Proponents of Intelligent Design, known as "ID," argued from a scientific standpoint: now that we had decoded the genome, it was obvious DNA conveyed encoded information. Information cannot come into being by itself—neither can it encode itself.

Now that scientists had observed the smallest particles of life, they discovered a threshold of "specified complexity," the crossing of which was the mark of an intelligent designer. And that threshold had been crossed, in the simplest living cell.

Individual cells were revealed to contain motors, pumps, power plants, supply lines with delivery vehicles and docking machines, messaging and labeling systems, recycling units, timing devices, sensors, even rotary motors with universal joints. Michael Denton pointed out that these cellular machines weighing less than ten-to-the-minus-twelfth grams (one quadrillionth of a gram) consist of some one hundred thousand million atoms, and are far more complex than anything ever devised by man.

The notion of "irreducible complexity," put forth by Behe, demonstrated that these workings could be reduced only so far, meaning that there was a particular point at which a minimum set of components would have had to assemble themselves simultaneously. The analogy of a bicycle helped her understand this: one can remove only so many parts from a bicycle before it ceases to function as a bicycle. Bicycle handlebars don't spontaneously come into being without enough of the other parts already there to justify their existence.

At the same time scientists were discovering the workings of irreducible complexity, paleontologists were unearthing the Cambrian explosion—the simultaneous appearance of all the major animals in the fossil record. This presented great difficulties for a Darwinian insistence upon gradual change.

The discovery that the major categories of life had appeared first, and then diversified was contrary to Darwin's predictions.

To make matters worse, ID researchers had uncovered an ongoing and systematic tampering with information for one reason: to advance Darwin's fallacies. The evolutionary charts Bryce had seen throughout her life in all her textbooks, laying out embryos and species side by side to illustrate progressive evolutionary transformation, proved to be false—doctored to support the Darwinian notion of common ancestry.

Darwin's own famous example of beak size among finches in the Galapagos Islands was found to be spurious. In the late twentieth century, researchers returned to Galapagos and ascertained that the change in beak size of the finches was cyclical, and merely allowed them to adapt to climatic variance. Yet, the National Science Association's 1998 booklet, "Teaching about Evolution and the Nature of Science," described the phenomenon without mentioning that the beaks returned to their normal size, instead encouraging teachers to urge students to contemplate the result of 200 years of such an increase in beak size as a catalyst for the evolution of a new species of finch.

Another often-used example of Darwin's theories was also shot down: that of peppered moths whose wing colors darkened during the Industrial Revolution, an adaptation attributed to the tree trunks they were accustomed to perching on having been darkened with soot. In 1999, researchers discovered that peppered moths don't perch on tree trunks. All the photographic evidence had been staged. A biologist at the University of Massachusetts came forward and admitted having glued dead pepper moths onto trees during the filming of a NOVA documentary.

The whole Darwin issue was so embroiled in deception and worse than that, it was committed to false teaching. It crossed her mind that removing a supreme being from the picture also served to remove a person's framework of any type of absolute morality. Preposterous lies were based upon other preposterous lies, *ad infinitum*; it was the proverbial "house of cards" effect.

Astronomer Fred Hoyle had summed up Darwin's macroevolution theory succinctly: "A junkyard contains all the bits and pieces of a Boeing 747, dismembered and in disarray. A whirlwind happens to blow through the yard. What is the chance that after its passage a fully assembled 747, ready to fly, will be found standing there?" The chance of that happening is the same as the chance of the spontaneous evolution of the basic enzymes required for life.

Darwinism was dead—at least any form of Darwinism that pretended to reach beyond micro-evolutionary matters.

Two weeks ago, that realization had rocked the foundations of Bryce's scientific mind. Now, as she scrutinized the small patch of vegetation with her high-powered binoculars, she knew she was seeing the clear confirmation of Darwinism's demise.

BRYCE CONSIDERED asking Earl about his first impressions regarding the garden in the crater below. Attaching a rope to a large rock on the crater's rim, he was testing it by pulling it taut near the edge of the rim.

She climbed toward him.

Believing the rope to be secure, he fastened it to his belt and leaned backwards.

Just as Bryce said, "Cole. I have a question for you," the rock slipped, and Earl disappeared over the rim of the crater with a look of surprise on his face. Bryce felt the blood rush from her face; she felt dizzy.

She rushed to the edge and smelled sulfur dioxide. She recognized the smell from a vacation she once took to the Kilauea volcano in Hawaii. Her nose made the connection the moment she peered over the edge. What she saw reminded her of the "skylight" she'd seen in a tube of a Pahoehoe lava on the southernmost Big Island of Hawaii.

The magma would be somewhere between 1,200 and 2,000 degrees Fahrenheit. It was neither dark red nor completely yellow-white; she guessed it to be around 1,600 degrees.

Then she heard Earl scream. He had fallen into the lava trough.

Serves him right.

She wasn't being cold-hearted—Bryce knew that such troughs had a skin on them that was very hot but rarely deadly. He might suffer some minor burns but nothing serious when he rolled off the trough.

The problem was that he didn't roll off. The flow of molten rock, continued back into the crater wall. Before he had time to react, a stream of lava disappearing into the wall caught Earl's leg, pulling him along. He was being sucked in!

Bryce recoiled as his screams grew more agonizing and then abruptly stopped.

◆ ◆ ◆

TOMMY HEARD EARL'S SCREAMS when he crested the crater rim. From his position at 10:20 on the rim, he couldn't see that the fall had been fatal. But he could see the church with its gold dome at the center of the crater, and he felt an urgency to reach the crater floor. Directly below him, he saw a mining cart. The cart appeared to be full of gold.

He studied the wall of the crater. The slope appeared gentle enough to slide most of the way. He sat on his leather flight jacket to protect his bottom. Inching his way over the edge, he gave one final push. He kept his eyes glued to the mining cart. The closer he got, the more he was convinced it was filled with gold.

The slide went faster than Tommy had anticipated. Close to the bottom, he encountered a rock protrusion that launched him spinning into the air.

Time stretched for the three seconds he was airborne, as he tumbled toward the largest beehive he'd ever seen.

Cone-shaped!

That morning, after passing Tatvan, he'd seen several villages consisting entirely of houses shaped like cones. Now we know where the Coneheads were born, he'd thought at the time.

Before he could appreciate the irony of this, he landed in the center of one of the hives with a sticky thud.

Mercifully, five thousand bees stung him simultaneously, and his breath failed before he could let out a cry.

The last thing his eyes saw was gold—the golden light filtering through the golden honey of the crushed beehive caving in on him. In the final moment of his life, the taste of the honey recalled all the Turkish aphrodisiacs he'd experimented with; nearly all were sweetened with honey.

Tommy Dorfler's life didn't flash before him, but as blood hemorrhaged behind his eyeballs, he imagined that his bright red Porsche did.

FIFTY-FOUR

B RYCE REALIZED SHE HAD better be careful when she climbed down the wall. Earl's fall had stunned her, and she moved away from where he had disappeared. She double-checked that she was firmly attached to her safety cord.

After checking everything three times, she rappelled down the side of the crater rim, landing behind the north observation tower.

No one noticed her as she stashed her gear and peered into the window of the circular research wing attached to the tower. Her heart skipped a beat when she saw the elevated diorama of the garden.

She yearned to be inside.

◆ ◆ ◆

DOBRO WALKED nonchalantly toward the crater. Having witnessed Bryce's change of position through his binoculars, he suspected she'd found the optimal location for her purposes.

He decided to climb directly under that spot, and made his way to the crater wall, his mind churning with conflict. If the golden church were on the other side of those rocks, too many people already knew about it.

◆◆◆

PHILIOS INTRODUCED HIMSELF to the travelers as "Pastor of this little community." Then he made the round of introductions. When he got to Stuart he leaned forward and whispered, "God is great," into his ear.

Suddenly, two women from the textile mill rushed to Philios. They whispered something to him.

Philios looked toward the north tower. His eyes were dark and his brow furrowed, but Stuart couldn't tell whether he was angry or worried.

"Excuse me," Philios said, motioning to Matthias. The two men hurried across the bridge.

BROTHER BARNABAS invited Father Romero for a tour of the library.

STUART CONTINUED talking with Meredith and his parents. Finally, he said, "I think the best thing to do is to show you."

"Show us what?"

"Follow me."

He led them along the path that cut in front of the Pastor's house. At the southeast observation tower, they continued along the stream into the garden.

Brad, Margaret, and Meredith were awestruck by the spiral of trees.

Meredith held Stuart's hand, and when she looked into his eyes, she saw the fire of belief within them.

DOBRO CAME over the rim when Bryce entered the observation tower. He saw the golden church and knew that in his official capacity, as Prefect of the Department for the Preservation of Turkish Antiquities, he had to protect the building with his life.

Although his shoes were appropriate, he hadn't been prepared for mountain climbing, therefore, his journey down the inside of the crater wall was painstakingly cautious.

Before he had climbed halfway down, he heard the beating of a helicopter rotor. Looking up, he saw a pilot and one passenger in a small two-seater flying in from the opposite side of the crater. The "RRR" logo was emblazoned upon the bottom of the chopper.

◆ ◆ ◆

RICHARD ROEBUCK'S HELICOPTER slowly circled the garden, following the spiral inward. Richard looked down.

This is spectacular!

From his position above the garden and level with the crater rim, he could see that the spiral of the trees did not represent an arithmetic progression. He immediately recognized the equiangular spiral to be the same as that of a chambered nautilus shell—or anything exhibiting organic growth that is proportional to its size—which he knew corresponded to that of a spiral galaxy.

Richard was well versed in the mathematical relationships of such spirals. They grew out of successive applications of the so-called "Divine Proportion"—one plus the square root of five divided by two—the only ratio in the universe reciprocating to itself plus one. The "Golden Mean" that allowed architects, painters, musicians, and poets, to create hierarchical forms reflecting the unique fractal-like relationships of nature, where the only rule is "the smaller part is to the larger, as the larger part is to the whole."

If any number could be considered God's fingerprint, Richard believed that it was the number that expressed the dynamic symmetry of the "Divine Proportion" of nature—1.618033989—represented by the twenty-first character of the Greek alphabet: *Phi*. Initially postulated by Euclid, Phi is the ratio of the length of one complete cycle of the double-helix spiral of DNA to its width; the number that Thomas Kepler said was one of the two great treasures of geometry—the other was the Pythagorean theorem.

This ratio determines the angle of every next branch a tree sprouts, and where and when to sprout leaves. Down the hierarchy, the ratio determined the branching of veins on the leaves, the petals of its buds, and even, Richard knew, the tree's cellular division. The design of bodies and body parts of every living thing reflected the ratio.

Artists had long ago discovered this natural law, and assuming it to be godly, had made efforts to apply it to their works. This included most of the artists and composers of the Renaissance; later Bach, Bartok, and Boulez; and the architects of the world's greatest cathedrals; the Parthenon, the Taj Mahal, and the Great Pyramid; even Corbussier's works. Durer's too. Dante had used the ratio as a deep structure in his *Inferno*.

In all his research, he had longed for the intersection of this principle with a topic he was researching. Until now, it hadn't happened. But, looking at the spiral below, he knew that finally he was seeing the fulfillment of his wish. And, he hoped, the extension of his life.

Richard was already convinced that here he would find his "Tree of Life."

But what if they wouldn't give it up?

Roebuck couldn't allow that to happen. He turned to the back of the helicopter and took stock of the munitions. Positioned by the side door was a floor-mounted machine gun. Stacked beside it were enough explosives to blow the crater to kingdom come. A single AP-107 impact explosive, dropped from the helicopter into the southern ravine would cut off all access to and from the crater. They'd be like sitting ducks for him to pick off at his leisure. The end justifies the means; everyone below him was expendable.

No matter. An earthquake was going to flatten this crater within hours...wasn't it?

He felt a twinge of remorse when it occurred to him that Bryce would be among the casualties, but he found it possible to erase that image by picturing the rainforest debacle. Since the "loss" of the Boalyptus team, he had discovered that listening to Barber's "Adagio for Strings" took his mind to a place of complete tranquility—and complete anarchy. He kept a copy of the recording nearby every CD player he owned. He put it into the helicopter's CD player at that moment, and routed the audio to his headphones. He turned up the volume.

It's all for the greater good after all...mine in particular.

◆ ◆ ◆

STUART WALKED with his parents and Meredith along the path leading to the garden. Calm on the outside, his thoughts were racing, trying to navigate a path through the barriers his parents had built between themselves and the Lord. Between Philios' house and the first observation tower, he noticed the beehives. One was demolished; it hadn't been that way yesterday. Now there were eleven, and this gave him an idea. The single, demolished beehive was precisely what he needed to make his point.

Stuart stopped and motioned toward the northwest wall of the crater.

"See those beehives?"

They did.

"See how one of them has been crushed by a boulder or something?"

They couldn't see Tommy Dorfler's swollen body beneath the ruined hive.

"I'm not blind." Brad stretched to see more.

"Those hives are in a dangerous place considering the rocks that fall during earthquakes in this region."

"So why build the hives so close to the wall?" Brad asked.

"I'm not sure, but I suppose the original hives were placed hundreds, maybe thousands of years ago."

"Your point?"

"Imagine that I am the beekeeper, and I discover a boulder poised to fall on that beehive in the next earthquake, like what must have happened there."

"It looks like this beekeeper wasn't doing his job."

"That's not the point."

"Go on," Meredith said. Margaret nodded.

"I would have a great desire to save my bees. They produce my honey and it's my livelihood, although they have no idea what I use it for, or that in the opinion of my customers, its sweetness is incomparable to anything else.

"I might try to pick up the hive, and carry it to a safe location, one where they would not only be protected, but closer to the flowers they need to make honey. But the bees would think I was threatening their home. They'd react by swarming and trying to kill me. They would have no idea that I had their best interests at heart. No matter how hard I tried to explain the danger presented by the boulder, they would never be able to understand me.

"So maybe I would build a new hive, in the middle of the field where they would be safe. There would be no way for me to tell them to move. I'd have to become a bee and bring the message to them in person."

"Bees do dances to share information with each other," Meredith said, captivated by Stuart's story.

"Right. But they probably do not have a dance for the concept of dislodged boulders that start rolling in the direction of their hive. As a bee, I wouldn't have any of my human powers available to make my case completely clear: no colored markers, no whiteboard, no little clay models with marbles representing boulders, no overhead transparencies illustrating plate tectonics…"

"Of course not." Meredith appreciated Stuart's new sense of resolve. She loved this "new" Stuart even more. *But does he plan to stay here? Will this affect our relationship?*

"So when I danced a dance telling of their hazardous situation, they'd become suspicious. They would wonder how I could know such things about the future, about the workings of the world around them, about the existence of a refuge that would save them all from annihilation.

"Many of them would pay no attention to me. Others would assume that I was a damaged bee, or insane, but anyhow useless to the community…so they would kill me. Some bees might join in the killing simply because I was not from their own hive.

"But before that happened, a few would get the message, a few would follow the messenger's advice, and be saved by their decision.

"For us, Jesus is that messenger."

"Uh oh. Here it comes," Stuart's father said.

"Dad!"

"You know how I feel about that kind of talk."

"I forgive you."

"YOU FORGIVE ME?"

"Yes—for raising me as an atheist."

Suddenly, Richard Roebuck's helicopter roared above their heads.

FIFTY-FIVE

PHILIOS AND MATTHIAS ran along the path. Stuart and his loved ones hadn't noticed the helicopter until it passed directly over them. It landed on the field between the garden and the bathhouse.

Bryce, having gained a better look at the plant in the center of the garden, climbed down from the observation tower and walked toward it, entranced.

Richard burst into the central clearing just as Philios and Matthias got there. They were followed by Stuart, his parents, and Meredith.

Barnabas and Father Romero approached from the library, oblivious to the rest of the goings on. Father Romero had found his book in the Recent Reading Room immediately, and his face was one big smile.

Dobro watched the developing scene from his perch on the crater wall. He continued down to the garden, as unobtrusively as possible.

RICHARD SMIRKED. "So. We're all here," he said. "Fancy that."

"And you are?" asked Philios.

"Richard Roebuck," he said, as if that said it all.

But, much to Richard's astonishment, it didn't say anything to Philios.

"I'm interested in purchasing this property. Name your price."

Philios was astonished. "It's not for sale."

"Oh come now. Everything's for sale, if the price is right."

He walked to the closest of the trees surrounding the cross. Reaching toward one of the pieces of fruit, he said, "I'll settle for the produce rights."

"Don't pick that!"

"Why not?"

"You heard the man." Dobro ran across the clearing with a gun in his hand and his other arm outstretched.

A shot rang out from Richard's helicopter. His bodyguard had remained on board covering the confrontation through the telescopic sight of his rifle.

Dobro fell to the ground, and squeezed off a bullet from his pistol. The bodyguard fell.

Father Romero rushed to his friend's side.

"Dobro."

"Rafael, my friend." He collapsed in a puddle of blood.

◆ ◆ ◆

RICHARD'S FINGERS closed around a piece of the holy fruit. His eyes showed the urgency of his craving.

A rustling, whispering all around them broke forth. It was like a thousand voices; all were saying, "Do not eat of the Tree of Life for surely you shall die."

Without knowing he was doing it, Father Romero murmured the words of Ezekiel, "The sound of the wings of the Cherubim could be heard as far away as the outer court, like the voice of God Almighty..."

The myriad whispering voices seemed to gather themselves together into the booming words, "Do not eat of the Tree of Life for surely you shall die."

Richard turned to Philios and yelled over the echoes, "Nice sound system."

Father Romero shouted the words of David, "The LORD thundered from heaven; the voice of the Most High..."

"I AM GOD!" Richard shouted. "No man in history has risen above me!"

Father Romero roared the words of Isaiah, "The LORD will cause men to hear his majestic voice and will make them see his arm coming down with raging anger and consuming fire, with cloudburst, thunderstorm and hail."

Plucking the fruit from the tree, Richard raised it to his lips. He rolled his eyes, and heaved his most annoying sigh; in the still of the moment, the rasp of phlegm sounded more like a death rattle. Its lack of effect upon those around him—their eyes filled with pity instead of frustrated subjugation—gave him pause.

He grinned and took a bite.

Later they would disagree about whether it had happened the moment his teeth had pierced the skin of the fruit, or when his lips had touched it. In any event, a bolt similar to lightning had come down from the Heavens; instantly Richard Roebuck was no more.

THE EARTH SHOOK. "Only when the Son of Man has returned, may you eat of the Tree of Life." The words themselves were shaking the earth, but when the voice paused, the shaking didn't stop.

WHEN BRYCE saw her benefactor struck down, she realized she had passed through the edge of her safety net, the safety net that formed the edge of her life. She had crossed through the border that defined and protected the secure insides of her refuge. She stepped outside that fragile bubble into the shaky and vulnerable realities of the world.

THE VOICE continued, and the earth shook more forcefully. "Know this. This place is only a copy, a shadow of what is in Heaven."

The ground moved like an elevator ascending—but faster than any elevator known to mankind. Elevator? It was more like a rocket—or the uncontrollable upward rebound of the carnival ride of all carnival rides, but without the feeling that you've left your stomach behind. For those present, it was as though the crater had turned inside out in an instant and they were now standing on the top of a mountain—and from that mountain they could see the whole earth with minute clarity.

THEY STARED at the cross: Stuart, Meredith, Brad and Margaret; Father Romero, Barnabas, Philios, and Matthias; Bryce.

Before their eyes, all the trees dissolved. In their place were angels: glorious ethereal beings dressed in garments of golden light, kneeling toward the cross—kneeling on their right knees with each left knee bent, each right hand wrapped around the grip of a mighty sword, blazing brighter than their cloaks, each head looking upward—and all their voices singing, "Holy, Holy, Holy."

Stuart, immersed as he was in God's grace through his recent salvation, saw the scene around him in sharp focus—more real than reality. He wept tears of joy for the first time in his life.

Meredith's eyes also overflowed with tears, but she didn't know why she was crying.

Father Romero's feelings recalled the day he entered the seminary. He stared at the scene before his eyes: one cross, not three.

Bryce was disoriented. She knew that science couldn't explain what was happening, and that terrified her more than the thought that they were, in all probability, in the midst of a massive earthquake.

Seven of the spectators fell to their knees, looking at the cross.

Brad remained standing. Margaret had been ready to join the others but Brad pulled her to his side. Nonetheless, he and Margaret joined the others in staring at the cross.

But the cross was dissolving, too. It was no longer a cross. It became a magnificent, golden throne.

And they knew this was what it had always been in Heaven.

Yet, this shimmering vision of the throne was empty.

THE WORDS BLARED through them: "The Son of Man will return soon!" Every cell of their bodies resonated.

"No one knows about that day or hour, not even the angels in heaven, nor the Son, but only the Father."
AND AGAIN, the kneeling angels sang "Holy, Holy, Holy."

The others joined their song.

◆ ◆ ◆

Then I heard every creature in heaven and on earth and under the earth and on the sea, and all that is in them, singing: "To him who sits on the throne and to the Lamb be praise and honor and glory and power, for ever and ever!" (Revelation 5:13)

EPILOGUE

A FTER THEIR EXPERIENCE in the crater, Stuart hoped that he and Meredith would be of one mind about God, the Bible, and Jesus. Yet, Meredith became quiet whenever he mentioned the subject. Yes, she admitted that something extraordinary had happened in the crater, but did it prove the existence of God? Or Jesus? Did it prove the Bible? Nonetheless, they had a wonderful relationship—"a relationship made in Heaven" they would come to say. Back in Los Angeles, with Meredith's Jewish heritage in mind, they began attending a Messianic synagogue in Culver City. Although she went through the motions, it soon became evident that Meredith was still seeking.

Much to Stuart's dismay, his father continued to maintain that everyone had experienced a mass hallucination. But the steam had gone out of his atheistic arguments—it was obvious to all that even Brad Pierce himself suspected that what they had witnessed had been real. That he agreed to limit all discussion of the experience to family members was some consolation.

By the end of the summer, the collision of Stuart's new found faith with his father's continual denials had created an untenable situation. Stuart tried to console himself with Jesus' words as recorded by Matthew: "Do not suppose that I have come to bring peace to the earth. I did not come to bring peace, but a sword. For I have come to turn a man against his father, a daughter against her mother..." In August, their differences of opinion caused Stuart to study another scriptural passage: "If people do not welcome you, shake the dust off your feet when you leave their town, as a testimony against them." With this in mind, he transferred to Boston University for his junior and senior years. Meredith joined him for her senior year, and they married shortly after they graduated.

Stuart's mother was a changed woman. Margaret Pierce returned to Los Angeles with a new air of assurance that most of her friends believed to be a result of her rugged adventures in the near east, but that Margaret attributed to God. She joined a local church and became an active member, ultimately taking part in several mission trips to South America.

TO FATHER RAFAEL Romero's delight, Philios allowed him to stay in the village for ten days. He spent most of that time in the library. The people of Stauros learned nearly as much from Father Romero's rekindled fire for the Lord, as he learned from his stay in the village. When he got back to America, he found a scroll in his suitcase; Barnabas had placed it there. There was a note that said: "If anyone asks where this came from—and they will—you can, in all honesty, say that someone must have placed it in your suitcase while you slept the night before your departure from Turkey." Father Romero used the information in the scroll—and notes he had taken while at Stauros—to write a book called "Simon of Cyrene—A Biography," the first scholarly work on the life of the man who carried the cross for Jesus on the Via Dolorosa. He then turned to fiction and wrote a series of novels called the "Apostle's Children Series." He became known for his "uncanny sense of what probably and plausibly *had* happened to the five Apostles who were not heard of after the Ascension of Jesus."

A WEEK PASSED before inquiries were made about Richard Roebuck's private jet at the Diyarbakir airport. By that time, Bryce Brinkman had forged a plausible suicide note for Richard Roebuck. In it, she described a dramatic escalation of his illness and a wish to tour the holy lands alone and by helicopter. The note closed with great ambiguity: "I will fly over the holiest sites in Turkey in hopes that God will heal me. If He doesn't (and I doubt He will), I might set down and let the buzzards eat me. Or, I might hover over the deepest part of a lake until my fuel gives out. Or, I might crash into a mountaintop. Or, I might head south until "friendly fire" of NATO forces releases me from this world. I will decide, when I decide. My affairs are in order." Matthias helped Bryce sneak into the airport runway and place the note on the night table next to the bed in the plane.

Neither Richard's pilot nor Earl Cole had any relatives. They weren't missed. On the other hand, Tommy Dorfler was missed rather quickly—until his car turned up two hundred miles away during a clash involving Kurdish rebels; they claimed never to have seen the young American consular officer, up until the moment they were executed.

Bryce Brinkman's world changed more than she thought possible. Her outlook on faith versus science made a 180-degree turn. Richard Roebuck had left no provisions for any of his ongoing research projects after his death, so her lab was soon dismantled. She could have found alternate sources of funding, but after her experiences that summer, she felt a strong pull to other branches of science. The trustees of Richard's estate held a meeting in July for all the former recipients of Roebuck's philanthropy. There, she met the director of the Scriptural Science Research Institute, the only Christian organization to receive a "Triple-R" grant—he agreed to hire her at the end of the coming academic year.

ON JULY 3, Dobro Suleyman had recovered enough to be transported in the horse-drawn wagon belonging to Achmed and Matthias bin Cyrene. They brought him to the medical emergency clinic of Diyarbakir. On the way, they had a long talk with him emphasizing the necessity for secrecy—they needn't have; Philios and most of the elders had met with him repeatedly after he regained consciousness. Dobro fully understood what was at stake. His zeal to protect the holy site surpassed the call of duty—he took helicopter lessons, received his license, and eventually returned to remove the unsightly machine from the tranquility of Stauros.

The glimpse of Heaven deeply effected Matthias. All doubts had been erased; the purpose of his family's obligation was based upon truth—he'd seen it with his own eyes. His yearning for another life in another part of the world faded. He and Ilana had a son the following year, the first of many children, and Matthias succeeded Achmed as Stuaros' primary contact with the outside world when his son reached the age of twelve. On the summer solstice of that year, he and his son watched the sunlight unveil the secret ravine, and as they followed the stream into the crater, Matthias said, "Now listen to this carefully: On the sixtieth day, shortly before dawn—" His son joined in, "three men rushed up the hill and took the cross…"

Hassan the goatman still wears the crucifix given to him by Father Romero. He never knew it contained a GPS location device, the battery of which had given out before the winter.

Moreover, the megathrust earthquake at Stauros—the displacement of the village to a height of nine hundred feet in the blink of an eye, and back again shortly thereafter—did not appear on the monitoring devices of any seismological tracking station in the world.

ABOUT THE AUTHOR

Chris Loveway was born in Cambridge, Massachusetts, and is the author or co-author (writing under another name) of seven non-fiction books and numerous magazine and journal articles. *Tree of Life* was written in the Netherlands. Chris Loveway resides in Maryland and has two daughters.

ABOUT THE SEQUEL

Tree of Knowledge, (Book Two of the Tree Trilogy), is forthcoming in fall of 2007.

Eden may be closed, but those who come across its remnants are still dangerously transformed by the Tree of Knowledge and must be stopped.

Newlyweds Stuart and Meredith Pierce search for Meredith's Hasidic roots in Antwerp. There, they encounter Reuben Yerushalmi, a charismatic rabbi with knowledge of the impending destruction—by a European Union oil pipeline project—of the remnant of the Garden of Eden. Meanwhile, Femke de Gier, working for a think-tank in Amsterdam that is trying to restore and secure Holland's destiny, has traced strategic technological breakthroughs and world-changing innovations to people whose paths have crossed the Eden region. Stuart and Meredith must overcome those who seek forbidden knowledge threatening to destroy humanity.